Philip Boast was born in 1952 in London and educated at Mill Hill. Finding writing incompatible with academic education, he left school at sixteen and sailed to the Galapagos Islands to study wildlife. Back home in London, he wrote at least two books a year and paid his way by selling origami paper and artists' materials, keeping chickens, working as a sanitary estimator, moulding asbestos sheet, and finally as a chauffeur. In 1976 his book *The Assassinators*, which he wrote when he was twenty, was published. Two years later he met his wife under very romantic circumstances in a well known south coast library, but his second love is London.

The Millionaire

Philip Boast

HEADLINE

Copyright © 1989 Philip Boast

First published in 1989
by Century Hutchinson Ltd

First published in paperback in 1990
by HEADLINE BOOK PUBLISHING PLC

10 9 8 7 6 5 4 3 2

ISBN 0 7472 3365 9

Printed and bound in Great Britain by
Collins, Glasgow

HEADLINE BOOK PUBLISHING PLC
Headline House
79 Great Titchfield Street
London W1P 7FN

For
my mother

THE FIVE FAMILIES OF BEN LONDON

The Millionaire's Family Tree 1575–1947

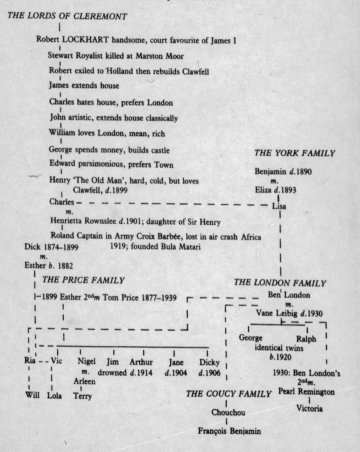

THE LORDS OF CLEREMONT

Robert LOCKHART handsome, court favourite of James I

Stewart Royalist killed at Marston Moor

Robert exiled to Holland then rebuilds Clawfell

James extends house

Charles hates house, prefers London

John artistic, extends house classically

William loves London, mean, rich

George spends money, builds castle

Edward parsimonious, prefers Town

Henry 'The Old Man', hard, cold, but loves
    Clawfell, d.1899

Charles — — — — — — — — — — — — — — Lisa
  m.

Henrietta Rownslee d.1901; daughter of Sir Henry

Roland Captain in Army Croix Barbée, lost in air crash Africa
           1919; founded Bula Matari

Dick 1874–1899
  m.

Esther b. 1882

THE YORK FAMILY

Benjamin d.1890
  m.
Eliza d.1893

THE PRICE FAMILY

1899 Esther 2ndm Tom Price 1877–1939

Ria — Vic   Nigel   Jim   Arthur   Jane   Dicky
          m.   drowned d.1914   d.1904   d.1906
          Arleen

Will   Lola   Terry

THE LONDON FAMILY

Ben London
  m.
Vane Leibig d.1930

George   Ralph
identical twins
b.1920

1930: Ben London's
2ndm.
Pearl Remington

Victoria

THE COUCY FAMILY

Chouchou

François Benjamin

PART I

THE SPARK

CHAPTER ONE

Midwinter 1924

Since Lisa had abandoned her baby on the icy steps of the London Hospital, she had not dared to live her life.

For twenty-five years she had kept her dreadful secret, even from her husband, but there was never a day when her heart was not broken.

She had built up a good life for herself, a comfortable life with a good man, without worry, without love, without pain, until she thought she would scream.

The low midday sun struck brilliantly across Regent's Park. Dressed in blue she sat alone on the bench near the gate. Despite the bitter cold, she wore no gloves. Her bare left hand was clenched like a fist at her side, and she stared motionlessly through the railings at Lockhart House.

When Lisa York was sixteen years old, she was so innocent and in love that the pride and heat of her passion blinded her to almost everything about Charles Lockhart except her desire for him. She was a parlourmaid, and he was married and soon to become Lord Cleremont, but they were in love.

He had been waiting for young Lisa at her secret refuge, the grassy knoll overlooking the mighty panorama of the Dales, since dawn, pretending to paint. She did not know what to say; but he did.

She remembered the brilliant sun burning on her eyelids and the cool drone of the waterfall, his fingers hot on her shoulders, then lower until she was gasping. The warm skin of his back began to move under the palms of her hands, and she felt the tension of his hard male nipples as their points furrowed her tingling breasts, his knees insistently pressing apart her thighs. Still he didn't say he loved her, but she knew he did. He jerked his hips, thrusting unbearably, and she was lost. 'Do you love me?' she cried. He said he did, he shouted it out, and in that moment she felt the warm, silvery flush of him as he melted in her womb.

Of course, in London he denied everything. Lisa was merely a parlourmaid seduced by Charles Lockhart and then deserted by him, condemned as a fallen woman by the high society he represented. He gave her ten pounds for an abortion.

Her dreams were ended, but the baby inside her was real. She wasted the money on a cape to keep her warm.

Alone, destitute and pregnant on the streets of Victorian London, Lisa gave birth to her son, and deserted him. She never forgave herself.

Who was he? What sort of man was the son she had left to die – or to live – in the dark squalor of London's East End? She never knew.

The elegant woman in blue, now forty-one years old, shivered, wondering what had become of him – wondering what he had become.

This morning in the East End the old porter she had traced from the London Hospital had shouted that he had found no child. She heard such hatred in his voice that Lisa had cringed, thinking it was for her wickedness, deserving such punishment. She had no rights. He swore there never was a child. That was the worst punishment of all, if she believed him.

Then a tear wound from the old man's one good eye and trickled between the scars that meshed his face. 'Poor old Peter Pungle,' he whispered, 'only worth a few coppers and sprowsie sixpences.' Then: 'Get out! Out!' When she offered him her address, he ignored it, tilting a bottle of Mackeson back into his throat.

Her boy *had* lived; but something terrible had happened, and the old man was hiding his guilt. Perhaps it was better not to know, but . . .

She had walked along Lichfield Road both wanting desperately to see her son and terrified that she would.

He could be any one of the customers going into the Lord Tredegar pub, any of the rough young workmen shouldering past her. She had no means of knowing him – his piercing blue eyes, but eyes changed. The mark beneath his right ear, but blemishes faded.

Charles never knew she had defied him. He knew nothing of his son. Pride, her old sin. Lisa sat in Regent's Park and stared through the railings at Lockhart House. Her blue eyes had lost none of their fire, and her striking features still revealed determination rather than submission, stamped with the power that derives from pain. She was thinking of Charles Lockhart all those years ago, feeling anew her rage of guilt, and loss, and fury at his weakness. She must love him still.

Today, her divorce from Edwin became absolute. There would be no going back. She wanted desperately to see Charles, but if he did not happen to come she might sit alone in the cold and sun until she died.

The park gate squeaked as a man came in. Charles? For a moment his eyes stared directly into her own, piercingly blue. No, not Charles.

The gate closed slowly behind him on its spring.

The man touched his hand politely to his hat-brim, and walked on.

The hinge squeaked metallically, then the latch clicked shut.

Charles had never moved with such powerful grace, such animal grace in a finely tailored suit, or worn a red tie in public, even though the Prince of Wales did.

She watched him walk. He was very tall. Charles had been tall.

But he was not Charles – not so prettily handsome as Charles had been – not the sort of man, this one, that a young girl would dare fall in love with lightly. Though his fingers were long and fine, his hands looked strong enough to crush, as well as to caress.

Like her, he wore no gloves. Like her, those eyes . . . those striking eyes . . .

Lisa stared after him.

He was striding swiftly down past the boating lake.

He was *not* Charles. Lisa put her hand to her mouth.

Suddenly she gathered up her handbag and umbrella. He was in the distance but she walked hesitantly at first. Only when people came between them did she begin to run, pushing them aside.

Too late. He was gone.

She flew, panicking, then glimpsed him leaving the park by York Gate. She saw the left side of his face as he crossed Oxford Street ahead of her, then she was running after him down New Bond Street, all gold and black with sunlight and shadow, solid with jammed traffic. London's most glamorous street, lined with its most exclusive shops: jewellers, couturiers, perfumeries. She dodged between the gleaming vehicles, then saw him crossing Grafton Street into Old Bond Street, but he was on her right, deep in shadow, and she was so blinded by the sunlight that she couldn't *see*.

A building came between her and the sun. Shadowed herself, she could see into the shadows. It was another world.

Instead of blackness she saw doorways, shop windows, the grim mouths of alleyways. Then she saw him walking just ahead of her. Lisa pushed past a fat woman window-shopping beneath the giant yellow canopies of London Emporium, and came up behind him. But he turned to go inside the store.

The Head Doorman backed to one of the great doors and opened it with a flourish. He actually saluted. 'Good morning, Mr London, sir!'

At last the tall man turned his head slightly to the right. 'Thank you, Hawk.'

Beneath his right ear, almost hidden in his hair, was a tiny red birthmark in the shape of a four-leafed clover.

Lisa gasped.

She had seen her son.

Hawk closed the door proudly behind the millionaire.

He eyed Lisa's reflection in the glass, then put his head back slightly and cleared his throat. Harumph.

Then he turned and stood, as always, to attention on his patch of polished flag in front of the doors to London Emporium. He had been Head Doorman nearly all his life, and he was sixty-four years old. Long ago the store had been called Leibig's Emporium, and the doorway had been smaller. His uniform had been imperial purple, terrifying with gold braid, to intimidate unsuitable customers (always called clients) from entering the Emporium – mostly women shoppers, especially those with poodles. Hawk detested poodles. He detested women too. He did not see the point of them.

Hawk's eyes glittered. Lisa stared at him, not lowering her gaze. Didn't she have anything better to do than stand and stare? Hawk shifted uneasily.

In the golden days of the last century there had been rules, and everyone knew their place. No modern liberal attitudes. Nowadays Hawk was obliged to wear a modern style of uniform in the house colours of yellow and navy blue, and to treat clients as equals. He had to smile at them. Greet them with a Good Afternoon. He had to allow the shining doors behind him to be opened to clients who did not deserve his respect, and he had to welcome them as though they did. He was still almost six foot five in his platform boots, with penetrating eyes and hooked nose in a predatory curve over his magnificent iron-grey moustache; clients did not take a welcome from Hawk lightly. Even in these egalitarian days it was a privilege to enter the most glamorous store on earth, and Hawk made sure they knew it.

'Good afternoon, Mr Sturgess,' he said, standing like a pillar, unmoving.

'Oh – good afternoon, Hawk.'

Hawk flicked his eye and one of the door-monkeys jumped to it. This damned girl was still staring. Hawk wished he could check if he had a button undone.

When Hawk's time came to be Called his dearest hope was that it would be standing here, chest out, elbows in,

13

faithfully doing his duty. Hawk was a past master – not merely a good Head Doorman, he was a great Head Doorman, and he knew it, and that pride was the ramrod that kept his back as straight as a drill-sergeant's. Mr London trusted him. Messes never happened outside the Emporium while Hawk was there. Never.

What hot eyes she had. He decided to clear his throat in explicit warning. '*Harumph.*' There was something about her, too striking to be beautiful – a face of power. *Terrible beauty*: Hawk understood the phrase. An open wound. Just standing there like she'd been shot in the giblets.

Hawk saw a thousand people a day.

He'd seen it all before.

Hawk had no children. His child was London Emporium. A few years ago Ben London had read the Riot Act to Hawk about his old-fashioned attitude to clients and his refusal to wear the new uniform. There were no threats. Ben smiled and chatted kindly to the lonely old man like an old and valued friend. Hawk, who all his life kept emotion locked in an iron heart, had been afraid he would literally cry – and he had felt human tears in his eyes, but Mr London had been generous enough not to notice.

Hawk's loyalty now was without measure, because he knew the millionaire understood him exactly. So Hawk, privileged, wore the new uniform. And smiled at clients too. Because now, Hawk thought, he understood what drove Ben London. Hawk knew, he thought, the millionaire's secret.

What had this woman seen in Mr London? He saw joy in her eyes. Amazement? And something frantic, almost like terror, like guilt, all alien emotions to Hawk. Such dreamers were dangerous. Once he would have ordered immediately: 'Move on there, madam!' These days he was supposed to sensitively inquire: 'May I help you, m'am?'

Hawk opened his mouth and said none of those things – she stood so close to him. Instead, incredibly, he said: 'Are you one of his enemies?'

'Tell me his name,' Lisa said.

Hawk put back his head. He surveyed her up and down with smooth sweeps of his eyes beneath the shadow of his peaked cap.

'Please tell me his name,' she begged frantically.

Hawk recognized hysteria. Bloody women. He laid a restraining hand on her elbow. She stared at him as ferociously as a wild animal – she might attack him with her teeth or knees, and he tightened his thighs automatically.

'Ben London!' Hawk said. 'That was Mr London.'

Lisa's eyes overflowed with tears. Hawk did not recognize such joy, a joy so great it hurt her like an agony. Lisa had found the baby she had abandoned.

'Has he been in love?' she asked, then pressed her fingertips to her lips. 'Tell me about Ben London. Is he – is he happy?'

Hawk told her the truth to get rid of her. 'Mr London's a gentleman, m'am, and he's the biggest bastard in the world, there's nothing we wouldn't do for him. London Emporium is his, I won't tell you what he had to do to get it.' Hawk swung his arm along the gleaming shopfront as proudly as if it were his own. 'He came from nowhere, m'am, and he doesn't have a father or a mother that he'll ever know, but now he's a millionaire.'

'You admire him,' Lisa said. Hawk was shocked. He would have died for Ben London. He was lost for words.

She asked eagerly: 'Is he married? Does he have any children?'

Hawk could not resist her. 'He married Vane Leibig, the boss's daughter, but she hates him for what he did to her . . .'

'What did he – '

'He loved her,' Hawk said. 'That's all. She hates him because she hates herself. Poor Vane. She keeps her twin boys away from him to hurt him.'

'Ben London has twin sons?' Lisa looked so joyous that Hawk opened up a little more.

'They're identical – can't tell them apart, young Ralph and George. Their Trust owns the Emporium technically,

15

I believe.' He coughed and lowered his voice confidentially, guiding Lisa into a quiet corner. 'I'll let you in on the secret – he has a third boy, by another woman. Kept out of sight down in the East End.' Hawk nodded. Bert Simmonds, the chauffeur, knew all about it.

'Apparently the mother is Ria Price – used to be a music-hall singer,' he murmured. 'She's a complete bitch and keeps the boy in poverty, Bert says, like you wouldn't keep a dog. She's a bloody East End slut. The Price family almost destroyed Ben London, but he loved Ria.' Hawk corrected himself: 'He loves her all right.'

'But he's still married?'

'That's why Ria turned him down flat.'

But that did not make sense, if Ria was the woman Hawk described. There must be so much more to this relationship than the solitary old Doorman understood, Lisa guessed. Yet she sensed an affinity with Hawk. His first question, *Are you one of his enemies*? had devastated her. Because it was true. She was.

Yes, I abandoned my tiny baby, Ben London. I left him on those snowy steps, I walked away from him, *because* I loved him – I knew I could not look after him. I have no rights over him, or any right to happiness myself. All I want is for him to be happy. But I am his cruellest enemy. I knew what I did.

Hawk said: 'Ria's brother Vic Price took this place over. They say he's a gangster. No one's sure how Ben London fought that monster – but Ben won, and that's all that matters,' Hawk bragged, puffing his chest out. 'They say Vic Price did the worst thing in the world to Ben once, though I don't know what that could be. But Ben did the worst thing too, to him, and that's how he won the Emporium back. Who knows? Revenge. Betrayal. Humiliation. He's the millionaire.'

'But he lost Ria's love,' Lisa said.

Hawk shrugged.

It was plain fact to Lisa that Hawk adored his master. But she did not believe this simple picture of her son he painted. Hawk's sentimental point of view did not ring

16

true to her ears – the loneliness of this man her son, his ruthlessness, the women who went to bed with him, his power over them, his millions, the cars this millionaire had, his horses, the sheer rootless devil-may-care glossiness of his diamonds-and-champagne life . . . Hawk was describing his own dreams, not the reality of her son. This was not him. Ben London had been a part of her, and however changed, she knew him.

One thing Lisa believed. The loneliness. That must be. When Hawk said *He came from nowhere, and he doesn't have a father or a mother that he'll ever know*, those words struck a perfect chord in Lisa, and she knew them for the truth inside Ben London's head. The loneliness.

She could never ever give him back the mother who had walked away from him all those years ago. She had deserted him, and now she must face her guilt.

But there was one thing she could give to her rootless, lonely, angry son.

She could give him his father.

Lisa lifted the polished brass lion's head that ornamented the front door of Lockhart House. Her heart was in her mouth. For a moment it seemed that nothing had changed, the years had not passed, and Charles would be as she remembered. He might sweep her off her feet.

She knocked once and heard the hollow echo inside. The door moved a fraction of an inch; it had not been properly latched shut.

Lisa walked alone into Charles, Lord Cleremont's cold marble hallway.

This was the smell of Charles: as institutional as an hotel, for he had so many servants. But Lisa's keen gaze picked out shabby dust along the skirting board by his study, and she discerned faint paths worn in the chequer between the doorways and the grand staircase. When she closed the door behind her the house was so quiet, because most traffic ran on rubber tyres nowadays, that the slow tocking of the grandfather clock was clearly audible.

It was not quite love which brought Lisa back now,

and it was not only guilt. Duty played a part: to at least tell the man she had loved that he had a child, though he was a man she despised, because he had not had the courage to love her. Charles did not deserve mercy from her, but she would not hold it back from him.

Was anyone at home?

And partly it was pity that forced her here. Everyone knew that Charles's son and heir from Clawfell, Roland, a charming boy and the apple of Charles's eye, was dead. It had been widely reported in the papers a few years ago. At the time many had criticized Lord Cleremont for the coldness of his indifference to his son's fate – the easiness, even the eagerness with which he accepted reports of Roland's loss as being of his sure death. The stiff upper lip was Lord Cleremont's credo. *Noblesse oblige*.

The plain truth, Lisa knew, was that Charles was mortally afraid of feeling. His public school education, his years as the virtual prisoner of his domineering father in the vast castle at Clawfell where Lisa had worked and starved, his stilted but voracious *nouveau-riche* wife Lady Henrietta whose appalling treatment of Roland he had been ineffectual to prevent, the façade of the exalted social position he had inherited and the dead weight of the handle on his name, had dominated Charles. Charles had always been a prisoner. Lisa had dreamed that they could escape. He had not.

That day high above the Dales she had wept '*Do you love me?*' and his handsome face above her cried, '*Yes, yes, yes!*' And she had felt the flash of conception. But that had been in the sunlight, not this dark hall. Later he had denied everything: over there, in his study, was the exact place.

Charles never escaped. He had become what he most feared: because she saw him now. A man had appeared in the study doorway, and it was Charles.

'Hallo – ' Then Lisa's voice croaked. Her mouth had lost its moisture, her tongue was dry ice. Time did not forget or forgive, and neither could her body.

He was so old. He had been such a talented artist. If

they had only dared break free together, he could have been a great man. Something in Lisa melted.

She did still love him. The years had not been kind to him, but the love that still welled up in her and drew her towards him was cruel, because she couldn't hate him as he deserved. She had to force herself to stop away from him.

He called in a dry, unconcerned voice: 'What can I do for you, my dear?' He thought she was selling something. 'You're supposed to go round the back you know,' he chided. Forgotten her completely; of course he had.

She had loved, *she* had suffered, not he. But he must feel something. She had always believed so. Perhaps she was a fool. She would gladly be a fool. Why couldn't he get someone to dress him properly? His tie was crooked and she longed to straighten it. She wanted to plead: 'Do you not remember me?' but her voice had betrayed her, thank God.

Charles smiled and his face broke into lines. He wore a grey suit and his dark green top-pocket handkerchief matched his tie. He crossed the hall and patted her hand. 'I am Lord Cleremont. What is your name?' The old magician's joints creaked, but he could still do magic. She shivered.

'I am . . . I am Lisa.'

'What a pretty name.'

Lisa tried to pull away from him. 'Damn you, Charles, I am *Lisa*.'

'Lisa.' He snapped his fingers. 'Yes, of course I remember you. What a long time ago, isn't it? A very pleasant surprise. How are you?'

Lisa could have killed him. She pushed at Charles, snatching back her hand from his grasp. He dropped his social smile and looked at her angrily. A Peer of the Realm.

She said: 'I see you have forgotten me.'

'Not at all. You are a parlourmaid.'

'I am the mother of your child.'

'My son is dead.' His voice was so cold; if only she could

warm him. As if her wonderful news could transform him back into the Charles who had loved her, she said gently:

'You have another child. He is London's child. He is yours. Ours.'

'Enough.' Lord Cleremont held up his hand. 'Enough of your lies.'

'You live a lie, Charles, every day of your life.'

He flinched, misunderstanding. 'My son Roland was killed in an aeroplane crash in Africa on the first day of April 1919. Burnt to a cinder, my dear. There was never the slightest hope.'

'I did not submit to your abortionist. I gave birth to our son and loved him. But I could not look after him. It was so cold. I wrapped him up warm and left him outside the London Hospital to be saved.'

'How charming. The perfect parlourmaid.' But his eyes gleamed. She had the power to affect him still. He had loved her . . . but not as much as he loved his own selfish life. Charles went into his study and she followed him. As she came through the doorway he was standing behind the sofa, dry-eyed. They spoke with the sofa between them, circling like matadors.

'Charles, today I saw him.'

'This invention is designed to secure money from me, I presume.'

'He is now a rich man.' Lisa came behind the sofa.

Charles retreated to his desk. As he bent down under the harsh light, his long hair looked white, and his pink, vulnerable pate showed through beneath. 'My wife is dead. My son is dead. I have no son.'

'You have Ben London!' There – she had given him his name.

Charles slopped brandy into an ordinary glass. As he drank the light crimped the smile-lines on his face into a net of black shadows, and Charles was suddenly his own father, he was the Old Man. Fathers never died. Lisa shuddered. Charles looked like the Old Man whose terrifying presence had ruled Clawfell, the aristocrat of the hard hills, indifferent to lesser beings. Like the Old Man's,

Charles's face was cracked and broken with the intractable lines of a shattering grief: the death of Roland, his first-born son, whom he had not dared love. And now Lisa stood before him, the second proof of his cowardice, for she was the second person in his life he had not dared to show his love. And still dared not.

'Charles, look at me,' Lisa said sadly.

He turned away and drank another glass.

The fine landscapes of his own that had filled his study in 1899 had been replaced by sugary portraits, none from his hand, and strange modern works. Lisa recognized Klee. And there was the distinctive OK signature of Oscar Kokoschka on a painting of a woman in blue, an ideal figure devoid of human passions and failings.

Charles must be a man in torment. How else could he cope, except with these lies and denials? His face worked.

'I despise you – ' Charles flung the glass into the cold fireplace where it exploded. Lisa hated sudden noises: perhaps he remembered.

The admission was jerked out of her: 'I deserve it.'

'A parlourmaid. You seduced me. You exploited me. When I didn't give you what you demanded you had yourself deliberately thrown out on the streets to force my hand.'

'No!' Lisa cried. But now he did speak a kind of truth. She had wanted the reality of her love to be exposed.

'Pride!' Charles shouted. 'Your damned pride – a parlourmaid!'

'If only you would understand.' Lisa almost collapsed.

Charles grinned. 'What is the worst thing a woman can do?'

'Charles, don't.'

'Abandon her baby.' He dismissed her with the back of his hand, contemptuously. 'Congratulations, Lisa. You've had your revenge. I am punished. You have hurt me deeply enough.'

She swayed, but he turned away. At last she murmured: 'You are right in everything you say.'

He laughed.

'Charles, forgive me.'

He said: 'I want never to see you again, you or your bastard son, is that clear?'

She said through her tears: 'Nevertheless, I am glad I came.'

He sat, dismissing her finally, then glanced up, and slurred: 'Poor Lisa, always did think she was so special.'

'The birth of my son makes me so.' Lisa would not give that up. Without his birth, she would be a parlour-maid still, never discovering her identity as a woman. She stared at Charles, and faced up to her failure.

'Did you never love me?' she asked finally. 'Never for one moment?'

He was silent.

'Goodbye, Charles,' she said. 'Goodbye.'

'Will I not see you again?' He watched her go to the door.

Then he simply called: 'Lisa.'

She looked at him over her shoulder in the doorway.

For once he almost treated her as an equal. 'Lisa. I . . . I don't know what I was supposed to feel.'

She closed the door. She had not come from love, or pity, or hatred, or revenge. The source of her guilt was that she had lived a happy life, she had not suffered. She sentenced herself: she would dare to live her life. By the time Charles appeared in the front doorway, Lisa had disappeared, and the afternoon was empty.

He returned to his study, picked up a pen, and began to write on a card in a neat, copperplate hand.

CHAPTER TWO

1

Hawk admired only one man more than himself.

Peter Aloysius Lucan Hawkins had lived alone above the stonemason's in Putney High Street since it had been built in 1886, when he had received his honourable discharge from the British Army for the missing finger that was his war wound and commenced his employment as Head Doorman – only doorman – of Leibig's Grocery. But Putney was his home, the place where he had been brought up by his aunts when it was still a village and they paid tolls to cross the bridge, and Hawk was too much a creature of habit to move merely for the sake of convenience. He walked those long miles to Piccadilly six days a week, and seeing his erect back and glittering eye many took Lance-Corporal Hawkins for a retired colonel of infantry. They assumed his missing finger was an injury from a Zulu spear or some desperate Afghan affray – by now Hawk himself did, though in fact it had been the result of an accident in the field kitchen, and the nearest he came to a foreign war in the Army was route-marching on the Brecon Beacons.

Only one man knew his secret.

Hawk was woken, as always, by the 5.03 workman's train chuffing noisily out of the station. He warmed the pot and spooned in less tea than most people would have, then while it brewed made his lunch out of doorsteps of yesterday's bread with cheddar cheese and thick brown pickle. He poured the tea, and London Emporium's finest Broken Orange Pekoe bloomed like a flower in his throat.

Beneath his white shirt Hawk wore a corset. A magnificent whalebone Victorian corset such as generals wear to regimental dinners, and doubtless the millionaire knew all about that too. There were no secrets from him.

Ben London understood Hawk's loneliness.

The end wall of Hawk's room – he only needed one room – carried books on sparse, undecorated shelves, because they were not decorations. Conrad's sea stories were the most thumbed volumes, often expensively bound. Hawk's father had gone away to sea and never come back, or if he had, Hawk did not know it. He rebelled against his father's memory, yet could not get him out of his mind.

Really his father would at the very least be an ancient mariner in his dotage, or most probably dead as Conrad was dead, but Hawk feared a wasted life so deeply now he was old too, that dreams comforted him. Like Joseph Conrad's heroes, old Hawk's young father sailed the Indian Ocean and the Yellow Sea still.

Hawk secured his starched white collar with studs, tied his black necktie, shrugged on his overcoat, fetched his stick, turned out the lights and departed. Walking over Putney Bridge, he was still groaning as his joints eased. After threatening snow last night the clouds had lifted and now under the stars a fine January morning was waiting for the sun.

In Fulham someone said, 'Morning, Colonel.' Hawk raised his stick in acknowledgement rather than greeting. Near the Brompton cemetery, he stopped. He looked at his watch. Dawn glowed faintly: he could see the smoke drifting, he could see the soot-blackened graveyard trees. He hesitated by a lamp post, sniffing the air like one of the dogs he hated, then came to a decision.

Instead of continuing along Fulham Road, he turned north. The streets grew wide, lined with fine white houses. Inherited money, generations of it. These were the types Hawk said Good Morning, Good Afternoon to all day. They held no mysteries for him. Mere money did not impress him. His face was set.

Hawk was a man's man: no woman saw past the guards to his heart, which was why he despised them. Only one

24

man could. Through Ben London, Hawk saw himself. Not the Hawk that was, the Hawk that should have been.

Because a millionaire was not a man like other men.

It wasn't money – a real millionaire didn't need a million pounds. Of course he got the most beautiful women, the fastest cars, the rarest champagne.

There was more to it than that.

The millionaire demanded loyalty, he commanded respect. He dominated his environment from the start. The millionaire forced the people around him to be special. He warmed everyone he knew, but he could burn them too. He was very, very dangerous. Because he knew what love was.

That was frightening. Hawk had never been in love. But he understood it could be everything, and understood what the millionaire had lost when Ria Price turned him down.

The millionaire was as fearsomely alone as Hawk.

Hawk knew he could have been Ben London. He could have come from nowhere and made his name. He could have been the millionaire.

Hawk came to Queen's Gate and stood shivering. Ben London would be slipping from the soft bed of some sighing ladyship. On Hawk's right rose the vast red roundel of the Albert Hall, on his left stretched the frosty expanse of Hyde Park. Sometimes men and women rode fine horses along Rotten Row for the pleasure of it. Sometimes Ben London did, but not for pleasure. Something else drove that man.

God, it was cold. No one would ride today.

A pair of number 9 buses appeared. Hawk let the first pass hopefully, then swung reluctantly aboard the second. He grunted his way up the back stairs and pulled the tarpaulin over his knees. The bus moved off along Kensington Gore with grinding gears.

Then Hawk's heart jumped as he looked into Hyde Park. Trust the millionaire to ignore the cold, as Hawk himself would have done in his youth: hatless, he rode a beautiful black horse in the grey dawn light. The horse,

25

a prancing Arab, a difficult animal, cantered on Rotten Row parallel to the bus. Hawk leaned forward. Horse and rider were one creature, elegant and powerful, gaining velocity together, galloping now, Ben London's white shirt shimmering in the slipstream and him standing in the stirrups, racing the bus. Hawk pushed the tarpaulin off his knees. The horse's neck stretched forward. The bus missed a stop. The horse pulled ahead, winning, clods of sand and mud flying. The speed, the power, the loneliness he saw in the man, made Hawk's day even though he had lost the race.

Hawk got off the bus on the corner of old Bond Street. In front of the brilliantly lit windows of London Emporium the cleaners were washing down the pavement. The post included a personal letter for Mr London, and Hawk noticed it because the name was written in a clear copperplate like Mr London's own hand, as though he were writing to himself. Hawk shrugged and had it sent up. In the cubby he changed into his immaculate uniform. Glancing outside to check that they'd done a proper job, he saw the cleaners had gone but that a group of women were gathering. 'Shop doesn't open for an hour yet!' he barked through the glass.

They ignored him.

Hawk adjusted his peaked cap in the mirror. He didn't like the look of those women at all – a dozen of them at least. Not flappers, either. Faces as stern and rigorous as his aunts' had been. He checked the gloss on his toecaps.

Hawk eyed the women through the glass, fearsome and fearful. They weren't clients. They were trouble. It was women like these, ordinary women with respectable values and impeccable morals, who had thrown stones through the windows of the Emporium during the War because Georgy Leibig had a German name.

Hawk heard Mr London's car – the distinctive bass rumble of the supercharged Bentley turning down Old Bond Street from the stables shook the glass. Hawk strode outside as the car pulled up, one of the fifty green tourers

26

built to contest – and win – Le Mans, the morning light glinting as yellow as butter off the nickel radiator cowling. The women unfurled a banner. Hawk cleared his throat warningly as he opened the car door. Mr London would know how to deal with *those* bloody women. Hawk felt privileged to witness it.

Mr London pulled up the outside handbrake but prudently left the car in gear, Bentleys had unreliable brakes. His eyes flashed a smile. 'Bright and early this morning, Hawk.' It was the only reference he made to the race.

'Thank you, sir.' Hawk glanced across at the women, but Mr London didn't look. His lithe form swung down from the car dressed in loose, rather modern clothes, still carrying the riding crop.

There had been dramatic new allegations in the sensational Billing libel case. Mr Noël Pemberton-Billing, the Member of Parliament, founder of the Supermarine Aircraft Company, and muckraking guardian of public morality, had accused the actress Maud Allan, playing the name part in *Salome* by Oscar Wilde in front of a private audience, of lesbianism. When she naturally sued him, he not only got the publicity he craved for his beliefs but also the freedom, protected by legal privilege, to slander whoever he wished. By now many famous names were being dragged in, but under English law they were not allowed to make a statement to the Court in their defence. Billing alleged that perverse sexual practices were rife amongst the 'First 47,000' names – the cream of society, most of the Government and even Mrs Keppel, mistress of the dead King – contained in a Black Book that had been brandished by a German politician in a Bavarian court as a symbol of the decadence of the British.

Ben London's name was in that book.

The case was one of those that achieved nothing and fed like a cancer, destroying lives and selling newspapers. Certainly it would go on from the magistrates' court to the Old Bailey. Hawk did not like newspapers, and he frowned at the indignant women. Ben turned towards them. They unfurled a banner in front of him.

The banner was painted with a single word in red, a ludicrous word that Hawk did not understand at all: REMEMBER.

Ben stared at it.

Remember.

He tapped the riding crop against his leg. Hawk smiled – now they were for it. He watched Ben walk slowly over to the women. The leader was an intimidating, county-featured amazon in tweeds, the sort Hawk feared most. But Ben treated her as an equal. She did not drop her gaze. Ben said something to her – maybe only half a dozen words, Hawk could not catch them.

She looked at Ben London incredulously, then her face broke into a smile – a reassured smile, a smile of relief.

Hawk cursed himself, stuck by the doors. By now all the women were gathering around Ben, and as they listened to what he told them, Hawk saw their faces reflect changing emotions of sadness, sympathy, horror – and finally, of understanding. They felt, they *knew* he told them the truth, and because they knew, they forgave.

No one had ever looked at Hawk with eyes like that.

For the first time in his life, Hawk realized he had missed something.

He'd thought he understood everything about Ben London.

Hawk did not know the first thing about him.

'*How could I ever forget!*' Not quite half a dozen words. Even the women had not understood them – they had read only the newspaper stories about Ben's tormented homosexual friend, poor Bertie Benton-Benson, who had saved Ben from the gutter.

High above the battlefields of the World War, Bertie's aeroplane had been shot up by a German ace. It caught fire, and Bertie, without a parachute, was being burned alive like a heretic. Ben turned his own aeroplane's guns on his friend, and killed him.

Ben helped the church group to furl their banner and

watched until they were out of sight, then let Hawk open the door for him.

'Good riddance, sir!'

'Shut up, Hawk.' That was the sort of language Hawk understood. Hawk had been found guilty of a mess.

'Sorry, Mr London, won't happen again.' Hawk stood stiffly to attention and saluted, ashamed. The millionaire had done his job for him.

Ben paused long enough for that to sink in. 'Next time,' he said, 'talk to them, Hawk.'

Ben London waved down Hawk's salute and brushed past him, going alone into the darkness of the great store that lay behind the blinding window-lights.

He stopped. This was home, the centre of all his hopes and dreams.

He looked down on the long dim lines of displays stretching away from him. He smelt polish: the cleaners had already done their job and soon the sales staff would arrive. The warehouse levels far below were already a swarm of activity: fresh produce would be brought up by lifts, fish coming in from Billingsgate since five, imported fruit and vegetables from Covent Garden, cut hothouse flowers – the forecast was for a fine day, and down in the basement the buyers would have adjusted their orders for buttonholes accordingly.

Then the doors would open, and the great store would wake up.

But for the moment London Emporium, the flagship of Ben London's name, remained dark and silent, and private.

He stood on the top step overlooking the main sales floor. His tall, muscular form was not elegant now. He stood with his fists bunched, and his shoulders were twisted, like a man remembering pain.

Remember.

He remembered Ria Price. He remembered her standing here after they had made love, her golden hair, her opal eyes as she turned towards him.

Ria Price's love would never die. But she refused to be

the second woman to Ben's wife Vane. She would not be second woman to London Emporium, Ben's dream of the most glamorous store in the world that she saw must crush her or squeeze her into third place. Ria would be number one in his life, or nothing. She saw the truth: Ben would be rich, and the millionaire alone would have the mansion that they had dreamed of together as children. His success would destroy them.

Because he could be happy without her, he had lost her.

He offered her everything, and she turned it down. Because she could not leave her mum and dad alone with her two brothers, Vic and Nigel – they were all her family too, and a family's love was not cheap to come by. And because she had given birth to Ben's son Will – and Ben would not, could not, stay in the East End to look after him: she was a prisoner for their sake. Because her brother Vic hated Ben. But most of all, she turned Ben down *because* she loved him.

So he knew she would never come back.

Ben walked along the line of the top step and pulled down the big brass switches on the lighting bank. The dark Emporium lit up by stages, bands of light spreading along the rows of counters piled high with goods until the entire sales floor was illuminated. His eyes glowed deep blue. The shadows were banished from his handsome face and now it was the eager, kind face that Ria loved until she hurt.

'I love you,' he murmured. He loved her fiery blue-gold eyes, her passion, her slim secret body, her fierce loyalty; he loved her love.

She thought the Emporium excluded her. Ria was so wrong. Love was the rainbow: lust, fury, compassion, pride, jealousy, hurt, rejection. Love.

'Oh Ria,' Ben London whispered. '*Oh, Ria,*' he shouted.

'You're my sister,' Vic said. 'I love you.'

Ria pushed round him. 'Let me get on with this hoovering, be a chum.'

He turned her new machine off at the switch. 'I'm going to make life easy for you, Ria,' he said in a quieter voice. 'I like to see you working at home.' But the little house in Havannah Street wasn't Ria's home – it was Mum's.

'Just let me get on with it,' Ria begged, 'she'll be back any minute!' She hated dusting in front of Mum; Esther always criticized.

Vic said: 'Don't forget who brought you the Hoover.' His gift was a lovely machine with a light on the front, but Ria stared at her brother with irritation in her opal-flecked eyes, knowing he literally meant brought, not bought. Vic was always literal. He observed her with his head on one side, his black eyes sparkling with life. 'I worry about you, Ria.'

'I'm all right.' Good old Ria. She picked up a duster to get away from him.

Vic said: 'You look silly wearing that handkerchief knotted over your head.'

'It keeps the bleeding dust out of my hair. What do you care anyway?'

'I care about you more than you care about yourself,' Vic said simply. 'You like the flowers I brought you, don't you?'

They looked nice on Mum's mantelpiece. 'They're all right,' Ria snapped. 'I mean, they must have cost a fortune!'

Vic knew when to close his fingers lightly over her wrist.

'I'm dusting!' Ria jerked free and flapped about, but Esther had some pretty china figurines on the window sill, and she had to be careful with them.

'I'm not a stone,' Vic said behind her, 'I know when you're unhappy.'

'I'm not unhappy.'

'Too busy to talk to your brother. Showing off.' Vic hated showing off.

'I'm working.' Ria dusted the photograph of Edward VII and continued along the sideboard through the rest of the royal family to the present King George at the end. The charming bachelor Prince of Wales and the Duke and Duchess of York hung on the wall. Esther adored the royals and regarded them as personal friends. She was dying for the young Duchess to have a baby so that she could write and congratulate her, but they hadn't been married long. Ria glanced nervously at her brother under her long lashes. Vic always had been kind, but he used presents to dominate people, and Ria wasn't having it. 'Mum will love the vacuumer,' she said.

'It's yours. This is your house as much as theirs. More.'

Tom's lovebirds twittered in the cage. Once her father's passion had been canaries, but Nigel had given him some lovebirds. That was something new, her quiet, clever brother Nigel giving presents to his dad. He'd grown closer to Tom since he began walking out with Arleen. Imagine, Nigel with a girl. Arleen was nice, Ria liked her. Marriage was in the air. Vic disapproved.

'Vic, will you please – ' Ria bit back her tongue, he hated women to swear. 'Just leave me alone!' She regretted her outburst at once.

He was genuinely concerned. 'What is the matter, Ria, darling?'

It was stupid, but Ria thought she was going to cry. She shook her head.

'You need your own house.' Vic understood. 'Not right, living with the old folks at your age.' Esther and Tom weren't old, but that was how they thought of themselves because that was how Vic treated them – he wanted people to need him. They didn't know what Vic was really like. For one horrid moment Ria thought he was going to suggest she move in with him and Nigel next door. 'You can't live alone,' Vic pointed out. 'Not right, a female on her ownsome.' He was well known for his puritan morals. In the sea of vice in which he swam it kept his head above water. He drank little, smoked not at all, did not so far as Ria knew supply drugs to the Limehouse Chinese, and was not directly involved in prostitution. In fact Nigel claimed that Vic's money was all legal, but Nigel was clever that way. They said Vic had killed a man.

'I'm happy here,' Ria said, but she wasn't. That single word: *marriage*.

'You're not happy,' Vic said with total conviction, knowing her.

'Now I've got a bloody Hoover,' Ria shouted, 'I am over the bloody moon!'

'What's the matter?'

'You're the matter,' Ria spat. Her temper ran away with her because Esther would be home soon, and there was her son Will to pick up from school, and she would go wild if she didn't get this stupid useless housework done in time for tea. 'Out! Get out of this house, Vic, please,' she ordered.

He stared at her.

Ria braced her hands defiantly on her hips.

Vic grinned. 'Ria. Darling – '

Ria stamped her foot.

'You'll feel better soon.' Vic nodded and left, but he slammed the door.

Ria kicked the vacuum cleaner, blaming it. 'Hell,' she said.

Mum's living room now sported net curtains. Ria peered along the grimy street. Esther was coming back from the shops with a wicker basket. Her plodding walk weaved genially, and her cheeks burned with two high spots of colour. Ria remembered to pull the plug from the socket then bundled the cleaner in a mess under the stairs. One day they would invent something better than electric flex.

'Just one little glass,' Esther claimed to forestall Ria's accusation, proudly thumping her basket down on the kitchen table – it was still a matter of pride to Esther that she had money to pay for her shopping. One little glass, Ria thought, but three or four doubles in it. 'I met Nigel

33

and Arleen,' Esther confided happily. 'Do you think there's a chance?' The single word again.

Ria tried to shrug it off. 'Them, marry? Depends how she looks after him.'

'You're much too earthy, Ria.' Esther bustled, putting things away.

Nigel had always been snotty to Ria about kissing, imitating his older brother Vic, keeping women down. In that way it was a pleasant revenge to see him in love. Arleen was petite but knew her mind, her black hair cut in the Eton crop that was all the rage, as short as a boy's. 'I hope they'll be happy,' Ria said.

'They are, she's so pretty, I saw them going into the Tooke Arms.' Esther looked reproachfully over her shoulder. 'She invited me in, I couldn't refuse.'

'I wonder what she sees in him?' Ria mused. Her own conviction was that Nigel had no balls, and she had said so once, but Arleen struck her as a warm, vital girl who liked everything in working order. Perhaps she dreamed of turning him round, they were hardly strangers. She'd worked in the Queen's theatre ticket office for years and Nigel had stacks of her old stubs.

'My son's a wonderful catch!' Esther sparked, getting past the booze's genial stage: Vic and Nigel were perfect. Only Ria, her last surviving daughter, wasn't good enough, daughters never were. 'Arleen dotes on him, he's much more confident with her now.' She looked longingly at the cupboard under the sink where she kept her secret bottle of gin that nobody knew about. That was why, Ria knew, it was kept wrapped in a brown paper bag as though it was the innocent bottle of bleach.

'I had a row with Vic,' Ria confessed.

Esther sighed. 'Vic is a saint to you,' she said.

'He says I'm unhappy.'

'I told you. Who else cares for you the way Vic does?'

'Don't start that again, Mum.'

'Ben London left you in the lurch.'

'I left him,' Ria murmured. She pulled off the handkerchief and tossed her gold hair. She wore it much longer and let the natural curls come out. It took ages to wash, but they had a proper bathroom now.

Mention of Ria's old flame got Esther going. 'I thought Ben was a nice boy! I brought him up like a child of my own, food, shelter, and they were hard times.'

'Mum – ' Mother and daughter were arguing again.

'And I thought you loved him!'

'Mum . . .' Ria threw up her arms, her cheeks flushing.

'Left you in the lurch,' Esther prattled. She never did know when to let go: 'I won't forgive Ben this time, and neither should you!'

'I've got to pick up Will from school,' Ria said distantly. 'I can't stay for a cup of tea.'

'I'm sorry, dear,' Esther sighed. 'I just want an easy life. I hate it when you row with Vic. You shouldn't.'

'This isn't a game we're playing, Mum.'

'I know it,' Esther shot back. 'Do you?'

Ben's bastard son Will attended, as Ria had when she was ten (when she wasn't playing truant), the Cheval Street school with its tall iron gates and high surrounding wall topped with broken glass. It had never stopped *her*, but Will wasn't like her, and you would never have believed that Ben was his father.

Will was quiet – quiet to the point of being passive. He never played hooky, he was a follower, not a leader. Will always *wanted* to understand, Ria thought angrily, but Ben, damn him, always understood.

Be honest – Ria blamed herself. She wasn't a good mother.

Mums liked picking their youngsters up from school, enjoying the excuse for a chi-hike now that so many of them were cut off in their homes by hot and cold running water and electric power. But Ria stood alone, away from the group. She told herself she found small talk boring, but . . .

If only I could be like them!

She was ashamed because she had no husband.

The wind blew off the hidden Thames, swirling behind

the warehouses, but she could smell its stink. A ship's bowsprit jutted incongruously above West Ferry Road. She could tell from its height over the house roofs that it was half-tide, falling. The man banging with a mallet looked as tiny as a doll.

Ria was alone because she was unhappy. Vic was right. She had lashed out at him *because* he was right. Ria no longer exalted unhappiness, willingly embracing it as a punishment for love. Now she had made her choice. She was no longer in love, she was tired of secrets, and she wanted no more memories to creep into her head in the night. She longed to be free of Ben London. And she was.

But here she was, waiting for Will to come out of school.

The bell rang and a racket of children's noise erupted as the gates were opened. A flood of kids swirled around Ria, squealing like piglets. They'd been allowed to keep their drawings to show their mums and dads. Where was Will?

Standing alone, she searched for his serious eyes.

The playground was empty. Ria's throat tightened.

Footsteps came running. But it was not Will who dashed around the corner of the wall – a boy she did not recognize. He pelted away along the deserted street.

'It's a surprise to see you, Mrs Price.' The teacher who spoke was Miss Leger, a tall willowy girl with spectacles and a flower-print dress. Ria's heart froze.

'*Where's my son?*' she screamed.

'I thought you had been called urgently up to London.' The Isle of Dogs prided itself on its separate identity, but to Ria *called up to London* carried a threat within its double meaning – London the place, or London the person.

'I'm sorry,' the teacher apologized, 'I must have misunderstood. William was picked up by his uncle.' Everyone knew Vic. 'It's quite all right.'

It was *not* all right. Ria was appalled at the teacher's innocence. She looked frantically around her, then drew a deep breath. 'Which way did they go?'

Miss Leger spun helpfully on her heel. 'West Ferry Road!' she beamed.

Ria ran. Traffic streamed along the road. Which way? North or south?

Then Ria was sure, beyond doubt, where Vic had taken Will. She turned north and ran with her skirt flapping at her knees. The street scrolled slowly past her, then a stitch jabbed her side cruelly. She forced herself to walk, holding the back of her wrist against her open mouth. Oh God, if anything had happened.

Vic had taken Will to the Limehouse lock where the great ships winched in and out of the vast tideless docklands beyond.

The same lock where her youngest brother Jimmy always played with Vic when they were children. The place Vic had never forgotten. When the men pulled Jimmy's drowned body out of the roaring waters, Vic had cried like a baby.

Ahead she saw Vic's white tourer parked on gravel at the side of the road. Will would do anything for a ride in a motor car.

She ran past the wall and skidded down the slope. The sunlight increased, then suddenly the wind gusted off the open river, stinking, whipping Ria's skirt around her thighs. She crouched, gasping, staring into the gushing pit.

Man and boy made an idyllic picture playing on the grass. Will was showing Vic something he'd found. Vic smiled and pretended to put it in his mouth. Will clapped joyfully. The gulls circled, the green water roared beneath.

Ria came crouching up to them. 'I'm sorry. I spoke out of turn, Vic.'

'Mummy!' Will said. He threw his arms around her neck. Ria cuddled him close, staring over the top of his head.

'I'm sorry, Vic.'

'We were playing,' Vic said, twisting round, fisting Will's arm playfully. 'We were just playing, weren't we, Jimmy-me-lad!'

'Yeth,' Will lisped.

'Yes,' Ria corrected without thinking.

37

'Yes,' Vic said. Jimmy had been just a lump floating in the water.

'I'm sorry, Vic.' Ria clasped Will tight. 'I was out of order.'

'All forgotten.' Vic stretched his mouth wide into a smile. 'I've enjoyed myself. Afternoon off from the pressures of work.'

But Vic never stopped working. Everything was work to him.

There was one thing Ria had to know. For a moment she dared to lift a corner of the veil of words that lay between them.

'Vic. You wouldn't, you wouldn't really have . . .' She held tightly to Will's small body, and glanced at the lock.

Vic's smile broke into a laugh at once. He shook his head and looked honestly into her blue-gold eyes. 'No.'

He was lying. Ria trembled, suddenly sure those rumours were true: Vic had killed a man.

'Be happy!' Vic said. 'I hate it when you're unhappy.'

'It's not a very happy world sometimes, Vic.'

'I know that,' Vic said. 'There's an old friend I want you to meet.' He looked behind her, and Ria turned.

Raymond Trott stood there. She remembered him as a mummy's boy, but that was before the War. He now looked aggressively male, almost as tall as Ben London.

He said very casually, trying to appear indifferent to her: 'Hi there, Ria.'

Raymond Trott, with his sunbleached hair and knowing eyes, his moustache as razor-thin as a film star's, had grown into the most handsome man she had ever seen.

CHAPTER THREE

1

We are alone, and no one on this earth knows us as we truly are.

No one knew the millionaire or understood what force drove him. The truth was love – love, that his wife Vane desired and feared. Love, that Ria feared to trust because that fierce, longing heat wears many faces, and not all are kind . . . love, that did not at all seduce Ben into the soft beds of sighing ladyships, as Hawk imagined, for Ben had led a chaste life since Ria left. They had both been burned.

Love burned.

Since Vane threw him out of Primrose House, Ben lived in the apartment above the Emporium converted from the old staff attic-dormitories. Peggy, his talkative and devoted maid, who followed Ben rather than stay with her ungrateful mistress Vane, was secretly ashamed of this large apartment. Despite an unparalleled view over the rooftops of the metropolis, it wasn't nearly as fabulous as it should be.

When people asked her Peggy said the rooms were terrifically grand with wonderful white furniture by Syrie Maugham, and an ebony-black concert Bechstein. Peggy's face lit up as she invented these lies. At his soirées famous men sipped champagne cocktails, and their pampered wives wore fabulous clothes. She told this to anyone who listened, even Hawk. Peggy loved working for Mr London. At last everyone listened to her stories.

In truth they were just a man's rooms, empty and sad without a woman's touch. He slept in a single bed, an ex-military bed that looked as hard as a punishment.

At six a.m. precisely, this and every other morning, Peggy checked that there was no lint on her black dress,

39

straightened her frilly white apron, then settled the silver tea-tray over her left arm. She knocked on the door and breezed straight in, knowing he would be alone.

He was working, of course.

'Good morning, sir!' She carried the tray to the long table, swept some papers aside, and put it down by his elbow. She cleared her throat.

He looked up with a smile. 'On time as usual, Peggy.'

'Drink your tea while it's hot, sir.' It was terrible working for a man.

The apartment was a mess, also as usual. Peggy opened the balcony window. It was still dark outside. A cold, gentle rain was falling, damping down the smell of smoke. He wouldn't ride today.

'I'll draw your bath now, sir?' He hadn't touched his tea, she noticed.

'I'll drink my tea when I come out,' he said, standing. Peggy was flustered: he always knew what she was thinking, he paid attention to every detail. They said he had been sold into the Workhouse when he was seven, and learned the hard way how to survive. Yet he retained a kind of unspoiled innocence, a warmth that compelled attraction. He could be hurt. He must have loved Ria very much.

While he bathed Peggy tidied up. Ben always complained he couldn't find anything afterwards, but if he was paying her wages she was going to do her job. Plumping up the sofa cushions, she caught her nail on a card that had fallen behind. She lifted it out then looked at it curiously.

It was undated, but topped with an embossed crest, and handwritten. *My dear London* – She glanced at the bathroom door and read the imperative line.

Kindly call on me at noon on Wednesday. Cleremont.

Blimey, what a cheek. But that name – and the impressive Regent's Park address – must mean it was from *Lord* Cleremont, because lords didn't sign their title, you were expected to know.

The bathroom door opened. 'A real lord!' exclaimed Peggy, then bit her tongue.

'I haven't forgotten,' Ben said mildly. Sometimes Peggy thought she was his only friend.

She burst out: 'And he's invited you over!'

Ben shrugged. 'He probably wants to sell his wine cellar. Aristocrats who haven't inherited plump property interests in London are feeling the pinch.' Of course; the millionaire had already checked up on the aristocrat. There was a copy of Burke's as well as Debrett's on the bookshelf.

Ben added: 'Especially when they own a castle in Yorkshire, too.'

'A castle!' Peggy gasped. Then: 'Will you buy his cellar?'

Ben smiled. 'He'll ask a very high price. Why didn't he send his butler to see me discreetly? Because he wants to impress me personally, and up the price.' He winked. 'I'll go, but I've got a busy morning first. Tell Simmonds to have the Rolls-Royce waiting outside at a quarter to twelve.'

'A real fairytale castle,' breathed Peggy, closing the door behind her.

'Probably a six-hundred-year-old stable without a roof,' he called through the panels, and heard her laugh.

His face changed.

We are alone, and no one knows us as we truly are.

Alone, he dropped the towel from his waist and strode naked into his bedroom. The four changes of clothes he would use today were neatly laid out. He cared nothing for this; he was bored. He dressed smoothly and in shirt-sleeves worked on papers for a further hour at the big table, leaving them in neatly labelled piles for Miss Cypress his secretary to deal with.

The teapot was cold – he had forgotten after all – and it was light now. Hooves clopped in the streets below, but fewer every year, and there was talk of closing Oxford Street to horsedrawn vehicles. He heard the angry buzz

41

of motors along Piccadilly. Hawk would be arriving for duty and the store waking up.

Ben went into the hall, opened the lift gates with a key, and dropped down through the still-dark sales floors of London Emporium towards the lowest level the shaft served, the upper basement.

Even larger than it looked from the outside, the Emporium had sunk its roots deep beneath the old cellars of Clarendon House into the clay of the stone-age village here long before London had a name: though that was one floor still further down, where the sub-basement warren of the Buying Department extended under the roadway and even beneath other shops. Here in the upper basement, Roman London was at the level of Ben's knees as he came out of the lift.

Now this modern, white-painted subterranean warehouse area was a bedlam of trundling sack-trucks and trolleys, piles of packing cases, tea chests, rounds of cheese, and cardboard boxes in teetering stacks that never quite overbalanced. Men worked with bulging muscles. Shouted orders flew above their heads. Milk churns were being run down the slope from the rear courtyard. Ben's gaze froze. 'That delivery is too late!'

'Sorry, Mr London.' David, the manager, came over looking harassed. 'There's a strike on the railway. The milk train was delayed.'

'Don't they want our business?' But Ben was pleased to see David Jones handling the matter personally, too many managers left these details to subordinates. That was not delegating, it was being out of touch – Ben approved of delegation, that was why he had made David manager, a man who owed him everything, a director he could trust. 'It was an unofficial action,' David said.

'Tell them I'll put a herd of cows back in St James's Park.' The manager smiled, but he wasn't sure if Mr London was joking – there had indeed been cows there in Spring Gardens until the War. 'I'll threaten them,' he promised.

'Warn them,' Ben said. 'Never threaten.' He smiled too

– but his was a sure smile. He clapped David's shoulder. 'Come and have breakfast with me.' Some crates had spilled over the painted line marking a walkway, and David knew that Ben had noticed. By the time they had eaten David would have quietly passed the word and the boxes would be moved. Ben banged through the swing doors. The canteen was hot and smelly, the tea urn bubbling steam. Ben took a tray to the counter.

'Wotcher Daisy, how are your knees now?' Daisy had been a cleaning chargehand until her knees seized up. Ben took advantage of her misfortune to promote her.

'I'm dancing again!' She looked at him, pleased he cared. Daisy's bad language had cleared up too – food and swearing didn't go together, though she could let rip if anyone backchatted her about stiff eggs or cold bacon. An army marched on its stomach, and so did a shop. The hard-working staff prized their food highly, but Daisy ruled the kitchen with a rod of iron and they had little cause for complaint. She was a good choice.

'What's the special?' Ben had been afraid the knee trouble was arthritis.

'Corned dog fritters.' She meant corned beef; the men here were all ex-Services and the girls had worked in factories – usually ammunition or armaments. By now their slang was nostalgic, their memories of the good camaraderie of the War rather than its horror – they still called the canteen the Naafi.

'Chips, beans and two slices please.' Ben took the heavy plate and mug of sweet tea to a centre table where he could be seen.

'I don't like this self-service,' a big man said loudly. He was sitting alone. 'It's like being in the bleeding Army again. Let's have the waitresses back, pretty little waitresses.' He looked at Ben out of the corners of his eyes.

'Come here and talk to me.' Ben poured brown sauce over his chips.

'Just tell us, why can't we have the skivvies back?'

Ben didn't look up. 'Pay me, Jake. How much do you want to pay?'

'Nah.' Isolated, Jake looked round for support.

'Who's going to pay for your waitresses then? Talk to me, Jake, tell me. How much do you want to pay? Penny a sausage, tuppence? Everyone voted, where were you?'

Ben let the others shout the man down: 'Give it a rest, chum.'

David slipped into the seat opposite Ben. He looked thin. His suit was always buttoned up, his eyes always restless. He felt he had been promoted above himself and he wasn't sure if he could live up to all Ben expected of him. Too young for the War, he hated the Naafi, and knew he could never have handled Jake as roughly and fairly as Ben had – or so he feared. Ben seemed to have no such fear, trusting David. David worked desperately hard to earn that trust.

Ben glanced at him, missing nothing. 'How is Harriet?' David's wife still worked downstairs in the Post Room. The head postal order-clerk's position was vacant, and Harriet was in line for it.

'I was looking for an opportunity of telling you.' David cut into his sausage but did not put it in his mouth. 'Harriet is expecting a baby in June.'

'Wonderful!' David smiled, pleased that Ben was pleased. 'I'm very happy for her,' Ben said, and that was true. He liked Harriet, but it suited him that she would not now fill the head clerk's job. Ben would tolerate no other dynasty but his own in London Emporium, even though his sons Ralph and George were only three.

He asked suddenly: 'Where do you plan to put the Inquiries desk?'

David was caught off guard. 'By the main doors.' But his voice lifted on the final syllable and made a question mark. That wasn't good enough.

'Put it over by the lifts.'

'Why?'

'Half the people will buy something on their way across,' Ben pointed out.

'If there's to be a desk at all,' David murmured.

Ben studied him. This was new. 'Mr Courtenay opposes

44

the idea of an Inquiries desk in the Emporium,' said David apologetically. 'They never needed one in the old days, he says.'

Ben did not underestimate Algernon Courtenay, he had brushed with the chief floorwalker before. But coming out into the open like this rather than quietly going his own way . . . that was new from Courtenay, and a mistake. Ben was sad. The older clients liked Courtenay, who exuded good breeding from his flared nostrils to his striped grey trousers, and he headed the considerable conservative faction within the Emporium, diehards like Hawk who had worked here for most of their lives. They were believers in the institution, and Ben respected them. In their way they were powerful, and he did not begrudge them their arrogance as long as they did not defy him. What would Courtenay's line be at the regular weekly meeting later this morning? Did he want to do battle with Ben?

'Tell Courtenay that he's making a mistake,' Ben said gently. 'He should not do this, I don't want him to. Make him listen.'

David looked horrified. Once Mr Courtenay had been young David's boss. 'I'm not sure he'd pay attention to me . . .'

That was the root of the problem. Courtenay should have been manager. Instead he was paid almost as much. And he was worth it, except that he wouldn't take orders. David looked at Ben nervously. Ben smiled.

'All right, I'll speak with Mr Courtenay,' David said resolutely.

'Don't speak to him,' Ben said coldly, standing. 'Warn him.'

He went back through the warehouse area. The boxes had been moved and the walkway was clear. He called the manned lift. 'My floor, Jim, please.'

'Yes, Mr London.' Jim had got over the pimples that afflicted him as a liftboy and now he was a presentable young man. They rose through the lower sales floor, toys, wines, guns, sports clothing, uniforms, funeral department . . . Jim shifted uneasily, self-conscious about Mr London staring at him.

'Main floor,' Jim said from habit, 'cheeses, cold meats, pâtisserie, general merchandise . . .' What a boring job.

'You know this shop like the back of your hand,' Mr London said.

'Yes, sir!'

'Where would I buy a number five shoe?'

Jim knew it was a trick question. Adult shoes were sold here on the upper sales floor. 'Lower sales floor,' Jim contradicted instantly. 'Number five is a child's size, sold down by the toy department.' He added: 'But if it was a woman asking, well, women often take fives or less, so Ladies' Shoes on this floor does stock the fashion range in those sizes. The answer depends who's asking, see.'

'You'll run the new Inquiries desk,' Ben said. The lift passed the top floor – now much expanded to take the Waterfalls restaurant on two levels, the offices and board-room beyond.

The lift stopped at Ben's private hall in the roof. He used his key to get into the apartment.

He undressed and changed into a comfortable tailored suit, selecting a dark, conservative tie. He stood looking in the dressing room mirror as he did up his diamond tiepin. He stopped, staring. The littlest things still reminded him . . . it was the tiepin that Vane had given him on their marriage, the B of his name symbolically enclosed within the outspread arms of the V of hers, all in sparkling diamonds, the physical shape of her hard, sparkling dreams for their life together.

Divorce was impossible. Vane hated him totally and used their marriage as a torment, never taking him back, never letting him go, keeping his sons to herself like property. It was her revenge for his takeover of the Emporium from her.

Ben stared in the mirror.

The V and B intertwined . . . not only V for Vane, but also Vic: for the lives of Vic Price and Ben were inextri-cably bound together by the crime Ben had committed many years ago in the East End when they were children. Ben only stole a couple of oranges and showed Vic up. But there was the root of Vic's envy, in that childhood moment when Vic realized Ben London would always be able to impress Ria more than he, her brother. All the terrible things that happened to the children grew from those roots.

Behind every great fortune, there lies a crime.

When David arrived in the boardroom he was surprised, as always, at how calm, relaxed and in command Mr London looked, because this meeting would be very difficult. In its first four decades of life the Emporium had been structured around the very stiff hierarchy favoured by the Leibigs. David now realized that Ben London had taken an enormous risk by his own promotion to manager – deliberately. Ben had planned this confrontation with Courtenay.

Ben welcomed the other directors filing into the room. They settled on the hard chairs around the walnut table. Alice Cypress, her formidable silver-rimmed spectacles glinting, sat by the wall to take the minutes. Ben chimed a tiny steel wand against his glass to declare the meeting open. 'We don't have much time this morning, so let's get on with it.' He was often direct, David knew, but this cold briskness was unusual.

The twins Ralph and George would not come into their Trust and inherit the Emporium until 1941. Meanwhile power was held by the troika named in cunning old Georgy Leibig's will: Ben, Vane who was never here, and sitting on Ben's right hand the accountant Clifford Ford, a shy red-headed Scot who was dominated (*persuaded* was the word they used) by Ben in the same way David admitted he was himself – eager to serve, wary of the alternative. Vane London's empty chair was on Ben's left. David remembered her precious, bone-china prettiness – she had the round, perfect face of an exquisite doll. Every man at the table had been bemused by her looks, except Ben, who paid her the compliment of treating her exactly as a business partner. But still she had turned him down.

47

Perhaps that was *why* she had turned him down – because he was not under her spell. Poor Vane, the only man she could not mesmerize was her own husband.

'Did you speak to Algy Courtenay, David?' Ben asked.

David tried to explain the older man's point of view. 'I think we ought to understand that he sees himself as the protector of the old ways – '

'I don't care how he sees himself,' Ben interrupted roughly. 'The past is dead. It's gone. All I care about is the numbers. We made a four per cent return on capital last year and at that rate we might as well keep our money in the building society where it's nice and safe.'

'Mr Courtenay opposes your plans to turn Warehousing and the Naafi into a sales floor,' David said in a muted voice. 'He also . . .' The list was long.

'We'll let him speak for himself,' Ben decided. 'Mr Courtenay!' He stood as the older man came in. Courtenay was a picture of refined elegance in his grey striped trousers and black tails, an orchid erect in his buttonhole. 'Sit down, Algy,' Ben said. 'Please explain your objections to my plans.' His manner was polite but his tone icy.

Courtenay spoke, as always, with pursed lips. 'You and young David, sir – ' A calculated insult, David was hardly younger than Ben, but Ben just nodded politely. 'I think you will find that you will learn by experience that a great store like the Emporium is an institution – and like all institutions – '

Ben had heard all this before. 'An organic growth,' he yawned.

For the first time Courtenay looked rattled. 'Not lightly tampered with.'

'What about the numbers, Courtenay?'

'There is more to life than profit!'

Ben said bluntly: 'No. No, there isn't.'

'Pile it high, sell it quick,' Courtenay sneered.

'Do you have a better idea? Would you rather work elsewhere? The other great stores make fifteen per cent. You wouldn't like it.'

'Is that a threat?' Courtenay asked in a high voice,

because he knew it was not. He was in great peril, but he could still draw back from the abyss. 'Are you asking for my job? Others will go with me.'

Ben said: 'I will have London Emporium be the greatest and most glamorous store anywhere on earth, so that people will gladly cross the world to come through these doors, and those who cannot will envy those who do. Algy, be a part of it. A whole new sales floor where Warehousing is now, more jobs. Buying moved upstairs. Lower stock levels, faster turnover. A better refunds policy, proper client services at an Inquiries desk that will also handle –'

'No,' Courtenay said. He would not draw back.

'Then you're out,' Ben said. He waited. Courtenay shook his head.

'Perhaps we could . . .' temporized David, then his voice trailed away.

Ben's eyes were fierce and cold. There was no emotion in their businesslike stare. Courtenay was out. Ben said: 'Yes, David?'

'Nothing,' David said. 'I agree.'

'I agree with Mr London,' said Clifford Ford, of course.

Courtenay cleared his throat softly. 'Numbers. It seems that no man can stand against *them*.'

'I'm sorry, Algy,' Ben said, 'you're finished. You'll be well paid.'

'Don't you have any feelings? I don't want your gold,' Courtenay said in a bitter voice. His lip curled helplessly and David actually thought the smart old man would break down. David looked at Ben for mercy but the millionaire's gaze was set like stone.

'Numbers,' Ben said. 'Don't you know what the difference between four per cent and fifteen per cent is? Three times the money for expansion. Jobs. Just numbers.'

A short way up exclusive Old Bond Street, outside a shop display of priceless *objets d'art*, a man with a white moustache stopped, and stared at the woman who was windowshopping there. Then he raised his bowler and the words simply tumbled out of him, breathless and spontaneous. 'Excuse me – you are the most lovely woman I have ever seen in my life.'

She acknowledged him gracefully as though she had never heard the compliment before.

'What a charming thing to say, thank you very much.'

He gasped.

Pearl Remington was more than lovely, she was beautiful. Everyone noticed how amazing she looked because she was so natural, so obviously unself-conscious about herself. Pearl radiated openness, so that desire was pleasure, and envy no jealousy. She was sensational – her hair was outrageous, seeming washed with light, yet real. Even pretty girls of her own age admired her as she passed the shop windows, and they would have sensed a fraud. Whatever price she had paid for such beauty, it had not been in a salon.

Sometimes she paused, and Miss Remington could have afforded to buy these Bond Street trinkets, for she was rich – so rich that she did not carry money.

She wore a simple black Chanel dress whose classical lines limned the form of her body stunningly – the rain had stopped and the people looking at her felt clumsy and oafish in their heavy clothes, but she had just stepped from a taxi deliberately a few yards from her destination, which was London Emporium. The old gentleman raised his hat to her and paid her the compliment which she would return with such grace.

A rope of gorgeous, priceless pearls encircled her throat. They did not only match her name: they also matched her amazing hair.

The proper word was nacreous. Her hair glowed with a subtle iridescence as pale as oystershell, yet imbued with such a rich deepness that it made a shimmering, fluid gleam falling over her shoulders. And that was why the old gentleman gasped.

Her hair swung freely when she turned, framing her face.

She has the face of an angel.

Hawk, too, knew it at once. He gazed at her with his heart in his mouth. She was the most beautiful woman in the world. He wished she would come up to him. She had paused under the yellow canopies of the Emporium, looking at the brilliant displays. He looked away from her, then looked at her again. With the whisper of an engine the Rolls-Royce slid up to the kerb, Simmonds arriving to pick Mr London up at a quarter to twelve. Two minutes early, to be on the safe side.

'Wotcher, Hawk.' Bert came round the gleaming bonnet of the laudalette and lit a cigarette under his hand. He was a small man in his seventies. Hawk towered over him despite the natty chauffeur's cap.

'You put that fag out on my patch and I'll have your guts for garters,' warned Hawk genially, without even looking at him.

'What about that?' Bert nodded at the Chanel girl. 'I bet she – '

'Don't you dare think one single dirty thought about her near me,' Hawk said.

'Would I?' Bert sounded injured. 'She looks like my Gloria.'

Hawk glanced at him with one eye. Bert's daughter Gloria was a fat pig and always had been, just like old Mrs Simmonds, God rest her. No one deceived men like women, in Hawk's opinion.

He stared at the wonderful girl. 'Isn't she simply spectacular?' he breathed. She had moved to the nearest window. In a moment he would open the door for her.

'I thought you hated women.'

'Not all,' Hawk said with dignity.

'Ha!' cackled Bert, 'Hawk's in love!'

Hawk thrust out his lower lip but before he could say anything Bert hissed, 'Look out!' and flicked his cigarette stub into the gutter. Hawk opened the door and saluted as Mr London strode out, dressed in dark clothes for a formal interview. He looked angry and withdrawn. The girl glanced over, her eye caught by his movement while her concentration remained on the display – a mouthwatering selection of the fresh food at which the Emporium excelled. She couldn't eat much with a figure like that. If Mr London noticed her he didn't even break stride. He stepped into the car and was driven away.

Hawk nodded to himself. So Courtenay was sacked at last and the Emporium was entering a new era. No one stood against the millionaire.

But Mr London hadn't looked happy. Men always were alone, Hawk knew; that was the hardest truth a man ever learned.

Someone lightly touched his shoulder.

'Excuse me . . .'

Hawk turned. 'Yes!' he gushed. It was her.

She smiled. 'My name is Pearl Remington. I wonder if you could help me . . .'

'That's my job, m'am,' Hawk said, saluting. She had a faint, attractive foreign accent.

She said: 'I am looking for Mr London – Mr Ben London.'

2

'I am Lord Cleremont.'

Ben had lifted the brass lion's head but before he could let it drop, the door swung open and there stood the peer. Cleremont smiled and took Ben's hand, shook it, held it warmly. It was an act he had rehearsed.

Cleremont's handsome, ruined face had fluttered many feminine hearts – rakishly winsome in his twenties, the dissolute, sophisticated air of his thirties and later years had still brought them fluttering, those young and innocent butterflies, giggling debutantes and shy maids, girls fresh from country life and girls who should have known better, but all with dreams of love in common, love that does not exist. In his fifties, this terrible life was what Lord Cleremont's face showed – or rather could not show, because he was smiling such a broad welcome to Ben as to reveal his teeth.

Yet Ben saw how smooth around that gleaming debonair smile Cleremont's face remained, hiding the years behind the veneer of his skin, which looked stretched, stropped, *polished* – shaved clean of the lines of age or suffering. Ben noticed his long fingers, with nails so cut back into the quick that they must hurt; and those porcelain-white teeth were surely false.

But Lord Cleremont was not false. His eyes were still the colour of melting ice – many women had willingly given up everything for those beguiling blue-green depths – but they were ice nevertheless. Within Charles Cleremont's chest beat a dinosaur's heart. Behind him stretched a dozen generations of cold, hard, successful men who did not marry for love. They married for blood, having only one duty in life: to inseminate a wife of good stock with a male heir. Roland, his son and heir, was dead. In the one thing that mattered, Lord Cleremont had failed his ancestors. He embraced that failure. Roland's unmarked grave was Charles Cleremont's revenge upon them all, as was his undirected lust, wasting himself in the sorrow of the women he took, his sweetest victory his refusal to marry again. He would be triumphant in death. But Cleremont was growing old, and such a life was a true horror.

His smile dare not slip.

He wore a green velvet smoking jacket and a cravat, very casual, almost indifferent. Ben felt overdressed.

'My apologies for greeting you personally – my butler is away.'

'You're very kind to see me at all.'

In the hall Ben wiped his feet carefully. The old boy was obviously fastidious, probably frightened of germs – germs, contamination by the lower classes, the invisible life that swarms and multiplies in dirt. So Ben thought, but he didn't know Cleremont.

Uniquely, the old man had deceived him completely. Cleremont knew all about the dirt the metropolis had to offer, but all Ben saw was the aristocrat, and he meticulously wiped his feet. Cleremont had outwitted his son in the game of lies even before Ben followed him into his study.

'Drinky?' Cleremont said over his shoulder. 'Sherry? Whisky?'

Ben sat in the overstuffed sofa by the fire. The room was gloomy, with too much dark wood.

'I'll have brandy.'

'Of course.' Cleremont held out a glass.

'Why of course?'

'I also drink brandy. Since we are related by blood, we must share other characteristics as well. Bottoms up!' He swigged from an ordinary glass, almost draining it, but not taking his melting-ice eyes off Ben, or losing his smile.

Ben sipped, showing no sign of the disturbance he felt, then put on a smile as broad as Cleremont's. 'I'm afraid you are mistaken. I am' – he forced the word out without apparent effort – 'a foundling. I do not know where my blood comes from.'

'I do,' Cleremont said. 'You'll believe me, my boy. Memory fails, but the blood remembers. The history of ordinary people disappears after a great-grandparent or two, they don't know what blood shapes them, what forces move them . . . but we . . . we are different. I am the eleventh Lord Cleremont, I know exactly what blood pulses in our veins. I can trace our ancestors to the 1570s, to canny Robbie Lockhart, favourite of King James the first. Then brave, brutal Stewart, and his son Robert the exile, and his son James the dreamer . . . and his son . . . I am your father.'

Ben studied him.

'How do you know?'

So easily, Charles lost control. He felt the floor open under his feet. His son was an adversary to watch. It was the question he had not thought to ask the parlourmaid. It had never crossed his mind. He had *believed* her.

Ben believed *him*. Hook, line, sinker. But Cleremont did not know that Ben was his son, any more than any father knew that what was his, was his; new life, life's oldest mystery. *I believe it because your mother believed it.*

Ben jumped up. He stared at his father. My God, he thought, it's true.

They didn't even look similar. The eyes, perhaps, but Ben's eyes had now turned from ice to fire, a hot blue his father's never burned . . . the long fingers, but the nails were perfectly trimmed . . . a mannerism here and there. The resemblances were true. Cleremont saw sparks of himself there.

He knew Ben London was his son.

I know you, because your mother knew.

I know you, because I remember my guilt. I remember my shame. Poor girl.

The most secret, smallest voice in Cleremont muttered: *I loved her, but I didn't have the guts to keep her.* He did not say it, and he never would. He had appearances to keep up; he would lose too much face.

Cleremont realized how much he feared Ben – his youth, his energy, his wealth. He feared Ben would see the truth: a lonely, frightened fraud who needed money more than love. 'Sit down.' Cleremont fought to establish control over his son.

But Ben stood by the fire. He said: 'Where is my mother?'

Cleremont shrugged. His smile showed shadows around it.

'Where is my mother, Lord Cleremont?' Ben shouted.

'I don't know! She went away, she's dead, she was a proud woman.' *She was a parlourmaid.* That would never do. Cleremont slopped brandy into his glass.

'Who was she?'

Charles Cleremont's debonair smile broke, and this convinced Ben. The words were dragged out of the old man's quivering mouth. 'I loved her.'

This was the simple truth. Ben saw it. He put his arms around his father.

They both cried – Ben thought his father did.

He could not see the intractable lines ruling the ruined

face that was pressed against his shoulder: the aristocrat of the hard hills, indifferent to lesser beings. Without lies, there was no respect. His bastard son was a millionaire.

'A princess,' wept Lord Cleremont, 'she was a Russian princess.'

3

I am not alone.

'Sir?' Bert Simmonds asked. The rain had passed and Ben stared back at Lockhart House shining in the sun, smoke drifting from half a dozen chimneys though there was only one lonely old man inside – and a few servants. And the precious memories of a love affair from the last year of the last century.

Love does exist.

'Where to, sir?' Bert Simmonds was holding the car door wide, looking worried.

'Have the rest of the day off,' Ben told the old man. 'Go home.'

He crossed the road and went into the park. The gate squeaked.

Love child.

He had asked Lord Cleremont: 'Did you love her?'

The voice against his shoulder muttered: 'Did I love her? Yes, yes, yes.'

Ben had said, 'I'm sorry if the memories are so painful. I have to know.'

'You have to know?'

'Everything!'

'There's not much to tell . . . I loved her.'

'But there must be more, Father. Was she beautiful? What was her name?'

'Beautiful! Her name . . . Princess Eléna Vasílyevna Kurágina.'

There it was. The beautiful Princess Eléna, a Russian Princess, his mother.

I am half Russian, Ben thought, staring at his hands. The waters of the lake lapped the toecaps of his shoes. The bare trees could have been Russian trees. He could have been standing by a Muscovy lake, but for an accident of birth.

'Tell me!' he had begged his father.

Cleremont spoke slowly, looking into Ben's eyes.

'It was an impossible romance, my boy. You understand this was before I inherited my title. Although my father insisted I spend most of the year at Clawfell, I had a few weeks here in the Season. I met her . . . never mind where. Such a glittering affair! You don't see its like nowadays. Love was hotter then. The jewels, candlelight, the solid gold platters on the starched white linen. Her dresses! *La belle Hélène*, I called her! High-born, rich, her estates were vast, love at first sight. You cannot imagine. Surrounded by protocol, head over heels in love! When we were alone together we were mad. We escaped! I . . . I was unfaithful to my wife. Forgive me.'

'Do you still love Eléna?'

'I still love her, but she is dead!' His father stared into the fire.

'When did she die?'

'It must have been in the Revolution. I don't care to know, and neither should you. I had to return to Clawfell, my father's orders. I swear I knew nothing of her condition, you know how these things are handled. Her maid left you discreetly outside the London Hospital. I knew nothing of it until a few days ago, when a letter was forwarded to me from that poor woman's effects. That is how I found out your existence.'

'Where is this letter?'

Cleremont gestured distraughtly at the fire. 'The shock . . .'

'You destroyed it?'

'I'm sorry. I shall be a good father to you now. I can be very useful, I'll do all the things I should have done – I shall introduce you to Society.'

57

But Ben said: 'I want to know everything about my mother.'

Cleremont said gently: 'It can do no good, Ben. May I call you Ben? Life is for the living. Why rake over those old coals of shame and unhappiness?'

'But you said you were in love.'

'Love,' Cleremont said. 'Yes, yes, yes.'

Ben walked out of the park and crossed the road.

Cleremont was self-centred and believed that he alone was enough. But Ben felt in his heart that his mother was still alive; by seeing her, he would see himself. Even if she were no longer living, he had to know. Now he had started, he could not stop. Already he must defy his father.

Ben went into the post office and phoned Bookkeeper & Bookkeeper, his solicitors. 'Charlie?' He raised his voice. 'I want you to trace Eléna Vasílyevna Kurágina, a Tsarist princess in London at the end of the last century.'

'A princess? They had thousands of them,' crackled the solicitor's voice. 'The Reds scattered or destroyed the imperial records, and they won't help us.'

'No expense spared. Please, please try.'

Bookkeeper heard something in his voice. 'You know I will. Who is she?'

'She was my mother,' Ben choked. 'She was beautiful.'

He dropped the phone and took a deep breath outside. If anyone could find her, Charlie Bookkeeper would.

When Hawk saw Mr London walking towards him, he shot his cuffs and saluted. 'Hallo, Hawk!' Hawk had never seen the millionaire smile so broadly before.

Hawk held his salute. 'There's a lady to see you, Mr London.'

'Who is she?'

'A princess,' Hawk said, dropping his voice confidentially. 'That's my opinion, I've never seen anyone like her.'

Mr London stared at him. 'What are you blathering about, Hawk?'

'A foreigner,' Hawk said, 'you wait until you see her, sir.' He added: 'She asked for you by name.'

*

58

Ben hardly noticed walking into the Emporium. He crossed the main sales floor without seeing it. Later he remembered that because the lifts were full, he took the stairs, two steps at a time, without pausing for breath on the landings.

He went towards the annexe to his office. A woman's voice was saying: 'Oh that's lovely, you look so good.' He stopped in the doorway. His formidable secretary Alice Cypress, who never let her guard down, had taken her glasses off and was primping her hair like a schoolgirl. She saw Ben and froze.

Ben was crushingly disappointed. Even from the back he knew instantly that the visitor who had spoken was no older than her late twenties, despite the so-pale wash of her hair. 'The foreign princess' was neither his mother nor a princess: her accent was American. He had been a fool to dream.

'I thought you had to wear glasses,' he snapped at Alice.

'It's my fault.' The newcomer turned and Ben's heart somersaulted.

Nothing for him, ever, for the rest of his life, was the same as before.

He gazed at her.

'Blame me,' Pearl Remington said.

She stared at his face.

'Blame you?' Ben hardly heard his voice. 'My God, I'm enchanted by you.' Was he really saying these words? My God, he was, and they were true.

'You're a fast worker, Mr London.' Her lovely creamy, soft-centred voice.

'Working? I'm not working.' He was dazed. He had received an electric shock – he had been struck by lightning. Twice in one day – he heard only her voice, hardly her words; hardly saw her, aware of her presence with all his senses.

She spoke again. 'We haven't been introduced.' Smooth and light, a femininity that he could have put to his lips and drunk. Not sweet, not cloying. A dry martini. A soothing sting of alcohol. A temptation.

He wanted to have her.

'I'm – ' his tongue failed him.

'Mr London,' Miss Cypress held up her glasses and read a card, 'this is Miss Remington to see you.'

'Pearl.' She held out her hand straightforwardly. He took it. 'So you're the millionaire.'

'Don't believe everything they say.'

'The newspapers? I take people as they are. Real surfaces are all that matter to me. What people really do, not what they say.' A nerve pulsed in her throat. Her hand was warm, her fingertips cool and smooth. 'I'm a surface person. And that's good grammar where I come from. Boston, USA. My family were British, they relocated there from Virginia about 1720 and did pretty well.' He didn't take his eyes off her. 'There's nothing complicated, not about me, though I've lived in Europe the last ten years.'

'You're beautiful,' he breathed.

'Since the War,' she said lightly, and stopped. Such an uncharacteristic withdrawal by this girl drew him on. The way the tip of her tongue touched her upper lip for a moment, the shine in her eyes on his. He had never seen her before, but he felt he knew her intimately, as if she had already taken off her dress for him. He felt her breathing, felt the warmth of her. Her hair – he had never seen such a shimmering perfection in his life before. He caught its natural scent.

He stepped back, still holding her hand with both his. 'Chanel.'

'Yes, this is one of Coco's dresses.' He tried to read himself in her eyes. The scent of her now filled his senses.

'You are wearing Chanel perfume,' he murmured.

'You know my secret.'

At her neck she wore the Coucy pearls – a sign, a borrowed talisman from the Countess of Coucy, who had taught Ben what love was during the War, when Paris was frantic with gaiety under the bombardment, and the Germans might enter the city at any moment. Chouchou had taken Ben, then a young airman, to bed and given him her passion, but there had been more to it than

60

that. *Shou-shou, shou-shou* . . . her gentle French name sounding across the years like the call of an exotic bird. The erotic, unforgettable scent of her perfume was mixed with darker memories. While they made love, her husband lay dying close by in a hospital. By such a hard choice, with the birth of her son François the tiger-eyed Countess saved her ancient family line from extinction. The blood would live on. Such a gift was worth almost any price, but Chouchou must have paid in her conscience.

Her son was Ben's.

Now Pearl was holding out an envelope in her free hand.

'I have a letter for you . . .' she said.

'You are wearing Chanel Number Five perfume,' Ben murmured. Her eyes widened and he saw himself in them. 'I did not know it had reached this country,' he complimented her. 'You are the first, Pearl Remington. You are unique.'

She was very amused. 'So you are an expert at perfume – as well!'

'As well?'

'As an expert at making love.'

'Love. Yes.'

She laughed. He was wonderfully arrogant, but with the self-confidence to let his feelings show, and she felt safe. 'I meant it in the European sense. The art of making beautiful compliments.'

'It's not art, it's real. Nothing's worth anything if it isn't real.'

He meant it. She stopped, and took him very seriously. 'Are you going to hold my hand all day, or are you going to let me go?'

'Yes,' he said, 'I'm going to hold you all day. I'm never going to let you go.'

CHAPTER FOUR

1

'Pass the chocs,' Arleen whispered to Nigel sitting beside her in the darkness.

Ria's youngest brother Nigel, his long thin frame bent uncomfortably into the cinema seat, was watching *The Gold Rush* for the seventh time. He did not like the film. Charlie's scene with the dancing bread rolls was good but the gold-digger's sick fantasy about eating people was repellent, and should have been censored. To Nigel there was something horribly real about the idea of people devouring people. People *did*. Not actually, but in the ways that mattered.

He wouldn't have tolerated the moving picture for a moment except that Arleen wanted him to, and he liked to do what she wanted. Was that love? He didn't know what he felt. Nigel was certain of this: Arleen, a girl, loved Nigel Price, loved *him*. It frightened him, because he was not worth loving.

'Chocs, Nigel,' Arleen nudged.

'You'll get fat.' And yet he wanted to be loved.

She pinched his knee. 'I want one of the sultana ones.'

'I am not joking, Arleen.'

'Neither am I.' She scratched her nails on his thigh. Nigel tried to catch her hand, terrified someone in the row behind would see. Arleen had wanted to go in the back row. Nigel was too old for that sort of juvenility. It had seemed dark in here when they first came out of the afternoon light – Arleen refused to give up her job at the Queen's, so they couldn't go out in the evenings until too late for film shows – but the picture cast a glow quite bright enough for anyone in the row behind to see what they were up to.

'Here,' he said, 'have the whole box. You look after it.'

'I don't want the whole box. I want you.' She smiled at his monochrome blush. She did love him. 'Only you, Nigel. You're my sweet, my love.' She snuggled against him. She could bring him round, just by being romantic and feminine, *different*. Too many girls tried to be like men.

Nigel was sensitive.

After a few moments he gave in and put his arm around her. He patted his fingers on her shoulder fraternally. Arleen smiled another little smile against his coat. She liked the film well enough, but her real reason for coming here was that it was the only place she could get Nigel away from Vic. Having decided that she loved Nigel Price, she must earn his love – in this world only things not worth having came free. He was still shy, a war hero shattered by the war (she could help him) and he must learn to trust her, a woman, and her feelings. And then, despite his horrific war experiences, she sensed that he would come to love her too. Even his male awkwardness was an engaging compliment.

She was a woman – to him, she was mysterious.

So she watched the dancing bread rolls out of the corner of her eye for the seventh or hundred and seventh time, and did not allow him to forget her, pestering him for the chocs, or an orange drink, or holding his thin right hand . . . and felt his fingers begin to curl around her own. She always sat on his right, because of the war injury from the German bullet through his left elbow which paralysed him of almost all feeling, and left those fingers icy cold.

'I like you, Arleen,' he whispered, 'I like you *a lot*.'

That was nice. Arleen didn't push her luck. They'd come to the part of the film which upset him.

The wind gusted over them as they came out of the picture theatre, but it had stopped raining. What had come over Nigel? Instead of walking her back to Havannah Street for tea, he turned the other way down West Ferry Road.

Arleen followed him uncomfortably – her shoes had heels for him, not for walking. This was a fine courtship. She didn't expect him to hold her hand in public, far less – yet – for him to peck her cheek. But she planned that he should at least have learned to treat her with consideration. Perhaps Nigel had a different plan – Nigel always had plans, they were his strength, his weakness. He stopped by the Seamen's Institute, waiting for her impatiently, the wind bending his long, light frame, looking so far away from her. Arleen held her collar down, frightened. The fear of losing Nigel touched her. He called, 'Arleen!' The wind whipped his words into a cry. She came up to him, uncertainty chasing over her face.

'Nigel, what is it?' He had decided on something. They were finished.

Behind them was the choppy waste of the Millwall outer docks, in front of them the roaring lock and the grey-green, windswept river Thames. Nigel's face was white, the wind had tangled his hair. She didn't dare reach up to smooth it.

He gripped her upper arms. 'I've got to tell you something you've got to know, Arleen. There's something you don't know about me. Something that nobody knows.' Was that true? – a frantic flicker in his eyes. 'I adore you, Arleen!'

'Nigel, I love – '

'No!' He hissed: 'I'm not a hero, I'm a coward, a filthy coward, you're the only person I've ever told. My wound – I did it. I shot myself in the elbow, Arleen. Myself! You had to know because I love you. I'm sorry. Go away. Go home. I'll have you driven home.' He let go of her arms, turned away, but she would not let him. It was almost funny, part of her thought, as they teetered together, him tugging one way and she back again. She held him against a railing, the palms of her hands enclosing his cheeks tight, their noses almost touching.

'I love you, Nigel,' she said simply.

'I'm a filthy stinking coward. I've never been with a woman.'

'I love you, Nigel.'

'It's always been Vic and Ria, never Nigel. I've never had anyone. I love you, Arleen.'

'Nigel, darling.'

'I love you, so I told you. Marry me, Arleen.' The way they kept saying each other's names.

'I will. I do. Oh, Nigel.'

He kissed her. Right there in the street – he kissed her!

'Congratulations, Nigel,' grinned Vic, 'congrats, Arleen.' So Nigel thought he could get a woman and get out of Vic's life. 'I'm very pleased for you – I am over the moon.' He grabbed Nigel and slapped his back. Nigel was tall and thin and pale. Arleen was short, high-coloured, with that horrid Eton crop. What a pair. Vic put his arms around her and pulled her against him. 'Arleen *Price*. I like the sound of that. You'll be very happy living here next to Mum in Havannah Street.'

Arleen looked at Nigel.

'We thought – somewhere with more room.' Nigel coughed into his right hand.

Of course. Vic felt sick and tired of them. He shrugged: If that's the way you want it.

'Well, Vic, is that all right with you?' Nigel persisted.

'You made your bed, you lie on it, I don't care where!' Vic laughed. Alan Stark was supposed to be here already, and on general principles he didn't want Arleen to see the flier. 'Look, *darling* . . .' Arleen was amazed: the same word that Nigel had used with such gentleness, such tenderness, had an entirely different force coming from Vic's grinning mouth, and she felt diminished. 'Here you are, darling,' he said, 'here's tuppence for your bus fare home.' He held it out.

Arleen wasn't having it. She felt her cheeks burning – they always did when she was angry or ashamed, and Vic made her feel . . . *feel* both these emotions. He was a master of manipulation. No wonder Nigel followed him, feared him. What drove Vic? Not what drove Nigel: Nigel could be saved – bright, intelligent, kind Nigel. Arleen almost cried because she was so happy and she hated Vic for putting it so brutally that she didn't deserve Nigel. *Tuppence for your bus fare.* He knew how to hurt.

'Nigel said he was driving me home,' she said, determined.

Vic shrugged. 'Go ahead, Nigel.'

'Well, don't you need me here? I thought we were meeting Stark.'

Vic said: 'Make up your mind.'

Nigel looked at Arleen. 'I've got to drive her home, Vic.' He held her hand. Arleen smiled: she had won. 'I'll be back as quick as I can.'

Arleen followed Nigel out, then turned at the door. 'I do deserve him,' she told Vic, alone. 'I don't care what you say.'

Vic surprised her. 'Yes, you do deserve him,' he said. For one moment Arleen thought she understood him – he was so sad. They said Vic was evil, said he was dangerous, they said Vic had killed a man. She was sure that he had been misunderstood. Vic had force: if only it could be channelled in the right directions . . . But it was Nigel she loved, not Vic.

'I'm sorry, Vic.' What she meant, in a kind way, was I'm sorry *for* you.

'I'll give you a grand wedding,' he promised, 'a real Isle of Dogs wedding, we'll have the whole street out! Your Ma and Pa are dead, aren't they? I'll make sure you get the whitest bridal gown that's ever been bought.'

Vic's smile did not move when she closed the door behind her and left him alone in the room. Vic was never really alone. He carried people inside his head and moved them around like chess pieces in a continuous battle. Arleen thought she was important, and he snorted with contempt. Even sorry for him!

Ben London, the Workhouse Bastard, was there in Vic's head, always there, bigger, stronger, more clever, more terrifyingly ruthless than Vic ever dared to be. And more vulnerable. More alone . . . yet he had married the white Queen, Vane. *Checkmate* – Vic controlled her.

Check: the Bastard had wrested control of the Emporium back from her. *Mate*: here was a hope for the future, their twin sons . . . and so the deadly game unreeled behind Vic's eyes. Not plans, not like Nigel laid. And not a game: reality, a deadly cocktail of opportunity and emotion. Vic Price had already discarded Vane – she had harmed Ben London, so she could harm him.

But there were others he must protect, however ungrateful they sometimes pretended to be – Ria, and Mum (Esther would be ecstatic to hear of Nigel's engagement, so it had done some good). Nigel himself: poor Arleen, she would find that Nigel was incapable of love. She thought she had won, but Vic would control her with his little finger. No woman could stand against Vic. She would learn.

Raymond Trott, the irresistible Douglas Fairbanks double, Vic thought contemptuously, had started walking out with Ria, and her moods had improved for his company. He was glad he'd introduced them – Ray hadn't been keen at first but Vic had persuaded him of the mutual advantages. Even knowing Ria as well as he did he hadn't been sure it would work, but in Vic's experience women liked to be told what to do and they loved a strong-looking man – Ray could do press-ups on one hand and he had a sharp sense of humour that would appeal to Ria. Any man could see at a glance what Ray was, but women didn't. If only she would get involved with Ray, that would be lovely: two birds with one stone, and still Vic would have her.

Because there was the long-running feud between Vic and Ray's father to consider. Ted Trott was proprietor of the Old Bull and Bush in Cable Street and a man of great power and standing in the community – and a man who had threatened Vic: *Get your eyes off this place, or I'll bury you*. That was seven years ago, but Vic had a memory longer than an elephant's. He never forgot, and he never forgave. Every man has a chink in his armour. One day, one way or the other an opportunity would arise, and Vic would be there . . .

Welcome to my family, Arleen, Vic thought.

'Are you in, Vic?' A knock on the door.

'In here, Alan.' Vic swung round at the rolltop desk.

Alan Stark sat down on the old hoop-back chair – Vic cared nothing for furnishings, Nigel had purchased the lovely Persian carpet. Stark crossed his legs. He wore an expensive herringbone overcoat, a gift from Vic. During the war in France his aeroplane had turned over on the ground and his two front teeth were capped with gold, another gift from Vic. 'I've got a job for you,' Vic said.

Stark inclined his head. He and Vic went back a long way – Alan had been a friend of Vic's sickly younger brother Arthur, back in the Canary Warren days. Stark had flown in Bertie Benton-Benson's squadron during the war, and had seen Ben London shoot his best friend, the man who saved him from the gutter, out of the sky.

'Fancy a nice holiday abroad?' Vic asked.

Stark hated turning Vic down. He clasped his hands eagerly over his knee, but said: 'It's a bit difficult, Vic, see, my wife Betty's having a baby – '

'I know what women fuss like,' Vic said flatly. 'You're going to Germany.'

'But – why?'

'Because the enemy of my enemy,' Vic smiled, 'is my friend. I want you to have a chat with the Hun ace Münchener, see what he says about what Ben London did that day of the dog-fight, because he must have seen as well as you did. In fact he was closer. It was murder, wasn't it?'

'No action was taken against London at the time. Münchener was credited with the kill in this country.'

'But actually London shot Benton-Benson down.'

Stark hesitated. 'He blew him apart at point-blank range.'

'Are you hiding something?' Vic demanded. 'Have you ever lied to me?'

'No! He shot him, I saw it.' He didn't mention that Ben and Münchener fought a duel later. Münchener's total humiliation then would ensure his co-operation now in bringing Ben London down.

Vic purred: 'London's name will be dragged through the mud at the Old Bailey because our crusading friend Pemberton-Billing alleges the Honourable Bertie Benton-Benson was a homosexual pervert. Named in the Black Book of forty-seven thousand names. London used him as a social ladder then got rid of him.'

'I don't know about that.' But it was safe to say anything in Court, where the laws of libel and slander did not apply. In fact Alan had liked and admired his flight leader. He was getting into deep water. But he knew Vic.

'Ben London was nobody before they met,' Vic explained gently. 'Afterwards, he was somebody. Lover's tiff, revenge, financial gain – London was left that Mantegna painting in Benton-Benson's will, wasn't he, and sold it to raise money and humiliate me in front of my family. And . . . other things.' There was the crux of the matter, Alan knew – Vic's sure belief that Ben took Ria by force, the foundling using the Price family too as a step on the social ladder. 'Who cares?' Vic smiled. He cared; he alone carried that heavy burden of care for his sister. She would not love Ben London when she saw him exposed.

'I'll bring Münchener back from Germany,' Alan said. 'He'll be eager to condemn his old opponent.'

'The truth doesn't matter,' Vic said. 'Do you understand that, Alan?'

'Yes.' Then Stark went quite pale.

'You do not understand anything in this life,' Vic said in a deep, terrible voice. 'Not one thing. You see it but you don't understand it. You are ignorant and blind and deaf and dumb. I want to see Ben London in prison as the murderer he is.'

2

Nothing for him for the rest of his life, ever, was the same.

'I am never going to let you go,' Ben said, and knew it was true. He burned for her, he had to have her, have everything Pearl had to give him. And she, beneath that calm surface, did she burn too? He stepped back, but only half a step; and let go of her hand, but not of her heart. They both understood. Her grey-blue eyes – he was seeing himself in them. His fingertips brushed her wrist and she shivered. He was holding her still.

'This is happening,' she said.

'It is true,' he said simply, 'love exists. This is us.' He sensed the heat of her skin beneath her dress. There was no space between them.

She murmured, 'I could never really believe . . . my sister fell for a man, it was during the war, she did crazy things for him, all for love. She loved him and I never believed that was all.' Her eyes searched his face. 'But it is.'

'All.' He enclosed her fingers in a caress. 'So you have a sister?' Talking just to hear her voice.

'My twin.'

'Two Pearl Remingtons.' Their hands lay warm and urgent between their bodies.

'Seventy minutes older, I'm not allowed to forget that! Mary is dark and – deep. She worries about me, she saved – ' Pearl's eyes sparkled as she looked over the edge of sorrow into an abyss, and Ben knew he loved her.

'Go on,' he said.

'Am I talking so much?' She smiled brightly. 'I'm so sorry.'

'Your voice is beautiful. You woman. Your hair – ' he reached up, she wanted him to – lovingly loosened the bonds of light and for a moment her hair parted in a fluid cascade, a breaking wave. She laughed, it framed her face with shimmering pale gleams. 'You are beautiful,' he whispered. 'You set me free, Pearl.'

Her gentle mockery: 'The millionaire is a prisoner?' She had forgotten her tears with laughter.

'I'm not a prisoner now. You are my future.' Her hair swirled on her shoulders, pearl: her name. 'You were named for your hair,' he said in wonder.

'My hair was dark when I was a . . . child.' She shook her head slightly and he was rebuked. He should not ask, not yet. 'My given name has come true since . . .' Again he felt that edge of tears, like a sudden blade between them.

'You have always been perfect,' he whispered.

'The art of beautiful compliments again.'

'You know everything about me,' Ben London said. As a woman, she hid much from him; she would come to it when she would.

'I'm so happy,' Pearl said, brushing her knuckles to the bright corners of her eyes. She wanted to share everything, but could not.

Ben was startled by a knock on the door. He held both Pearl's hands in his and stared into her eyes.

'I will understand,' he said softly.

Alice Cypress came in – they had not noticed her leave, or that she had tactfully shut the door behind her. The overhead lights glittered uncomfortably on her glasses. 'Excuse me – the time . . .' Alice packed up at four. 'Will there be anything more, Mr London?'

'That's all for today. Thank you very much, Alice.'

Her face contorted with a wry little smile. Pearl let go of Ben's hand. 'Remember, Alice, you only need the glasses for reading, so why not take them off and rest your eyes elsetime?' That was a very Pearl word, a signature already as clear and personal to Ben as if she had signed her name. 'You look really good and you don't need them, you know.'

Alice bobbed. 'You're so kind, Miss Remington. Yes, I'll try to remember elsetime. Good night. Good night, Mr London.'

'Good night,' Pearl said, and watched the door close. 'She loves you. She wanted to be jealous.'

'Because you're so beautiful.'

Pearl said: 'But everyone is beautiful, if only they can discover it.' And because she said so, it was true. There seemed to be no darkness in Pearl's world. She had the long, casual grace of a couturier's model: cool poise and perfect elegance. She was too beautiful to have suffered. She was bright and liberal and kind because that was the way the world treated her. Nor, Ben knew, had pennies bought that classic Chanel dress.

'Alice loves you,' Pearl said lightly, 'she frightens people to protect you.'

'Let's have tea together.' He touched Pearl's waist. 'I shall show you my proudest possession.'

'London Emporium.' She knew men's pride.

'You see?' he laughed. 'You *do* know everything about me.' He opened the door, turned along the corridor towards the Waterfalls restaurant.

As they walked he observed her – the scent of her, the sway of her hair, her grace: not Russian, but a princess indeed. An American princess.

'You said you have a letter for me.' Then they came into the restaurant, and she gasped and grabbed his arm.

'Whoopee! Ben, it's magnificent!' She gazed up with the expression of awe and delight people always did on entering the Waterfalls at the very top of the Emporium for the first time. He enjoyed her open amazement at the smooth, silent arch of shining water that spanned the skylit dome above the tables, the fountains of yellow flowers and subaqueous blues and mauves of the watersilk pillars reflecting in her eyes. 'Real water! It's impossible! Ben, how's it done?'

He led her to a white linen table in the centre and pulled out her chair before the waiters could beat him to it. From Anton, the obsequious head waiter in bow tie and tails, he ordered tea, coffee and choux pastries. When they were alone, he followed Pearl's gaze upwards to the astonishing water-arch. 'The principle is called a Rumney Waterfall,' he explained, 'invented by Marcus Rumney for agricultural irrigation – never splashes a drop. Something to do with surface tension. Rumney was a genius.'

'Any relation to Nurse Edith Rumney who looked after you as a baby?'

He took his elbows off the table, startled. 'The Countess told you?'

'Everything,' Pearl said.

'I'd like to think they were related, second or third cousins maybe. We'll never know. Marcus Rumney went mad, he blamed himself for the World War. The awful thing is, perhaps he was right. He and a German chemist, Ullwig, dreamed of mass-producing artificial nitrates for fertilizers, turning the world green.'

'Nitrates as in high explosives?'

He looked at her with new respect.

'The German did a patriotic bunk home and had a chemical town named after him, Ullwigshaven. The Kaiser could manufacture all the explosives he wanted, didn't have to sneak minerals through the British blockade. So instead of the Germans running out of ammunition by Christmas the war dragged on for four years. Mice and men. Ullwig was a national hero and Marcus Rumney drank himself to death.'

'But he created beauty,' Pearl said, gazing up at the extraordinary water sculpture.

Anton brought the trolley and they chose from the enormous selection of exquisite shapes wrought by the pastry-chef from fragile choux – sailboats, flowers, as insubstantial as air, stuffed with whipped cream. 'Cream cakes, whoopee – I'll have just one, promise.'

Whoopee, another Pearl word.

'Have one,' she insisted, 'don't be a stiffy.'

Ben only toyed with his cake. Rumney's story had saddened him. 'Are you going to give me that letter?'

Pearl helped herself to a second pastry, then reached forward with her napkin and casually wiped a speck of cream off his chin. She slipped an envelope out of her handbag. Ben stared at the graceful script of the address,

73

England written *Angleterre*, and recognized Chouchou's writing.

'The Countess of Coucy,' agreed Pearl. 'Coco Chanel's old friend. And yours. I know all about it, Ben. Her child.'

'I hardly knew her.'

'That's not what she says,' Pearl said blithely, and then took mercy. 'Don't worry, I alone know.'

It was incomprehensible that Chouchou would have told anyone. Yet she had told Pearl. Ben dropped his eyes, more impressed than he could say.

He opened the letter from France.

> My dearest Ben London,
> The bearer of this letter is Pearl Remington, whom I love. It would please me if you cared to use her talents, which are extraordinary, in any way you wish to her advantage. One day you will understand the secret of her beauty – as you, alone of men, understood mine.

'My pop knew the old Count years back through the Rothschilds,' Pearl said helpfully. 'I thought it would be nice to see the Coucy castle he talked about, but the Boche had blown it up. It's too big to rebuild so Chouchou renovated the château and lives there with her son the young Count – it's beautiful inside, she's so aware of fashion. That's how she paid for it, she's a respected doyenne now, very thick with Coco. People don't argue with *those* two.'

What had Chouchou seen in this spectacular girl, a foreigner, an American, almost a stranger, twenty years younger than she – but so compelling, so *special*, that the patriotic Frenchwoman risked so much? *One day you will understand the secret of her beauty*.

> Now, my friend, to business. Pearl Remington is too brilliant not to be bored, and boredom is dangerous in a beautiful girl. I have given her the occupation of bringing civilization to your barbaric country.

Ben frowned.

Pearl sensed a misunderstanding. 'You are my occupation. Only you, Ben.'

But he held up his hand, and read on.

A revolution has occurred in the art of perfumery that makes the scent last. Therefore only a little need be used, of exquisite quality and very great cost. Coco Chanel now creates a range of the greatest scents in the world and we would appreciate your advice –

Ben's eyes blazed. He was furious. He didn't read the rest of the letter but tore it up savagely and scattered the pieces on the table in front of Pearl.

'So that's the secret of your beauty!'

She shook her head, but she couldn't speak, he was so wild with anger.

'A product which you wish to *sell* to me! I believed in you, Pearl. In *you*. What an act! How many bottles shall I buy?' the millionaire demanded fiercely.

'No, don't, Ben.' Pearl's eyes became luminous and did not move, fixed on him.

'The softest of soft sells,' he said bitterly, 'very clever. A sales rep! I bet you catch a lot of business this way. What commission are you on? Twenty per cent? You're worth a hundred,' he added brutally.

Pearl laid her hands flat on the table. 'Isn't this lovely?' she said brightly. 'Our first public row. I like a man who lives up to his reputation.'

'Wipe those tears off your face.'

'*You* wipe them off.'

'Go to hell. You want to sell me perfume, all right, I'll buy!' He took her wrist and swept her to the lift. 'We'll go see the buyers right now. Satisfied?'

'I'm crying,' Pearl said. 'You, Ben, only you.' She turned her face towards him, openly streaked with the undeniable truth of her tears, but he looked away, and then the lift doors opened and he pulled her inside. They went down through the floors, the other passengers trying to ignore their emotion, embarrassed in the British fashion. 'I love you,' Pearl said.

'Sell it to the buyers.'

'I love you!'

'Shout all you like.'

'Isn't it a wonderful world? I hurt you, so I know you love me too,' Pearl wept gaily. 'Otherwise you wouldn't have been hurt.' The lift stopped at the lowest sales floor and the other passengers got out. 'Answer me, Ben.'

He ignored her naked tears. 'Go on down,' he ordered the liftboy.

'Don't make me face this,' Pearl said clearly. 'Don't do this to me.'

The doors opened on the warehouse area. Pearl fixed her eyes on the ramp up to the courtyard, the bright lights glaring in the open night out there. But Ben had walked to the stairs leading down to the warren of cellars below, where the buyers had their offices. He looked back.

'I can't do it,' Pearl called. 'Even for you.'

He held out his hand.

She put her foot on the first step, and then the second, and followed him down. She did it for him. The cellars were ordinary rooms, brightly lit and freshly whitewashed. Clerks scurried to and fro in their smart suits and shiny shoes, and chirpy messenger boys scampered past. But the ceilings were curved like cellar ceilings . . . and there was a very faint earthy smell . . .

Pearl smelt blood and earth and the fumes of high explosive. The walls were splashed with yellow chemical. The cellar was full of dying boys. She screamed.

3

Pearl struggled upward from the dark. She did not dare look down. Above her, her hands were being held by someone. 'Where am I?' she called.

There was something hard under her head. Pearl struggled to see. It was a bolster in rough white linen, practical but spartan. 'Welcome back.' Ben London held her hands gently in his. 'You're in my apartment. The nurse is here.'

Pearl heard a woman's voice. 'Her blood pressure is fine now.'

'You fainted,' Ben said. 'You frightened the living daylights out of me. Pearl, I'm sorry. I'll never forgive myself, I didn't mean the awful things I said. It's just that I love you. And I thought . . .'

'What is it, Ben?'

'Women have always betrayed me.'

The vapours evaporated from her brain. 'But I never will.'

His eyes, which had blazed with such a furious blue heat, now smiled.

'No. You never will.'

'I'm glad we got our first row out of the way,' Pearl breathed. 'It'll be all plain sailing now. But . . . suppose I did?'

'We would not survive.' He wasn't joking. His love would destroy her, she could see it in his eyes and felt it in his hard hands. 'I love you to death, Pearl.' Then he smiled again, and she felt the caress of his fingertips circling over the backs of her hands, infinitely gentle. He loved her enough to die for her, she was sure of it. The certainty of her power over him, and so her responsibility towards him, thrilled through her body.

'I was blind and stupid,' he blamed himself. 'I should have guessed you suffered from claustrophobia, you were so pale.'

'Claustrophobia?'

'You passed out. Don't you remember?'

'I remember . . .' What did she remember? Something so horrible that her mind wanted to shut it out. Not claustrophobia – a memory.

Ben understood – she felt it. 'Memories do make us what we are,' he said. 'We are what we remember. But some things we'd rather forget?'

She nodded.

He touched his finger to his lips, then leaned down

close, his powerful features almost touching hers. 'One day, when you're ready to love me fully, you'll tell me what happened to you.'

'I want to tell you now!'

He leaned back, held out his hand, palm up. If you want.

'She's got her colour back,' the nurse said, 'it was just one of those things. Nothing that a good night's rest won't cure.'

'I'll have my maid Peggy sit with her until she sleeps,' Ben said.

'I'll pop in tomorrow morning. Good night.'

'Good night,' Ben said, and the nurse left them alone.

'I can't bear to remember,' Pearl said with her bright smile, her hair shimmering around her face. 'Do you mind, Ben?'

'You're gorgeous,' he said. 'Of course I don't mind. Don't be so serious.'

'So this is where you live.' Pearl looked around her.

'Not in this room.'

'Good, because it's a real pit,' she said. 'I wouldn't like to think of you living in a dump like this. Is this mattress stuffed with straw?'

He looked offended. 'What's wrong with it?'

'And the bolster is a rock.' She smiled contentedly, looking at him with one eye. There were certain things he was going to learn about living.

'All right,' he said, giving in surprisingly easily, then springing his trap. 'Since you're staying here, do it up how you want. No expense spared.'

'You can be so charming when you try. I'm convalescing here and living at my own place, am I?'

'I said I would never let you go, and I never will. You and I will never misunderstand one another again. Let people talk.'

'So it's true what they say. You really don't care. And you a married man. Don't underestimate them, Ben.' But she loved him to talk like this. It warmed her blood and sent a cool chill up her spine, and she felt alive, and safe.

'Pearl, understand me.'

She did; this was the millionaire's voice that made Hawk salute, and Simmonds stand to attention at the Rolls-Royce's door, and made all things possible.

Ben said simply, fiercely: 'There is nothing I will not do for love.'

CHAPTER FIVE

Nigel was terrified. Today he was getting married.

The Isle of Dogs changed little, summer or winter. Spring was in the details – people started leaving their doors open and beating their carpets out of the windows. The few trees showed black shoots. Budgies and canaries were hung out in their cages, preening their yellow feathers and trilling cheerfully, each one stalked by a semicircle of half a dozen hungry, hopeful cats. At last the lovebirds Nigel had given to his father were making love instead of fighting. Making love – which Nigel would have to do tonight in a strange hotel, in a strange bed, to Arleen. It was a dreadful mistake. He was going to call the whole thing off. Better to disappoint everybody than to disappoint her.

He had tried to explain. 'I want to be friends with you, Arleen.'

She didn't laugh. 'I want you to be *you*, Nigel.'

He lit another cigarette. He wished he could tell his wife-to-be about the full horror of that night in the latrines with the gun rigged to point at his elbow: just before the German attack started, Raymond Trott had seen Nigel shoot himself. Trott had returned to London and was living only a few miles away with his father at the Old Bull and Bush in Cable Street, learning the ropes. There had long been a certain secret agreement to ensure Trott wouldn't talk about what he had seen. Nigel almost confessed to Arleen that Trott was blackmailing him.

He pulled back from the brink. 'You might not like me.'

'Nigel, do you find me attractive?'

Arleen could be so breathtakingly direct. Nigel crossed his legs defensively. 'Arleen, this is the truth. I simply cannot believe my luck in you.'

'Trust me, Nigel,' she said, touching his nose, 'trust me.'

He trusted her.

Today was the day, and tonight was the night, and he trusted Arleen blind, but he was a born failure, Vic had said so, and he knew it wasn't going to work.

Nigel put a cigarette tin in his pocket, called to Vic that he was just going out, and clattered downstairs. It was a clear sunny day. He went next door and knocked. 'Mum?'

'You can't come in!' called Esther, sounding alarmed. Arleen was being tarted up – here because she had no family of her own – and it was unlucky to see her. The women had spent a fortune on dresses that they would only wear once. But young Will opened the door, freshly scrubbed and red-cheeked, bouncing up and down, and Nigel noticed that Ria hadn't even bothered to try and comb her boy's hair yet. Will worshipped Nigel and they got on really well. Ria wasn't a good mother. He'd told Ria that, and he'd told Will too. Nigel took out his comb and did Will's hair, to his disgust.

'I'm ten,' Will complained.

'You're never too old to have your hair combed.'

'Nigel, you're so *careful*,' Will said, and Nigel was startled. It was true.

'Call him Uncle Nigel,' came Ria's voice from upstairs.

'I've lost my pins!' screamed Esther.

'I'm just popping down to the newsagent,' Nigel called up, 'I wondered if – '

'Bring me back a paper, would you!' shouted Ria.

'Can I come in the motorcar, Uncle?' Will ran outside.

'Not today.' Nigel pulled him back.

'Why not, you always let me!'

'Not on every fourth Saturday.' Nigel pointed his nephew firmly back inside.

'Why not?'

'Because, because,' Nigel said. 'That's all.'

'Spoilsport!' A word his mother had taught him; Ria lost no opportunity to mock Nigel. *Only lucky ones like you get it in the elbow, Nigel – others get their balls blown off. Don't suppose you'd notice any difference though.*

Nigel drove to the newsagent's – not because it was far, but for the pleasure of driving the car when so few other people had one, and even more for the sense of disconnection it gave between home and what would happen next. He parked outside the shop, warned off the dirty-faced kids who gathered round, and went inside. He bought a tin of cigarettes.

'And *The Times*.' A small revenge: Ria hated *The Times* because it had hardly any pictures.

Raymond Trott came into the shop. 'I'd give her this one,' he said. 'Nice pictures in this one.'

Nigel stared at him. Recently Trott knew all too much about them. 'What's it to you?'

Trott shrugged. 'I'm dying for a smoke.' Nigel followed him to the alleyway outside. Trott held out his hand and Nigel passed over the empty cigarette tin in his pocket. Trott snapped off the cap in his strong hands and pulled out the roll of one-pound notes, licked his forefinger delicately and counted them to fifty. 'Price is going up next time.'

'I can't hide any more, Vic will find out.'

'Cooking his books are you, Nige? You're a very naughty boy. But so clever. You'll find a way.' He clicked his tongue at a girl walking past and she smiled then glanced at her reflection in the shop window as she walked on. He whistled and she looked back.

'You're cruel,' Nigel said.

'Nice bum,' Trott said. He had to pretend. He called out: 'Love you, darling!'

'Ray, for God's sake.'

'Hundred quid.'

'Can't do it.'

'Not a penny less. Not one penny.'

Nigel tried to persuade his blackmailer of his sincerity. 'Ray, if Vic found out about this, he'd – '

'He'd strew your cowardly guts over the Isle of Dogs,' Ray said cheerfully, fitting the notes comfortably into his back pocket. *Strew* was one of those fancy words he'd picked up from Lawrence of Arabia in Jerusalem.

'You wouldn't be safe from Vic either.'

Ray was amused. 'Who's my daddy? If Vic lays one single digit on me, Ted Trott's mob will come down and eat him for breakfast.' He clapped Nigel's shoulder. 'Confidence, that's the key.' Ray Trott liked taking risks, Nigel thought bitterly as he walked back to his car, liked skating on the very edge. His own nature was exactly the opposite.

Yet here he was, getting married today.

Nigel looks sick, Ria thought with satisfaction as she came into the church. She wore a lovely crimson dress, tight on the bust and loose over the hips, that floated like a dream around her knees. It was a gorgeous colour like sunburn, and it set off her opal blue-gold eyes to perfection.

'It's indiscreet,' Nigel had hissed, 'where did you get the money for a dress like that?'

'None of your business.' Actually Raymond Trott had given it to her. She wondered what he wanted. Her? But she'd accepted it, and Vic hadn't kicked up about it either. Raymond Trott had kissed her cheek. *You look terrific.* He was interested in clothes, and he certainly had good taste as well as being the most attractive man she had ever seen. He had asked her to walk out with him – they'd go to a show, something glittering in the West End. That was cunning. Ria adored shows, and she could wear the dress. She had refused, but only just.

Mum wore purple with a brown hat, brought by Vic. Tom, now grey-haired but still with a docker's enormous shoulders, wore a suit two sizes too tight. When Arleen was escorted in by Stanley Kirschbaum from the Queen's, she looked very proud in her white bridal dress, carrying a bouquet of white flowers.

'My son Nigel, getting married!' Esther whispered to Ria. 'I would never have believed it. St Luke's is too small. I wanted St Paul's.'

'What, the cathedral?'

'A cathedral is the only proper place to get married. A cathedral is God's palace. I'm going all the way to St Paul's this evening to thank God.'

'Here's good enough.' Ria had dreamed of getting married here once.

Tom whispered: 'St Luke's is God's single-storey outhouse.'

'If you can't say anything sensible, Tom,' Esther said, 'don't say anything.'

The married couple were seen off in a car with a chauffeur and white ribbons over the bonnet. Vic tied a dustbin to the rear bumper, and Nigel looked embarrassed, but Arleen laughed. They drove off with the dustbin clattering and banging behind them.

'Rubbish for rubbish,' Vic joked.

The hotel in Southend overlooked the long pier – the fairylights looped away into the deep dark night over the Thames estuary. Nigel's shadow did not move from the window. 'I wonder if we've done the right thing.'

'I don't wonder, Nigel.'

'I wish I was as certain about everything as you are.'

'It's a certain world. You love me.'

'I do!' he cried. 'Is that all?'

'Yes,' Arleen said as she took him in her arms. 'This is all.'

And it was so easy.

Ria lay in bed. She was naked.

Her crimson dress hung from the back of the door, but she could not see it. Her room was not dark; the bedside light illuminated it. She could not see because she was holding her pillow over her face with her clenched fists, making everything as black as it felt, determined not to cry.

At last she rolled over and lay with her head over the side of the bed, staring down at the newspaper on the floor – the picture-paper Nigel had bought her that she hadn't had time to look at until now.

MILLIONAIRE TO CLEAR NAME AT OLD BAILEY!

Page three, the gossip column, carried a large photograph of Ben London. He looked angry, the harsh flashbulbs picking out the muscles bunched along his jaw and the smooth satin lapels of his dinner jacket. He was pointing straight into camera. The woman behind him was laughing, and she was an incomparable beauty.

Pearl Remington, shining-bright and shallow, and not deserving, and happy.

Happy.

The tears trickled up Ria's nose and slid up her forehead into her hair. If any dreams had been left her, they ended now, and she had no more illusions.

It was all over. Ben London was finished. She shut him out of her heart.

Ria sat up defiantly and stared at the back of the door.

CHAPTER SIX

1

'People.' Vane London yawned, patting her red-varnished nails to her pouting red lips. 'The world and his wife are here today.' The two women sat together in the back of Marcelline's Lanchester limousine near the Old Bailey. There was talk of a General Strike and the whiff of garbage hung on the air.

Once they had been lovers – to Vane their romance had been her whole life, to Marcelline merely an exotic sensual spice. Vane envied and adored men, but Marcelline used them confidently: now she was the wife of Henry Stoughton, the Member of Parliament for Haworth and Clere, who served on many important committees. She did not love him but she admired his gifts, and he gave her everything she needed in return: money, respect in Society, freedom. (Doubtless he had mistresses on the side, too.) Most of all, he had given her Broze, the young daughter who was such a source of pride to Marcelline. All without love.

'Broze sucks her thumb,' Vane said. She yawned again. 'Are you tired?'

'I was dancing until dawn, almost.' *With a wonderful man*, Marcelline thought, completing what Vane left unspoken. It was always a wonderful man. Poor Vane, thought Marcelline smugly, all she wanted from life was love and joy, and very little would have satisfied Vane's cold heart; but they were the two things denied her – except Ben London, who she kept enchained in their loveless marriage, and perhaps she squeezed a little joy out of that sterile revenge. The rest of her life was the pursuit of pleasure, and it must be a kind of hell.

Vane was still perfectly pretty, Marcelline admitted: she

was like a china doll, and the bright lipstick and dainty carmine nails suited her white skin. There was something porcelain-hard about her that men must find attractive – they must surely want to break that fine shell of cold reserve, but would find no warm feminine heart beating behind those stiff round breasts. Vane's dream of love was a misty romance, not the real business of giving. Marcelline nodded wisely. Vane didn't dare fall in love, and she never would.

Vane pointed at the reporters gathering on the steps beneath the ornate arch of the entrance hall. 'Look, the grubs of Grub Street! I hope they eat him alive.'

Marcelline tried to feel sorry for Vane. Ben lived openly with Pearl Remington, thus turning Vane's sword against her with his public rejection of her – Vane could do nothing about it, her only weapon against him was divorce, and that was what he desired. Stopping Ben marrying Pearl was a hollow victory, and its price was Vane's public humiliation, which had drawn her here today. Vane had come to see Ben London suffer – and to suffer herself.

'You don't have to do this,' Marcelline said.

'Yes, I do. I'm doing it to him too.'

'He'll hurt you,' Marcelline said.

Vane turned and looked through the back window. The twins, *her* twins, Ralph and George were playing on the pavement under the watchful eye of Miss Lorre, their present nanny – none of them lasted long, although they always seemed sad to miss the children when they left. Vane called them governesses. 'I hope that stupid woman keeps George away from those church railings – he'll get his head stuck.' Ralph, the friendly one, was playing with a blond-haired boy who looked foreign. Ralph was far too friendly, Vane thought. Such cheery openness was dangerous, you never knew who he would meet, he gave away too much. George, on the other hand, she trusted. He kept himself to himself.

'Why did you bring them?' Marcelline asked, and knew the answer immediately from Vane's ingenuous smile. She wanted Ben to see them. They got out of the car and walked to the children by St Clement Dane's church.

'Mama, he doesn't speak English!' Ralph greeted them enthusiastically and introduced his new friend. 'His name's Fritzi. I've taught him to say hallo.'

'Now teach him to say goodbye,' Vane said. She held out her hand until Ralph took it.

'Miss Lorre's giving in her notice next week.' Ralph grinned up at her, and Marcelline laughed out loud. Vane sulked, then called George and went towards the waiting crowd. Marcelline stayed where she was, where she could better observe the ebb and flow. That strong-looking woman with the hopeful eyes and blonde pigtails must be Fritzi's mother – Marcelline's lips widened in satisfaction as the blonde woman adjusted the collar of the boy's cheap new suit, then gave his face a quick spit and polish with a handkerchief.

And this was the German ace, Adolf Münchener – the father of the boy. What an interesting face he had, Marcelline thought, with its sword-slash scar down one cheek, broad forehead and arrogant smiling mouth dominating a narrow chin, his hair slicked back over a thinning crown, a cruel stereotype of a killer. Such men had been heroes; now they were mostly out of work. When a man in a herringbone overcoat took him by the elbow and led him up the steps, Münchener did not resist. He had fallen on hard times. A few flashbulbs popped.

Marcelline recognized the next man all right – his dark eyes, his flat red cheeks. He looked back at her mockingly, taking in her wide mouth and sensual curls, her hungry eyes. Vic Price grinned, forcing her to look away. Unlike Vane, Marcelline knew all about men. She was a wise and earthy creature with a sophisticated taste for forbidden fruits. But she feared two men in the world, and one of them was Vic Price.

He has no sex about him – she had once tried to explain to Vane. Vane had tangled with him without harm. But Marcelline would not – she knew she could never control him. He was a taker. Like a vacuum, his sexlessness

88

would suck her dry of her identity as a woman. Vane had survived him because she too was a taker – but for Marcelline, Vic Price was a man of terrible force.

That grin did have a certain voracious attraction.

Then Vic walked inside. No flashbulbs popped for him. Where was Nigel, Marcelline wondered – Nigel had always been Vic's *alter ego*.

She heard the rumble of a motor and craned forward to see a green Bentley sweep past her, braking hard. The photographers rushed forward and jostled around the parked car – Marcelline bit her lips, she could not see. Then Ben London appeared, pushing them back. He took off his driving coat and opened the passenger's door.

So this was Pearl Remington. She was as beautiful as they said.

The photographers fell back. Pearl stepped elegantly down. It was impossible even for Marcelline to feel envy – they were so obviously happy together. He held her arm, his eyes a hot blue. Her hair shone with a wondrous filmy glow. She must have sold her soul to the devil for hair like that – if the devil could have sold such a heavenly radiance. Pearl laughed aloud at something one of the reporters said, and for a moment Ben's eyes touched Marcelline.

She looked away. Ben London was the other man in the world she would never bed. He was dangerous, because he attracted her, and he did not lie. Marcelline knew what she was; the romantic force of his love would illuminate her soul. She feared him because he would not love her lightly and discard her – his depth of commitment frightened her.

Yet she was so tired of discarded love affairs; she was so tired of not loving poor Henry.

When she looked again Ben had answered the reporters' questions. He and Pearl crossed the pavement, his hand resting lightly over her forearm, she looking relaxed and happy, he smiling into her eyes, plainly in love. But Marcelline was wise, knowing men, knowing women, seeing beneath the surfaces. She sensed something between them

– an invisible pane of glass, a fascinating refraction that for a moment revealed a broad distance, and Marcelline was absolutely certain that they were not lovers – they were in love, but not lovers. Pearl was graceful, but her walk did not have that delicious fluidity, her skin that radiant glow from the heart that lying with a man gave . . . they did not sleep together. Marcelline's eyebrows twitched.

Love and celibacy! How rare!

Love so deep was love indeed. Marcelline shivered.

'Don't make trouble, Vane,' she whispered to herself. She began to walk along the pavement, searching for her friend. Ben and Pearl were going up the Old Bailey steps – they looked back from the top, and there was a crackle of flashbulbs. Marcelline's feet crunched on thin, broken glass, and she felt her ruby necklace swinging at her throat as she began to run. Vane and the children were on the pavement to one side – the children innocent, but Vane smiling her prettiest smile. Marcelline turned and saw Ben's tragic face.

There on the top step, head and shoulders above the reporters pushing and shoving around him, he had seen his family. He had eyes only for his two sons.

Vane would not permit him to visit them – they hardly knew him.

Marcelline said: 'Vane, stop it.'

Ralph and George would spend their lives wondering about their father – as Ben still wondered about his mother. She was teaching him revenge indeed. Marcelline shook Vane's elbows. 'Take that bloody smile off your face!'

Vane's eyes refocused slowly. 'But he tried to destroy me.'

'You idiot,' Marcelline said, 'he tried to *love* you.'

Vane began to cry.

Counsel for the plaintiff completed his long speech to Mr Justice Darling. He would taint the credibility of Pemberton-Billing's allegations from the Black Book on the basis of palpable untruth. Pilot Officer Stark had already made his statement and now the German was in the witness box.

'Herr Adolf München.' Counsel peered over his half-glasses.

The German looked around the foreign Court with its single judge and ranks of prosecuting and defence lawyers in black silk and white wigs. The public gallery was packed. But for him the whole Court centred on two faces, and he sensed the battle going on here between them like a pressure on his skull. There was Ben London, his enemy; and there was Vic Price, his friend.

Counsel said impatiently: 'You are Herr Adolf München.'

'*Geschwader*-leader Adolf München. That is correct.'

'You are a member of the Nazi Party. Yes or no?'

'The Nazi Party has no members, it is a banned organization.'

'Yet you admire the ideals of these thugs.'

'I admire the ideals of patriotic Germans.'

'We English never used the cult description *ace* of our fliers – '

München's English was excellent. 'You did by the end of the war. And if you are going to mention hero-worship, as I suspect you are, I saw Ben London's face spread across the English newspapers we received through Lisbon.'

'I stand corrected. You were an *ace*. You shot down forty-nine Allied aircraft.' The face of Sir Ozwald Benton-Benson, Bertie's father, stiffened.

München said: 'Now you are correct.'

'Are you proud of these *kills*?'

'Naturally.'

'You were following orders, fighting your enemies.'

'What do you expect?'

'I'm not criticizing you or your new Nazi friends, Herr München. By the way, you flew with Hermann Göring I believe.'

'He was my wingman.'

'Your Honour,' explained Counsel, 'another man now senior in the hierarchy of this party of thugs, lucky to have escaped prison. Have you ever met Ben London?'

'Only in combat.'

'There is communication without words. You hate him, don't you.'

'Yes.'

'I do not think the jury heard you.'

'Yes! I hate him more than any man in the world.'

'So I wouldn't expect you to say anything good about him.'

'Why should I?' Münchener clamped his fists to his chest. 'I am a poor man from a defeated and exploited country, a mere thug who you are pleased to insult, desperate to clothe and feed his family, to keep them warm against the winter winds. I have nothing. Of course I will say nothing good about the man I hate for how he left me – without pride, without honour!'

Ben squeezed Pearl's hand. 'We fought a duel,' he whispered.

'Look at him,' sneered Münchener, 'the millionaire in his fine suit!'

Counsel traced his fingernail over a piece of paper. 'Thank you, I think you have made your feelings quite clear. Another witness, Mr Stark, has testified that he saw Ben London shoot down his friend and alleged lover, the Honourable Bertram Benton-Benson, after you had broken off your combat with – '

Münchener held up his hand. 'Benton-Benson's machine was on fire.'

'Yes, but – ' Counsel waited cunningly.

'You have never fought in the air, lawyer. You do not understand what it is like to fight in the great abyss, or to be on fire three miles above the earth – and no parachute . . .' Adolf Münchener shuddered, his eyes far away. 'Stark was a novice pilot, easy meat for me, but Benton-Benson, damn him, would not let me have him . . . he came between us, time after time, baulking me of my prey.'

In the gallery Alan Stark's face was white, his knuckles braced stiffly over his knees. Münchener had changed his story. He was telling the truth.

Vic stared at Ben.

Münchener sneered: 'Stark saved himself by hiding in cloud. I turned on Benton-Benson's machine and shot it up badly. It sparked and began to burn. Stark was so poor a pilot that he could not fly by instruments in cloud – he span out into clear air. I would have had him too. But then Ben London came.'

'The man you hate.'

'Yes.'

'You are admitting your hostility to him.'

'Yes. London followed his burning friend down, round and round.'

'Did you see what happened next?'

'Ben London opened fire on his friend and killed him.'

There it was in stark words. Vic grinned at Ben.

'You must have been appalled.'

'Yes, I – ' Münchener stopped.

'You were naturally horrified. Please carry on.'

Adolf Münchener looked at Ben with wide, hurt eyes. *A man of honour cannot lie – but I have no honour – so I can lie!* Defeat and victory chased themselves across his tormented face.

Münchener chose. 'I would have done the same thing,' he said aloud. 'What Ben London did was not murder but mercy, and I am proud to have witnessed such a selfless, brave act.' He could speak no more for the hubbub that broke out. He glanced at Alan Stark, offended that Stark had once had the temerity to think they had something in common.

Adolf Münchener stepped down from the witness stand with pride. His admission of the truth had lifted a great weight off his back. In front of everyone, he had earned back his lost honour. No longer ashamed and humiliated in defeat, he had earned his right to hold his head high again.

I am a man of honour.

*

'Mr Ben London.'

'Yes, that is my name.' Ben curled his hands around the cold brass rail. Since his advocate had informed Mr Justice Darling that his own name appeared in the Black Book, permission had been allowed for Ben to make a statement.

While the judge looked on approvingly Counsel said: 'Words have been spoken against you on another day in this Court that have received wide and regrettable publication in certain sections of the press. You have asked for this opportunity to clear your name. I must ask you, are you, or have you ever been, of the homosexual inclination?'

Ben nearly laughed. Nowadays they claimed that Bertie had been homosexual – and they alleged the great Lord Kitchener had been – it was the newest, brightest, shiniest invention of the Roaring Twenties. People were obsessed with talking about sex. Every secret must be revealed, every locked box had a Pandora to burst it open. Guilt, sin, all could be explained and sanitized and made devoid of meaning. The façades were being ripped down and an open society erected in the air in their place.

It was fearfully dangerous, because it was a dream. There would never be a world without lies. Ben knew this, and so he spoke the truth – very slowly and simply. It was their hearts he had to win over, not their minds.

'No, but I loved him. In a way we were both orphans. We were like souls.'

With fine words Ben did his last duty to his friend and cleared his name.

Poor Bertie. The truth was that he had wanted to die.

2

Lisa held the newspaper in her hand. She was smiling, and she was proud.

Sunlight made golden slants across her spacious front

room from the elegant bay windows. A tug hooted on the river, startling her. Lisa crossed from her desk and looked out over the walled garden. The rosebeds had been dug up, and it was full of children playing. This was heaven.

Many of the children had thin dirty faces and scarred knees, but every one was kitted out in clean second-hand clothes with good stitching and no missing buttons, and the food was filling and nutritious.

One little boy swung from a branch of the mulberry tree. Lisa could hardly bear to look in case he fell, but his face was joyous. Many of them would never know their mummy or daddy, many had been deserted, but most had mothers who could neither support them nor let them go, and must do their best by putting their kids on the street.

Lisa did her best, too. Her face was tired, but she looked happy.

'The post has come, Miss York.' Helen was unemployable as a maid with anyone else in this fine part of Chelsea because of the disfiguring strawberry birthmark that covered more than half her face, yet there was nothing wrong with her brain.

Lisa sighed. Most of the envelopes were brown; heaven was an expensive place to run. 'Leave them on the desk, please, Helen. Tell me, are you happy?'

Helen looked frightened. 'Yes, m'am.'

'It was just a question. You are safe here.'

'Thank you, m'am.' Helen cleared the tea things and left. Shrill cries from outside – Lisa closed her eyes, probably the little boy had fallen. Then laughter, so she knew he was all right.

She turned back to the paper. Her smile was for her son, and her pride was in him. *I loved him.* There was arrogance in those words of his, ruthlessness, pride. And strength: he dared say what few men would.

She had left her son to live; he dared to live. He had won.

He was truly hers. In her foundling son she recognized herself.

Every secret Lisa found out about him was a secret she found out about herself.

Yet she had failed.

PART II

THE FLAME

CHAPTER SEVEN

1

Pearl's own scream woke her. The dream skidded out of her consciousness and sank at the back of her brain. She lay in her bed, staring up, her heart ticking frantically and the perspiration trickling from her long, slim body into the satin sheets. *What had it been?* She was terrified in case she ever knew.

'Calm down, Pearl,' she told herself, 'it's today. Attend to the business of today.' Her own voice comforted her and she sat up. The room was not dark – Pearl dreaded the dark, she was a creature of the light – a childish night-light still burned even though morning showed around the curtains. She threw back the sheets and sat up in her silk nightdress, yawning. Silk and satin, two products the Emporium sold of superb quality, the silk as fine as gossamer yet strong, and the satin never feeling cold even at first touch. Anyway one of the first things she'd made Ben do was turn up the heating. The British always kept their rooms too cold, and they loved draughts.

She jumped out of bed and slipped into her dressing gown, padded through to the lounge but was disappointed not to see a white-shirted back bent over the papers on the huge onyx table (the intimidating walnut one had been banished to the boardroom). Ben loved work – Pearl had never needed to work, but she liked to keep busy and it was easy for her to get jobs, her success always attracted employers. She worked as she loved – wearing them lightly and leaving.

Nothing was serious in Pearl's life.

(But your own scream woke you.)

The Emporium, work, was Ben's passion. She never let it come between them, because it was a different love from his love for her, or hers for him. It was *passion*. Looking for him, Pearl held the palms of her hands lightly over her breasts, her need for passion, for love, the real thing, intense.

Yet she ran from reality – didn't she? Remember . . .

She shook her head, her gorgeous cloud of hair.

She took one thing seriously: her love for Ben London.

They had not made love. What had always seemed so easy, he denied her. He was loving, but he would not release her from the tension she felt rising within her day by day, the need in her sometimes almost intolerable when he kissed her lips or touched her face and arms with the very tips of his fingers, her sighs shared, her passion shared, until she felt she would cry out – biting it back – and knew he felt the same too, and yet nothing happened. The tension was winding her up like a spring, she could feel its coiled energy within her and within him and knew he loved her *but there was no release* – until she thought she would scream – they would scream together. She loved him. He loved her. It wasn't that simple. There was more. But what?

Pearl trusted him. One day she would know.

He was probably working down in the Emporium, but she went to his bedroom door and knocked. When there was no reply she went in. This was a room she never entered when he was there, yet it already carried the definite stamp of her personality, showing her characteristic care in the choice of its surfaces and textures – the soft velvet drapes hanging sensuously beside the hard shiny Russian lacquer of the dressing table, the deep creamy carpet that she felt warm between her toes offset by the smooth pale tiling of the en suite bathroom (and the entire place had been served by a single paltry archaic bathroom once, another British eccentricity). And Pearl's personality showed, too, in its dry joke – for his walls she had chosen Emporium navy blue, for his sheets Emporium yellow. The Emporium, the other woman in his life. She never felt a touch of jealousy, because she had made the Emporium hers too.

She worked to make his life hers.

She worked to know his mind even though she didn't know his body. Ben London knew love. She had faith in that. *I loved him* – all the different sorts of love. And had he loved Vane? Yes, though everyone said he'd married her to use her, to get the Emporium. Vane didn't bother Pearl, she didn't need a contract to be in love. And had he loved the girl called Ria? Yes, and he had never forgotten her.

Pearl had asked gaily, because that was her way, 'Do you still love her?'

Ben said: 'Why do you need to ask? You are my pearl, my Pearl, and my life.' That was beautiful, and she brushed her knuckles across his chin.

'Does she still love you?'

'Who knows,' he said, 'a woman's heart?'

Ben never forgot anything. *Remember* was engraved in darkness on his heart. Pearl was happy not to know why, because there were things it was better not to know. That was love too. His masculine life was not a slate to wipe clean.

Pearl knew what was important without asking why. She knew he loved her *because* they did not make love.

The time would come when she knew it was right.

Constantly he surprised her. At some god-awful hour last Sunday morning he'd knocked on her door in the dark and told her to get dressed in warm clothes. 'You'll need them.'

They'd been dancing at the Troc until a couple of hours before but Pearl loved adventures and he never disappointed her. Twenty minutes in the roaring Bentley through the darkened streets brought them to Hendon Aerodrome where he kept his Tiger Moth biplane. Pearl didn't like heights, but as she surveyed the intricate machine against the dawn's glow nothing would have persuaded her to back down.

Pearl knew how important it was never to say no.

So she always said yes. When he handed her a leather flying coat she knew it would be tailored to fit perfectly, and it was. He had even thought of a scarf for her hair. The engine was noisy, but he was a superb pilot and she was not sure of when they left the ground – suddenly they were flying. The metropolis was a spectacular panorama tilting beneath the lower wing, then the sun rose behind them over open countryside. At Bristol they ate bacon and eggs at a table set up on the grass while mechanics refuelled the plane. By midmorning they were over a waste of sea, Pearl's scarf blowing in the slipstream like a banner, tippling brandy from his flask as the coast of Ireland rose out of the mist. A map of emerald fields unwound slowly beneath them, then two dusty roads scrawled a cross. Ben checked that her seatbelt was tightly fastened, then flipped the machine over in a looping curve as Pearl screamed with ecstasy.

'Thought you were scared of heights,' he said when they had landed in a field near the village and the engine was silent.

'Not now,' she said, jumping down into his arms, then followed him across the grass. Every door in the village was a different primary colour and remained closed, the locals seeming little interested in their arrival. Then a big white-haired woman wearing a black ring on her finger greeted them.

'Colleen!' Ben called, lifting her up and spinning her round like a girl. 'Are you well?'

'I'm so happy to be home after these long years, as you knew.'

'I wanted to hear it from your lips,' Ben said, introducing them, 'this is Colleen O'Keefe, an old friend.' He never forgot his friends. Pearl noticed what lovely hands Colleen had. Up to them bounded a vast ginger dog with a white muzzle and crotchety joints, proudly showing a bone in his mouth.

'Hallo Sam!' Ben tousled the long ears and Sam's tail flapped so that it seemed it must come off for joy, and they rolled together in the grass.

'Come on, Pearl,' Colleen said, 'with your figure you

couldn't touch my chocolate cake I suppose, but it's Ben's –'

'It's my favourite too!' Pearl exclaimed.

'You didn't need to come all this way,' Colleen told Ben, 'the phone . . .'

'No,' he said. 'It wouldn't have been the same.'

No, it wouldn't have been the same.

Pearl could no longer imagine life without Ben London. They flew back in the evening. Now Pearl touched his bed, then left his empty bedroom.

She went through to her bathroom, and after she had bathed, slipped into a blue-grey dress the colour of her eyes. Slinging a sapphire necklace round her throat, she went to the lift. Since the Inquiry desk had opened the old Edwardian concertina-gate monster was replaced by two modern Otis lifts with automatic doors. Pearl inserted her special key then thumbed the button for the warehouse basement. She hoped he hadn't gone down further – she wouldn't willingly go lower.

The warehouse was brilliant lights and bedlam, as usual – she wanted to put her hands over her ears. 'Wotcher Alf, seen the guvnor?'

The porter jerked his thumb upstairs. 'Just missed him,' he shouted.

'Thanks.' Typical of Ben to use the stairs when they'd just had the new lifts installed. Pearl found him two floors up, holding a dress in front of him in the mirror.

'You look sweet, ducky,' she puffed. Shoppers pushed past them. A tall thin lady posed with a cigarette holder and a poodle, then flounced away when Ben didn't notice her. He knew who not to notice.

'Seriously, what do you think of the dress?' He always asked Pearl's opinion because she told him the truth.

'Bit dowdy,' Pearl said, recovering her breath, 'okay for Aunt Moss.' Aunt Moss was anyone they didn't like. 'Hemline should be an inch higher. They'll go up to the knee, I guess.'

'Quality's good.' He fretted at the hem, then turned politely to the matriarch in the tweed cape who swept imposingly along the aisle. 'Good morning, Lady Winshume.' She stopped, flattered. They exchanged pleasantries, and Ben watched her go. 'She steals,' he said.

Pearl couldn't believe it. 'But she looked so wealthy.'

'She is. Her husband is an hotel director. That cape has poacher pockets hidden under it.'

'Will you confront her?'

'That would be very bad for our reputation, she's a famous hostess. She steals for the thrill of it, Pearl. Every month we send an itemized account which her secretary pays. At the Emporium the client is *always* right.'

He looked at the dress in his hands, frowning.

Pearl said: 'It's not the dress itself – but that they all look the same.' She gestured at the neat rows of racks burdened down with earth-coloured clothes. 'More range, Ben, more choice. Elegant chic, and nice interesting clothes, as well as the solid stuff.'

'Lots of money, Aunt Moss.' He handed the dress to an assistant for ironing.

'Broaden her horizons. Excite her!'

'Most women don't want to shop for excitement.'

'How wrong you are,' Pearl said. 'Just give us the chance.' They walked along the bustling, busy aisles between the counters. Tills rang. With flashing, nimble fingers girls folded purchases into neat parcels of yellow paper and navy-blue bows. 'Good morning, Judy. Larger bows, Molly.' He knew them all by name.

He turned back to Pearl and took her hand. 'Shop For Excitement,' he said like a banner headline.

'I like it,' Pearl said.

They walked to the perfumery counter. 'Exciting enough?' he said.

'This?' she scoffed at the straight lines of bottles. 'It wants to be brighter – *brilliant*, and more gorgeous, more . . . everything. You're selling dreams. And nearer the doors. Girls will walk in just to breathe the wonderful scents.'

'The Chanel's selling extremely well,' he admitted. 'But

perfumes – ' It seemed impossible that sales could continue to rise so fast.

'Taken a walk up Bond Street lately?' Pearl advised. 'Yardley's at number eighty, Elizabeth Arden's just opened a salon at twenty-five. Fenwick's are talking about enlarging in a big way. You must have a perfumery department.'

'A whole department. By the main doors.'

'Better than the smell of cheeses and coffee. The coffee here tastes crummy, by the way, did you know? You Brits get wonderful coffee beans from Kenya and Jamaica and you make lousy coffee.'

'Let's go to the Waterfalls and have a cup of lousy coffee.'

'Thought you'd never ask.'

They crossed the shimmering subaqueous daylight of the Waterfalls to their usual table, saying hallo to the people they met on their way. Charles Cochran the impresario was at his regular table with his regular cigar and the Gish sisters were sipping tea in the corner, observing everything. Later the matinée idol Noël Coward might drop by on his way to the Savoy Grill – he had written an extraordinary play about drug addiction and homosexuality, and Ben had raised his eyebrows when he heard about it. 'Nonsense – dear chap,' said Coward (who never really said *dear boy*), 'nonsense, we'll even talk about *alcoholism* on the London stage next.'

From where he sat, Ben could see three lords and a cabinet minister. The Waterfalls was fashionable, but it was also discreet.

Ben said: 'I'm going to see my father later today.' *My father* – how strange it still felt to say it. 'He must know more than he says about my mother – he loved her, for God's sake.'

This Lord Cleremont must be a swine, Pearl thought, and the princess – abandoning her child in midwinter like someone out of a horrid Grimm fairytale – even worse. Ben couldn't give up his need to find his mother, but could he love the monster he found?

Time more than distance separated Pearl from her wealthy parents; the European war had come between them like a wall separating the future from the past, and Lowell and Dizzy Remington were isolated on the far side of more than just an ocean. Pearl, swept into a European war in an age of change, had the luxury of growing away from her parents naturally, but Ben had been totally denied and rejected by his. She couldn't imagine his loneliness.

He sipped his coffee and made a face. 'I only know her name – ' He turned as a waiter in bow tie and tails arrived, incongruously holding a telephone on a silver tray.

This time the line was better. 'Charlie Bookkeeper here.'

Ben put his hand over the mouthpiece. 'Bit of luck – it's Charlie.'

'Look, Ben,' came the solicitor's voice, 'my man can't find any trace of the name you requested, but we did turn up a Prince Krópotyna, Naval Attaché at the Russian Embassy from late 1899 to the end of 1904. Sent packing after a diplomatic incident.'

Ben was doubtful. 'The names aren't similar enough.'

Charlie said: 'The funny thing is, I'm sure I *have* heard of an Ellen Kurágina.'

'A princess?'

'Yes, I'm quite sure. I don't know, in a book or somewhere.'

Ben hung up the phone and the waiter took it away. Pearl touched his hand sympathetically because he looked so depressed. The forces that drove him could so easily turn on him – he could spend his life chasing an obsession. He wrapped his hand around hers. 'You are my obsession,' he said. 'Loving you. You are my future.'

Pearl put her head on one side, smiling. 'And your past, Ben? What did you say your mother's name was?'

'Princess Eléna Vasílyevna Kurágina.'

'That's nice,' Pearl said. '*La belle Hélène.*'

Exactly the same phrase Cleremont had used. Ben closed his eyes. Exactly.

'Ben, I'm sorry!'

'How *could* he? My father lied to me,' Ben whispered incredulously. 'I believed him, I forgave him, and he lied to me.'

Unconsciously he was squeezing her fingers tight but Pearl let him, wanting to share his pain and by sharing, diminish it.

'Prince Vasíly's daughter,' she said gently, 'Pierre's girl in Tolstoy's novel.'

Ben released her and stood. 'I am going to face him right now.'

'Not without me,' Pearl said. He mustn't go to his father alone.

'I'm going to squeeze the truth out of him.'

'Not without me.'

He turned. 'This isn't your fight, Pearl.'

She held his face. 'It is,' she said. 'Ben, everything about you. It *is*.'

Ben ignored the knocker and rapped straight on the door of Lockhart House with his fists. When the door was opened Pearl followed him past the frightened housemaid across the chequer. Cleremont was in his study, and he was drunk.

'Are you really my father?' she heard Ben demand.

The old man drew himself up. 'Yes.'

Ben threw open the curtains and light flooded into the room. Children were playing in the park. Traffic rattled and flashed under the sun.

'But I am nothing like you!' Ben said.

'Aren't you?' Cleremont poured a brandy with shaking hands. 'Men destroy what they most love, and become what they most fear.'

'That's a lie,' Ben said.

'No, it's true,' said Pearl. Her voice trembled. The peer turned to her.

'Oh, my dear child!' exclaimed Cleremont, downing his brandy, 'how I pity you!'

'Save your pity for yourself,' Ben stormed.

Cleremont held his arms wide. 'Look at me.'

'Damn you, who is my mother, where is she?'

'Dead, she's dead.' They argued with rising voices.

'Only dead in your heart,' Pearl said softly to the old man. Her words dropped into silence. 'She wasn't a princess, was she, Lord Cleremont? She was someone . . . anyone . . . ordinary.'

'No.' Ben shook his head. 'She was special. My mother was special, wasn't she, Father?'

Cleremont said: 'I told you the truth, I loved her. But it could not possibly be.'

Pearl moved gently between the two men. 'Anything can be. She wasn't high-born, Lord Cleremont, she was low-born, and you were ashamed of your feelings.'

Ben stared at her. Pearl had taken control. Constantly she surprised him.

'You're beautiful,' confided the old man. 'I had to lie to him. But I knew I would be found out. It was the first name that came into my head.'

'It was your cry for help,' Pearl said.

'Don't you hear it? Help me!'

'Yes!' said Pearl, holding his dry, withered hands. 'You wanted your son to admire you.'

'Now the opposite has happened,' Ben snarled.

Pearl said over her shoulder: 'He's just a lonely, ordinary old man. Help him.'

Lord Cleremont inhaled a breath. 'She was a parlourmaid,' he said.

Pearl drew him down beside her on the sofa. 'Lisa,' he confessed. 'Her name was Lisa. She must have got married later – I saw a wedding ring on her finger. She was a woman of terrifying spirit and determination, but when I had her I saw only a shy girl . . . hardly a person . . . they were always so thin. So thin and so hot, such a burning heart, and so shy. Her last name, I don't know, Lisa, Lisa . . . Do they have last names? She was just a serving girl.'

'You must have records,' prompted Pearl quietly.

Cleremont's head nodded sideways. 'Staff records! No, not since Crane died.'

'Did Lisa work here?'

'Mostly at my other place, at Clawfell, in Yorkshire.'

Pearl asked: 'May we search for her there?'

'You won't find her,' Cleremont said. 'I was good to her, as good as I could be. But a relationship is two halves. And she was the stronger half. Now you know my secret. I love her. Forgive me.'

Pearl looked up at Ben, waiting for his response.

2

'I don't care that she isn't a princess,' shouted Ben.

'What?' Pearl called, laughing, her hair streaming around her ears.

'I don't care that my mother isn't a princess, all I care about is her!'

The Bentley thundered past the afternoon traffic along Prince Albert Road, the sun-flashing red in their eyes. 'Go faster!' Pearl cried.

'I don't care how ordinary she is – she's *alive*.'

Ordinary? Even Ben had to have the obvious pointed out to him sometimes: 'Don't you understand?' Pearl laughed, 'she's an extraordinary woman! She was only a parlourmaid, she didn't have much education, but she knew what she wanted and by God she nearly won! She defied the great Peer of the Realm. She fought him for love, and when she lost she did what she felt she had to do, even though it was almost the worst thing in the world.'

'I suppose you're right,' Ben said, cutting past Lord's cricket ground and turning down the Edgware Road.

'She must have been scared out of her mind,' Pearl said softly. 'Can you imagine it? Wandering the streets of London in midwinter, cold, dark, with a baby inside you about to come and no friends, rejected by everyone, even by – *especially* by – the man you had loved . . . no, Ben, she isn't ordinary.'

Pearl had never seen his face so full of emotion. 'I love her, I love you, Pearl.'

She kissed his cheek. 'We're out of our minds with love,' she said.

He slowed the car on Park Lane and pointed at the old Londonderry House Hotel. 'We're going to celebrate. We'll go dancing tonight.'

'Ritzy,' admitted Pearl. 'But I want to go somewhere deep and dark with you. A nightclub, huh?'

'Classy dame,' said Ben. 'I've already ordered Simmonds to get the Rolls out. Tonight, we're puttin' on the Ritz.'

He was as good as his word; Simmonds was busy polishing the big black laudalette as they drew over the cobbles into the Emporium's rear courtyard, and a couple of hours later, after bathing in her separate bathroom and dressing in her separate bedroom, Pearl found herself sitting in the back of the Rolls as it glided through the night. She wore a stunning off-the-shoulder ballgown in midnight black and silver that revealed the graceful curves of her neck and throat clustered with diamonds – the constellation glittering in her hair was also diamonds. Ben lay his hand on hers.

He was dressed with classical elegance in white tie and tails, his hair swept back, his top hat and stick laid on the seat facing them. The hotel's brilliantly lit façade rose out of the night above them. 'Based on the villa Farnesina,' Ben said casually, 'but with an added dash of florentine, I think.'

Pearl flashed him a look. 'I didn't know you knew about architecture?'

'There are one or two things about me you don't know.' The ultimate mystery of his sex, the source of her faith in him and his power *for* her, for her protection. She was safe. She relaxed, laughing.

'Where did you go this morning when I couldn't find you?'

'You've already guessed.'

'I don't believe it,' she breathed.

The commissionaire opened the laudalette's door and saluted. 'Good evening Mr London, sir. Miss Remington, welcome.' They went up the steps into the foyer, almost blinding with white, scarlet and gold, and entered the swirl of people.

'Two hundred bedrooms,' Ben said. 'Hallo, good evening.' He nodded from side to side. 'Hallo. Good to see you. How are you.' Staff and guests parted in front of them as they went up the grand Wyatt staircase to the first floor and Pearl found herself in a magnificent ballroom lined with Canova statues, with an orchestra waiting at the far end. 'Smile,' Ben murmured. 'Hallo! Great pleasure . . . You are radiant, darling,' he whispered, 'and I love you.'

They left everyone behind them and crossed the expanse of dance floor to its centre. 'I hope you can dance,' he said.

'I hope *you* can.' She was still relaxed, still laughing.

Ben turned to the conductor. 'The Charleston!'

Pearl gasped as he swept her into the dance. He was a superb dancer, he could have made a professional living. 'I sat in with Cochran and Astaire at the World Solo Charleston championships at the Albert Hall when the third judge fell ill.'

'Who taught you?'

'Chouchou.'

Pearl missed a step, and Ben covered by leaning her back on his arm.

'Let's say she commenced my interest,' he said.

'I'm sorry,' she said.

'Chouchou knows what suffering is,' Ben said. 'So do I. So do you. You are a woman. Yes, you do.'

'But I'm so happy!'

'I'll tell you my secret,' he said, 'if you'll tell me yours.'

He swung her gracefully around him as though she were flying.

'Tell me!' Their faces were close.

'I bought this hotel this morning,' he said. 'It's all ours. Share it with me! This is London's.'

3

'Tell me,' Ben said.

It had been a wonderful evening, the most wonderful of Pearl's life. She had danced as she had never dreamed of dancing before. She had won the admiration of high society, the food was light and delicious, the champagne exquisite. But even the last waltz ends, and now the last bottle of Krug *Grand Cuvée* was placed upside down in its cooler and the waiters were yawning.

'Tell me everything about yourself.'

'Oh, Ben, I can't. I wish you'd understand. I just can't.'

'I love you. I must know everything about you, feel everything you feel, I must share your life.'

'You do share everything, almost everything,' Pearl said softly. Some things could never be explained. 'But you're a man, and I am a woman. You'll never understand.'

He raised his hand and waiters scurried around them.

He must have sent Simmonds home earlier, because a valet delivered the Rolls-Royce to the steps as they came out into the cool night air, and Ben drove. The front seats were in the open and Pearl looked up at the stars as the car whispered through the silent streets. Ben stopped by the Thames and turned off the engine. This was the Embankment, and the river slid darkly by. A waxing moon rose late beyond the black dome of St Paul's.

'I will understand.' He was staring at the river.

'It's locked up inside me, I *can't* tell you – I can't even tell myself.'

'You told a little of it to Chouchou, knowing she would understand. You felt safe with her.'

'But Chouchou is a woman.'

'Do you think I love you so little?' He laughed. 'Only a man.'

She shook her head, mute.

'Once upon a time . . .' Ben said, 'once upon a time, the girl called Ria said I raped her – at least, that was what she allowed everyone to believe, because she was frightened.' Pearl didn't have to ask *Did you?* and he did not have to say *No*. 'She was frightened because she loved me. She had dreamed of and desired love in a romantic way, but when it actually happened, the real thing, it frightened her.'

'Love exists.' Pearl smiled faintly. She curled her fingers around his. The moon had moved clear above the dome now. 'I want every night between us to be here, now. The river, the moon. It's a good world.'

'Evil exists in this good world,' Ben said. 'I don't mean bad intentions, I mean real evil. A force as inexplicable as love.'

'We mustn't believe that.'

'Let me finish telling you,' Ben said doggedly. 'I'm talking about Ria's brother, Vic Price, and his evil. Vic is an evil man, Pearl.'

'I sensed that in Court.' She shivered; his black, intense eyes had touched her like a stain. She had not been able to look away from him.

'Maybe he was born evil – but can we believe that on a night like this? His parents are harmless folk. Perhaps I myself made him what he is. Vic *believes* in rape. It's real to him, just as love is real to us. He believes in the worst.'

Pearl said suddenly: 'Don't tell me, Ben.'

'In the distance, just to the right of the moon – that's Tower Bridge. Close by, at this time of night, on a secret platform above the river, Ria took me and made love with me there. I was fourteen. She was fifteen.'

They looked out over the river. 'This meant so much to you,' Pearl said, and wiped her eyes. 'Don't tell me any more.'

He did tell her more, it was engraved in darkness on his heart. 'Ria fell pregnant. She couldn't hide our secret. She couldn't stand up to Vic or dare tell him anything but what he believed. Rape. Force. Lust. She denied love.'

'Don't tell me about Vic,' wept Pearl.

He told her everything.

'Vic caught me and dragged me to the exact same place

Ria and I made love. There, while Nigel held me, he crouched and . . . covered my face with the palms of his hands . . . and forced me to swallow . . . to eat . . . his excrement.'

'I love you,' Pearl wept. She flung her arms around him. He cuddled her, saying nothing.

'I know you,' Pearl said. 'I'm so ashamed of myself.'

'Tell me everything.'

A siren hooted on the water.

Ben said: 'Tell me the secret of your beauty.'

She must finish what he had started. Pearl squeezed her eyes shut.

'I want you to take me to bed,' she said.

Tell me the secret of your beauty.

She stood in the moonlight from the open drapes, then crossed to his bed and slipped inside. His earthy, masculine smell on the warm yellow satin sheets she had chosen for him; the hot hard curves of his body beneath his soft cotton pyjamas. She wore her wild-silk nightdress, so fine that if he touched her, he would leave his fingerprints on her body, and her heart would melt. But she trusted him. He held only her hand between them; he did not touch her.

She lifted herself on one elbow and looked down at him in the moonlight. *That blessed mood, in which the burden of the mystery, in which the heavy and the weary weight of all this unintelligible world, is lifted.* Talking to him, her life began to make sense.

'Until I was twelve years old,' Pearl whispered, 'I sincerely believed that everybody had a house on Fifth Avenue, a summer house on Rhode Island and an ocean-going yacht. Of course we did – Mary and I were brats, we had no reason to think otherwise. Everyone we knew was like us.'

He nodded, listening.

'One day the chauffeur taking Mary to French lessons got lost. When she came back we sat on the stairs, whispering secrets, our skirts around our knees. The poor existed. They lived in ghettoes. She had seen them – unwashed, violent, *alive*, living a kind of hideous opera on the street, in filthy tenements racked up to the sky, in their hundreds and thousands. The poor, in their *millions*. As we whispered we realized that they were all around us. They supported us. We were the object of their dreams, we were their envy and desire. And they hated us. We deserved it: look how we lived. We were guilty, Mary said. We were guilty because we were . . . born the way we were.'

For a long time she said nothing, caressing his hand. 'We could never be *us*.' He saw her gorgeous hair in the moonlight.

Ben murmured: 'So you escaped?'

'So we escaped, at the age of twelve? Where to? My Daddy is a fine and gentle man, but he owns fifty thousand apartments in New York City and real estate all over Boston, railroads . . . The only place we could escape to was Europe. The answer was education. European manners. Pops couldn't resist the idea. We were fifteen, and it was the Golden Summer. Perhaps we'd marry dukes – there's quite an export market for American heiresses – it cost Vanderbilt ten million to marry into the Duke of Marlborough's family, they say, and he thought it was worth every cent. We could see the same gleam in Lowell Remington's eye. Mary had different plans, and I tagged along. She looked after me. I wasn't alone.'

'But when the War broke out it caught you over here.'

'Queen Alexandra's and the VAD turned us down as nurses, but we smuggled ourselves into France anyway. Natalie Barney looked after us and we drove ambulances between Paris and the Front with Jean Cocteau, society girls doing their bit. We spent the summer months with Lily de Clermont-Tonnerre by the railway station at d'Aubervilliers-La Courneuve. Aren't those lovely names? We could smell the gangrene on the air before the trains pulled in. But it didn't really *touch* me. Mary said it was our duty.'

'Always Mary.'

'Well, bossy older sister and all that. Always looking after me.'

'Never being alone must have made all the difference to your life.'

Pearl ran the palm of her hand over his face, then rested it flat on his warm chest, staring into the moonlight blindly.

'Then I was alone. I was at the battle of Loos, Ben.'

He waited.

'Everyone knew an attack was coming. When we heard the boys complaining that their mail was stopped, we knew it was happening any day. Civilians lived right up to the line, remember? So we tramped across the fields. Fine idea for a fine day, it was windless, the end of summer. But I got lost when darkness fell and the bombardment started. I couldn't find the hospital. Everything didn't look so neat then. For the first time in my life I was alone and *I was terrified*!'

She stopped. 'I stumbled through the dark.' She stopped again.

He reached up and touched her breast.

'Guilt,' Pearl shuddered. 'The loss of my virginity.' He noted that: not of her innocence. Even now, Pearl was innocent.

'In the cellars?' he said.

She nodded, sitting clasping his hand to her, her head thrown back, her hair a shimmering wave. She looked – not elegant – elemental. He desired her mightily.

'The cellar of Loos château was a death cavern of men and boys. They had run into their own gas. Eight thousand dead in three hours, and the battle going on and on. The village burning, the stink of flames and blood. A hole had opened in the ground, I slid down a coal chute into the cavern. Down there I was as deep as my womb, the thudding of the guns, the heat, and I was a woman alone amongst them. All those poor boys dying. I could not give them life.'

He put his hand behind her back, supporting her.

'The walls were splashed with yellow lyddite from

explosions. The men wore kilts, the first Camerons, how white their knees looked. Snipers got from Hill 70 into the houses further down, we were trapped – a dying boy was shot in the throat in my arms. We put the dead in another cellar for as long as we had the strength. It was lovely in there, that silence, terrible peace. As more died, more were brought down from the wasteland.'

She walked to the window and opened the sash. The moon was high and blue, but grey dawn lit the skyline. The breeze set the silky nightdress wafting around her body, and her hair billowed.

'On the 28th of September conscientious objectors of the fifth Forward Ambulance Unit from 47 London Division reached us – a man slid down the coal chute. Frankie was a pacifist, very intelligent, very religious. Family man, he had a wife and three girls. Pretty, he showed me their photographs. My age.'

'You fell in – '

'No, I fell in . . . into affection with Frankie.' She ran her fingers through her hair in the first rays of the sun, and he saw the silhouette of her body clearly beneath her nightdress now, everything. She came and sat on the side of the bed, tucking her long legs under her, resting her elbow matter-of-factly on the sweep of her thigh.

'He was thin and tall, not strong, but over the next few days Frankie worked like a Hercules, dragging a stretcher and bringing in wounded all the time. He went trembling with fear, knowing he would be killed out there. His nerve went, he was a dreadful sight. I begged him to leave those men out there. I needed him to be a coward. To save Frankie, to prove there is something more than death.

'I wanted to give myself to him. There was a place kept locked, a narrow room with a curved ceiling, the wine cellar, I'd found the key. We would go in there, I would let him love me, keep him with me. Life for him. One lifetime saved out of this horror. Yes, for his tender caresses, for his life, I would have let him have me, willingly.'

Pearl looked at Ben.

'Don't tell me,' Ben said. He dreaded what she would say.

'He wouldn't,' Pearl maintained. 'He was marvellous and understanding. "Give me the courage to go," Frankie said gently. "Tell my wife I love her. Tell my girls to be always as beautiful as you are now." '

Pearl stopped. She did not go on. She began, then stopped again.

Ben waited.

'He kissed you,' Ben said. 'And that was all.'

'He went out and I never saw him again,' Pearl said.

'He may have survived nevertheless.'

'I was in the cellar for another twenty-seven hours. Then Mary found me. She had been sheltering with Madame Moreau in a cellar in another part of the village. "What's happened to your hair!" Mary screamed when she saw me, and I knew I was free. I was free of her and everyone. I had earned the name I was christened with. Pearl. I had achieved my own identity, my own femininity, even though I had lost.'

'Suffering is your secret, the source of your beauty,' Ben whispered. 'Of course Chouchou understood. She recognized suffering.'

'I love you,' Pearl murmured.

'No woman is born beautiful, beauty is earned.' He held her gently against him. 'Pain and compassion made you what you are. Pearl, you earned in full, and are rewarded in full.'

She has the face of an angel. Her sleeping features were framed by her spectacular hair. She lay warm and safe in his arms. The sun had risen into the window, and somewhere close to it in the blue he knew the moon burned with a paler light, invisible and forgotten by most people as they hurried to work. But all over the world the tides were rising and falling, dominated by its hidden force, and people too, as the calendar ticked on.

He held her and they slept.

CHAPTER EIGHT

1

'No!' Ria said. Mum had come up to Ria's bedroom to help her choose what clothes to wear for Ray tonight, not that she had been asked, but Esther liked to feel that she was close to her children. They thought they didn't need her, but they did, although only Vic was nice enough to say so outright. Esther even enjoyed Ria's flaming tempers in their way, because they were a symptom of love. Love for Mum – and possibly for dashing Raymond Trott, who would be a wonderful catch. He always kissed Esther's cheek, and always brought Ria flowers. So Esther was actually smiling at Ria's tantrum.

It was when Ria was quiet that something was wrong.

'I only suggested,' Esther said, 'that you wear your nice electric blue.'

Ria's eyes flashed and she tossed back her golden hair. 'It's old,' she said.

Esther held it up to the light, there was nothing wrong with it, and the cut was so out of date it looked almost *avante-garde* again. 'No!' Ria snatched it and turned away for a moment, then stuffed it in the cupboard. Esther understood.

'I know,' she said, 'you were wearing it that morning Ben London brought you back for the last time. Memories, is that right?'

Ria's cheeks flushed scarlet. 'Mum, do you have to trample? Give it a rest. Why do you have to say everything out loud!'

Esther changed the subject. She could hear children laughing outside and supposed young Will was playing. 'What a lovely warm evening, isn't it? You could wear something quite off the shoulder. Ray will be here soon.

119

What about that nice crimson one he bought you? That would be a compliment to him.'

'I don't want to *compliment* Ray, he's an adult man.'

'But he's so polite.'

'Men don't like compliments in words, Mum,' Ria snarled, 'they like them in kisses.'

'Don't think you're shocking me.' Esther folded her arms. 'I have been in love too, my girl.'

Ria closed her eyes. Mum was going to guff on about Dick, her first husband. Esther liked Tom, her second husband and father of her children, she liked him very much and was happy with him, but Dick had been the flame of her life. When he died of peritonitis Esther married Tom on the rebound, even though it meant a big drop in her circumstances. She never regretted marrying Tom, but she had burned for Dick.

'I'm not in love,' Ria said.

Esther nodded wisely. 'Of course you aren't, dear. I should wear the crimson, he'll like that.'

'Ray isn't really my type.'

'He's ever so attractive! There's terrific competition for him, you should be grateful he's so attentive, obviously he's head over heels for you. You must be blind. He's a good prospect too, seeing who his dad is.' Esther was always practical in her way. 'Ted Trott owns the Old Bull and Bush outright, it's a free house. It'll be Ray's one day, my girl. You could set up together, him doing the bar, you the food, and make a good living like Dick and I did.'

Ria had to admire Mum's cunning, though she had no intention of spending her life as a waitress. She threw her arms around Mum. 'Ray wants to set up a nightclub,' she confided. 'We'd call it Trott's and we'd be up West, attract the toffs and all the fashionable people. And he says I could sing.'

Esther's eyes shone joyously. *We* – twice Ria had said *we*. Ray was closer than she had thought.

'Not your type!' she scoffed, hugging her daughter. 'Why, you've always dreamed of singing again.'

'If only Ray can get the money,' Ria said anxiously.

'He always has plenty of cash,' Esther pointed out.

'That's not the same thing.' Ria pulled the crimson dress out of the cupboard and started undressing. Esther went downstairs, eyed the sink cupboard and resisted a slug of gin, and made a pot of tea instead.

She only really drank spirits when she was unhappy, and nowadays she had nothing to be unhappy about. Nigel was married and living his own life with Arleen. That was a weight off Esther's mind – Arleen was such a good influence, and she fed Nigel properly so that he had put on pounds and looked much more relaxed. He'd almost lost that haunted look he'd worn since his experiences in the war. Esther approved of Arleen because she so plainly loved Nigel, and had turned him from a lonely boy following Vic in everything into his own man.

But what Esther had fought tooth and nail was Nigel's ill-advised move (at Arleen's insistence) to a house in Greenwich, south of the Thames. True, it wasn't far, and connected by a footpath under the river, but to move from the Isle of Dogs was in Esther's view very nearly traitorous, and she had not forgiven Arleen for it. Vic had merely shrugged.

'Let him go,' Vic said, 'he's so clever, isn't he? Let them be clever.'

Esther didn't see what was so clever about it – with the river between them, it meant Nigel saw even less of Vic.

Ria came in wearing the crimson dress. 'I should put your hair up,' Esther said, filling the flower vase. They heard the clatter of an engine and Raymond Trott arrived by taxi. He was dressed in a slim black dinner suit and looked smart enough to put on a chocolate box. And he was carrying a large bunch of flowers – which, bowing, he handed to Esther in the hall.

'These are for you,' he said seriously, and kissed her cheek.

'Ray, you shouldn't, what a lovely surprise, you are thoughtful! Come in the front room.' He knew how to get on the right side of his future mother-in-law, and Esther liked him to take the trouble. He was a wise boy. 'Ria,' she called, 'Ray's here.' Then to Ray: 'She knows perfectly well,' she apologized.

'I know Ria,' said Ray Trott indulgently. He rested one elbow on the mantelpiece, his other arm tucked behind him.

Ria came in. 'Wotcher, Ray. Are we going up West?'

'Dancing until dawn,' smooched Ray. Both the women pretended not to notice the package he held behind his back though they were dying to know what was in it. 'However,' Ray wagged his finger, 'I cannot permit you to wear the same dress twice. Once is magnificent. Twice does not do you justice.'

Ria tried to keep her eyes on his. 'You speak so smooth, Ray.'

'Isn't he a wonderful lover?' Esther said. 'Like Valentino.'

At last Ray held out the surprise. It was a dress box done up with an enormous ribbon. 'With my compliments.'

'Oh, Ray, you shouldn't.' Ria knelt and undid the ribbon lovingly, then pulled out a long green dress with a gasp of admiration. 'Oh – *Ray*.' She held it against her.

He smiled and she offered him her cheek, but he kissed her on the mouth – there was a certain lack of innocence in that kiss. Ria glanced at him out of the corners of her eyes while she examined the dress. From the black hem contrasts of very dark green rose and intertwined like jungle plants, tormented exotic blooms twining like flames past the knees and less round the hips, all but disappearing as they reached the pale green bosom. 'It's a dream,' Ria said.

The Greenwich to Island Gardens footpath under the river was over twelve hundred feet long and glazed with two hundred thousand white glazed tiles, and in Nigel's opinion it looked like London's longest public urinal. Arleen didn't encourage that sort of joke (he justified his prudish manner by sticking imaginary inhibitions on his wife) so he said nothing. She fussed his tie straight as they went up in the lift at the far end, attentiveness he pretended to find irritating but was grateful for. As they came out into the sunlight Arleen said: 'That place always reminds me of an enormously long public toilet.'

Nigel laughed, unbending. 'I thought so too.' He looked down at her, loving her afresh. He was always finding out about her, some tiny new surprise that caught him and made him realize all over again how lucky he was in their small pleasures, in her – and realized how much he had missed before he met her.

She tucked her hand in his elbow as they walked to the car. 'Nigel, I know you do tell me everything, don't you?'

'Yes.' That said it all.

'You don't have to work for Vic.' She looked up at him – so small, so vivid.

'I do,' he laughed.

'You're intelligent, you're easily clever enough to work anywhere you wanted. A bank or an insurance company, anywhere.'

'He needs me,' Nigel said, and that said it all, too. He pointed at a bush, changing to a more congenial topic, one that Arleen never tired of dreaming about. 'Look at those berries. If you get a passion for berries, we'll have to come here at midnight so you can eat that bush.'

He helped her into the motor car then swung the crank and drove up West Ferry Road, noticing Arleen's eyes turn, as always, to the mudchutes by Millwall Docks where he had proposed to her. It was a revelation to Nigel, as always, that he was precious to Arleen – that in her love he had achieved the happiness men crave most and he deserved least. That her eyes always turned to him. There was only one insignificant secret between them – that he was being milked by Raymond Trott, a purgatory he merited. Nigel realized that he had just technically lied to Arleen. *You do tell me everything, don't you?* But it was such a tiny secret.

There had to be secrets: in their line of work he and

Vic probably kept thousands, all indistinguishable from truth, if truth existed.

'I was talking to Alan's wife yesterday,' Arleen said. She meant Alan Stark's wife Betty. 'Alan hasn't phoned her or anything, and there's the baby.'

'Vic will look after her until he gets back.' Vic had been peeved with the German flier's evidence, the opposite of what Alan had led him to expect. Alan was taking a holiday during Vic's displeasure.

'Back from where?'

Nigel shrugged. 'Does it matter? Wherever he's gone. Look – there's Will.' He braked. The boy was sitting on a low wall with his bare knees drawn up to his chin, staring past the cranes to the river. Nigel left the engine running and went over, then crouched by Will's shoulder, sharing the view.

'Does Mummy know you're here?'

'She thinks I'm playing with friends.' Will didn't lisp away from Ria. 'But I haven't got any friends.'

'What are you doing here?'

Will pointed. 'That's China.'

'That's Rotherhithe,' Nigel said, 'the Chinese live in Limehouse.'

'The Great Wall. Coolies in enormous hats. Rice fields. We're in China.'

'Your mum ought to knock some sense into you,' Nigel said bitterly. *Someone ought to knock sense into Ria*, he thought. He held out his hand. 'Come with me. Bloody China! You ought to have your bum smacked.'

'I don't want to go back to the house.'

Nigel was subtle. 'You want to ride in the motor, don't you?'

Will jumped up. 'Yes!'

When Nigel swung the car into Havannah Street he had to park behind a taxi waiting with its engine ticking over. Ria opened the house door. Will dashed past her and his feet thumped upstairs.

'Ria, it's *lovely*!' squealed Arleen at Ria's green dress,

124

holding out her hands and leaning back in ecstatic amazement. 'Wherever did – ?'

'Ray bought it for me,' Ria said as Nigel pushed past her into the hall.

'Ray who?' said Nigel, coming into the front room.

'Nigel, old fruit, what a treat it is to see you again,' Raymond Trott said, and Nigel's heart went cold, 'after all these years.' That was all; Ray, leaning languidly against the fireplace, gave an ironic wave, but Nigel was too sick to feel relief.

'What are you doing here?' he hissed, going so close that he could smell Ray's eau de cologne, their faces almost touching.

'Your charming sister has consented to go dancing with yours truly.'

'I don't want to see you here again,' Nigel said, stepping back and waving his hand in front of his nose.

'Who do you think you are?' demanded Ria. 'I go out with who I want.'

Nigel sat down trying to ignore the sour taste in his mouth. 'You don't know what you're getting into.'

'Bugger you, Nigel,' Ria said. 'Get out of my life!'

'I expect we'd like a hot cup of tea,' Esther said eagerly, bustling to answer a knock on the door. 'I expect that's Vic.' She glowed with pleasure to see her family gathering in her home. 'Come in, come in.'

Vic rubbed the palms of his hands. 'Evening, all.'

'Hallo, Victor,' Ray drawled, and Ria's ears pricked up, liking that defiance. Vic's name was Vic, everyone learned that.

'Raymond, old mate,' said Vic chummily, taking no offence.

She looked at Ray with new respect. He was one up.

'Now that Vic's here – ' on the sofa, Arleen dug Nigel's ribs. 'We have a small announcement to make.'

Nigel stood up. 'Mum, you'd better sit down . . .' He cleared his throat. 'Arleen and I are going to have a baby.'

Esther burst into tears and blew her nose, then

embraced Arleen. 'At last, a proper baby,' she snuffled joyously, 'a proper baby, born in wedlock.'

Ria hid her pain – she hadn't realized that Will's illegitimacy was such a constant grief to Mum. She turned to Nigel, but Ray spoke first.

'Congratulations, Nige,' Ray said, 'I didn't know you had it in you.' Ria looked at him, amazed – that was exactly what she had been going to say.

'I wanted you to hear it, Vic,' Arleen said deliberately.

Vic nodded, grinning, his black eyes not leaving hers.

Arleen said suddenly: 'Nigel might be getting another job, Vic. Insurance, the City, we don't know yet.'

'We haven't discussed this in fact,' Nigel explained, glancing between the two of them.

'We have in principle,' Arleen said, and Nigel nodded, agreeing.

'You'd have to consider such a big decision very carefully,' Vic said, and Nigel nodded. That also was very true.

Esther struggled up from the sofa. 'I forgot all about the tea.'

'Not for us, we're off.' Ray slung a white scarf casually from his neck. 'I and your sister are going dancing, Victor.'

'So that's what she's dressed up like a dog's dinner for,' Vic said, letting Nigel off the hook. Ria bridled.

'Arleen and I found Will dumped outside,' Nigel said. 'You ought to stop thinking of yourself all the time, Ria. There's more to life than pleasure.'

'What are you ganging up on me for?' Ria said tearfully, feeling for Ray's hand. 'It's the first time I've been out dancing for ages and ages.' She felt Ray's arm around her shoulders, turning her to the door, and let him lead her out. Ray knew best, there was no point in having a family set-to in public. Ria felt tired; and she had been looking forward to her evening out so much.

'Don't pay any attention to them, Ria,' Ray murmured. She held his hand gratefully, looking up at him. Ray was strong and very attractive. It was lovely to be seen out with a man again.

'Mind she doesn't stand on your toes, Ray,' Vic called after them in a jolly voice as the taxi pulled away. He knew it wasn't the discipline of the dance Ria liked – she liked the holding, the closeness, the dark.

Vic stared after them along the street until the taxi turned out of sight. He knew his sister as well as he knew himself.

He chuckled as he came back into the house. Everything was going very well, and he even beamed a grin at Arleen. She who dared defy him. He hoped she was enjoying her victory while it lasted.

2

The holding, the closeness, the dark.

There were hardly any lights on in the nightclub and the dance floor was darkest night. A swarm of shadows rotated slowly around them, warm and intimate, other dancers; Ria was flying on cocktails, and she held Ray's taut body in a fierce hug, letting him sway her round, holding him close in the dark in her lonely centre of the universe, never wanting the night to end.

'You don't understand,' Ray confided, his lips in her hair, 'you come from such a good family. Your mum adores you, so does your dad. Nigel's wet, but Vic would do anything for you. But I'm an only child. I haven't got anyone.'

'Oh Ray. I do understand.'

'My father's frightening,' Ray admitted. 'I don't want to follow in his footsteps. I want us to set up on our own.' Ria's heart thrilled, sharing Ray's dream of their own nightclub. She pressed her face against his chest and inhaled his scent. Someone bumped into them and Ray snapped out – he had a sharp tongue, and he wasn't afraid to use the edge of it. But then he was gentle again, sinking

127

his fingers into her hair, turning Ria's head up. She sensed the shadow of his head. 'Vic would lend us the money.'

Ria's eyes popped wide open. 'He'd never let us – '

'If we were married,' whispered Ray's voice out of the dark. 'He trusts me. Vic knows you'd be safe with me.' And she knew he wasn't frightened of Vic – he'd defied him, and Vic had taken it on the chin without a murmur. Such dangerous courage was a compelling excitement, and Ria felt its attraction.

She stared up, wishing she could see Ray, feeling his strong fingers winding in her hair and his hard, arrogant body against her. She wanted him. Marriage, they were talking about. Need, that wasn't enough reason to marry. She tried to concentrate. She needed him. God, how she needed someone.

You don't know what you're getting into, Nigel had said. *Bugger you, Nigel*! Yet Arleen had transformed Nigel, and not only his appearance – he was much kinder, a more complete person. Men needed women. Ray was not without his faults, but they added to his attraction, she could turn him round. As his wife.

'Ray, I want to go home,' Ria said uncertainly. She had to think.

'Got to ask Vic's permission?'

Ria stepped back into a pool of light. She pressed the heel of her palm to her forehead. 'I don't know,' she said, 'I don't know. It's all so sudden.'

'It's what you want.' Yes. She clung on to him. 'He's promised me the money already,' Ray said. 'It's not a dream. It's real.'

'Please,' Ria begged. 'I don't know what I feel.' But she did.

Ray fetched his coat and they went out to the taxi. The headlights glowed enormously but cast no beams; a thick fog was rolling off the river. Ria watched the outline of the driver hunched over the wheel as the taxi crawled through the invisible streets, intensely aware of Ray sitting beside her.

'He won't get there for hours,' Ray murmured. He kissed her hand. 'I'm saying I want you to marry me.'

She almost swooned. At last she had heard those simple words.

Marry me. She whispered: 'Do you love me?'

'Yes, yes, yes.' He leaned across the leather seat and caught the nape of her neck in his hand, crushed his mouth to hers. Ria struggled, then arched her back. She held his head between her hands, pushing him down, overwhelmed by fiery need for his lips against her throat and her breasts. The thought of marriage, an end to her loneliness, filled her with lust, the need to give, to share, to take.

'Is it a deal?' he said.

'I don't know!' Ria gasped. The need to be a woman; a full woman.

He brushed his lips against hers. 'Marry me, Ria . . .'

She kissed him wildly, almost crying, his handsome face smiling above her in the glowing fog, intensely desirable in the way he withdrew from her as she advanced. 'Yes!' she cried. 'Yes! Yes!'

'Darling,' he said, stroking her hair. 'Darling, no, we mustn't. Not now. This is a holy moment.' He kissed her again; she felt the erotic promise in that kiss. 'We must save ourselves.'

'What for?'

He kissed her for a third time. 'For our marriage bed,' he said.

Ria flung her arms around him, crying openly. He had proved how much he treasured her.

Vic toasted Ria. 'I'm glad you're going to be happy now.' They chinked glasses.

'Another wedding,' Esther fluttered. 'I can't believe my luck.'

Even Nigel said something nice. 'You and I have had our differences, Ria, but I hope this will bring us together. I hope that Ray will make you as happy as Arleen has made me.' He would have to break it gently to Will that his mummy was getting married. *Raymond Trott!* he thought, appalled, *getting married to Raymond Trott!*

Arleen kissed Ria. 'I hope you have a baby soon,' she said. On her slight frame her bump showed already. They were standing by the bar in the Tooke Arms. Ria eyed the fireplace where Ben London had struck Vic down . . . *Ria's all girl. She can't live without a man, but she has a deep and tender heart, and she is so easy to hurt that she must live hiding it deeply inside herself, or she would scream . . .* but now Ria smiled, and the fire was cold.

'Cheers, all,' she said, and downed her sherry in one.

'Getting married in a cathedral like your mother wants?' Tom asked gruffly. When Ria shook her head he said: 'Told you, Esther. St Luke's again.'

'No,' Ria interrupted, 'I don't want to get married there. Ray and I thought a registry office. Something simple and quick and, you know, modern.'

Esther was horrified. 'But it isn't *right* if you don't get married in church. It isn't sanctified, it won't be a sacred union.'

'I just don't want to. Ray agrees.'

'You've always dreamed of getting married in church,' Esther accused.

'Yes, but – I suppose I've grown up, Mum.'

'Let her have her way.' Vic hugged Esther. 'They're just dying to get married, they can get a special licence in a few days, no need to make a song and dance about it.'

Arleen took Ria aside. 'If you're honeymooning, Southend's so lovely. Nigel and I never regretted it.'

Ria told her the secret. 'Vic's booked us into the most expensive hotel in London. It's his present. We're looking for a place to set up our nightclub.'

'I'm so happy. Everything's coming true for you – everything you've ever dreamed of, Ria.'

Ria downed another glass. 'That's right, Arleen.'

'It's so kind of Vic to put up the money. He's turned over a new leaf.'

On Saturday Ria married Ray Trott at Poplar Registry Office. There was a football match on and the streets were empty. Ria wore lemon-yellow, the nearest she dared to white. As the taxi jarred over the cobbles by the Work-house she turned to Vic. Her hair was a stream of golden curls and she felt as though she was floating – it was really happening at last.

'Should I do this?'

'You look terrific,' Vic said. 'You were so unhappy.'

'Was I?'

Vic kissed her cheek. 'You're safe with Ray. I wouldn't let anything happen to my sister.'

Ray was waiting on the steps. He wore a smart grey suit, practical and businesslike. Esther was dressed in pink and blue, bought for her especially by Vic, but she still looked glum about it not being church. Ray's father Ted Trott was there, a vast man with an overhanging belly and several little men swarming around him like the suck-erfish that service a shark. His face broke into an implac-able smile. 'Afternoon to you, Vic.'

'Afternoon, Uncle,' Vic said.

Ted laughed boomingly. 'That's true, I suppose.' He didn't introduce his wife, a thin creature in a big hat with royal-blue feathers, but Ria heard Vic call her Lydia. Vic knew more than she did about her new family of in-laws; Ray had barely introduced them. He despised his parents and they opposed the marriage. Ray frankly didn't give a damn; that was attractive, too.

'We should get together sometimes,' Ted told Vic grudgingly. 'Come and see me for a talk, friendly-like, when you've got the time.'

'Five o'clock,' Ray said, looking at his watch, 'last wed-ding of the day.' They went inside, and when they came out it was five twenty, and raining. They got back in the taxis, Mr and Mrs Ray Trott riding together this time, and jarred back to Havannah Street for the wedding breakfast.

'Nice little place.' Ted Trott stood in front of the window and darkened the room. Arleen offered round the platters of Lyons canapés. Lydia chattered to Esther about making ice cream, she had a refrigerator. Ria had no

131

appetite, but Ray cheerfully ate all the shrimps. Ted's cigar stank.

'Come on,' Ria said nervously, 'let's go.' She hoped Vic wasn't going to tie a dustbin to the bumper. But outside, Vic was serious, even sad, and he was the last to say goodbye to Ria as she climbed into the car.

'I love you,' he said. 'Remember.'

It was like a dream. The hotel couldn't have done more for them. Their suite in white, scarlet and gold held a magnificent view across the treetops of Hyde Park and the tables were a mass of white roses. Champagne was waiting, wrapped with a samite-white linen napkin in a bed of ice, and the glasses were finest crystal – Ria tapped one with a fingernail and it rang a lovely deep note. No expense had been spared, no corners cut. They ate in the à la carte restaurant where Ria had the hors d'oeuvre, including caviar, and then ordered the first steak she had ever eaten. The waiter flambéed it in an enormous copper pan at the table, the golden flames briefly hissing higher than their heads, and Ria had never tasted anything so delicious. Ray ate casually, toying with his food, he'd always had plenty of cash, this was nothing special to him. But Ria's eyes sparkled as she looked around, several times pointing out people she recognized from the picture papers. Later they went upstairs and danced with those same people in the ballroom. Afterwards a jazz band played in an island of light and in the dark they drank cocktails, Ray leaning back in his chair with his legs apart, and Ria sucked an olive. Its exotic scent filled her mouth and she studied Ray's floodlit profile. She wanted to go to bed with him, she longed for his kiss.

They went up. Ray put his arm around her shoulder and she giggled as they swayed along the corridor. Ray couldn't get the key in the lock and Ria was helpless with laughter. She put one hand on his chest and one on his back and kissed his shoulder. Ray swore and got the key in at last, and they stumbled inside. 'Leave the lights out,' Ria whispered.

Ray turned them on. The maid had been in to draw the curtains and turn down the bed. Ria's nightie was neatly laid out. 'You won't need that,' Ray said. This was just what Ria wanted to hear. She went into the bathroom to undress, and when she came out, she was naked. The lights were down, moonlight showed in the tall windows. Ray had opened the curtains and she saw his shadow against the neat squares of shining glass.

'Go to bed,' he said without turning. 'I like you, Ria. Don't let's play around any more. I don't love you, and you don't love me.'

'We need each other.' Ria wasn't ashamed of her nudity; she was proud, and the feel of the air was sensuous on her hot, bare skin. 'Turn round, Ray.'

He turned easily. Their bodies glowed blue under the moon – he was as naked as she, but muscular and flat, his lean chest as hairless as a Greek athlete's. She touched her voluptuous curves to his straight lines, reaching up, caressing his lips with her fingertips and then her mouth.

'I do understand,' she murmured. His chest felt smooth and cool. He returned her kiss with his own, sharp and mocking. And yet erotic: that lack of innocence that she longed to share – enhancing him with her femininity – breaking his masculine shell. Making him alive, giving him life, making him not alone.

He laughed in her mouth and snatched a step back from her. Suddenly they were apart, and eighteen inches was an abyss she could not traverse.

'It's all right. Just hold me,' she whispered.

'You won't get me that way.'

'Am I so ugly?'

'All women are ugly.' Ria trembled. 'Your charms are a perversion of nature, your whole body is, you're soft.' He brushed his hand against her intimately. 'You have no substance, Ria, darling. Do I make myself clear?'

'You married me.'

'Now, I wonder why I did that?'

'Love. A little bit of love.'

'No such thing. I don't know two married people who

love one another, do you? Grow up, Ria. My dad doesn't love my mother, they don't love me, I don't love them, I don't love you. Why are you shivering? Put some clothes on.'

'Hold me.'

He held her. He was as limp as a dishrag and proud of it.

'Vanity and arrogance, you women make me sick, it's not my fault how you suffer. You made your bed, now lie on it. You deserve everything you get.' He pushed her back, but not hard enough to hurt her – he didn't hate her. He was teaching her. 'You thought you could turn me round?' He held one hand above his head and twirled like a ballet dancer. 'You knew exactly what I was from the very first day you saw me, down there by the lock, and you knew exactly what the game was. Don't try and change the rules. We can have a good life.'

Ria sat on the corner of the bed. She put her head between her bare knees and felt sick.

Ray knelt and lifted her hair. 'You know why you married me really.'

Sex. Ria couldn't say that. The truth was unbearably brutal: to get away from Vic. To get their own nightclub. To sing again. To have the hope of love. And to get away from Ben London, his memory.

I love you. Remember.

'You're dirty,' Ray said.

'Ray, these are tears I'm crying. Leave me alone.'

'No tantrums – married woman now.'

'I despise you.'

Ray laughed. 'You despise yourself,' he said.

Ria lay staring up into the dark. Yes, she had not married for love. The penalty was not hate – it was hell. She couldn't hate Ray for being what he was, but she could blame herself, she could burn in this hell of her own making. Of course, it was bearable. It was even comfortable, lying here in bed, her husband snoring beside her, she could even smile. And it was all her fault.

134

She had chased a dream. Love does not exist.

She tossed her head on her pillow. Vic saying: *I'm glad you're happy now.* Happy? Or had he said: *Safe?*

Ray saying: *Vic knew you'd be safe with me.* She covered her eyes.

I'm Vic Price. Remember me.

Ria got up in the morning. She brushed her teeth. She washed her face. She combed her hair. She went downstairs with her husband and ate breakfast, cornflakes and cream, sausages and egg, tea and lemon. The waiters treated them like normal people. Today they would go and look at a couple of promising cellars in the Strand that might be suitable for a nightclub.

And Vic would lend them the money. He was in with Ted Trott now, and Ria was *safe*. Two birds, as Vic would say, grinning like a cat, with one stone.

'Damn you, Vic,' Ria said suddenly, and knocked over her teacup. Normal people did that sometimes.

As they went out through the foyer, Ria felt the blood drain from her face, seeing someone she recognized – and she would have fallen, but caught Ray's arm. He said: 'Seen a ghost?'

Ben London was standing by the main desk talking to the concierge. He looked at her and their eyes locked – that hot, burning blue struck her to her heart, recognition flashing between them at the speed of light. Then the doors swung and a wall of shining glass separated them.

'No one you know,' Ria said. She looked up. Workmen had replaced the letters of the Londonderry House Hotel with an arch of brilliant lights: LONDON'S.

'Damn you, *Vic*,' wept Ria, '*damn you, won't you ever give me peace?*'

CHAPTER NINE

1

'Ben, are you upset?' Pearl asked. Sitting by the bright window with her legs crossed, she was as rakishly elegant as a fashion picture in her long Burberry ulster, cap and brown leather kneeboots.

'Do I look upset?' He threw a couple of shirts into his Vuitton suitcase.

'Love,' Pearl sucked an olive, 'think you can fool me?'

'No.' He kissed her. 'Do we have to talk all the time?'

'Yes. I'm so happy, I want everything out in the open. Did I tell you yet the lobes of your ears are lovely? Nibbleable.'

'I was in London's and I saw Ria across the foyer. I'm sure it was her, I checked the register. She's married.'

'Another one bites the dust. Your socks are in the third drawer.'

'She looked so sad.'

'The travails of the marriage bed. Everyone goes through them.'

'Except you and I.'

Pearl paused, then licked her fingers. 'Does that bother you?'

'I love you,' he said fiercely, tenderly. 'I want us to be married.'

'We can't be, so we don't have to be, it doesn't bother me. Ben, I've got love, that's everything to me, I don't care about paper. Everyone thinks we're living in sin anyway, so let's.'

'Living in love,' he insisted.

'People don't believe things like that,' Pearl winked, 'about people like us.'

'Cynic,' he said, kissing her and snatching the last olive. 'It's true.'

'The alternatives are much more interesting.' Pearl wiggled her eyebrows then washed up the dish while Ben closed the suitcases and hefted them. Pearl's was the size of a wardrobe. He rang down for Hawk to send up a couple of extra doorboys. Peggy arrived with them, looking anxious.

'I do hope you find your mother at Clawfell, sir.'

'If she doesn't want to be found there's very little chance of picking up my mother's trail, I'm afraid. But she worked at that great house in Yorkshire for at least half her life until she was sixteen, and we may find a clue. We're just trying everything.'

'Pressing every button,' Pearl said.

'Good luck, sir. And you, miss.' Peggy curtseyed. She adored Pearl. At last the apartment was as it should be. The *au courant* white leather sofas and new white carpet, pure hell though they were to keep clean, still thrilled her. 'I've telephoned the butler at Easton Manor to expect you.' Ben and Pearl were breaking their long journey halfway at the country home of Sir Ozwald Benton-Benson – Ben owed the magnate an overdue apology for the way his son Bertie's name had been dragged through the newspapers. Although Ben remembered the old man's face betraying no sign of his feelings in the courtroom, he must have been in torment. Bertie's death, and his bequest to Ben of a priceless Mantegna nativity painting, had set Ben on the road to fortune. He and Sir Ozwald had never got on; they understood each other all too well.

'Goodbye, sir,' Hawk said downstairs, saluting Ben, 'I hope you have a good journey.' He gave one of the boys a quick clip round the ear for not strapping down the big trunk properly on the back of the Bentley. The Rolls-Royce was at Mulliner's having its coachwork rebuilt down the side after Simmonds cut one corner too many. Bert was pensioned off, still living in Lisson Grove, but now a gentleman of leisure.

'I hope it doesn't rain,' Ben said, going round to the

137

driver's side. Hawk was honoured to close Pearl's door, and he caught a glimpse of her ankle.

'Ta-ta, Hawky.' Pearl smiled beautifully, and Hawk almost melted like wax.

He cleared his throat. 'Rain, sir?' The Bentley had no top. 'Fine run of autumn weather, sir, depend on it. I have a nose.' He tapped his nostrils.

'Bye, Hawk.' Ben started the engine.

'Good luck, sir.' Hawk returned to his patch of polished flag. Yorkshire; that was a world away. He couldn't imagine it.

It drizzled by the time they reached the Great North Road but Ben kept going, the rain flying over the tops of the Bentley's aircraft-style windscreens. By lunchtime it was pelting, so they stopped under the lovely redbrick curve of a country railway bridge and raided the famous Waterfalls hamper, eating Parma ham and melon in their fingers, smoked salmon cornettes washed down with hock, a small-boned roast poussin, profiteroles and brandy. Then they leaned back with their arms round each other, the transmission tunnel between them, one of Pearl's long legs casually thrown over it, staring up at the dripping arch.

'That's the last time I trust Hawk's nose,' she giggled.

'It'll stop, there's blue ahead.' He kissed her and they drove into the sun. The A1 was tarmac nowadays, a narrow black thread winding between the fields, though some of the villages were still cobbled. When they saw a petrol station Ben let the air pressure out of the tank and put in thirty gallons of Pratt's while he had the chance. Evening found them searching amongst the lanes and hay-stacks of Lincolnshire for Sir Ozwald's Elizabethan manor house near Stamford.

While Pearl changed into her evening clothes Ben, already dressed for dinner, stood with the magnate looking through the ancient leaded windows towards the distant chimneys of Burleigh House, just visible beyond a ridge of autumn trees.

'So you sold Bertram's nativity picture,' Sir Ozwald grunted. 'Knew you would.'

'We all have to do things we don't want to sometimes.'

'All the times,' Sir Ozwald said. 'Always.' He was a hard, corpulent man, hypertensive and driven, immensely rich and with nowhere to go except old age. Now that he had effectively retired something had leaked out of him. He seemed to doubt his entire life, his wealth, his religion, himself. The veneer that had once protected him, the invulnerable armour of success, had thinned and softened with the years and now Sir Ozwald seemed dubious of every truth and all the rules he had lived by.

Once Ben had dreaded becoming this man. He could almost sympathize with the Sir Ozwald he saw, but still he dreaded becoming him. He was grateful when Pearl appeared. Sir Ozwald kissed her hand without emotion.

'My dear, you are extraordinarily beautiful – may I say so, Ben?'

'It's true,' Ben said. The sapphires she wore matched her eyes.

'This is a beautiful view,' Pearl said.

'Burleigh and Elizabeth I tolerated our family,' Sir Ozwald explained, 'though of course times had been much better under Mary, herself a Catholic. James did not like us and my ancestor Robert Benton was tortured to death in the Tower for his part in the plot to blow up the Protestant Parliament. Of course all this was three hundred years ago.' His eyes said it was yesterday.

He stopped. A maid brought them drinks. He did not talk in front of servants. When the age-dark oak door closed he said: 'My wife was beautiful, too. She never loved me for myself, and I'm glad she died five years ago, less than sixty years old, while she was still beautiful. She was not like you, my dear. It meant a lot to her, you see.'

'You have a rather harsh benevolence.' Pearl could say such things.

Sir Ozwald was not enraged. 'It's a cruel world. One has to be harsh to be realistic. Softness and success do not go together.'

'So you have no one now.'

'Not even my son.'

'Were you glad when he died?'

Ben stared at her, shocked that she could say something so terrible.

'Yes,' said Sir Ozwald. 'His life was the failure mine is now.'

'You never failed at anything,' Ben scoffed.

Sir Ozwald smiled tolerantly. 'I know he wasn't my son. He was nothing like me. He wasn't a man. Even Bertram's name – *Bertie*, his mother always called him, rubbing salt in my wound, my shame. She was part of the Prince of Wales's set, you know, of the 1890s. His nickname was Bertie of course.'

Pearl gasped: 'You mean the one who was King Edward VII later?'

'Yes.'

'How terrifically *glamorous*,' clapped Pearl, 'I *love* it.'

'I know my own father now,' Ben said, 'and I'm nothing like him.'

'Aren't you? I knew you'd sell that painting,' Sir Ozwald said, turning to Ben. 'The highest ideals always come to the least, my boy. Baggage to be sold. I have worshipped my God who sees into every heart all my life, confessed my sins, and never once betrayed the ideals my ancestors lived and suffered and died for. I know the truth. My son, last of my line, was the bastard of the Protestant King.'

'Maybe you want to believe that,' Pearl said, 'because you are a bitter man.'

'And maybe I know more about life than you do, my pretty girl.'

Pearl laughed. It was such an easy, natural laugh.

'Dinner is served,' Sir Ozwald said, flushing.

One habit Sir Ozwald had not lost: he still tried to dominate his guests with his awful food, a lukewarm turbot and a blackened leg of lamb. But Pearl's good nature was irrepressible and by the time the excellent vintage claret was opened, Sir Ozwald was her slave. When Ben raised his glass it was her he silently toasted.

Dawn was cloudless and still. Their boots crunched loudly on the gravel as Ben strapped their suitcases on the back of the car and Pearl wiped the dew off the seats. He thumbed the starter and they drove away from the manor house. Pearl shook out her hair luxuriously in the cool air as they picked up speed.

'Did you believe him last night?' she said. 'Or was he just being grandiose?'

'Sir Ozwald has made a virtue of protecting himself from people all his life. Nothing could have hurt him more than opening up and telling us what he did. The biter bit. His wife's contempt. Her mockery of everything precious to him and the failure of his life.'

The engine note rose. She tied back her hair. 'You knew all the time, Ben.'

'Where everyone knows everything, in the back of my mind.' He glanced at her as he drove. He was certain that Pearl had not told him the whole truth about the cellar. She hid nothing from him; she could not tell it to herself. Whatever the secret was, he prayed it would remain for ever buried. He lightened the subject, needing to see her smile. 'Sir Ozwald thought you were terrific!'

She laughed and kissed him. 'You were the son he wanted.'

'I have my father,' he said grimly, then shared her laughter. 'We're going to find my mother today – at Clawfell!'

For your sake, Pearl thought silently to herself as they flew north along the main road, *I hope we do find some sign of her*.

They lunched at a rustic stonebuilt inn by a stream then crossed the packhorse bridge, wasp-waisted in the middle to stop medieval farmers risking too-heavy loads (as always Pearl knew much more about English history than he did) and drove up into the pennine backbone of England. And so they came to Clawfell.

It was strange and beautiful.

The moor sweeping high above them was purple with heather, the autumn bracken as amber as whisky. They could hear birds singing above the rumble of the motor, though there were few trees. 'This must be so bleak in winter,' Pearl said, pointing at outcrops of harsh millstone grit. Green valleys climbed towards the rim of the moor like fingers, but never reached it. Streams glinted in them. On their right was a magnificent view over the Aire dales. They turned along a bumpy track, following a smooth leat of running water – and came to the ancestral home of the Cleremont family.

On such a day as today, it was a fairytale castle.

'Whoopee!' Pearl clapped her hands.

Ben stopped. So this was where his mother had worked as a girl.

Sunlight glinted off the turrets and the many windows glowed red with the setting sun. Not a real castle – the house had not always been this romantic vision of a Gothic dream, turreted, crenellated, and vast. The Saxon barn mentioned in the Domesday Book had been a stone farm-house by 1189, and four hundred years later the first Lord Cleremont chose this place to build his dynasty. The simple farm was dramatically expanded into a Jacobean country house, but survived now only as a proud detail in the background of family portraits. In the last century the eighth Lord of Clere Mount, Blane and Clawfell, at a cost reputed to be over one hundred thousand pounds, commissioned his dream. This stone pile, both ugly and beautiful, was what they saw before them now.

'Does it have a ghost?' Pearl asked, then bit her tongue.

'My mother,' Ben said.

As they drove past the Home Farm and the medieval fishponds, the heavy walls rose above them. Ben stopped the car on the weedy drive and Pearl followed him to the entrance in the pillared porte-cochère. The enormous studded door was pulled open by a flustered maid. 'Honoured to see thee, sir.'

'Thank you.' Ben looked past her, then around the vast

stone entrance hall with its grand staircase rising into the shadows. He shivered.

'I'll get stable-lad to carry in cases,' the maid bobbed.

'He isn't going to bite you,' Pearl said. 'What's your name, honey?'

The girl looked surprised. She was just a serving girl. 'Eliza, please, miss.'

Ben was on the staircase, looking around him at the dark portraits – his family. He felt the weight of their gaze. Lifetimes; centuries. He felt the slow tocking of remorseless time – there were no women in the pictures. The Cleremont wives must have had daughters; but they and their fleeting lives, their beauty, their eyes and smiles, their feminine hopes and desires, were as unrecorded now as they had probably been unnoticed then. Ben was chilled.

'These guys did all right for themselves,' Pearl called. She jumped as her voice echoed. 'Look at the rings that one's got on his fingers.' Ben backed down the stairs, then turned to her.

'What a dreadful place,' he said.

'I've only worked here this year,' Eliza confided to Pearl. She showed them round some of the ground floor, turning with a shy smile to watch their faces as she opened each door on the room beyond. Three hundred and sixty-five windows, each representing a day of the year, and God knows how many rooms. A library of mouldy books, no electric light, but at least there was running water from tanks concealed in the turrets.

'My mother was a parlourmaid here,' Ben said. 'Is anyone still working here who would remember her?'

'They say everyone was put out of work when his Lordship made his main residence in London, sir. That was about the turn of the century. Half the houses in the village are tumbled to rack and ruin from that time. They had to move away when he did.' She touched a work-chapped finger to her lip: 'Mrs Parkinson might have an idea, now – she's come up to cook thy tea, special. She knows all the secret ways of this place.'

'You mean real secret passages and everything?' Pearl was delighted.

Eliza tapped the side of her nose. 'A girl could live her lifetime in this place,' she said, 'and she'd never be found. No one would ever know.' She smiled sadly: look at me. Pearl held Ben's hand.

'Let's go and see Mrs Parkinson,' he said.

They found the cook down in the kitchens. The nooks were green with wet and the cavernous room was cold despite the iron range roaring – it had clearly been lit specially. Mrs Parkinson turned from feeding the fire and wiped her hands on her apron. She was a big, rough woman shrunken by years, her neck showing wattles below an angry red face. She had lost an eye and obviously found it more intimidating not to wear a patch.

'We're plain honest folk,' she greeted them, 'thee won't find airs and graces down here.'

Ben asked directly: 'When did you lose your eye?'

Mrs Parkinson was taken aback. He sat at the big oak worktable and gestured his permission for her to sit. She looked at him then sat obediently. 'I'm eighty-one years old,' she said proudly. 'Lost it during the war, working on the land. Newfangled machinery. But I were head cook here for eleven year.'

'Until when?'

'Until we was Let Go.' He waited. 'Midsummer's day, 1899.' She smiled bitterly. 'The very day the Old Man died. Young Charles never did like this place, sneered at us folk, hated every thing and every one. And himself. He loved London, it was in the blood. Only the girl ever understood him.'

'His wife – Lady Henrietta?' Pearl admired the long rows of saucepans, coppers, ladles the size of soup plates, a spit in the hearth big enough to turn oxen whole. 'I fed two hundred here many a time,' Mrs Parkinson bragged to her, 'not including servants. *We* never counted – and it wasn't so long ago that even our slops were left out in a bucket for the poor. Lady Henrietta, you said? She was

144

of no account except as a misery. If only she'd made young Charles happy . . . but it was not to be.'

Ben asked: 'Does the name Lisa mean anything to you?'

'Lisa – his doxy girl. Aye, I remember her.'

'What about her?'

'She was the cause of all our misfortunes!' Mrs Parkinson's face twisted and she slammed her hands flat on the table. 'Remember her, the little whore, aye!'

'Be careful what you say,' Ben said mildly.

'Why should I be? We were all out of work, but *she* didn't lose her job.'

'She was a parlourmaid, I believe.'

'That's the one. She knew what side her bread was buttered on. Frantic to get him, she was. And she did. They were mad with it.' She gave a horrid wink with her unsighted eye. 'We learned to knock before going into a room, I tell thee straight!'

'You've done enough of this straight talking,' Pearl said.

'I'm not afraid.'

'She was my mother,' Ben said.

'Maybe I would have done the same thing at her age,' Mrs Parkinson admitted tiredly. 'She was striking. But a lord's a more dangerous catch than a stable-boy. She believed his lies, I daresay. Followed him down to London. She thought he loved her, poor girl.'

'Did he?'

'The way men always do. Loved himself more!'

'What was her name?'

'Oh, she was the teacher's orphan.' Mrs Parkinson snapped her fingers. 'Thee means Lisa York. But thee knew that, surely.'

'Lisa York,' Ben said. 'Lisa York.'

'I know my mother's name. We can find her now,' Ben said, turning from the window. A dull red fire burned in the grate of Pearl's bedroom – the stone room was cold though the night outside was warm and autumnal, and he had seen meteors flashing from the constellation of Orion; it was the time of year. Pearl lifted the copper warming pan from her bed and snuggled down, her hair spread over the pillow like flame. Ben crossed the flickering light. 'I love you so much, Pearl.' She kissed him sleepily. 'I've come home,' he marvelled.

'I'm your home,' she murmured. No; he did not know her fully. He kissed her neck, her shoulders. Her breathing came quickly and he caressed her mouth with his lips. 'No – not now,' she whispered against his cheek. He respected her, but it was a dreadful effort to ease his passion back from her warmth, her need. 'It wouldn't be right,' she said, 'here.' Her intuition was right. *We learned to knock before going into a room*! Pearl's eyes gleamed as she touched a knuckle to his lips. 'Now we know your mother's last name, we can trace her. Your father said he saw her wedding ring, so we know she married. All we've got to do is go to Somerset House when we get back home and look it up in the records.'

He kissed her knuckles. 'I love you, Ben,' she said tenderly in a breaking voice. 'I want you to take me walking over those beautiful moors tomorrow. We can be on our own.'

'Today,' he said.

'Today,' she said. 'Take me today.'

He understood. He kissed her lips and returned to his own bedroom.

And he did take her, and they knew it was inevitable, although neither of them knew how it would happen. They were in love and would let the skies fall. The day was brilliant and all around them the fields rose green between drystone walls, and the leat was a silver line of water far below them reflecting the sun. Far above them the rim of the moor was like a breaking wave of purple and gold against the ultramarine sky. Pearl's hair and her long ulster were swept out by the breeze as she leaned into a shepherd's crook, and her face glowed with the exertion of the climb. He lifted her easily over the walls; there was no end to his strength today. Finally the slope steepened and they rested on the last wall before the open, windy moor, eating oranges out of Mrs Parkinson's packed lunch.

'I'm pooped,' Pearl said, staring upwards.

'It'll be easier if we follow the ghyll.' He pointed to a grassy cleft cut in the hillside by a hissing stream. It followed the natural line of the slope and made climbing easier. They clambered up to a level grassy knoll to find a deep green-blue pool enclosed on three sides by rock – the outer edge was a magnificent view over the Dales. Out of the wind at last, Pearl thought.

'At last we're out of the wind,' Ben said. 'Why are you laughing?'

'You read my mind. This must be our secret place,' she said. 'I bet you don't dare dive in off that rock.'

He stared up. 'I will if you will.'

'You must be crazy!'

He said seriously: 'We'll be crazy together.' He slipped off his rucksack and undid his clothes. When he was naked he said: 'You don't have to if you don't want to.'

Her voice shook with fear. 'Try and stop me!'

He found a steep grassy path up the side of the vertical slab and climbed up, then stood at the top looking down. This was madness. Pearl had no head for heights. He couldn't see her anywhere below – perhaps he had pushed her too far, he had no right to do this to her, she had run away. Then he saw her clothes already piled on the grass and heard pebbles sliding behind him. Naked, she was climbing up. He laughed and reached down but she shook her head, teetering, her white teeth bared with concentration or fear, then swung herself up. She stood beside him on the very edge, pale and statuesque. Perspiration slid between her fine breasts. He admired her, adored her, he didn't even try to make her back out.

'Only one way down,' he said. She gripped his hand with soft, hot fingers.

'Love you!' she screamed, and jumped out into the empty air, tugging him after her, and down they plummeted together. The water roared in her ears, then Pearl opened her eyes on a cloud of silvery bubbles that flooded

147

away and left her floating with warm hands deep in the cold clear water – Ben was holding her hands, then his lips were hot on hers. She had never felt such fear or such joy as she felt then. She gave herself up.

They lay on the grass and the sun was burning hot and he was like a flame inside her at last. She felt an exultant wild heat, the sun burning swirling patterns of red over her closed eyelids, and he didn't say any rubbish like *Do you love me*, and she didn't have to mouth platitudes like *Yes* because it was all so breathtakingly affirmative in her that for one long pulsing, excruciating moment she knew this is the world where only love exists and she felt something like a brilliant flash illuminate her womb, and knew it was the moment of conception.

2

'I'm so looking forward to it,' Esther said, 'a proper baby at last.'

'Will's all right,' Nigel said sharply, 'don't you say a word against him.'

Esther hugged him. 'He's a lovely little boy, of course he is. I wouldn't say a word against him. It isn't his fault he isn't proper.' She held Nigel at arm's length then sat him down in the kitchen chair while she made the tea, glad to have him to herself. 'You've changed, Nigel. Arleen's changed you for the better. That's ever such a nice suit. How is she?'

'Blooming – she says having a baby is a woman's natural condition, she's never felt better. Her face has a wonderful glow . . .' Nigel glanced at his watch, he had to collect some debts for Vic.

'I'm so glad you're happy, Nigel. There were times when I despaired you ever would be. You were such a frail child.' She put his tea in front of him and stirred in sugar fondly. 'You and Vic always get on so well. And now you've got Arleen too. What are you going to call the baby?'

'If he's a boy, Arleen wants Terence. Terence Nigel. If she's a girl, Rachel. We're going to have at least three, or four. I want a big family. Arleen's already thinking of a bigger house and we're getting a maid. I want a house with a wall round it and apple trees in the garden.'

'There aren't many of those on the Island of Dogs.'

There were in Greenwich. This bone of contention between him and Mum; Nigel didn't know how to explain how much happier he felt living away. It wasn't just Arleen and their tender love together, the way she tried to have a hot supper waiting for him when he returned home tired, or the joy of caring for her and anticipating the baby together, cuddling her warm belly in bed . . . the delicious feeling of responsibility that they shared. Nigel examined the cuffs of his new suit which Arleen had insisted he buy for his interview. Nigel had gone along with it tolerantly. To his shock, the insurance company in the City had offered him the job. He didn't know what to do about it. If he talked to Arleen, he would take it. If he talked to Vic, he wouldn't.

'I don't know, Mum.'

'You stick close to your family,' Esther said firmly.

'But I love you all, I need you all – yet I want a family of my own too,' Nigel tried to explain.

'You'll always have a home here,' Esther snivelled, pulling a tiny handkerchief out of her sleeve. Nigel put his arms round her.

'I love you, Mum,' he said. They looked up, hearing banging noises from upstairs. Ria was moving out – that was the real cause of Mum's tears and all this about sticking close. Her family was breaking up, but her children meant more than anything in the world to Esther. They were the survivors, and each departure was a little death for her. Nigel made a mental note: he and Arleen would be enduring this process in twenty-five years' time. 'I'll go up and say goodbye to her,' he said. Mum hugged him tight. Maybe he could do some good.

Dust flew around Ria's room, glinting in the chill sun from the open window. She had tied back her golden hair in a practical knot, which always meant Work In Progress. Nigel choked, fanning his hand in front of his face.

'Hallo Nigel,' Ria said, 'goodbye Nigel.' She rolled up the rug and gave it a couple of good kicks to get the string pulled tight.

'Don't be nasty to me, I'm not nasty to you,' Nigel said. 'I am capable of being friendly, you know.'

She braced her fists on her hips, then nodded. 'I know, it's me, I'm sorry.' Her eyes shone very blue in her grimy face. Marriage suited Ria – she looked very good, damn Ray Trott. Perhaps it was just the excitement of setting up the nightclub. *I was wrong about Ray*, Nigel admitted. Nigel had not seen him since the wedding; the newsagent's had been empty. Nigel went there every faithful fourth Saturday, but he was starting to hope Ray had turned over a new leaf.

He searched for something to say to his sister. 'You've got a great smudge of dirt on the end of your nose.' Ria sniffed. 'When are you moving?'

'All this week, all next week, God knows. Ted's lent us a room at the Old Bull and Bush. There's a mountain of redecorating to do at the Club before we can even start on our own flat. We're worked off our feet.' Ria wiped her nose then plonked herself down on the rug and put her feet up with a sigh of relief. Nigel glimpsed an embarrassing length of leg and sat down quickly beside her where he couldn't see. Ria leaned her elbow on his shoulder. 'I expect Arleen's looking quite big now?' she said wistfully.

'It won't be long before you're in the club,' Nigel said encouragingly. He always tried to talk like Ria when he was with her, but in fact his feelings towards Arleen's pregnancy were close to reverence. *A proper baby*.

'We're too busy for that for a while,' Ria said briskly. 'You'll love our place, Nigel. Trott's Nightclub on the Strand, we're going to be terrifically fashionable.' Of course; that was Ria's new baby. 'Ray's a natural. We've got the licence and everything. The cellars were only used for storage before, it was a stroke of luck. Everywhere around there has enormous cellars because the river bank used to be along the Strand, see, the Vikings and Romans and those used to pull up their boats on the sand and eat oysters, so there's oystershell everywhere, it supports the floor bricks.' Nigel could not deny the enthusiasm he heard in her voice. 'The river bank's been built out so far see, Nigel, with the Embankment now and everything. But the old level remains below, and that's where we'll be. In the cellars of the old Lamerts Blacking Factory. Below.'

'Dancing and drinking. What about Will?'

Ria took her arm off his shoulder. She looked guilty – Ria's feelings were always so easy for her clever brother to see and manipulate.

'What are you going to do about him?' Nigel demanded. 'You won't get out of bed before noon, and it's no life for a boy. It's not a *proper* life. Why didn't you think about him when you had him?' That was unfair, but it was time someone was unfair to Ria and stuck her with a few home truths. 'Just face up to your responsibilities, Ria. All you care about is yourself, you aren't sensitive to other people's feelings.' He felt justified in that because he *was* sensitive, and she had been terribly cruel and unfeeling to him on occasion. 'Fine for you, living the life of Riley! But you're a married woman now, as well as a mother.'

'Will always talks about you,' Ria said sadly. 'You're his hero, it's always Uncle Nigel this, Uncle Nigel that. It's so bloody unfair.'

Nigel couldn't understand. 'Why?' He glanced at his watch – it was time he got back to Arleen, and he hadn't done Vic's work. He was going to be late again.

Ria said: 'Because you have everything, Nigel.' Yes, it was always greener on the other side of the fence. Suddenly Nigel was sure that in the end he was going to turn down that insurance job. He held Ria's hand and spoke into her wonderful opal eyes more tenderly than he had ever said anything to her before.

'We're family,' he said. 'Ria, we must never fight, we must stick together.'

'Ben,' Pearl said. 'Ben. I think that's baby's name. Excellent pedigree.'

'I just can't believe it's happening. You must have caught at once.'

She kissed him. They lay tangled nude in each other's arms in a mass of satin sheets and plump feather pillows. The flat sun glittered across the frosty rooftops outside, but she kept their bedroom at American heat. 'I felt it happen.'

'I'm so ashamed of myself. I should have taken precautions.'

'I'm glad you didn't. I'm so happy!'

'If only we were married. Look, I could go and see Vane. Maybe she'd understand, and let us go.'

'You don't understand the jealousy she feels,' Pearl said.

'But a little baby! It isn't his fault – or her fault.'

'Him, Ben's a boy. You'd be making a very great mistake,' Pearl said firmly. 'Why humiliate yourself by begging? It wouldn't do any good, and it's just what she desires. Or are you ashamed of me?' She patted her naked tummy – already they could imagine it was slightly rounded, though really it was flat.

'Don't joke. What did it *feel* like?'

It was always such a mystery to men. Pearl looked up dreamily. 'It felt . . . it felt like the beginning of the world.'

'You're so lucky.' He lay his head on her tummy and curled his fingers in her hair. 'I just don't want – '

'I know what you don't want,' she said gently. 'Hey, I suppose you could always bump Vane off. It's the only way she's going to let you go.'

'I don't suppose Ralph and George would approve.'

'Or you could offer her lots of money.'

'She's getting lots already. I'm overextended enough. Do you know how much the extra floors we're building

152

on top of London's are costing? How much carpets cost per mile?'

'Don't work too hard.'

'You can imagine what the gossip columns will say about us when you show.'

'People will be horrified. They will despise us. Trade will flourish.'

'That horrid Mrs Parkinson despised my mother. But the more I heard about Lisa,' Ben tried to explain, 'the more I admired her.'

'I did too,' Pearl reassured him gently. 'I love her already. Are you trying Somerset House again?'

'The mills of God and bureaucracy grind slow, but fine. They should have found something in the records by now.'

'I won't come. I get tired and I want to take things easy. I'm breeding.'

'I'll be back in an hour.' He jumped out of bed and she watched him cross to the bathroom. Men's bodies were supposed not to be erotic, but Pearl always loved to see the curves of his back and buttocks, the rigid outlines of his abdominal muscles below the dark curls of his chest; sensing the hardness of his thighs and the strength in the firm grace of his movements, so unlike a woman's soft voluptuous sway.

'I don't want to leave you,' he said, turning.

'I don't want you to go.' She held open her arms.

Afterwards Ben drove to Somerset House, parked by the statue of George III in the courtyard and went into the General Register of Births, Marriages and Deaths. The archivist showed it to him in black and white: Lisa York married Edwin Petherton on Saturday 21 April 1900 in Newport on the Isle of Wight, they had no children, they lived apart for more than seven years in a divorce action (English law required a guilty party, his mother, and the innocent party was Edwin Petherton), and though their differences were irreconcilable they seemed to come to a quite amicable settlement for such a necessarily nasty business. The decree nisi was granted in June 1924 and became absolute six months later.

Ben returned home. 'But *why?*' he wondered aloud to Pearl while she dressed. 'Why take such an extraordinary step as divorce? There was no mention of another man.'

'You,' Pearl said. 'You are the other man.'

'Come off it. Just a baby. She can't have cared.'

'Perhaps she cared too much. Perhaps she didn't love Edwin enough. Perhaps she was bored with him. Perhaps . . . she hadn't suffered enough.'

'That's hardly a reason for going through all that dreadful business.'

'To a woman . . .' Pearl splayed her fingers. Perhaps. 'You'll know her, Ben. Lisa Petherton is special. She's strong, determined – and guilty. Write to her. Petherton will forward it.'

Ben hesitated. 'Suppose she doesn't get in touch? Suppose she isn't interested in me?'

'She's interested in you all right,' Pearl said.

He admitted: 'Suppose she rejects me for a second time?'

'It's going to be the hardest letter you've ever written.' She kissed his forehead. 'I'll bring you a big mug of coffee.'

But it wasn't hard. He dashed the letter off before Pearl even started the coffee, simply by writing what he felt.

Mother
I love you, I forgive you, we need each other.
For God's sake write to me.
Your loving son,
BEN

He addressed that envelope *Lisa Petherton – please forward* and enclosed it in a letter to Edwin Petherton at The Chine, Blackgang, Isle of Wight.

'Suppose he doesn't know where she is?' Pearl asked.

'Then I'll go down and see him after the Christmas rush.'

154

The inner envelope was returned in a couple of days marked Forwarding Address Not Known.

Vic Price and Family. Vic tapped the invitation card with his fingernail. Ted Trott was holding his private Christmas bash on the Monday, when trade was quiet at the Old Bull and Bush. Could he trust the cunning old gangster? Ted and Vic were related now, but only nominally, not by blood, and it was ties of blood that really counted. And *that* knot would never be tied because Ray was as queer as a fourpenny piece, a bit of gaudy rough stuff who would never lay a finger on Ria. But Vic trusted Ted enough; he had worked hard to earn Ted's trust, and this invitation meant he must be more than halfway there now.

The women sat in the back of the Vauxhall tourer and Nigel drove anxiously. 'Are you sure Ted's absolutely safe? Arleen – ' He flicked his eyes back. Arleen was enormous with child, and there was still a month to go. In the driving mirror the pools of gaslight sweeping by made her face look drained.

'Enjoy yourself,' yawned Vic. 'How are you, Arleen?'

'Don't worry about me. Nigel, please don't drive so fast.'

'Isn't she big?' said Esther proudly. She wore a hat with feathers in, bigger than Lydia's at the wedding.

'Slow down, Nigel,' Vic said, 'you heard the boss.'

The Old Bull and Bush was a big pub on almost its own traffic island near the end of Cable Street, the sort of place where posh people came down East to go slumming. Vic helped his mum down and took her in. It was nice, all red flock wallpaper and dark wood inside, but the wide floor area was bare boards and sawdust for the sake of authenticity. An ex-prizefighter pushed the punters smoothly aside ahead of them, his menace giving no offence. The private party was held in one of the back rooms deeply carpeted in red, with dark green walls. Vic knew it would be for illegal gambling, probably high-stakes bridge. Unlawful gaming in fixed premises meant

Ted had the police in his pocket in a big way – in the West End too, how else had Ray got a booze licence?

'Good to see you, Vic,' rumbled Ted.

Vic shook hands. The women separated into a group with Lydia on one side, but Vic, nodding and smiling to Ted as they talked around items of mutual interest with hints and winks and unspoken understandings, missed nothing. He observed them all. To Vic the social side was just as much business as the business was – it was all the same. That was what clever Nigel had never learned, too bloody intelligent. Without Vic, Ted Trott would have eaten Nigel alive by now, gulping him down in his mouth like one of those giant horrible fish in the *National Geographic*. Not that Nigel feared Ted Trott, he was too ignorant. Vic knew that in this world the worst things did happen. But Nigel, drink in one hand, chatted to Ted as cheerfully as if they were at a cocktail party.

Lydia wore a tight cloche hat with purple sequins to outdo Esther. 'Here come the lovers,' she said as the door opened. Ria came in holding hands with Ray. Vic smiled openly, no one was as ignorant as parents: Ray was still Lydia's sweet little boy. Undeniably the pervert was attractive, plenty of girls would want him, and would envy the girl who held his hand.

Ria greeted Lydia with the warm smile she reserved for people she loathed, and Vic knew Ray had taught her his secret, and she had learned to love the lie. In human relationships the carrot and the stick never failed.

Nigel looked anxiously at Ray, twitching his damaged fingers, and Vic wondered why that was.

Arleen sat in the corner, safely on the sidelines, hands clasped beneath her bosoms and knees slightly apart, looking as pregnant as you could get.

Mum glowered at Lydia's hat.

Ted put his arm proudly around Ray's shoulders.

Vic kissed Ria's cheek and started to enjoy himself. Life was looking up.

156

CHAPTER TEN

1

She was striking. But what was his mother really like?

One thing he was sure of: Lisa Petherton was a driven woman.

Ben stared from the speeding train, hunting clues to his mother's personality in the snowy midwinter landscape beyond his own reflection in the glass. She must have known this journey, travelling on this very train, perhaps putting this same teacup to her lips. There might be a hundred other women like her on this train, sitting patiently, or knitting, or reading a book like the woman opposite him. Ben surveyed her unconcerned expression detail by detail, the smile-lines in the corner of her mouth, her taste in earrings, the pleasing way she chose to wear her hair. She was not his mother.

She was not *like* his mother.

What terrible force drove Lisa Petherton to be what she was?

Leaning on the railing of the steamer to Ryde, he wondered what he would find when he met Edwin Petherton, and it began to snow again.

There was no motor-taxi for hire on the quay in January, so he had to make do with a trap, glad for his fine leather coat and gloves. 'Motor wouldn't have got you there,' the driver spat, 'pardon me. They can't take the drifts. A horse has more sense. More ground clearance, too.'

'Do you know Mr Petherton, The Chine?'

'Pardon me. Climb up sir, I'll take you there, don't startle the horse. The Chine? Horse knows the way. Always taking people there before the war.' He spat for the third time. 'Women, mostly.'

Ben offered his brandy flask. 'Didn't think much of them?'

'That type? Jailbirds,' the old man said, 'pardon me.'

In this weather the journey took three hours through pleasant, wintry scenery. The snow eased and Ben enjoyed the hedgerows and undulating hills. In the summer he imagined it must be an idyllic setting. The horse clopped through a grove of trees and Ben drew a startled breath: as if a sharp knife had been drawn across the landscape, it simply disappeared. They were very high, looking down on nothing, a waste of sea.

'The cliff edge,' the driver said. 'Sea don't stop until you get to Antarctica.'

The track turned inland. The Chine was set in a hollow, a haven of leafless trees on the brink of the great expanse.

'Wait for me,' Ben said, and the driver touched his whip to his hat. The house looked comfortable and inviting – it might have been any vicarage with a good living, except for its large outbuildings. *Who's Who* described Petherton as an inventor, and the Patent Office confirmed several hundred applications before 1920 – the most important was a kind of slatted metal track unrolled behind a tank for infantry to consolidate a breakthrough. He had also written two books of poetry – Ben had no idea of poetry but Pearl said the first was liberal but forgettable; the recent second much darker and more powerful.

'I'm Ben London,' he said to the man who opened the door.

Edwin Petherton was about sixty with white hair and a red jolly face. He wore a cardigan, a crooked tie, slippers. His friendly handshake was warm and genuine, but confusion showed in his gentle soft eyes as he searched his stepson's face. 'I had no idea – she never told me.' He showed Ben through the living room, a dusty mess of books and papers, into a bright solarium. 'Her favourite room.' Ben sat in a deckchair. Though the room was heated by steam for the sake of the many plants, he felt chilled: Petherton spoke of his mother as though she was dead – as though he had never really known her.

158

'I had no idea of your existence at all, Ben. I feel awful about it. She hid it from me all those years. I could have – *would* have done something, anything. Of course that's why she didn't tell me. I failed her. Now I've lost her.'

'Perhaps she'll come back.'

Petherton shook his head firmly. 'It was my fault. I did everything for her. Money, of course, my father lived in Hong Kong all his life, made his fortune from the opium trade I believe. As the second son I was educated in this country, he was a stranger to me . . . I feel so guilty about Lisa. All those years I never knew her.' He laughed as if such a thing was of no importance.

Ben looked at the photographs: so that was what his mother looked like. Striking, eager, innocent – wearing the same happy expression in portraits, or with the Mayor of Southampton, or at Edwin Petherton's side. The face she wore for the camera. He recognized it in himself. It was the same face he had worn, so often, to protect himself from the world as a child.

'You have no idea where she is?'

'I don't know anything any more.' Petherton jumped up and pressed a switch. Ben expected a maid to appear, but Petherton said: 'Automatic teamaker. Trinket. Got to keep busy. Where she is? I wish I did know for your sake, but for mine . . . I'm glad I don't. Never had a clue, all my life, of all she hid from me.'

'Perhaps she hid it from herself.'

'Don't try and explain it, dear boy, don't be rational!' Strange words from an inventor. The kettle bubbled boiling water into the pot. Petherton turned with a little secret grin of pleasure at the flawless operation of his toy.

There was something very suburban about Edwin Petherton. He was harmless, a gentle, childlike eccentric. Yet here he was, without a patent registered for half a dozen years, a poet, living in this charming house on the bourgeois edge of madness, offering his guest a cup of tea.

'I would have jumped off that cliff for her, Ben.'

'Did she know it?'

'How would I tell her?'

'You could say the real words to her.'

Petherton raised his white eyebrows. 'She was never my equal. Lisa had fire in her belly, she was a driven woman, like an engine inside her, but with a woman's heart. She got so exhausted. The moment I met her, I fell in love – except it wasn't falling. I was uplifted, never deserved her. She was so vulnerable, so easy to hurt. I never would, of course.'

Ben waited. They sat staring at the whirling snow outside.

Petherton said: 'It was a frosty morning.'

'It was a frosty morning and I had spent Christmas comfortably with friends at their house in Essex. The plan was that I should return on New Year's Eve to my house in the suburbs of Southampton, quite an ambitious journey for those days, but my motor was of my own design – the vanity of youth. Of course the thing broke down before I got so far as Romford, and I welcomed the New Year in whilst kneeling in a ditch with a spanner in one hand and an acetylene lantern in the other. At first light I got going again, the only vehicle on the Mile End Road. You understand I had lived a very sheltered life. She was running along the road in front of me – just running. Gradually I caught her up, a girl in a dark dress, her hair wild. She kept looking back: the expression in her eyes. Terror. I was ashamed. I wasn't threatening her in any way; just the rough noise my vehicle made, and of course I was wearing goggles. I stopped the engine, tore my goggles off, held my arms wide. I don't know where we were, Whitechapel, Aldgate. Her face was white, she was panting, a cornered deer, she had that look in her eyes, except that they were so blue. She said: "*Help me!*" I held out my hand. "*Trust me,*" I said. And slowly she reached out, and took my hand – and collapsed.'

Petherton glanced at Ben. 'She never did trust me. I see that now. Why should she? But I didn't know that at the time.'

'You had a whirlwind romance?' She had trusted Edwin Petherton all right. She had collapsed, hadn't she?

'She said she was a parlourmaid with a brutal master, he had attacked her, she had run away. I believed her. I was all for storming back and punching him on the nose, but instead . . . I realized that I would lose her. It was better to let what had already happened, simply happen: fall in love with her instead, and ask no questions. She judged me right. I was much older than she was, but much younger up here.' He tapped his head.

'So she lied to you to love you.'

'She needed me – someone like me. That was no lie. And she never *lied* – it was simply the force of her personality made me incapable of disbelief. Besides, who looks love in the face and counts its teeth?' Petherton shook his head. 'At first I had much to teach her. Eastern religions. Astronomy and astrology. Mathematics, the theory of mechanics.'

Ben nodded. The abstracts, safe distractions, a refuge in Petherton's safe and kindly, and boring, little world of numbers and ideas.

'Then she began to teach me about people,' Petherton said. 'She took me by storm. She loved Southampton, but she loved the island too. Her energy was colossal – as if she was not giving herself time to think. As of course she was not. How blind I was! Yet I thought I was creating her, and I was happy to have this place built for her. She was very much *au fait* with the Women's Movement which, along with some other like-minded men, I of course supported. I had long been friends with the Pethwick-Lawrences. This house – Lisa's house, rebuilt from a ruin – was often used for meetings, and latterly as a recuperation centre for women released from prison under the Cat and Mouse Act – the police came here to re-arrest them as soon as the poor girls recovered their strength.'

'Recovered?'

'They starved themselves in prison. The authorities did

not wish any to die on their hands. They released them, let us feed them up, then rearrested them.'

'Was my mother ever sent to prison?'

'Several times!' Petherton smiled, remembering. 'I used to send her Fortnum's hampers to tempt her will. Never succeeded.'

Of course not, and now Ben sensed how far apart Lisa and her husband had grown by that time. Petherton's loving good intentions, encouraged by the authorities she hated, must have seemed stupid and gross, a personal insult. 'She always took herself so seriously,' Petherton said, not understanding. Lisa had known her identity, and Petherton still searched for his. Ben felt sorry for this gentle man. He had not deserved Lisa, and she had almost destroyed him.

'I never realized that things were so bad between us,' Petherton said. 'I gave her everything. My life. I don't give a damn about the money. But she grew away from me, I could not control her, I could not make her understand I loved her. We were very polite together but I felt like a dilettante. As though she was in the real world, and mine was not real. In the war she worked in an ammunition factory filling shells. At night she slept like a dead person. I felt like a pariah.'

'And when the war ended, she started divorce proceedings.'

Petherton said: 'I have no idea why she did it.'

Ben could see exactly why Lisa had needed to divorce Edwin Petherton. Every secret he found out about his mother was a secret that illuminated himself.

In a quivering voice Petherton said: 'Why did she leave me?'

'I have no idea, Edwin,' Ben said, gripping the older man's hand reassuringly, 'I have no idea.' He felt like a cuckolder.

Ben leaned on the ferry railing. Edwin had no idea where Lisa Petherton was, but Ben knew. She was in London.

He comprehended his mother's reasons for freeing herself from Petherton, from her safe home, from her happy life. Those things were not enough. She had stepped over the cliff. Her destiny was London. He knew it; so must she.

He gazed through the train window at the speeding landscape. Finding her would be easy. Her name would be in the phone book, or a street directory, or a property document – Petherton had settled a generous sum on her.

She had not quite broken free: she took the money, and Cleremont had seen her still wearing the wedding ring. Ben frowned. That was out of character for the woman he understood his mother to be – the woman who ran heedlessly down the middle of the broad Mile End Road – just ran.

He slept dreaming that he had put an advertisement in *The Times*.

He woke, yawning and contented, as the train drew in to Waterloo station. He stood and buttoned up his coat, then bent down and peered through the window looking for Pearl. She was late, though he had telegraphed his time ahead from Portsmouth. He grinned as he pulled on his gloves, she was always late. With the baby growing so rapidly inside her it was time she stopped driving herself anyway. He would get another chauffeur to replace Simmonds.

He walked along the platform, searching for her unmistakable hair above the heads of the passengers streaming through the gate.

He didn't see her.

He handed in his ticket, then looked up.

Peggy said: '*Ben!*' Not Mr London. *Ben*.

She shouldn't be here.

She held out both her hands towards him, her face distorted with grief.

'Oh – ' he said, 'oh no.'

Peggy wept openly. Ben put his arm around her and led her out of the crowd. 'What happened? Something's happened to Pearl? Is she all right?'

163

'Sir, she – ' Peggy sobbed, she could not speak. 'The poor – the poor – '

Ben shook her. 'Is she all right, damn you?'

Peggy wailed: 'The p-poor little b-buh – poor little *baby*!'

She's lost the baby.

'No, no, no,' Ben said.

'I came as soon as I heard – ' David Jones, the manager of the Emporium, was running across the concourse. 'A messenger caught me up on my way home.'

'I was in the train. I was asleep. Oh my God.'

'Listen, she's all right,' David said, showing Ben to the car. 'Peggy found her lying on the floor when she brought the tea . . .'

'Thank you, Peggy,' Ben said.

'She was bleeding.' Peggy was trying to be so calm. 'I got the nurse up and called the Harley Street doctor. An ambulance arrived in ten minutes.'

'Where is she now?'

'B-but she's lost her little baby boy!' sobbed Peggy.

'She's at Guy's,' David said. 'Private room, top consultants.' The car cut across the rushhour traffic, street lamps reflecting bruised light over their faces.

'All she needs is rest,' Ben said. 'She was so careful. I'm just grateful it didn't happen when she was driving to meet me. I should have known.'

'What could you have known?' David asked.

'I should have understood.'

'It's just one of those things, I'm sure,' said David, looking away.

'I should have *understood*!'

'It's not your fault that you're not married, sir,' said David, mistaking him. 'Everyone knows who is to blame for that.'

Ben whispered: 'I should have understood what Pearl was trying to tell me.'

'He was a boy,' Pearl murmured.

He clasped her hand.

'I know. Peggy told me.'

'It wasn't your fault. It was mine. You couldn't know, I couldn't tell you. Now there will never be another Ben. My fault.' Pearl opened her eyes and smiled brightly for his sake, but she looked very pale.

'There will be other times.' *Will there?*

'There will never be another Ben. I'm sorry, I'm so sorry.'

'I'm to blame, not you. I should have understood you because I love you, I should have known everything. I knew you held something back.'

'Because I love you.'

He kissed her hand. He thought she slept. The room was full of flowers; silent as midnight.

She murmured: 'Did you find Lisa?'

'I feel closer to my mother all the time.'

'I'm so glad. Cheer up, Ben, I'm comfortable, I'll be out in a day or two.'

He said: 'Tell me about Frankie now.'

'It was worse than you can imagine. I *tried* to tell you.'

'Yes, I know.' *He kissed you, and that was all* – Ben himself had interrupted her, trying to save her the pain, but made it so much worse.

'The truth was he took from me by force what I would have given him willingly.'

Ben stroked her hand.

'Every time he went out I prayed he'd survive and come back.'

'Of course you did.'

'He was a brave man.'

'Yes, he was.'

'Isn't that the most dreadful thing in the world?' She put her knuckles in her eyes.

'I'm sorry,' Ben said. And now this had happened. 'I love you.'

Sir William Blizard was the royal gynaecologist, the most eminent that money could buy. He was a confident, practical man with a quiet manner. Morning light slanted through the window behind him.

'Probably a fifth of all pregnancies end in miscarriage and often the girl doesn't even know. Of those that are known, miscarriage is most common in the third and fourth months.' He twirled a paperknife in his fingers.

'Like now.'

'It simply happens. Babies are complicated, sometimes one and one doesn't make three, that's all. Chance, injury, disease, alcohol, too hot, too cold, guilt, who knows. There is no particular reason for miscarriage to be habitual in Pearl's case.'

'Go on.'

'But you are aware that she shows minor internal scars?'

A previous miscarriage, or an abortion. Ben put his fist over his mouth.

'Not so minor,' he said.

That terrified pacifist, family man, snatching courage from a woman's terror and compassion, taking by force what would have been freely given. He had raped Pearl, raped her terribly. Ben couldn't imagine a more thorough betrayal of everything that everyone, especially Frankie, supposed that they stood for. Betraying an act of love with an act of hate, betraying courage with fear. And now, because of it, an innocent love child dead as well. Ben hoped Frankie's soul burned in flames in hell.

'I hope I've been of help,' Sir William said, standing.

'You've been a great help,' Ben smiled.

Pearl was wrong. The most dreadful thing in the world was death and the end of hope. But they had hope. They had life, they had love, and for them everything was possible. Outside, the day was bright.

The millionaire checked his Blancpain watch. He would drop into Cartier and buy her something pretty, then check over the redecorations at London's – if the builders weren't on strike again – before returning to the Emporium. There was always plenty of work to do. He must remember to order a ton of flowers for Pearl's return

166

home; she would like that, and he thought of the happiness and amazement that would light up her face.

2

Esther opened her front door and looked down the street. 'Still no sign of Nigel,' she told Ria, coming back to the kitchen. It was Saturday and Will was doing his weekend homework, the textbook propped against a jar of honey.

'Do you understand fractions, Mum?' he asked. Esther almost replied – she was so used to being called Mum around here.

'What, love?' Ria said. *She* was Mum now. 'No, not a clue.'

'You're stupid,' Will said. Esther boxed his ear. 'Go and do it in the front room. *Go on!*'

Will rubbed his ear and lifted one leg. 'Can't I stay?'

'No,' Ria said. 'Do what Granny says.' Alone, she looked up at Esther. 'Did Nigel say he'd be late?'

'I don't know where he is,' fretted Esther.

'Probably collecting off the floaters.' The street bookmakers. Esther looked at Ria reproachfully. Her boys were never involved in crime. Ria worried her more – daughters were so easy to understand compared to sons: though they were complex creatures they were driven by simple forces: men, babies, families, homes. Not Ria. Ria had to be different, Ria wanted a career, yet she had a husband in Ray Trott who was as close as a girl ever got to perfection: gave her plenty of freedom, yet she always had a roof over her head. But Ria was too modern to want a baby, a *proper* baby, and a family of her own. She always wanted the forbidden things – the things she couldn't have. She wanted to be herself.

'Vic laughed when Arleen telephoned to say she thought she'd better get to the hospital,' Esther said – she didn't keep a phone, but Vic next door did. 'I wanted her to have the baby at home, you know.'

'Arleen likes to have everything organized.' Ria helped herself to a biscuit and put her feet up on the side of the table.

'It's more homely at home,' Esther said. 'Friends are what you need.'

'It'll pop out in no time,' Ria said.

'That's all very well for you to say, sitting ever so comfortable now, but I remember you screaming your head off when *your* time came. Arleen's got slim hips,' Esther added.

'So Arleen had to call up Vic when her contractions started?'

'She trusts him. He said he'd try and get in touch with Nigel to take her to the hospital. When her pains came down to twenty minutes she rang again and said she'd better get a taxi. Vic said no, he'd come to Greenwich and drive her himself. Wasn't that nice of him?'

'She'd have preferred Nigel.' Ria opened the honeypot and scooped, sucking her finger luxuriously.

'Don't do that,' Esther said, 'it's not nice.'

The door slammed and she jumped up. Nigel came in wearing an expensive beige British warm and carrying a bag, his fedora tilted stylishly. He looked like a very elegant version of an American film gangster. 'Nigel, I'm so glad!' Mum embraced him and Nigel kissed her cheek. 'Arleen phoned,' she explained breathlessly. 'She's started.'

At first Nigel was calm. 'Did she get the taxi to the hospital?'

'Vic drove her.'

'I left her the number for the taxi and everything,' Nigel said anxiously. 'I shouldn't have left her alone.'

'Don't be stupid, Nigel,' Ria said, 'it's just a baby.'

'She's got all the baby clothes and everything,' Nigel said. 'I just hope she remembered to take them. I left the shawl in the airing cupboard, I wonder if she noticed. And her suitcase weighed a ton.'

'Vic will have carried it,' Esther said. 'Sit down and

have a cuppa. Young fathers should conserve their strength.'

'I'll just phone the hospital and check everything's all right.'

Esther asked Ria: 'Do you want some bread to go with that honey?'

Nigel came back from next door. 'Everything's fine,' he admitted. 'Her waters have broken.' He shrugged uncertainly.

'Relax,' Ria said. 'We've been doing this for millions of years, you know.'

'It's the men I feel sorry for,' Nigel said, drinking his tea nervously. 'We have to pretend we're so calm and relaxed. I don't feel that way.'

'Brace up,' Ria advised, 'go and have a steak.'

'I can't help worrying,' Nigel said. He bent down with a grin. 'All right, thanks for keeping me on the tracks, Ria.' He kissed her cheek.

'She's quite thoughtful really,' Esther admitted. 'All Ria thinks is feelings, that's all.' So did Vic; in a way Nigel, not Ria, was the odd one out after all. Esther looked at her eldest child and felt a stab of guilt about her.

Ria kissed Nigel on the lips. He said: 'I know I sometimes appear, well, cold.'

Ria clapped his shoulder. 'Go on, go and worry about Arleen!' she said.

They watched him drive away, then returned inside, shivering although it was a bright, sunny day. 'He's forgotten his lunch.' Esther snatched up the bag Nigel had left on the table. Too late to catch him. Ria opened it. Arleen made Nigel spectacular sandwiches, and she was hungry. She looked inside, then closed the bag up quickly. 'It's nothing.'

'What is it?' Esther said, taking it back. She couldn't resist a peep. Inside the bag was more money than she had ever seen in her life.

'It's nothing, Mum,' Ria said firmly. 'I wonder if Arleen's had the baby yet?'

*

It was all planned; that was what bothered Nigel as he automatically turned left at the end of Havannah Street towards the tunnel. It was all planned, yet already the plan had gone wrong. Vic had driven Arleen to the hospital, not him, and they'd planned he and Arleen should drive there together. He would have been telling her not to worry and she would have cut sandwiches to keep him going.

Nigel parked by the public gardens and walked quickly into the circular entrance building. The lift was at the bottom so he took the steps down, round and round the liftshaft, going faster until he was running.

And once he was running, he couldn't stop.

He ran along the white tunnel under the river with his coat flapping behind him.

He ran up the stairs at the Greenwich end, gasping, his legs trembling, then jogged tiredly past the Union pub, feeling a fool, but still he couldn't stop.

The hospital was modern and white. Everything was calm and professional, and voices only murmured. They even had flowers in the waiting room. 'What's the matter?' Vic said.

Nigel could not reply.

'Don't worry about a thing,' Vic chuckled. 'Everything's fine. She's in the delivery suite now. Let's go to the Union and eat some whitebait.'

'I'll stay here.'

'Read a magazine,' Vic advised.

When Vic returned from lunch Nigel was still turning the pages. 'She's fine,' Vic said, 'I just asked the nurse.'

Later Nigel found the nurse and asked: 'Isn't anything happening?'

'These things always seem to take a long time at first,' she said.

Vic went to the main building and brought Nigel a cup of tea from the Hospital Friends stall. It was dark outside: he could see the riding lights of boats waiting for the tide.

The night nurse looked in. 'Haven't you two gone home? Mrs Price could be in labour for several hours yet.'

'Don't want to miss the excitement, darling,' Vic grinned.

Nigel remembered his manners. 'Thanks for staying, Vic.'

'You are my brother.' Vic folded his jacket for a pillow and lay down across the seats. How could he sleep at a time like this?

Nigel was woken by footsteps. A doctor went past. Nothing else happened.

There was a dreadful scream. It was dawn. Nigel jumped up. 'Did you – '

'I didn't hear anything,' Vic yawned. He went out to wash.

Again the scream, rising to a horrible gasp. Nigel stumbled into the corridor. Arleen's voice; he knew it was. He didn't know what room she was in, there were so many doors. 'It's a painful business, you know!' the nurse told Nigel. 'Now you mustn't make a fuss.'

'Where is she?'

'She is getting the best of attention.' She pointed Nigel firmly back towards the waiting room.

'Perfectly normal,' smiled Vic, 'they always scream.'

'I almost hate the baby for what it's doing to her!' Nigel burst out.

'What are you going to call the little bugger?'

'Terence, or – '

'Terry,' grinned Vic, 'that's nice.'

'Terence, Arleen insists on it. What was that?'

'You wouldn't think one little woman would be able to shriek her head off like that!' said Vic easily, and squeezed Nigel's shoulder. 'Don't worry, it's natural.'

Later Vic said: 'Don't worry, the doctors here are very good.'

Yes, but they dealt in averages, like insurance actuaries, but people were different, and Nigel wondered if the doctors and staff weren't making it up as they went along, because no one in the whole world was exactly like his wife, and he wondered if it wasn't unravelling. The screaming wasn't so frequent or so loud now, and paradoxically that worried him more.

Finally there was silence, and Nigel was almost frantic. He stuck his head into the white corridor. The nurse noticed him, and a little later a doctor in a suit came to the waiting room.

'Mr Price?'

'No, that's the one you want,' Vic said.

Sitting in the corner, Nigel didn't get to his feet. He looked up sickly.

'We can't quite get the baby to come out. We're going to perform a Caesarian section,' the doctor said.

'What's that?' Vic asked.

'Do it,' Nigel said. 'I don't care about the baby. Just do it.'

'It's a perfectly standard operation.'

'Yes, I know. Get on with it.'

Alone again, the two brothers sat together. 'I'll never be clever like you,' Vic said, 'I'd never heard of it.'

'What time of day is it?' asked Nigel wretchedly.

Vic looked out the window. 'It's night again,' he said.

'She's exhausted,' Nigel said.

'Don't worry.' Vic put his arm around his brother.

'Vic – I don't know what I'll do if . . .' Nigel looked awful, his flesh had sunk in between the bones of his face and his eyes were staring. 'If.'

'Everything always turns out for the best,' smiled Vic.

They heard the rattling of a trolley – stainless steel trolleys these days, not tin. The doctor came in. He was carrying a small white bundle in his arms.

'Go away!' shouted Nigel.

'You have a baby boy.'

'Terence. Oh God no.' Nigel broke down, his elbows on his knees, the palms of his hands covering his face.

Vic looked back, then lifted the baby from the doctor's arms.

'Terry,' he said.

Nigel grabbed the doctor's arm. 'Tell me where she is.'

'I'm very sorry.'

'Tell me where she is!'

'She's – '

Nigel dashed into the corridor. Someone tried to stop him and he thrust them aside. A trolley crashed over. Somebody said: 'This behaviour is totally unacceptable.' Nigel heard his breath yelling in his throat. He kicked open doors. He owed it to Arleen.

He found her outstretched on a white porcelain slab, defenceless and ripped.

Her eyes stared blankly into his.

Arms grabbed Nigel from behind.

'She trusted you!' he screamed.

Needles. Sedatives. Nigel wrestled. He saw Vic standing calmly in the doorway, holding Terry. Nigel fought drugged sleep as it advanced. This was what they did to you if you moved away. His gaze wandered around their sympathetic, professional faces. Our brave new world, and Arleen was dead.

'She trusted you,' he whimpered, 'she trusted you.'

'Poor bloke,' said Vic. 'Only thing worse than the death of a baby, the death of a mother.' Nigel was falling asleep now.

Vic smiled.

CHAPTER ELEVEN

1

If there was one thing Vane London hated, it was missing out on a chance to dress up, and she was dressed to kill tonight. It had been a glorious summer and she loved the heat, yet Marcelline thought how sad Vane looked.

'You look lovely, darling,' she said reassuringly, glancing across as she drove.

By the lights of Piccadilly flashing past the windows, Vane's perfectly pretty doll's face smiled for her only friend. White suited Vane, and tonight she wore precious and incredibly expensive white sable fur – an ankle-length fur coat, puffball fur hat, perhaps even fur shoes for all Marcelline could see. Vane ought to look sensational; she looked like a drowning woman. Marcelline didn't like to be so close.

'Darling, do try and enjoy yourself,' she said, 'promise you won't be unhappy.'

'How can I be unhappy?' Vane cuddled the furs luxuriously, but her voice was hard. 'Look!' London Emporium shone like an oasis of light ahead of them.

They drew under the floodlights illuminating the façade. Society women flashing smiles and diamonds were stepping down from their limousines – Vane could see at least half a dozen Rolls-Royces, a Cadillac, a Bugatti, a flame-red Hispano-Suiza – and Hawk, saluting them, looked magnificent. 'How could I be unhappy?' purred Vane. But she was: once a glittering ensemble like this would have filled her with ecstasy at the opportunity to shine. A valet took their car and flashbulbs popped, covering the paving stones with a confetti of glass. Marcelline wore brown and red.

'You won't photograph well,' Vane said, crossing the

pavement, waving indifferently to the crowd. Her furs were strikingly cut, and Marcelline wondered how many hundred animals Vane wore.

'Hawk!' Vane said. Her lower lip trembled.

Hawk smiled. 'Welcome back, Mrs London.' He had known Vane Leibig, as she was then, before she could walk. He opened the doors for her personally.

'I wonder if he supported the communists,' Vane whispered as they went in.

Marcelline laughed. The years of disillusionment and industrial unrest after the War had come to a head in the General Strike, and she was proud that it had been broken by people like them – Marcelline herself had driven a bus, and the revolution Lenin had predicted for Britain had failed, thank heavens.

'I wish Lenin won,' Vane said bitterly. 'They'd have torn all this down.' She swept a glass of pink champagne off a tray and narrowed her eyes against the glare of the giant room.

This evening everything was changed – the displays were gone, the counters concealed beneath the enormous neon-lit stage at the far end of the auditorium. Tonight the Emporium was launching the Lyonnais couturier Jean-Marie Jolie's new fashion range, and a long catwalk ran between lines of gilt seats. The rest of the floor was a huge party. Along the walls looped brilliantly designed pastiches in shining neon, yellow, blue, red: *Jolie at the Emporium*.

'This has cost Ben a fortune,' Marcelline said. 'Isn't it fantastic?'

Vane sulked. She snatched another glass and crossed the floor. How had he got such wonderful people to come? She recognized Bendor the Duke of Westminster and his girlfriend – extraordinary. That must be the dashing Lord Cleremont. And over there was Nancy Astor in a lovely gown. Vane would not have been surprised to see the Prince of Wales; she saw any number of lesser luminaries – that was definitely Anita Loos, who wrote exposés about people such as these; William Hickey from the *Express*, and elegant Cecil Beaton without his camera chatting with Lady Diana Duff-Cooper, said by some men to be the most conventionally beautiful woman in the kingdom, though Vane thought she had a face like a sheep. A blaze of light surrounded a film crew from the Pathé news.

Jean Jolie was standing under the kliegs giving an interview to be subtitled later. Vane heard him say: 'The clothes she wears are a woman's statement about the life she lives.' He used the extravagant gestures of a dandy, dressed in a ritzy white alpaca suit such as men wear in the tropics, complete with rakish white hat. 'Fashion? There is no such thing as fashion. A wonderful dress is like a beautiful woman – beyond time.' Vane knew that the frenchified gestures would look well on film, and despite the blazing lights he was the only man in the room to keep cool – Vane felt perspiration sliding over her skin beneath her furs. 'Nothing is worth anything unless it's real.'

How I hate you all, Vane thought.

'What do you think?' Marcelline asked. She raised her eyebrows at the Frenchman. He would be an excellent lover – suave, considerate and unsentimental.

Vane tried to tell the truth. 'I want . . . more.'

Marcelline laughed. 'You married Ben – and he was too hot to handle.'

Vane stared at her. It was a revelation. Marcelline was jealous.

The lights went down and Jolie, introduced by Ben London at his most authoritative, gave a short speech from the stage. Vane squeezed Marcelline's hand: so Marcelline was a coward about men. She took them lightly and left them lightly not from sophistication, but from fear.

Mannequins sauntered and twirled on the catwalk. Hemlines were shockingly above the knee. Chiffon was the *dernier cri* this year, brown the favourite colour, and Marcelline coveted a lovely earth-coloured chiffon dress embroidered in chain stitch with green and crimson silks. Vane watched her applaud.

I have courage, Vane thought, *and she envies that. The great Marcelline envies me, poor Vane*. How patronizing Marcelline was to her!

The show built up to its climax. Ben came on stage. 'And now, I give you – Natasha!' No one knew what to expect, and there was a gasp as the lights came up on the forward-striding, confident figure of a black girl. She wore a hip-hugging gold lamé evening dress with a plunging cleavage, and her prowl along the catwalk was sinuous and showstopping.

Vane turned away and found some more champagne.

'Hallo,' said a beautifully light, smooth voice, yet Vane felt its sting. 'I'm Pearl.' Vane was stunned by her nerve.

Ben's mistress looked like a million dollars in her frankly outrageous, but gorgeous, flower-embroidered *crème chocolat* Chanel trouser suit with Cartier bangles. Her tall elegance, her poise, made Vane feel uncouth. 'So pleased to meet you,' Vane said.

'I hope you enjoyed the show. It was my idea to invite you.'

'I'm sorry you lost your baby,' Vane said viciously, and heard Marcelline gasp. Pearl went quite pale, and a bright scar of pain flashed in her eyes.

'I had to meet you,' she said.

'Frankly I'm surprised you've got the guts, Miss Remington,' Vane said.

'Won't you just listen to me? Can't we at least talk like rational people?'

Vane was perfectly rational. 'I don't want to,' she said.

'*Let him go*,' Pearl said quietly.

Vane stared up at her, then laughed. Marcelline tugged her arm. 'Come on, Vane, let's leave.'

Vane shook her head. 'I'm not afraid of her.'

Pearl said gently: 'I don't want you to be afraid of me. We aren't competitors. I love Ben. Please let me have him.'

'Beg me, if it means so much to you.'

'Vane, I beg you,' Pearl said simply.

'You don't love him,' Vane said, 'as much as I hate him.'

Pearl shook her head. 'That cannot be true.'

'It is true,' Vane said.

Pearl made a last effort. 'Because we lost our son, Ben feels . . . he feels it was his fault. He blames himself because, well, we aren't married.'

'So sorry,' Vane grinned insolently.

'I hope you feel happy,' Pearl said.

Vane's mouth twisted. 'No,' she said, 'I am so very unhappy.' She wanted to tell Pearl how unhappy she was – Pearl, standing so tall and bright and happy even in her distress, because she had Ben, his love. And Vane was truly glad that Pearl had lost her baby, because that was fair and just.

Marcelline said sympathetically to Pearl: 'I apologize – '

'Shut up, you gutless wonder,' raged Vane. 'This isn't one of your pretty affairs, this is important, this is between her and me, it's real. Real.'

'Vane,' Pearl said, 'I am sorry for you. Don't you have anything more in your life? Find yourself a man.'

Vane, with tears standing out in her eyes, could have thrown her drink. Instead she turned on her heel and stamped away half a dozen paces, then stopped when Marcelline did not follow.

Pearl said politely to Marcelline: 'I don't think you've met my father, Lowell Remington.'

'Pleased to meet you,' said the distinguished man with swept-back silver hair. 'Lovely country you have here,' he continued in his cultured voice.

'You Americans have such adorable manners,' Marcelline said. If Lowell Remington disapproved of his daughter living publicly as a mistress, he showed no sign. But he did disapprove. It revealed itself in a hundred little ways – he smiled at Pearl's mouth not her eyes, he looked down when she touched his shoulder. Pearl was so dazzling that he seemed merely ungracious.

Dizzy Remington, a fiftyish blonde with dark eyes and a perky manner, showed no such reserve, hugging Pearl and stroking her. 'I hope we didn't interrupt anything, honey?' She glanced over at Vane.

'Charmed to meet you,' Vane called, very British. 'Cigarette smoke gets in my eyes.'

'Lowell's been boring the pants off Ben about the stock market,' Dizzy said.

'Not at all.' Ben kissed Pearl's cheek. 'This is the age of mass capitalism. Every man and woman in the street owns shares.' Only Pearl detected the flash of amusement in his eye: Ben had not relished his lecture from the stately Bostonian, who talked of everything but matters that concerned his daughter and her lover.

'And mass fashion,' Pearl added into the silence.

'The showing went very well,' Ben said. 'I think Jean Jolie will be a big name.' He held out his hand. 'Congratulations, Jean-Marie. May I introduce – '

The Frenchman swept off his white hat and kissed Marcelline's hand. 'Enchanté, mademoiselle.'

'Marcelline's husband is up for a knighthood,' Ben said.

'Well,' simpered Marcelline, 'we're not supposed to talk about that.'

Dizzy laughed and drew on her cigarette. Vane turned away. 'Who's the nigger?' she asked.

He towered head and shoulders above the pale crowd like an African chieftain, coming towards them, dressed in the Emporium's yellow uniform. He looked as magnificent as Hawk. 'My chauffeur Simmonds disgraced himself,' Ben explained. 'Dillibe is Cadillac-trained so he can handle the Rolls. He's Natasha's husband.'

'He was a war hero,' Pearl said, 'I found him polishing shoes in Piccadilly.'

'Dillibe is his intimate name. He calls himself Pineapple. Is it raining?'

'Coming down cats and dogs – you asked me to fetch you out if it got wet,' Pineapple reminded Ben. 'Hawk's keeping a watch on the car.' His voice was rich and deep and his eyes sparkled with good humour. Long ago his ancestors had been enslaved and converted to Christianity, and he was devout.

'Ben, where are you going?' asked Pearl.

'To my club,' Ben said. 'It seems that Nigel Price wants to see me.'

'You aren't really going to go?' Pearl followed him through the crowd. Ben smiled, affected by her concern. 'I thought he was the scum of the earth.'

Ben turned and kissed her. 'Tell you all about it when I get home.'

Dillibe Dpinyabe respected the millionaire: the only white man ever to trouble to find out how to pronounce his name then say it publicly, and the glottals were difficult. Pineapple feared that closeness (though he said he feared nothing) and on the whole he preferred to be as always called Pineapple. 'Give them symbols,' Hawk agreed. 'Aloysius Hawkins – that's my real name. But Hawk – everyone remembers Hawk, famous across London Town. Well now – ' Hawk said, 'a chauffeur's as much a public figure as a Head Doorman is, a man apart, he's got to be respected or the taxis cut him up, and you can't have *that*, can you?'

A man apart.

Hawk didn't have the colour of Pineapple's skin; he didn't have the wonder of such a woman as Natasha sharing his marriage vows either.

Pineapple swung up the umbrella, opened the door of the Rolls and saluted Ben London. He liked a man who ordered up his Rolls to drive him a hundred yards to his club – that showed style.

'Remember to drive on the left,' the millionaire said.

Before the war Pineapple had been manservant to a busy New York businessman, a Jewish bachelor who needed a general factotum who could iron shirts, cook, and arrange steamship tickets as well as drive. Eight months after the war started they had been in Germany touting for orders – America not being at war with the Kaiser – but things had got a little rough and Pineapple ended up fighting for the British in France. The British were not grateful, and

Pineapple drifted from job to job, an alien in an alien land.

They said Ben London was an orphan. Pineapple understood that.

The Rolls swept across the traffic coming along Piccadilly and turned down St James's Street. 'White's Club, sir.'

'Don't you ever cut across traffic like that again,' the millionaire said in a very low voice. 'Is that clear?'

'Sorry, sir.' Pineapple opened the door, surprised.

'Unless I tell you to,' the millionaire said. Pineapple saluted. For the first time in his life, he had apologized and meant it.

White's was London's oldest, most famous and most fashionable gentleman's club. The porters were regimental sergeant major types with that air of bluff authority Nigel remembered from the trenches. Sitting in the waiting room, Nigel heard footsteps and looked up apprehensively. He remembered Captain Lockhart saying: '*I think you've got a bit of a barrack-room lawyer here, Sergeant?*' and Sergeant Rhys-Davis said: '*I know how to deal with them, sir.*' Nigel trembled.

The door opened and the porter said respectfully: 'Mr Nigel Price, sir.'

Ben London said: 'Come with me.'

Nigel followed him. 'They made me wait in there!'

'You aren't a member of the club,' Ben said. He sat in the bow window. Rain starred the glass. Once Lord Arlington had bet £3,000 on which of two raindrops would reach the bottom of the pane first. Nigel sat nervously. Ben crossed his legs and casually signed for a bottle of four-diamond Courvoisier. 'You wanted to see me? Do you want a job?'

'I've gone back in with Vic!' Nigel confessed.

'I didn't know you'd been away.'

Nigel was crushed. He'd assumed that Ben kept an eye on everything that happened in his life. It seemed not. 'I want to be friends, Ben,' he gulped.

'We've never been enemies.' He had never rated Nigel high enough.

'Vic would do for me if he knew I was meeting you,' Nigel bragged.

'I won't tell him.' The millionaire poured more snifters of brandy.

Nigel tried to reach him. 'I heard you lost your boy.'

'Ben. Yes, his name was Ben.'

'I'm sorry!' Nigel said. Emotion threatened to overwhelm him, he had to fight it down. 'I – I married.' He couldn't bring himself to say *was*.

'Yes?' Ben said politely.

'We'd moved to Greenwich. She's dead.'

Ben put his hand over Nigel's. He didn't need to say anything – that awesome power he had always had. Nigel struggled to control himself. He stared at the trickling raindrops, then drained his brandy.

'Arleen loved me,' Nigel choked. 'Why did she die?'

'Don't give her up for Vic,' Ben said, leaning close.

'What else?' whispered Nigel. 'She let me down, poor Arleen. I'm in the vortex.' He tried to sound cheerful. 'Mum's looking after the baby. Terry.' Nigel gave a twitching smile. 'Terry the Terror - right little terror he is! Don't cry much though. Good old Mum.'

Ben poured more brandy.

'How is she?' *You can call me Mum*. Ben remembered Esther's kindness as though it was yesterday. But he was not a little boy any more, and suddenly he hated what time did to them. 'Does she ever talk about me?'

'No . . .' Nigel didn't say that Mum hated Ben for the way he had treated Ria, using her to humiliate Vic, then leaving her in the lurch. Nigel thought that it was the other way round – Ria using Ben – but it was better not to rock the boat. In the end it was Esther's simple faith that held their family together, not Vic. Mind you, sometimes Nigel saw a strange look in Mum's eye nowadays, when she thought he wasn't looking, as though she were sizing him up in a different light. He should never have left that bag of money with them – Ria had been bound to open it. There were so many lies.

'It's all in the past,' Ben said sadly. He had guessed what Nigel was thinking about him. None of the Price family except Ria had accepted the truth or even comprehended it: that what had happened between him and Ria had been simply love.

'All past,' he repeated.

'That's what I wanted to speak to you about. It isn't past. Christ, Ben, you haven't even asked me about Will! He's your son too.'

Ben flushed. 'Of course I think about him all the time.'

'He's growing up like an orphan,' Nigel said, 'he's growing up like you did. You don't want to let that happen, do you? It's not his fault he's illegitimate.'

Ben said seriously: 'Have you spoken to Ria about this?'

'She'd never listen to me, would she? The busy hostess of Trott's Nightclub in the Strand feels as guilty about Will as you do – she snaps my head off. But Will and me get on and I care about him. He isn't like you, life is hard for him, Ben. He doesn't understand it like you. He needs discipline, but it wouldn't be fair to suddenly send him to a classy school.'

Ben nodded. 'Thank you for telling me this.'

'It's not for you, it's for him. There's enough misery in the world.'

'Maybe I misjudged you, Nigel.' Ben stood.

'No,' Nigel said, standing, 'you haven't. I give you fair warning if we meet again. I'm Vic's.'

Ben stuck out his hand. Nigel hesitated, then took it. They shook hands.

2

Rain drummed on the umbrella as Pineapple sheltered Ben between the door of White's and the Rolls. 'Where to, sir?'

'Drive,' Ben said, 'just drive.' Nigel had landed him with an awful problem.

The car whispered down St James's Street into the square, circled in front of Spencer House, then turned down the stableyard towards the street lights of the Mall. 'Stop,' Ben said.

Rain sheeted across the stars of light. Beyond lay the darkness of St James's Park and almost straight ahead he sensed the outline of Westminster Abbey, with the glowing face of Big Ben to its left showing midnight. *I never knew the numerals were coloured blue*, gasped his young voice across the years. *None of it's ordinary*, Ria laughed, *it's all extraordinary*.

Somewhere out there they had bought tumblers of milk from the Spring Gardens herdsman – gone now, a casualty of the War, or of time. Ben remembered pointing at Buckingham Palace on the right. They had been changelings, half child, half adult, and would be fully adult before the evening was over . . . but at that moment they had still been children. Closer on the right was Stafford House where they had stuck their heads through the railings, dirty-faced pauper urchins gasping with wonder at the sight of a glittering gala of footmen and coaches, a Cinderella ball. Bendor and the Astors were his friends now, but Ben would never forget his wide-eyed wonder and his sure, certain knowledge that he would one day buy this house.

The two children had exchanged dreams and secrets. *One day*, Ria said, *I'm going to have a tiara with diamonds as big as eggs*.

Ben said: *I'm going to have this house*!

Ria said sadly: *You wouldn't let me in*.

Even then girls were so much wiser than boys.

Nowadays Stafford House was falling into disrepair. The Bath stone walls were flaking and the gutters were blocked: water spouted in a dozen places down the impressive façade. Once the most magnificent house in London, it had been bought by Sir William Lever, the soap magnate, and for some years used as a museum. Now no lights shone and it looked derelict and sad.

Such memories, such dreams.

Nowadays his son Will was almost as old as he and Ria had been then, and it had taken an enemy, Nigel, to point out to Ben that he was making a mess of his son's life. Will knew him no more than Ben had known his own father, and that was terrible. Did Will think of him? Yes, children dreamed. But in this one area Ben was almost helpless to act. If he told Pearl he had to see Ria, what might she imagine? If he did not tell her, what was he hiding?

The only safe thing to do was not to see Ria, and to desert his son.

That was the last thing he wanted.

The last thing Ria wanted.

And the last thing Pearl would want.

Ben dragged his eyes from the crumbling façade. He opened the voice tube. 'The Strand,' he said. 'Take me to Trott's Nightclub.'

3

'I've slept with Ria.' These magic words were supposed to jump anyone who shouted them to the top of the queue into Trott's. But now it was very late and this young toff, his dinner jacket undone and his starched white collar sticking up like a crest, was drunk enough to struggle with the bouncer. The password had started off as a joke of Ray's, but it had worn very thin with Ria. Still, it amused the clients. Ria, dressed in a slinky hostess gown, left her champagne cocktail at the bar and sauntered over. The young man had been drinking elsewhere all night and someone had whispered the magic words to him when everywhere else was shut. Ria preferred more loyalty in a drunk.

'Now now, this is a private drinking party,' she chided him.

'I slept with Ria!' The young gentleman peered across the smoke-filled cellars with their dark walls and curved ceilings. A few people were dancing in a daze but it was three in the morning and a weekday, so the barman was polishing glasses and yawning. In one or other of the alcoves Ray was drinking with his pals, sharp types with eyes like broken glass, and lovely boys in equal numbers, and he would probably go on all night, and then he would sleep all day. Ray had a reputation for cutting up rough that attracted young drunks like this boy, who had a good-looking girl behind him. Ria wondered what she thought of the password, as humiliating to her feelings no doubt as to those of Ria, who had no feelings.

'Who's Ria?' Ria asked the boy gently. 'Where is she?'

'She's here somewhere,' he slurred, staring past her.

Ria took mercy. 'Take your girl home,' she said, and told the bouncer: 'Get that sucker out of here.'

'Thanks,' the girl said.

'Look after him, darling,' Ria said.

She found Ray and told him she was going up. Ray stood to attention mockingly and she ignored him. She went between the pillars into the middle cellar where the dancers staggered to gramophone music, cigarettes hanging from the men's mouths, and their girls had taken their shoes off. Earlier there had been a jazz band – Ray had excellent taste in jazz, Jelly Roll Morton and the Red Hot Peppers played here last month. Tonight Ria sang songs from the shows, but she needed to work out a style suited to the intimate atmosphere of a nightclub – she had learned to project her voice and body from a lime-lit stage to an audience of up to a thousand, and now she had to scale that right down for a venue little bigger than a living room, singing from the mouth not her throat, toning the act right down for an audience close enough to touch. She went to the piano and silently fingered a riff.

'Night all,' she said. She unlocked the private door and went up the narrow brick steps. The odour of sweat and cigarettes was replaced by a lovely earthy smell and her feet tapped on the stones. At ground level she came out in the hall and her feet echoed on boards. She climbed the first few flights of stairs.

'Ria.' His voice.

She sensed his presence below, a shadow moving amongst the shadows on the landing. 'Ben, is that really you?'

'It's me.' He clicked his lighter and for a moment she saw his face, ruthless and dominating, terrifying with success, an ironic smile on his lips, a curl of dark hair over his forehead, his eyes a deep and hard blue. The lighter clicked off and Ria clutched at memories. Once those eyes had melted her.

'Go away!' Ria called. 'I don't know you now.'

He didn't reply. Perhaps he had gone. No, she felt his presence on the landing below as if they were close enough to touch, but it was as dark as the ocean between them. Their contact was all in feeling, but Ria had no feelings.

'I hear you're a millionaire now,' she said coldly.

His voice echoed. 'My fortune is as large as my credit is limitless. I am what I have to be.'

'I told you,' Ria said. 'You've got everything you wanted. Are you content? No. Happy? Yes, I can feel it – ' but Ria had no feelings. She bit her lip. 'I'm glad she's making you happy, Ben.'

'I love Pearl.'

'I respect that,' Ria said honestly. 'I'm married too.'

'I'm pleased you got what you wanted, Ria.'

'I'm over the moon about him. Your mother – have you found your mother?'

'I was sure I would, but nothing works.'

She's hiding, Ria knew, *she's terrified of him. Her baby who is now a man. What has she created?*

Ben said: 'She did not reply to my advertisements in *The Times*.'

'God,' shouted Ria, 'do we have to go on talking like this!' Their voices sounded so flat and cold, skirting every emotion, banishing everything real. Ria held out her hands, but his shadow did not move. There was nothing between them.

'Nigel came and saw me.'

Ria was amazed. 'Blimey, that was brave of him. Vic thinks Nigel wouldn't fart without his permission.'

'We still have Will between us, Ria.'

'He's all right. Reads too many books, that's all! I take him round Trafalgar Square some afternoons. He loves boats, last month we went on the river.' She stopped. 'I know, but what else can I do?'

'If I find a suitable boarding school, will you agree?'

Ria said: 'Do you want to see him?'

His voice came drifting sadly up the stairwell. 'He must have changed?'

She beckoned him, opening the door behind her, then stepped back as he came up. Ben went inside her flat but Ria stayed in the doorway, arms crossed, her expression as withdrawn and unemotional as Ben's face was as he pushed past her.

Will was not the young boy peacefully asleep that he remembered tiptoeing to see in Havannah Street years ago, long dark eyelashes curled above lovely red cheeks chubby with puppyfat. Now he was a young adolescent. The boards creaked gently as Ben leant over his son. He did not know what he saw – his son Will, but he did not know him. Ben did not know what he felt.

Suddenly Will's arms came around his neck and the boy hugged himself up against his father. His skin was hot. Ben felt his son's ear crushed against his mouth and his tears against his face. Will trembled with love and need. Ben wrapped his arms around him and they rocked together.

'Daddy,' Will said. 'Daddy.'

'Son,' Ben said.

'I knew you'd come back, Daddy.'

'I told him about you,' came Ria's voice. 'We cut your photographs out of the papers together and pasted them in a book.'

Suddenly she stepped back and closed the door behind her, leaving them alone.

Ben held his son. They both cried.

If he told Pearl he had to see Ria – what might she imagine? If he did not tell her, what was he hiding?

His only safe option had been not to see Ria, to desert his son. He had not done that, and he was glad.

But would Pearl understand?

The lift rose smoothly, the doors whined open, then clacked loudly against the stops, and the lights glared: this was the darkest hour before dawn.

Only the soft orange glow of a night-light burned in their bedroom – the night-light Pearl was not supposed to use since they slept together.

'Did you see Ria?' Pearl's naked body lay like velvet amongst the rumpled satin sheets. She was lying on her back with her hands over her breasts.

'Yes.'

'I knew the moment you met Nigel Price. I just knew.' She closed her eyes.

'I had to see Will.'

'Of course,' she heard herself say calmly.

She heard him undressing. Was she the second woman to hear those soft sounds tonight? Pearl tried to keep calm. *You don't love him as much as I hate him.* She pitied Vane and understood her: the borderline was that sharp.

He undid his buttons, and she heard the tap of his two collar-studs on the dressing table, then his gold cufflinks that she had given him, and the whisper of his shirt over his broad shoulders.

Pearl whispered: 'Did you enjoy your visit?' and hated herself.

'Yes.' His hands stopped on his belt. 'I did see Will, and . . . it was very emotional and wonderful. Wonderful and terrible. So many years wasted.'

'And Ria?'

'Do you think I slept with her?' He took off his trousers.

'You knew her . . .' Pearl tried to explain her anguished

feelings. She loved Ben, she trusted him, she was sure nothing had happened. It could have happened; it hadn't. But her heart needed to feel it. But how could a man prove himself innocent? 'I'm sorry,' she said, 'I sound such a jealous bitch and I'm not.'

Ben sat on the bed and kissed her navel. 'Yes you are.'

'Yes I am! You can't help wondering, Ben. You have to know.'

'Who are you?' Ben said tenderly. 'Who am I with?'

'I know. I love you so much I hate myself.'

'*Who are you*?' She felt the palms of his hands touch her nipples.

'You know who I am.' She dug her head back in the pillow and bent one leg.

'Tell me.' He caressed her.

'Pearl. Pearl Remington. I love you,' she sighed.

'Ben loves Pearl.' He brushed his lips against her mouth. She wrapped her arms around his head, his shoulders, crushing their mouths together in a breathless sensuous kiss, his palms making a smooth glowing line between her breasts and loins, her secret places, making them his.

'Pearl loves Ben.' She felt his heat and ran her fingernails down his iron-hard belly to where men always told the truth.

'Actions speak louder than words,' he said, agreeing. 'Believe me.'

She believed him, holding him and giving herself, melting where he was hard, feeling him fill her, taking him. His thrust seemed to go forward for ever. They began to tremble, their bodies locked in love and the act of truth, his loving eyes so fierce with passion, so gentle. Pearl quivered, leaning back like a pulled bow. She inhaled a long gasp.

'Pearl loves Ben!' he demanded.

'I love you!' she cried. He shouted and threw back his head, and his hot flood into her womb was her release too. Her screams, her tormented writhing, were for joy. There was nothing left secret between them.

She clasped him lovingly to her.

190

'I love you, Ben.'

He slept.

She ran her fingers through his hair, kissing his shoulder.

Dawn rose in the window, the blinding sun silhouetting the roofs of London.

She cuddled him against her, soft and hers. She would never doubt him again.

This time she had not felt the flash inside her, but now she knew the time would come.

CHAPTER TWELVE

1

Every Christmas each employee, past and present, of London Emporium received a complimentary turkey, a prized Waterfalls hamper full of rich dainties, and a bottle of wine.

Hawk took Christmas seriously. He made an event of it every year and savoured the ritual. Firstly he rose late, as late as nine o'clock, and put the turkey in the oven. Then he drew a hot bath in which – ultimate luxury – he actually shaved lying down, with the soapy water lapping around his throat. He dressed formally in a dinner suit, wearing a white apron to carry the turkey to the table, then carved it with expert sweeps of the blade. Surveying his filled plate with satisfaction, before he ate he lifted his glass of fine wine and proposed the toast: 'To you, sir. God bless the millionaire and all who sail with him.' Then Hawk sat down, and ate, and drank himself into a happy stupor.

Bert Simmonds opened the hamper bitterly. It was much too big for him, who did they think he was? The turkey would feed ten, it was stupid. How did they expect him to cook it on a single gas? It would just cap this awful day if that fat pig Gloria came round with her kids, messing the place up, bossing him about. He was happy by himself, didn't she understand? Annie was his favourite daughter, but he wasn't speaking to her. Bert lit a cigarette and stared at the offensive turkey, coughing. One little scratch and he was given the push. Ungrateful bastard. He'd driven more vehicles than Ben London had eaten hot dinners.

Esther always got tiddly at Christmas, the perfumed scent of gin preceding the goose, the ham, the pies and puddings. Dick, her first husband, always believed in entertaining friends on a Pickwickian scale, and that was a part of her memories Esther never wanted to relinquish. Her family always ate in the sitting room with decorations and coloured lights and this year Esther had wanted to sit facing her proudest possession, the framed letter on the wall from the Duke of York's private secretary, thanking her for her best wishes on the birth of the Princess Elizabeth. But Vic said no.

'Ted and Lydia Trott have invited us to the Old Bull and Bush and we're going.' Esther was heartbroken. It was unlike Vic to be so very unfeeling, and she had cried a little. Vic hugged her. 'We'll have a lovely Christmas, all of us together!' he promised her, 'but not on Christmas Day, that's all.' He knew how to get round Mum. 'I'll buy you a hat.'

'A proper hat?' Esther said.

This really must mean a lot to Vic, because he fetched her a magnificent hat in a lovely peacock blue, with real peacock feathers. Esther had no dress that really went with it, but she would gladly have gone dressed in a dishcloth in order to wear that hat. As it happened Ria saw a dress in Mary Walker's window and made it Esther's Christmas present – she had a little money of her own now the nightclub was turning out a goldmine.

At the Old Bull and Bush Ted Trott was as forceful and exuberant as ever. Lydia was completely put down by Esther's hat. Nigel danced with Ria across the boards and sawdust, she was a crazy dancer with such vitality that no one could look away, and she knew all the modern dances. Later she sang 'Show Me the Way to go Home'.

'What's the matter, Mum?' laughed Vic.

'Nothing.' Esther blew her nose. 'It's just that I'm so happy.'

'She's lovely, isn't she?' Vic said.

'Oh, Vic,' Esther snivelled, 'if only you knew.'

'Knew what?'

'Nothing. What mothers know, that's all.'

'You girls love your mysteries,' Vic grinned.

'Ray's so handsome,' Lydia said. But later Ray had an argument with his father about something or other, and Nigel asked Vic about it on the way home.

'Nigel, you fool,' Vic said, 'I've been putting the word in Ted's ear that Ray's in with some pretty low types, that's all.'

'You set this up,' Nigel said.

No one was so incredibly ignorant as Nigel. 'I'm glad you're back in the fold, Nigel,' Vic said. 'I can confide in you. The nightclub's more successful than Ted anticipated, God knows how, and now Ray won't follow in his father's footsteps. Also Ray is a fairy queen and big hard Ted doesn't like that. So he's been grooming someone else to take over in due course and the fullness of time, to keep him in his old age. He'll take the money, they'll do the work. Not Ray.'

Nigel was amazed. It was all so clear to him now.

'You!' he said. 'You've squeezed Ray out, and you're going to work for Ted!'

Vic said: 'Ted Trott is a barrel of lard, and the day Vic Price works for him is the day hell freezes over.'

Nigel looked appalled, shaking his head. Vic's game didn't add up to him, but Vic had his own way of doing business. When he wanted Nigel's help planning the details, he'd ask.

'One day,' Vic grinned, 'you and I are going to have a little talk with Ted.'

But it was that *God knows how* the nightclub was successful that had chilled Nigel's spine. Because he knew why it was doing so well: Ray Trott was creaming money off him again, every fourth Saturday, in the cigarette tin. And last month Ray had confidently demanded a round thousand pounds in back payment.

Nigel had been almost hysterical. 'I can never hide that!'

'You'll do it somehow.' Ray whistled at a girl. She hitched her hips and looked away, giving him the come-on, but of course Ray never did.

And Nigel had managed to get the money together

somehow. Vic never checked the books anyway. He trusted Nigel.

The canaries were out in their cages and a warm, smelly wind blew off the river. Nigel was walking Terry in his pram, the same pram that had served Will so well. He felt silly – a grown man, and all the mums watching. He pushed Terry around Island Gardens and tried to admire the view of Greenwich opposite, the maritime museum, the observatory on the hill, the rooftops of the town shining under the spring sun. He had never returned there since Arleen died, selling their house without even cleaning up. Esther had done that, taking Terry through the tunnel to the house that should have been his home – the thought of what they had lost broke Nigel up, he couldn't face it. He made one last self-conscious circuit under the amused eyes of the young mums, then turned the pram towards his car.

'Nigel.' He turned. It was a moment before he placed her, a strong-faced girl with a mole on one cheek, long brown hair and chestnut eyes. Betty Stark was wearing a yellow print dress, carrying a child on her hip.

'Yes, Betty?' He always felt a bit defensive since Alan Stark had deserted her after the business that went wrong about the German flier, although he knew Vic saw she was looked after.

'I liked Arleen,' Betty said. 'I'm sorry. Looks like we're in the same boat.'

Nigel joggled the pram. 'Alan will come back, I'm sure of it.'

'Well, you'd know more about that than I would, wouldn't you?'

Nigel was baffled. 'What do you mean?'

'Being so close to Vic.' She touched his elbow. 'I don't mind. Alan wasn't a good husband. But you were so happy with Arleen, weren't you?'

She was attractive; undeniably so. And she was hungry, sucking Nigel in – it was always a surprise to Nigel that he was regarded as a catch, since he wasn't a womanizer.

Arleen had been the love of his life, and he would never love again.

'Well, goodbye,' he said, and loaded the pram into the car.

Betty watched him drive away. She knew that the world is divided into two halves: the surface, and the depths. The loved, and the unloved. She knew Alan was dead. He had been a monster: a weak man made wicked by despair, and although she had tried to love him, he had beaten her until she did not know which way to turn. Now, freed of him, Betty saw clearly again and was glad. Nigel had known love with Arleen and Betty dreamed of love; Arleen had made him happy and Betty dreamed of giving happiness like that. And all the young mums watching Nigel had agreed that he had been a good and kind husband. Because he was kind was enough for Betty.

Will started at Training Ship *Mercury* on the river Hamble in the autumn term. Ria cried and embarrassed Number 3081 by kissing him goodbye in front of everyone at the station – him thirteen years old and gawky in his navy blue cadet's uniform, with a bag of oranges and *Tarka the Otter*, Ria's gifts, in his kitbag, and a lovingly cut packet of sandwiches in his hand. Mothers never loved you as much as when you were going, Will decided.

'*Sandwiches*,' gasped another cadet. 'They won't let you take *those* aboard!'

'Why not?'

'Food's against the rules,' the boy said. His name was John Storks. 'Everything is against the rules.'

So there were rules: Will heaved a sigh of relief. They would be told what to do. They were indeed, and those sandwiches were the last time he had enough to eat for many months, for the ship was not run by the godlike Commander Fry whom Ben and Will had met and trusted in the Waterfalls, great cricketer and friend of Churchill's, but by his domineering wife Beatie, disgraced and demented by a teenage love affair in the last century. She gave birth to her last child at the age of forty-eight and treated children with the great brutality which Will understood to be the backbone of a good education: this confused, semi-illiterate martinet wanted to improve him. He was a savage; she cared about him. Will's head was shaved and his boots were taken. Summer or winter, half-starved and exhausted, up the mast or down, he ran barefoot.

Rules; there were enough rules even for Will and no time for dreams of China. The Hamble was isolated, the ship remote. Inspection parades lasted two hours, and God help any little boy whose pyjama bottoms showed evidence of *beastliness* to Beatie's eager eye, or who had to ask the Night Watchman for a urinal ticket, or forgot to sign for his bowel motions in the book. There were punishment fights rigged so that the young offender was battered bloody, or boys were simply tied over the gun barrels and beaten.

Will understood. They punished him because they cared about him.

One day he would be good enough. By now he regarded his mother as a bit of a sissy and he knew she would never believe him, so he didn't bother to tell her what it was really like. *Dear mum*, he wrote home, *I am well. Please send cake.*

One dark night when snow was blowing in the wind Lord Cleremont came to dinner with Ben and Pearl at their apartment. He was developing a cold and the brandy fuddled him. He stared at Ben, trying to see himself in his son, feeling as distant as if Ben were a stranger. To be truthful Ben frightened him.

He owed much to Ben's generous gifts of money, but Cleremont felt he had repaid that in full, more than repaid, with his introductions to those who counted in Society. He felt that Ben was not grateful enough. But Cleremont liked talking to Pearl, her conversation shone, and she smiled when he patted her hand.

She had excellent taste: their apartment was extraordinarily elegant, just completely refurbished in the new Art Deco style, stylish geometrical shapes beautifully lacquered and cleverly lit. The tables looked like black mirrors, but they were of wood so subtly decorated with precious veneers that the more you looked, the more you saw in them.

After the meal – he didn't remember what it was, caring little for food – Cleremont sat by the fire snuffling into his handkerchief, and Pearl picked up something that had fallen out of his pocket. Ben was pouring liqueurs. She saw a photograph of a man in his late twenties wearing the uniform of a captain in the British Army. 'Who is he?' she asked, curling her legs under her by the fire.

'My son,' Cleremont said, holding out his hand. 'My son Roland.'

Ben came up behind him and gave Pearl her Cointreau. 'So that's my half-brother.' Pearl handed him the photo and he examined it.

'He's dead,' Cleremont said, still holding out his hand.

Ben stared at that face. The moustache, the betrayed eyes with the lines of exhaustion below them – he did not recognize those features, but the face was familiar. Memory played strange tricks – Ben heard the thundering melody of a calliope, saw an enormous crowd dressed in old-fashioned clothes, a Zulu chieftain . . . the Hampstead Easter Fair. Within a week of that day he was an inmate of the Workhouse. But that last sunny day . . . he had seen someone . . .

'Roland Lockhart, my son and heir,' Lord Cleremont said, 'he should have been the twelfth Lord Cleremont. Not to be.'

The grainy print did not reveal the long eyelashes (just like Will's), or Roland's sensitive mouth – 'He was tall,' Ben said. Roland was the boy he had seen in the crowd that day, and envied. He was sure of it.

'And intelligent,' Cleremont sighed. 'Too bloody intelligent.' He took the photograph back and held it close, not admitting he needed reading glasses.

'I saw him once,' Ben said. 'He was with a nanny.'

'His governess, Miss Bell. After Henrietta died I brought her back, only woman bright enough for him.

She'd learned her lesson, cynical woman, and controlled her damned wit the second time round. Made a good mix with Roland, he was always serious and – dreams and stuff. A dreamer.'

'An idealist,' Pearl said. Cleremont put the photo carefully away.

'Too good for this life. The war turned his mind, you know. Four years solid, Béthune, Arras, the Breastworks at Croix Barbée. Roland gave up. After the war he threw his DSO medal off Brighton pier, burned his uniform. He was going to build a new life in Africa. Plane crashed, pouf, all our dreams up in flame.' He blew his nose. 'Sorry. Cold.'

When they were alone again Pearl put on soft music and danced with Ben by firelight, kicking off her shoes and resting her cheek against his shoulder.

'Poor Cleremont,' she whispered, 'he and Roland both gave up, didn't they?'

'Art Deco is so beautiful by firelight,' he murmured. 'I would give it all up for you. The Emporium. London's. Success. All this.'

He felt Pearl smile. 'How would we live?'

'In love.'

Later she mused: 'I can't imagine you giving up.'

'Would you mind?' She did not catch the seriousness in his voice.

'Darling,' she joked, 'I could only love my millionaire!'

He laughed, and they danced.

Lisa sat by her smoking fire, a cardigan draped over her shoulders. The children's Christmas Eve nativity play and party were over, the last jelly dishes cleared away and washed up – work shared with the faithful Helen, who had moved with her here – and she must remember to return the empty pop bottles for the pennies . . . Lisa was exhausted. The rooms she rented were rather large for two women, and difficult to heat without a man to carry the coal up.

'You do look puffed, ma'am,' Helen said, 'you ought've let me. I'm used to it.'

'Come and sit down, Helen.' Lisa raised her eyes from the paper. The classified advertisement was the same that ran every Christmas through the New Year. She toyed with her mother's wedding ring.

'Anything interesting in the paper, Miss York?' asked Helen, stretching out her legs with a groan. 'Did you see that little bugger flicking jelly with his spoon? It's all over the ceiling. I didn't half give him a piece of my mind.'

'Nothing of importance,' Lisa said. She re-read the advertisement, and her brow furrowed with anger, then resignation.

> LISA PETHERTON
> Mother
> I love you, I forgive you, we need each other. For God's sake write!
> your loving son
> Ben.

Lisa crushed the page and dropped it on the fire, then leaned forward, putting the sudden flame of burning paper to good use: warming her hands.

Vic kissed his mum. 'Next year,' he promised, 'we'll celebrate Christmas at home, just our family, all of us together. I'll find us the biggest goose on the Island, Mum, and we'll have ham and pies just like the good old days!'

Esther embraced him joyfully. 'But what about Ted Trott?'

'He's getting old,' Vic said, cuddling Terry, who was walking around unsteadily towing a toy wooden boat, Vic's present, 'not like this little chap!'

'But Ted's awfully strong.' Esther felt driven to play devil's advocate in the face of her own joy, because she knew Vic wouldn't let her down. 'He's very successful, and he'll insist we come, what with you two being so close now.'

'I heard he's got a disease,' Vic said sadly, grinning at

Nigel. 'Heart disease.' He kissed Terry on the lips. 'Next Christmas at home, Mum. Promise.'

Esther was overjoyed. Vic's family came first, last and always. His promises always came true.

2

'I don't know how the hell you're going to persuade Ted Trott to let you take over the business,' Nigel said worriedly.

'I have a silver tongue,' grinned Vic. Nigel's lips looked blue by the gassy light of the street lamp, but his face was as white as paper. So he had guessed.

It was two o'clock on a foggy night. The foghorns on the river echoed haunting cries across the invisible rooftops. No lights showed in the Old Bull and Bush, of course. They heard footsteps and a copper strolled by on the other side of Cable Street, looking in the doorways. He didn't see them in the alley.

'Christ, Vic, you've got a nerve,' Nigel murmured.

'He had his baton strap showing,' Vic said. 'One of mine.'

'Do we have to do this? Can't you just talk to Ted?'

By now Nigel feared the worst, Vic knew. He had started to shake.

'That's all I'm going to do,' smiled Vic, 'talk to him! What did you think?'

Nigel sighed. 'I – I'm sorry, Vic.' He was probably remembering old Blumenthall, the first man Vic had murdered.

'That was an accident. You were as much to blame as I was,' Vic said.

Nigel knew that. 'I'm sorry,' he said. 'It's just – '

It hadn't been an accident.

'Listen,' Vic said soothingly, 'you've got it all planned out. To persuade Ted to retire we've got to catch him at the psychological moment. Right word?'

Nigel concentrated. 'Psychological, yes.'

'The psychological moment when he's tired, like now, and it's dark, like now, and he wants to get home, like now – all he wants is to get in his car and there we are talking at him. A chat by night is worth four by day. Right?'

Yes. Nigel's own words. But he had been just speaking, spinning ideas – and it had been broad, sunny day. This was night, this was real. 'I went to the town hall,' Vic said, checking his watch. 'Had a look at the old drawings. Always wondered why the Old Bull and Bush stood alone.'

Nigel had never thought about that. 'What did you find?'

'In the last century that site was occupied by something no one wanted to live next door to, what's the word, slaughterhouse?'

'Abattoir.' Nigel felt sick.

'That's it. An abattoir on that site.'

'Let's go home,' Nigel said.

'We are home. This is our home from now on.'

Vic held a finger to his lips. The minder with a prize-fighter's battered face, Nigel didn't know his name, came out of the side alley beside the pub and checked the street. A few people came down the steps and dispersed. The prizefighter walked back to Ted's Daimler waiting in the alley. No sign of Ted.

'You know how Spike got so battered?' Vic sounded amused. 'He was no bloody good.' So Vic knew his name; he was always interested in people. Probably they were even friends, though Spike's face turned Nigel's blood cold.

Spike waited by the Daimler, his foot on the bumper, yawning. 'Let's give him a cigarette,' Vic said. Suddenly he crossed the road with smooth strides. Nigel ran after him. Spike unfolded his arms menacingly, then recognized Vic and smiled.

'You're out late, Vic.' Vic was a good friend, and often bought him a drink.

'Something's come up, I need to talk with the great man.'

'He'll be out in a minute. Do you want me to fetch him?'

Vic held out a packet of Woodbines. Spike took one and opened his mouth to put it in, and Vic hit him, breaking his jaw. It was that simple. 'Spike will laugh when he feels better,' Vic grinned at Nigel, holding the groaning man up, 'he taught me that trick himself.' He patted Spike's back. 'Now you go quietly home, old boy. And keep that jaw wired tight shut, right? Good boy. Off you go.'

Nigel let the fighter stumble past. 'Christ, he must be in agony.'

'Better than the alternative,' Vic said, then ordered: 'Get in the car and lock the doors, then keep your head down.'

Nigel didn't understand. 'Why lock the doors?'

Vic gave him a look. Nigel got in and Vic heard him clicking down the locks. Vic went behind the car and searched in the dark by touch: grimy brick gave way to wood, and he found the outside door to the beer cellars just where it should be. He turned. In the mouth of the alleyway the car shone in an angle of gaslight. Wiping his hands, Vic stepped behind a pile of beer barrels waiting for the drayman's collection. It was very dark here.

The side entrance opened in a blaze of light, and Ted Trott's shadow rippled ahead of him down the steps. Vic silently reached out and swung the door shut behind him. There was still that bluish slant of gaslight against the car, and the fat man hesitated, then turned, illuminated. 'Who's that!'

Vic smiled. 'Got some business.'

'What are you doing here, Vic?' Ted rumbled. He looked relieved.

'I'm not here,' grinned Vic, his hands stuffed casually in his pockets. 'I'm at Trott's Nightclub on the Strand.' Ted's face began to freeze. 'It's Ria's night off,' explained Vic, 'so I'm drinking with your charming boy Ray and half a dozen of his best friends at this very moment.' His alibi.

Ted fumbled for the car door behind him. Vic took his hands out of his pockets. Between his grimy fingers poked a shiv. This was Vic's silver tongue. It was less than three inches long.

Ted tugged at the car door. It was locked. He battered at the window. Nigel's terrified face looked out. 'Nigel, let me in, for God's sake let me in.'

Nigel shut his eyes.

Ted Trott slowly turned around and stared at Vic.

Vic put his hand against Ted's chest. The fat man looked amazed at the rage in Vic's voice. *'The day Vic Price worked for you, you barrel of lard, was the day hell froze over.'*

Vic twisted his hand, his fingers making a grubby circle on Ted's white shirt beneath the bow tie, then blood gushed out between them. Staring at Vic, Ted slid down the side of the car until he was sitting on the stones. His eyes lost their life and his mouth slowly opened.

Vic tapped on the window. 'You can come out now, Nigel.'

'Did you have to?' Nigel said.

Vic misunderstood. 'Here, you mean? Got to be economical, got to do them where they're going to stay.' He clapped Nigel's shoulder. 'Come on, give me a hand. You know what an oubliette is, clever boy like you.'

Nigel thought about it. 'The cellar beneath the dungeons in the French Bastille used for dropping bodies into. Oh my God, Vic.' They were dragging the body across the cobbles. Nigel tried to concentrate on the Bastille.

Vic opened the door to the beer cellar and let Ted Trott's body flop down the steps. 'Not just that. An oubliette was also a deep hole packed with straw and used for storing ice in. I checked.' Vic grinned. 'And meat.'

And of course the abattoir had an oubliette.

Vic took a steel measuring rod and thumped it into the earth floor, then handed it to Nigel and sat on a beer

204

barrel, watching him. It took ages, but no part of the floor resonated. 'It's deep,' Vic said, 'deeper than anyone would ever dream of looking.' Nigel tried again, driving the rod deep into the earth. A wall divided the cellar almost into two – it must have been built later, because Nigel felt the faint resonance almost underneath it: that was where the ceiling of the oubliette was highest. He dug down through earth and rubble to a roof of curved brick. He began to lift them out one by one. Echoes came up from below, then a foul stench.

'Get on with it,' Vic said.

Nigel lifted out the bricks, concentrating on his work. This was not so bad. It was not as bad as Blumenthall's murder had been; those clutching hands around his neck, the soft plop into the water, still woke him in a sweat. And it was never as bad as digging up the French gold had been – that awful moment when they opened the box. And it wasn't as bad as shooting himself in the elbow. No, it wasn't nearly as bad as that.

'It's ours, it's all ours,' Vic said. 'Everything Ted Trott had. We're rich.'

Nigel pressed the back of his hand to his mouth. 'Vic, I want to go home.'

'This is home,' Vic said.

3

Esther's Christmas dream came true: all her family were gathered around her in her living room, eating roast goose off her laden table. Outside it was snowing a blizzard, but inside she felt warm and proud. Vic had kept his promise.

'Got you the biggest goose on the Island, Mum.'

He sat next to Ria, who wore a chocolate-coloured skirt and a white top with a golden topaz necklace that matched her hair. Her eyes sparkled as she talked about singing to her father, Tom, who was carving the goose. 'Have another sherry,' Esther beamed.

Next to Nigel sat Will in his sea-cadet uniform with TS *Mercury* on the cap – it was against the rules to wear that indoors, but he set it by his plate where it could be admired. He was drinking beer, and Esther felt a tear in her eye: they grew up so quickly. Ria had been wrong to send him away. A son's place was with his mum. She'd be sorry when he grew away from her, though Ria had thought she was doing the best for him. Already his talk was all of ratlines and luffing. It was that stupid Nigel who'd started it off, and Esther patted Ria's hand sympathetically.

'Don't smoke so much, darling,' she said.

'It's to make her voice husky when she sings,' muttered Tom.

'It's the modern way,' Ria said defiantly, 'it sounds intimate.'

'I'm just telling you because I love you,' Esther said.

'You're right, Mum,' Vic said, 'and I don't like some of the people she sings to. No offence, Ray.'

Ray was sitting next to Terry, who was in his high-chair having his food cut up. Ray was good with children, and Terry was quiet with him, his dark eyes fixed motionlessly on his uncle. He was going to be a tall man – on his second birthday Esther had measured Terry over three feet long, which according to the old wives meant he would grow up over six feet tall, and he had Nigel's slim build. Esther thought it was such a shame that Ray and Ria hadn't had a baby yet, but he had taken over a half share in the Old Bull and Bush with Vic, as well as building up the nightclub's business. Too busy.

'Perhaps Ria will have a baby this year,' Esther told Vic hopefully, but Vic laughed. 'Anyway, there's plenty of time,' Esther said, 'I just hope I live long enough.'

'None of us will live that long,' Vic said, 'what, Ria?'

'Leave me alone, Vic.' She was the only one with the guts to talk to Vic like that – even Ray didn't go that far. But from his sister, and her alone, Vic took it. In fact he smiled – genuinely smiled from his heart.

Ray did not possess her; Vic's secondhand possession

of his sister, his male domination of her life through Ray's indifference, was his victory. She danced to Vic's tune: he enjoyed her defiance, her outbursts of flaming temper, her hatred for him and fear of him, because her struggles only increased his power over her.

No one knew him as well as Ria.

He loved that, and feared it too.

She alone was everything good to him.

Vic stood and raised his glass in a solemn toast. 'To Mum and Dad. To us – to all of us. Our family. To Ria. May God bless us in the coming year as He has in this.'

'Amen,' Esther said, and drained her glass merrily.

CHAPTER THIRTEEN

1

My fortune is as vast as my credit is limitless.

Pearl lay beside Ben watching him work. In the past few months he had taken to going over papers in bed, leaving reams of reports, minutes, balance sheets, conveyances spread over the covers. It was not an efficient way of doing this kind of work. It was a sign of strain, a call for help. She was there, lying beside him, her hand on his chest. But would he listen?

He glanced at her. 'What is it, darling?'

'Nothing, honey. I am with you, that's all. All the way.'

Ben started a fresh pile, initialling each page, his propelling pencil flashing.

At first the papers called it a *technical adjustment*. Then a financial panic, then a crash. By now it was a recession. Nobody wanted to say the word *depression*. But it was here: Depression. You had only to read the obituaries.

'London's room occupancy rate was down again last week,' Ben said. 'It should be going through the roof at this time of year.'

'Sell the car!' Pearl said cheerfully.

'I'd have to pay someone to take a 1912 Rolls off my hands.'

Ben lay back against the pillows. For a moment he looked truly tired, and Pearl put her arms around him. Only she ever saw him like this.

Ben had not followed Lowell Remington's advice about the stock market so he had lost little real money. The problem was that all over the world governments had clamped down on their spending, so the banks were not lending – simply, he could not obtain the credit he needed to service his debit.

But he had followed Lowell's advice about [   ]
and land: 'They don't make it any more. There's [   ]
way it can go, Ben, and that's up.' True enou[   ]
large tracts of London housing were for sale as th[   ]
inheritance taxes broke up the great families. Ben ⸴as
sure he had made a wise investment in the long run but
for now his money was locked in by falling prices – he
couldn't sell, and he still had to meet the mortgages. Many
tenants couldn't pay their rent. He put off repairs, it was
the only thing he could do.

Pearl cuddled him. '*Illegitimi non carborundum.*'

Don't let the bastards grind you down. That was true.
The worse things got, the more important it was to keep
up appearances. He snapped his fingers. 'We'll have a day
at the races!' He tickled her and they rolled around in
bed, knocking papers aside, then slipped to the floor. 'My
God, you're so beautiful. I love you, Pearl.' Her eyes
shone.

'Ben,' she said, 'don't you ever bring your work to our
bed again.'

She wagged her finger. She meant it.

'Fine set of people you see at Royal Ascot,' Pineapple
said. 'Nearly midsummer, very strong sun. Mind you
don't get sunburn now.' He opened the car door, saluting.
Pearl glanced at him as she got out onto the grass. She
was never sure if he was joking or not. Ben knew.

'Better watch your shoulders,' he agreed as they walked
through the crowd. Pearl wore a stunning dress of fla-
menco red, very flounced and nearly off the shoulder,
with a curvaceous white hat that set off her looks and
figure to perfection. It was spectacular but outrageous,
and everyone looked at her. 'I know,' he said, 'even
though you're wearing a wide brim to keep the sun off.'
So Ben had noticed what Pineapple had not. And long
white gloves to protect her arms – he had noticed them
too. Pearl could hardly hide her happiness. There was
never a moment when Ben did not show his love for her.

They watched the horses being shown in the paddock.

studied the jockeys as much as the horses. Horse races were about people, the jockey's feel for his horse, and Ben won more often than not when he gambled.

'Are you betting this year?' she asked as they strolled towards the finish.

'Only what I can afford to lose.' He casually put a thousand pounds on the electric tote – it was essential to be seen not to care about dropping real money.

He hid his eyes behind binoculars. He would never lie to Pearl, but the truth was all much worse than he dared tell her. The top two floors of London's were fabulous, but fabulously expensive, and with interest rates sky high he needed an incredible eighty per cent occupancy to make money – last week averaged less than half, in the cheapest rooms, and they ate off fixed-price menus too.

Pearl came back. 'I put two and sixpence on the bookie for you. Three to one, but I liked the jockey's colours.'

'Thanks.' He didn't take the binoculars from his eyes.

In the Emporium he had reacted as he had in the recession of the early twenties, by cutting prices. But this was a Depression, it was different. People weren't buying even the cheapest stuff, they just weren't coming into the shop.

So many businesses were going broke that everyone was under suspicion. Just one late or forgotten payment could start the rumour mill these days, and before you knew it a nightmare swarm of creditors were camping in your office for cash on the nail. No business could operate like that.

So far his reputation as a winner had saved them.

Ben felt that he was holding up the whole edifice by force of will alone.

No sign of strain showed in his face. He looked calm and relaxed.

He dropped the binoculars and Pearl gasped. 'Darling – don't frighten me!'

'What is it?'

She held his elbows, staring up into his face. 'For a

moment you looked *terrifying* – please, never look at me like that again.'

Only the woman who loved him saw into him in that way: actually saw his driving love for her revealed, his ruthless will to win – as he had won her, taken her as his mistress heedless of what the gossips said. *She* saw the iron determination behind his gentle, loving smile. His eyes were a deep and subtle blue, tender for her alone. But for a moment she had felt their true heat – felt herself burn. He loved her. There was a terrifying side to love, it was a flame that could burn as well as caress. She demanded nothing less.

'Business is hard,' he said.

'I'm guilty,' she confessed. 'I've kept a little secret from you.'

The crowd moved suddenly, almost separating them, and above the excited murmur of voices he heard the thunder of hooves.

'What secret?'

She laughed. He could see her mouth moving, but could not hear her words above the roar of the crowd as the horses flashed past the post.

'. . . four months,' she said. 'I couldn't bear to disappoint you again. I spoke to Sir William Blizard and he says it's going fine, I'm past the danger point.' Pearl laughed, holding out her hands to him: 'I'm going to have another baby!'

Ben hugged her and spun her round. The people tearing up their betting slips thought he had won again. So he had; so he had.

'Why are you so upset?' she asked in bed, tracing her fingernail across his chest. Their bedroom was filled with translucent midsummer twilight.

'I'm not upset.'

'Yes you are. Loosen up.'

'Damn Vane!' he said bitterly. He walked to the glowing window, his feet making no sound on the soft carpet. 'I'd give up all this – to marry you.'

Pearl understood. 'You want the baby to work right so badly this time. But why do you feel so guilty we aren't married?'

'Because it isn't fair on you. I haven't got a baby growing inside me – I can do what I like and you can't. That's not a fair relationship.'

'I'm not jealous,' Pearl said mischievously, 'you're only a man.'

'I want to tie us together. I want a family with you and – what's his name?'

Pearl tapped her nose. 'I'm not counting my chicken until it's hatched this time. He or she is Bump.'

'I want Bump to have a fair chance.' He caressed her belly with his palm and did find a slight bump. 'Hey!' He tried to hear the heartbeat.

'It's much too early,' Pearl laughed.

Ben admitted: 'I've decided to talk to Vane.'

Pearl stopped breathing. 'Do you have to?'

'What choice do we have, darling?' He looked up at her.

'I just feel so terribly sorry for Vane,' Pearl said.

'Everyone always has. Not as much as she does, believe me. She's got everything, looks, money – my money – but she won't face the real world.'

'She seems to have done a pretty effective job of making your life as hellish as she can. Maybe that gives her enough pleasure.'

'It can't be enough.'

'She can't live with you, she can't live without you.'

'I shall be very calm,' Ben said.

'Be an utter bastard.'

'That's what she loved about me.' He shook his head. 'Yes, that's nearer the truth. Hatred. Contempt. Worship. That's what she wanted, and wanted to give.'

'God, if only people wore the colours of their souls like jockeys,' Pearl said. 'You must have been mad to marry her.'

'Desperate,' Ben said. 'Desperate.'

*

212

It was such a lovely afternoon as Ben walked to Vane's house. The children playing on the hill took his mind off his troubles. From the outside Primrose House looked immaculate, freshly repainted in primrose yellow, and Vane had added white shutters, as though she feared a hurricane. The lawns were fastidiously clipped, and a small fountain now played below the front door. Ben rang the bell and looked round. So this was Vane's life of exquisite luxury he was paying a fortune to maintain. He wouldn't have minded so much if she'd enjoyed it, but she took his money as her God-given right, then hated him for it.

The door was opened by Ralph, who was eleven years old. 'Hallo, Papa,' the boy said at once, 'I'm Ralph.'

His son felt he had to introduce himself politely to his father, in case Ben didn't know him. They shook hands curiously.

How could Vane be so cruel! Ben wondered what lies had she fed Ralph and George about their uncaring father – he didn't know, but he imagined them. The truth was simply that they had both failed the twins . . . but by now the threads of such tangled mischief as Vane would have wrought could never be undone.

Vane had succeeded in her terrible revenge.

Ralph wore neatly ironed grey flannels and a prep school First XI cricket blazer – she would be sending them to Westminster School later. His hair was slicked, his face scrubbed, and his blue gaze straightforward.

Ben said: 'I know that you've got a mole on the side of your leg.'

Ralph was interested. 'Which leg?' he asked quickly.

'Right calf. Show me.'

Ralph hitched up his flannels and laughed. There it was. If school didn't beat his unforced natural manners out of him, with those looks he'd break girls' hearts when he was older.

Ben crouched and took a serious risk.

'I love you, Ralph,' he said.

Ralph understood. Tears trickled down his face. 'I knew you did really.' He neither embraced his father nor pulled away, staring into Ben's face. For both of them it was like looking into mirrors.

Ben dared hope that one day, perhaps he could draw his family around him.

'Will you take me flying?' Ralph asked.

'Does Mother approve?'

'I love her, and I love you,' Ralph whispered. He didn't know where his loyalties lay. He said anxiously: 'She doesn't know about aeroplanes. I think the Supermarine's good for three hundred and fifty miles an hour, don't you?'

They went into the hall. George was sitting on a white velvet chair by the telephone table, watching them. He was identical to Ralph, without the mole, but now growing slightly heavier, and redder in the face.

George said: 'It's always Ralph.'

There was distance in his eyes, a drawing back where Ralph came forward.

'Never George and Ralph,' George said.

'Rubbish,' Ben said, and felt the distance between them increase.

George said quietly: 'Why won't you leave my mama alone?'

This would be the first time Ben had seen her in three or more years.

'You're never out of her mind.' The boy sat with straight arms, his fists on the seat of the chair taking the weight of his upper body. His dark eyes glanced towards the french windows at the back of the house. '*Leave her alone!*' He stared at Ben defiantly.

Ben gave a soundless clap of his hands and smiled with his whole face – a beautiful happy smile, and the same smile spread across George's unhappy face, and he gave the same clap, then stared down at his hands in obvious bewilderment.

'I love you too, George,' Ben said, 'don't you remember

– it was a game we played when you were a baby.' He smiled again, but this time George was ready, and scowled instead.

Ben said goodbye to the boys and went through the french windows.

Out in the garden, surrounded by flowers, Vane was sitting in a loose cream gown under a fringed sunshade. On the table stood a tall carafe of orange juice. Ben called her name then crossed the manicured grass. Vane turned and for a moment she looked startled and afraid, as though he had caught her out in some secret vice. *You're never out of her mind*. She pretended to be surprised to see him.

But she had expected him – Alice Cypress had phoned to say he was coming. Ben sat down in the cane chair opposite his wife.

Vane looked older. She had started exposing her face to the sun, as if to make herself look less precious. Its rays had bitten petulant lines around her nose and mouth, but when she smiled they would crinkle alluringly and add character and maturity to her doll's face. And perhaps replace her flawless prettiness with something more attractive.

Yes, she still stirred him. But Vane broke her spell with her very first words: 'So she's left you,' she said victoriously.

Ben did not understand. 'What?'

'Your Pearl beyond price!'

He shook his head.

She didn't believe him. 'I knew you'd come crawling back one day.' That was what she wanted so much that it might happen any moment – day or night – a knock on the door and he had come back to her. Perhaps here, now.

He said: 'Have you ever been in love, Vane?'

Her lower lip trembled – he could hurt her so easily. She stared into his opaque eyes. 'You know I have.' With him. She remembered the swelling voice of the lovely Renatus Harris organ, her breathless affirmation: *I do*.

'No,' he said gently, 'you loved a dream. Not me.'

'A beautiful dream.'

'Dream, nightmare, but not real,' he said with crushing brutality. He had no idea how delicate her feelings were. She did not know how to coarsen herself enough to communicate with him. She shouldn't want to. But she did.

'You wooed me so beautifully,' Vane heard herself say. 'It was your fault. Any girl would have done anything for you but it had to be me, and I was so afraid. I couldn't give you enough, you took everything. I don't know. It was my fault. I don't know anything any more.'

She fell silent. He waited, then said: 'You must know why I've come.'

'Will you promise to love me?'

What the hell was she talking about?

'I've been so lonely,' Vane said. 'Marcelline had a beautiful love affair with that Frenchman, your couturier, he was a wonderful lover and considerate and bought her flowers and sent her secret notes. Jean-Marie treated her with reverence. Little gifts, a gold bracelet, perfume . . . perhaps a kiss. At last they arranged to meet in Paris and there he took her to the finest restaurant, and afterwards seduced her all night long with loving caresses. When she woke, he was gone. There was only a magnificent spray of flowers left where his head had rested on her pillow. The perfect affair. She took a single red rose and pressed it between the pages of a book to remember him by for ever.'

Vane poured herself a glass of orange juice and sipped it. 'I just want you to treat me as I deserve.' She looked at Ben.

'That man doesn't exist.'

'We can start again,' she said. 'Promise me.'

'Vane, it cannot be,' he said gently. 'I love Pearl Remington and I want to marry her. That is why I have come here. You and I have lived separately almost long enough in the eyes of the law.'

She looked at him uncomprehendingly.

'Divorce,' he said.

'But I thought – you've come back to me,' she said.

'I want a divorce, Vane.'

'You've made such a success of things,' she said eagerly. 'I can see you were right in all sorts of ways.'

'That isn't love.'

'But we could travel. The whole world is our oyster, we could go to Paris. Or Cairo, even more romantic. We could learn to get along.'

'Vane. I do not love you.'

She clapped her hands over her ears. He almost caught her falling glass, but it shattered on the cane arm of her chair, splashing orange and broken crystal across her lap.

'Promise me you're lying!' she screamed.

'I have never lied to you.'

Vane whimpered then scratched at the stain in her lap, slicing her fingers on the fragments of glass. Ben jerked forward and grabbed her wrists.

'You're mad!'

'Without you,' she hissed into his face, then sobbed. 'Without you.'

He held up her bloody fingers between his hands.

She looked past them into his eyes. 'Do you believe me now?'

Without him, she hated herself.

He took out his handkerchief and wiped her fingers carefully. He found only shallow scratches. They would hurt her later, but of course, that was what she desired.

Ben said: 'Pearl is going to have a baby.'

'An illegitimate baby,' Vane said, and hurt Ben as much as she hoped. Then she shrugged. 'I wish I cared,' she said dully. 'Why can't I?'

'Let me go.'

She said despairingly: 'You're all I've got.'

'Don't be silly.' They were leaning forward, her splayed fingers between them, their faces close.

'Come back to me, Ben. Give her up. What's she got that I haven't? I'll be as good in bed as she is.'

'That's got nothing to do with it.'

'I'll do anything for you,' Vane murmured, 'I'll be your whore. That's what you all want, isn't it?'

217

'I want to marry the woman I love.'

'Love,' Vane wept. 'Oh, how I hate you all!'

'Vane, I beg you, free me.'

'Never!' she ranted. 'Never. Never.'

3

Ben's shoes tocked on the grimy pavement as he walked: never, never, never. Vane would never divorce him. He looked around him, he did not know where he was. A moving column of smoke spouted above the wall beside him, showering him with cinders, and he realized he must be near Marylebone station. He found a pub and went into it. Never, never, never. 'Double brandy.'

'Don't do brandy,' the barmaid said.

'Give me gin.'

After a while she said: 'You want a room, we got rooms to let.' She touched her hair.

'Go to hell.'

'Looks like you're there before me,' she said spitefully. 'You want to be careful round here, dressed like a millionaire like that.'

Suppose his unborn child died?

Ben couldn't face that again. He went to the door. Never, never, never.

As he reached out the door opened from outside, barking his knuckles. 'Knock me down with a teaspoon,' a voice drawled, 'it's Ben London, right?'

Ben squinted against the evening sun. The gin fumes swirled in his head.

'It's me, mate! Peter. Pete Mackelroy. You saved my life and I've never forgotten it. The Germans fell on us out of the sun, remember?'

Ben stared at the big, blunt Australian. The Boche fighters had swarmed like tiny red gnats around the slow-moving British FEs, machines as stately and helpless as green butterflies. In the abyss of air a mile above France, they had witnessed a massacre. Mackelroy gripped his elbow.

'Christ, mate, you look a sight and a half. You sure you're all right?'

Ben said carefully: 'She won't let me go.'

'Women, forget them,' Mackelroy said cheerfully. 'Smell like a distillery, you do. Let's have a drink.'

'Not here.'

'No trouble. I've been staying here waiting for something to turn up, and the bedbugs are as big as the cockroaches, believe me. Come on.'

Peter Mackelroy was a rugged man, with narrow blue eyes, blond eyelashes and short sandy hair. He looked rough and tough, and his handshake was like an assault, but beneath this forceful masculine veneer Ben knew he was intelligent and sensitive. Mackelroy had antennae: even buried as deep in the Western Territory as Waramgiri, he had sensed the war coming to Europe.

They found another pub and stood talking at the bar.

'I went back,' Mackelroy confided. 'The desert's one bloody hell of a hole of a place, I can tell you. But prospects. Prospects, get my meaning?'

Ben stared into his glass. He remembered a khaki-green butterfly sliding below him, Mackelroy standing up in the cockpit, his legs stained with blood, firing back with the Lewis gun mounted over the top wing. Machines had been falling in flames all around them. Ben had pulled his own triggers, firing until the gun jammed. Mackelroy had looked up as he passed below Ben, their frail machines swaying together in the insubstantial air. 'I owe you one, mate!' Mackelroy had shouted.

I owe you one, mate.

'Have another drink,' Ben said.

'Frankly I'm a bit short of ready at the moment.'

'My treat.' They drank brandy for a change. Mackelroy rolled it on his tongue.

'My place is bloody useless for sheep. You can drill down a thousand feet and still won't find a sip of water. I tried. Found something else though.'

219

Ben wasn't interested. 'Let's find another pub.'

They were walking along a lane in Soho and by now Mackelroy limped badly. 'Those French doctors took an inch off my left leg. Let's sit awhile.' They found a noisy place and carried their beers to a table.

Mackelroy put his arm around Ben's neck and whispered in his ear: 'Golden minerals.'

'You found gold?'

'Sssh,' Mackelroy said, then shrugged. 'Stuff's there.'

'You found the seam?'

'Drilled straight through the lode. Damn sure. Raising the bloody money to make certain, that's the nub. Don't want to give it away to the mining conglomerates for a half one per cent.'

'You're imagining it,' Ben scoffed. Or else it was a confidence trick. Yet Mackelroy had frank eyes to go with his open manner. And Ben *had* saved his life.

I owe you one. Mackelroy was paying back the debt. He wasn't lying.

'A swagman's dream? Too right. Maybe I am dreaming, sport. I ought to settle down with a good woman. Christ, it's dark already.'

'Last orders,' called the publican. Someone told them where to find a club. They went down some steps and sat at a tiny table. Mackelroy clapped and whistled at the striptease artiste and she flaunted for him. Ben stared into his drink. Mackelroy stuck his elbow in Ben's ribs – sometimes he thought Ben London was very drunk, and sometimes he thought he wasn't drunk at all.

'She's taking her tassels off,' Mackelroy said. 'Come on, enjoy yourself.'

'I want to marry the most beautiful woman in the world,' Ben said.

'No worries,' Mackelroy said, 'they're all the same. Close your eyes.'

Vane had said almost the same thing, but it wasn't the same. Making love to Pearl was like coming alive, entering her like being born again, a deep and potent and unique celebration of a beginning and an end together.

'It isn't the same,' he said.

'Well,' Mackelroy said, 'you must know more about them than I do.' He didn't believe it.

But Ben tried to explain. 'Vane doesn't love me and I don't love her. But you know how human nature works. We can't let one another go.'

'Love 'em and leave 'em,' Mackelroy bragged. The girl smiled at him.

'Vane's got her picture of what life ought to be like, and it isn't, but there she is. So she's going off to Cairo, but she won't escape, because she'll still carry her picture inside her. And no one can live up to a dream.'

Mackelroy half-stood, clapping. 'Come on, Sheila, get them off, don't muck about!' The blonde girl kissed the air coquettishly, then as she finally swept the last tassels off, the lights went down at the same moment, and they saw nothing.

'What do you think?' Mackelroy said. He thought he had glimpsed her nude.

'I'll give you a thousand pounds,' Ben said in the dark.

'No, of the sayeeda bint, I mean.' The lights came up and Mackelroy nodded at the empty stage, then registered what Ben had said. 'What, you'll stake me?'

Ben shook his head. 'I don't lend money to friends, they don't stay friends. I give. I don't want control – if you give me forty-nine per cent, fine. If you don't, fine. It's enough to get you back to Australia, anyway.' He casually scribbled a cheque.

'Bloody hell,' Mackelroy gasped, 'you must be rich as Croesus.'

'I can afford to lose it.' As long as his cheques didn't bounce, he could. Maybe next week the market would turn back up.

But the Depression did get worse. In two months the number of claims for unemployment benefit doubled. Taxes were three times what they had been before the War, with the new surtax on top of that, all rising rapidly along with interest rates. With the Labour Party in power Ben's Workhouse friend George Lansbury had been made Minister of Works, allowing children to play games in the parks, and at 'Lansbury's Lido' the Serpentine was opened for bathing. The *Daily Herald* published a photograph of Ben without a care in the world, up to his neck in water, with a little orphan girl sitting cutely on each shoulder.

The Home Office estimated that seven hundred men committed suicide that year because of unemployment.

Ben slashed the number of hourly-paid staff working for him in half and was widely reviled for his ruthlessness. Better they should accuse him of that than know the truth: he was broke. It was a secret he dared not reveal even to his closest friends – the merest hint of doubt would breed instant loss of confidence and bring the whole London edifice crashing down around them. The smiling, confident face of the millionaire alone made disaster impossible. In fact they were on the brink. The only department in the Emporium doing well was shoe repairs – the shoe department was selling almost no new shoes, but people still had to have footwear. Knitting wool also sold well as people made their own clothes. But these bright spots did not, as Ben explained one by one in his office to the people being fired, even cover the Emporium's lighting bill.

Then he went to London's and told the hotel staff. The hotel normally had a one-to-one ratio of staff to guests, but if occupancy rates at the height of the season were only thirty per cent, as they were, then sixty per cent of the staff had to go – and they did.

They blamed him.

Sometimes men shouted abuse or shook their fists at him across the street, disgusted by his aura of success in a world of crumbling industries, soup kitchens and hunger marches.

Only Pearl knew the truth. She had seen into Ben that day at Ascot: his ruthless love, his terrifying determination. At some point very far back in his past Ben London had made a decision about his life: whether to win or lose. He didn't mind sacrificing a battle here or there, if necessary he didn't mind losing every battle, except the last. That, he would win.

His total creed was to win the war.

He would never lose, because he would do anything not to lose.

He would pay any price.

Pearl feared that, but respected it. When he tumbled despairing and exhausted into bed, she held him and soothed him, assuring him of her love, cuddling him tenderly through the short, short night. Whatever happened to them, would happen to them together.

Vic lay in bed alone. It was a drowsy warm afternoon at the Old Bull and Bush, and when the bar closed at three he'd ordered Spike to wake him at five.

Nigel's book-filled rooms on the floor below were more comfortable, but this hot attic bedroom was where Ria had slept when she and Ray were waiting to move in over the nightclub. She had slept in this very bed.

Vic imagined that.

He lay on the coverlet with his shoes on and his hands behind his head. He couldn't sleep. Beside him was the socialist rag, the *Daily Herald*, with its pretty picture of Ben London up to his neck in water.

If life was fair he'd be up to his neck in excrement.

Vic groaned aloud. *Ben London's never going to let me forget him – the seducer of my sister, rubbing my face in it day after day. In my mind he'll always be there on the steps by the river, Ria's lovely body squashed beneath him. She struggled, she cried, but her blows were unavailing, and he ruined her.*

Vic could never forget his guilt. He had not come, and

223

she had been crying out for him. He was sure she had. There was never a moment when that knowledge was not at the forefront of his mind and of his heart.

The memory was as fresh as if it were happening now. His failure tormented him.

In every other way except this most important one, Vic's life was a success. He looked after his mum and dad and made sure the old folks got anything they wanted. Even Nigel's gift of the lovebirds that Tom doted on – there were now over a dozen of them – had been Vic's idea. Then after Ted Trott's sudden disappearance he had taken over not only the pub, in half ownership with Ray, but also effective control over the real life of the Isle of Dogs, Poplar, and much of Limehouse and Wapping. While Ray packed his mother Lydia off to live with her sister in Merton, Vic took control over the organization and the income from the rackets. In addition he had Trott's nightclub as a base to consolidate the West End when he was ready.

Vic glanced at the inside pages of the paper. They'd had an election in Germany and the Nazis were bouncing back. The Depression was good for them – Nigel had tried to explain why – all Vic knew was that six million votes, up from less than a million in two years, wasn't smoke without fire. Vic hadn't forgotten Adolf Münchener letting him down without warning, but Hitler hadn't made a man he didn't trust editor of *Voelkischer Beobachter*. Now he was a deputy in the Reichstag, representing the movement in the important Foreign Affairs Committee.

Vic got up and ran the palms of his hands back over his black hair, then yawned at his face in the mirror. National socialism was a good thing. Its blend of mysticism, paternalism, blind hatred and thuggery made it his sort of politics – so Nigel joked. Nigel was getting too clever for his own good. Vic did not like to be patronized even by his own brother.

There was a knock on the door. 'Five o'clock, sir,' came

Spike's distinctive hiss. He still spoke through his teeth – his jaw had not set properly.

Vic went downstairs to the bar. Young Terry was sitting on the sawdust floor eating a bag of crisps. When he saw Vic he ran over to him. 'Give us one,' Vic ordered. Terry held out a single crisp.

'Offer the packet!' Nigel said sharply. He was going over books at the table. 'Manners, Terry.'

Vic laughed and swept the boy up in his arms, then sat beside Nigel on the red plush banquette, listening to Nigel's pen scratching. Since the Companies Act came into force all businesses, even private ones, had to keep proper accounts. Vic tried to make Terry laugh by tickling his ribs. Almost fifteen years ago Vic had insisted Nigel keep proper balance sheets and channel as much of their income as possible through legitimate sources. Thank God he had, though the details were awesomely complex. That was perhaps the way Vic was most lucky: he had Nigel.

'We'll pay over seventeen thousand pounds in income taxes this year,' Nigel said as he worked. Vic paid, knowing it was stupid to evade taxes like the Chicago gangsters did, that was how they got caught. Besides, it was immoral. In this locality Vic was more important to the ordinary people than the borough council, but he had an even wider duty. Vic cared about his country, and paying a little income tax, even if it was only the tip of the iceberg, made him feel patriotic. Several friends, including Labourites like Sir Henry Stoughton and Sir Oswald Mosley, were Members of Parliament.

'What's this?' Vic's blunt finger stabbed the densely covered page.

'That's a payment to Rixby,' Nigel said calmly.

'A hundred pounds every four weeks to that old fraud? Christ, we're spoiling him.'

'It's a technical adjustment,' Nigel said. 'It only has relevance in the context of accounting procedures.'

'Is he trying something on?' Vic demanded.

'No,' said Nigel casually, 'the situation is under control.'

'All right,' Vic agreed, and played with Terry again. 'How are we doing?'

Nigel pointed out a total that contained seven digits. Depressions, taxes, laws and wars were the best friends of organized crime.

Vic called laws R&Rs – rules and regulations. They were good for business. Many people who had tasted their first cigarette in the trenches were now captive smokers, and rising tobacco taxes encouraged the tobacco smuggling which was so enormously profitable. 'Just like tea in the nineteenth century,' Nigel had explained eagerly, 'and salt and pepper before that.' No one smuggled salt nowadays, too cheap. Crime was a matter of adapting to changing tastes and the fashions of government policy.

'People in work have got more money to throw around,' Vic grunted. It was months since he'd seen a woman completely without shoes, or a child with legs bent by rickets, and in his own childhood before unemployment insurance they had been common sights. Fresh fruit was in the shops all year round, and milk was clean.

'Contraband gin's doing well,' Nigel said. A lot of the old folk weaned on gin couldn't live without it, and it was a pricey drink nowadays. But the bulk of Vic's money came as always from the lovely business of perms and pools, totalisators and twiddlems, street betting, gambling clubs and prostitution. And from fear.

'All right,' Vic said, 'I'm going to get some fresh air and meet some people.' He took Terry out, leaving Nigel as always feeling mildly put down and wondering how he could serve Vic better. The pub was opening for evening trade and Nigel packed up the books, then took them upstairs. It was bad luck Vic catching on to that hundred-pound payment, but Nigel was sure he had satisfied him. And if Vic did take it further, old Rixby knew what to say. Nigel washed his face and returned to the bar just as the door opened and Betty Stark looked in.

'Hallo, Nigel.'

He liked her and was flattered that she had set her cap for him. She still had not remarried, though he couldn't imagine why, she was an attractive woman. 'What will you drink?' he asked.

'Gin-and-splash.' Nigel nodded at the bartender and sat opposite her. It never went further than this, opposite sides of the table, yet Nigel felt a faint thrill of pleasure just watching her. He supposed she felt the same. Once she had kissed him, then understood that she had taken it too far. In a very real sense, Nigel was still wed to Arleen.

'I like you, Nigel,' she said kindly. 'I like being friends with you.'

He was flustered. There was a new Shaw play on, *The Apple Cart*, and he wondered whether she'd like to see it, but he was too shy to ask. 'Why me?' he said, covering his confusion by sipping his drink.

She smiled and shook her head. 'No reason!'

'Betty,' he said.

'Yes, Nigel?'

'I wondered – we could see a play. I don't know if you like Shaw.'

Her face was transformed with pleasure. 'I do!' she said, 'with you.'

CHAPTER FOURTEEN

1

Peter Mackelroy had shaken the dust of Marylebone, England off his feet with relief. He made a holiday of his long journey, travelling slowly south through France, taking in the sights and battlegrounds he knew from the War, but staying in the best hotels this time. A thousand pounds was a fortune. Mackelroy felt guilty about such a favour. A man liked to work for his money.

He took ship from Marseilles. Already he'd had one shipboard romance, women found him irresistible, he knew what they wanted. He was bored with her already, but she was the clinging type – smiled at him across the dining room, bumped into him on the boat deck.

Dressed all in white, Mackelroy leaned on the ship's guardrail and let the hot Egyptian wind from Port Said blow in his face. It stank bad, and the old ship would be stuck here ten days for new shaft bearings. Bumboats selling women and trinkets circled the anchored vessel, the crew keeping them off the loading ports and gangways with boathooks. Ten days of this would be no fun at all. But that wind . . . beyond that awful human stink Mackelroy could smell the dry, clean, burning breath of the desert.

He watched a spout of smoke traverse the embankment over the low fields of the Nile delta. It was the train from Jerusalem, and this evening it would go on to Cairo. *My wife's going to Cairo*, Ben London had said. A thousand pounds was nothing to him, but everything to Mackelroy. It was burning a hole in his pocket and he felt demeaned by it. He could take the train, see if a millionaire woman had tits like other women. He was a real man.

*

Vane London stayed at the lovely Mena House Hotel in Giza. A short taxi ride from Cairo, surrounded by desert, the wild scent of burning sand mingled with a heady perfume of bougainvillaea and jasmine in the formal gardens, where the water sprinklers clicked all day and cicadas chittered all night. The Mena House had class, and the view of the pyramids was spectacular – a mile beyond her second-floor balcony Cheops was a brilliant yellow cone between the desert and the sky.

Vane changed before dinner, holding a selection of evening gowns against her in the mirror before deciding on a cool pale blue. She put on her face then went down the corridor to the twins' room. The governess, a practical sort called Miss Barker, was giving them a mathematics lesson. The boys were returning home in a week, having already missed more than a month of the September term.

Miss Barker stood up and Vane kissed her boys carefully. 'Bed after supper.'

'If it's that fish again,' George sulked, 'I won't eat it.'

Ralph said forthrightly: 'Mama, is the man who came up to our table at lunchtime a friend of my father's?'

'*My* father's,' George said. Ralph picked up a pillow and pretended to hit him.

'Stop it!' Vane said. Miss Barker's discipline was no better than that of the others. 'Mr Mackelroy saved your father's life during the war. He was shot in the knee by a famous German ace, which is why he limps. He is very brave.'

'Did he really save my father's life?' asked Ralph.

Vane frowned. 'Of course he did. Why on earth should he claim otherwise?'

'Because he likes you,' Ralph said.

Vane was flustered. Mr Mackelroy was simply a breath of fresh air. He was utterly unlike the fawning lounge lizards who oiled their way across the hotel's public rooms, whose eyes lay on a woman like sweat. Mr Mackelroy had an honest face and manners as blunt and genuine as a Yorkshireman's. Yet his voice and rugged, sunbrowned features made him excitingly different, and the tiny lines around his eyes hinted at a great experience of life.

So he really did like her – Ralph was perceptive about such things.

'There's nothing wrong with it,' Vane said uncertainly.

Ralph simply winked. It was the great tragedy of Vane's life that her boys were not girls. Daughters she would have comprehended.

'Oh, go to bed,' she instructed, and shut the door on their chorus of complaint. Putting them out of her mind in the lift, she thought of Mr Mackelroy.

'Come off it, Peter's my name,' Mackelroy said. 'You Brits are always so formal and distant.' He bought her a green minty cocktail with a maraschino cherry in it.

'We like it that way.' Vane found the drink very pleasant, the tiled lounge high-ceilinged and cool.

'Why not break out?' Mackelroy dared her. He was tough and very masculine, polite and almost rude to her at the same time. He both treated her with respect and didn't give a damn about her. That gave him away: she was by far the prettiest woman in the room, the other men had all noticed her. Peter snapped his fingers and the Arab boy in the colourful *galabiya* brought them another drink.

'I couldn't possibly manage another,' Vane said politely.

'Just eat the cherry,' Peter said, looking at her over his brandy. He was wearing a white alpaca lounge suit with Italian shoes. Unbidden to Vane's mind came Marcelline's voice saying *suave, considerate, unsentimental*. None of those words quite described Peter Mackelroy, but she couldn't get them out of her head. Egypt was far more romantic than Paris. Her fingertips tingled.

'I'm going sailing on the Nile tomorrow,' Peter said later. 'Come with me.'

'Oh, I don't know . . .' But how could she refuse such a dream of an invitation?

The day was a peerless arch of Egyptian blue and the felucca heeled dangerously as it tacked between the shimmering sandbanks, but Peter only smiled. The fellahin crew looked like rogues, but Peter didn't take any non-sense and soon they retreated to the bows. Vane held up a parasol against the sun. She thought she would die of the heat, then glanced at him and shook out her hair, trailed her fingers in the water. 'Enjoy yourself,' Peter said. 'I'm going to have a go steering this ship.' He stood at the tiller, legs apart, the muscles bulging in his brawny arms and the desert wind blowing his sunbleached hair.

'You look rather piratical,' Vane said. She held his gaze for a moment before dropping her eyes. Peter widened his stance, more piratical than ever.

They grounded on a beach and walked to the end of the island, finding a cool glade of tropical flowers. Mackelroy opened the hotel hamper and they picnicked looking along a magnificent blue vista of the Nile, the bordering green fields and lush vegetation growing to the very edge of the burning desert, then chopped off as though a line had been drawn.

'Just half an hour's walk,' Peter said, 'and a lonely man could die out there, amongst the dunes, surrounded by nothing but sand.'

That was a surprisingly sensitive remark, and Vane looked at him.

She stayed awake while he dozed, keeping the flies off his face, thinking about him.

That evening they returned to the cool arched rooms and tiled courtyards of the Mena House. Vane wore her pale-yellow chiffon. She watched Peter eat his dinner through the glittering silver cutlery and gleaming linen that separated them. In her confusion her pleasure was in watching him eat. He liked her dress, she saw him looking at it as he drank his wine.

Beyond the verandah the pyramids were red as blood in the setting sun, then faded away, and the orchestra began playing under the purple, starry sky.

Peter danced clumsily and she had to help him. The problem was his left knee. 'You have very little articulation,' Vane said.

'You know about that?'

'I used to be a nurse.' She enjoyed helping him. He needed her.

'You can nurse me anytime,' Peter said.

'Don't be naughty,' Vane said. He clasped her to him a little roughly, and a shiver of ecstasy ran abruptly down Vane's back. She stared at him, shocked.

Peter could not be shamed. He smiled broadly. Finally the corners of Vane's mouth twitched. 'You're quite a woman,' Peter whispered as they danced. 'You act so cold, such a lady all the time, but you're on fire.'

She jerked away from him but Peter almost fell, then held his knee. He looked up at her admiringly.

She relented, and they danced again. 'I'm sorry. I forgot about your injury.'

'Well, and I had half a bottle of cognac before I came down.'

She laughed. 'You wouldn't be able to dance at all if you were drunk.'

'A man in love can't get drunk,' he murmured.

This was fearfully dangerous.

'No, don't,' Vane said, turning her face away.

'Why shouldn't I say what I mean? I'm falling in love with you.'

'We mustn't keep meeting.'

'I want to kiss you.'

'Not here,' said Vane desperately. They danced, his arms enclosing her, his unflinching eyes filling her gaze. She could not look away.

'Your husband wants to divorce you. You don't love him – do you? What are you frightened of? That I've been sent to spy on you?'

'Of course not.'

'Or afraid of not being a proper woman?' Peter said: 'Don't be afraid.'

They sat drinking liqueurs with a tiny table between them. Below, the world was lost in black. Above them arched a shimmering blaze of stars, slowly rotating. It must be very late by now. They didn't say a word. Vane was all in confusion at such an intensity of silence between them under the face of such glory. She felt everything. Her mind was too full to speak. Words would break the spell, she would not know what to say, only feel. They must not meet again; they must.

'Good night,' Mackelroy said. He saw her to her room. She turned her face up to him. 'I'm going to examine those pyramids tomorrow,' he said. 'Want to come?'

'Yes.' He leaned down, but an Arab boy came along and Vane turned away.

Mackelroy walked off along the corridor. His room was on the floor above.

Vane undressed. A fan whirred slowly in the ceiling. She turned the lights down and stood looking out over the balcony, almost falling. Falling in love.

If he *had* kissed her, would she have returned his kiss as ravenously as she felt, transforming her lonely life for ever with the heat of her passion for love?

Vane lay down, staring up at the fan and at its rotating shadow from the street lights of the road below, her hands clenched behind her head in the hot, perfumed night. That was how she lay until dawn, sleepless and alone.

After breakfast she went to the twins' room and kissed them. They were looking forward to a trip on a paddle steamer all day. 'Don't let them go near the railings alone,' Vane told Miss Barker.

'Can we go out on camels in the desert tomorrow?' Ralph asked.

'The desert is a very dangerous place,' Vane said.

'If you marry Mr Mackelroy,' Ralph said, 'does that mean we won't ever see my father again and we'll have to go and live in Australia?'

Vane blushed. 'I am certainly not going to marry Peter!' A new life; she had thought about it all night. Suppose he asked her? Would it really be such a terrible thing to give up her hatred for love?

Back in her room she tried on a bright gown in the Arabic style, silkily light and flowing, such as Isadora Duncan might have worn. She wound a pale chiffon burnoose around her head that would fly in the wind, then

233

smiled at herself in the mirror and went down to the lounge.

Peter looked amazed when she made her entrance. 'You are spectacular.' He had hired a driver and carriage but the sun's heat was too fierce to leave until after lunch. They had drinks and he touched her elbow, shy and possessive. 'I enjoyed dancing with you,' he said quietly.

The pyramid rose up vast and dark red as their carriage approached its shadowed side. Peter swung her down easily and they walked around the deserted ruins, staring up in awe. He'd brought a Thermos of iced tea and they drank it amongst the giant blocks, the sun casting long shadows around them.

'Let's climb up,' Peter said, 'it'll be a terrific sunset from the top.'

'But your leg.'

'You'll have to hold my hand,' Peter smiled.

She found the pyramid was not so smooth as it looked from a distance, and even though they climbed in shadow it was very hot. This made the peak above them all the more attractive, and Vane was determined not to give up. She helped Peter up the crumbling sections, and he swung her easily up the steeper blocks, her clothes filling with the cool breeze, fluttering around her legs.

'You're a damned beautiful girl,' Peter said.

They stood on the pinnacle with the world stretched around them in a stupendous panorama, the wind blowing smoothly over them. 'This is so beautiful,' Vane breathed. Below them the sun glittered on the horizon like a fierce jewel, crowding the red desert with the half-moon shadows of dunes. The lurid illumination faded and now it was all darkness down there, leaving the two of them up here alone bathed in the soft, amber rays of sunset.

'I love you,' Mackelroy grunted.

He kissed her. Vane swooned. Her head was back and she felt his powerful fingers in her hair, the chiffon unravelling, blowing out in a long streamer, and the hot flaky stone gritty beneath her shoes. But that was only for a moment: then all of her was concentrated on his kiss.

'Let's do it,' Mackelroy said.

She knew what he meant. He was talking about her body, not her heart.

'It's too soon, Peter, it's too sudden.'

He kissed her again, and Vane shuddered with desire. He put his hands in the small of her back and pulled her against him. 'Come on, don't you care about me?'

'It's because I do care about you,' Vane whispered.

He laughed. 'You've been leading me on, now you're backing off.' He kissed her throat. 'Don't pretend. You're hot for me, you're dying for it.' He groped under her clothes as possessively as though they were his own.

Nothing is worth anything unless it's real. Vane's gown fluttered in the wind. *I'll be as good in bed as she is!* But that couldn't be all. *I'll be your whore – that's what you all want, isn't it?*

She couldn't get Marcelline's voice out of her head. *Suave, considerate, unsentimental . . . arranged to meet in Paris . . . seduced her all night with loving caresses . . . when she woke, he was gone. The perfect affair.*

'Promise me you won't leave me, Peter!' she cried.

'Sure, I promise.'

'We mustn't – not here. I don't want an affair,' she said. 'I want – I want your love,' she tried to explain.

'You were going to get it.'

'No,' she said gently.

Mackelroy wiped the back of his hand disgustedly across his lips. 'Not here, not there, not anywhere I bet.' Mackelroy let her go. 'So that's the way it is,' he said bitterly, 'you're playing with me.'

No – she was saying how serious she was about him. The wind unravelled her burnoose and it flew into the void. Vane clamped her hands to her head and cried.

'You're a bloody flirt,' Mackelroy said. 'Let's go.' He started down.

'Peter!' she said. He carried on without her.

She tried to say she was sorry. It was her fault; she was to blame.

'I got a telegram,' Mackelroy told her roughly in the

carriage. 'The ship's repaired earlier than they thought. I'm leaving tomorrow.'

'Don't leave.'

'Want some more sport? No thanks, lady.'

Vane tried to make him understand. 'I'm not a coward. I just want – more.'

'Leading a feller on then cutting him off must make you feel bloody superior.'

Vane said: 'I want a man who knows how to treat me.'

'You've found him. Me,' said Mackelroy, paying off the driver and going up the marble steps. 'I know how to treat flirts like you. Bye bye, darling.'

She ran after him. 'But Peter – '

'Shut it,' he said without looking back. Then he did look round. They talked between two pillars. 'Sure, I would have loved you,' he said.

She humiliated herself. 'Stay,' she begged.

'Give me a reason.'

Surely he must understand what she couldn't say out loud? But Mackelroy only shrugged, then disappeared into the bar, leaving her alone.

Vane went up to her room. Men were like that. It was no use expecting them to be like women. She tore off her lovely clothes and kicked them away, flung herself down on the bed and wept genuine, desolate tears. If only she had let him love her in the way he wanted, she could have taught him to give her the love she needed. She had so much to give.

Thinking everyone was at dinner, the maid came in using her master key to turn down the bed. Vane sat up, ashamed, wiping her eyes.

Mackelroy got up to his bedroom at some hellish hour after the bars closed. All the hotel corridors were bright and quiet. He put his finger to his lips. He was very drunk, but it only showed in his limp, as usual, and in his broad smile. He fumbled for his key, but his door swung open as soon as he touched it.

The room lights were out, but the dim glow from the

street lamps below revealed the fan and its rotating shadow on the ceiling.

Like a dream of desire, the millionaire's wife was lying on his bed.

'Bloody hell,' Mackelroy said.

She sat up, her pale hands clenching the sheet against her body.

He stared, blinking. 'What the bloody hell are you doing here?'

She threw out her arms. The sheet dropped. She was naked. Mackelroy didn't know whether he was dreaming or not and he didn't care. He stripped off his tie and headed for her.

She had lovely breasts and she was as pale as a stone goddess, but when he touched her he felt her trembling. Then she kissed him ravenously, pressing her lips against him in a desperate embrace, trying to make him feel her passion. He tugged at his trousers, embarrassed. He couldn't respond.

'Hang on a minute,' he said.

She fell back from him. Her face was dark with shame. She had failed to arouse him.

'It's your bloody fault,' Mackelroy said cruelly. He wasn't about to admit he was that drunk. Let her take the blame.

Vane gave him an exhausted look.

'Who the hell do you think you are?' Mackelroy demanded.

'Love me,' Vane said. 'That's all.'

Mackelroy threw himself face down on the bed and began to snore.

'Love me,' whispered Vane into the air.

2

Ben and Pearl sat with his office desk between them. They were both looking at the letter lying on the blotting pad.

It was a surtax assessment from the Inland Revenue of Ben's taxable income for 1929. That had been a good year.

'Can you meet it?' Pearl asked.

He had never seen her more beautiful than in this final month of her pregnancy. Pearl was blooming, her hands resting protectively over her Bump, radiating contentment. But now a questioning frown furrowed her brow. Ben hesitated, looking at her. And then he lied to her.

'We can manage somehow.'

It was impossible. He hadn't even told her about the four other notices of assessment in the desk drawer. Within the month, he would almost certainly be bankrupt. All doors were closed to him now. Even Lowell Remington had lost his cash on Wall Street, and saddled with his enormous property holdings, he found himself in the same corner as Ben: paying for the good years in the bad.

'I can always sweep floors,' Pearl said, heaving herself up and waddling round Ben's desk. She held his head against her Bump. 'Don't try and protect me from the truth, darling. I can face it.'

Ben opened the desk drawer and pulled out the whole sheaf of papers. He sent them fluttering across the desk then smiled up at her. 'The truth is that we don't have a hope. We're bust.'

The inter-office phone rang and Ben picked it up. His secretary Alice Cypress said: 'Mrs Marcelline Stoughton is here to see you.' The door opened and Marcelline stood there looking frightful, her hair hanging down the side of her distorted face. It was obvious something terrible had happened.

'Marcelline!' Ben came round the desk and helped her to a chair. Pearl poured her a glass of water from the carafe. Of cynical, wise Marcelline there was now no trace: her eyes were raw with hurt, and tears had runnelled her makeup.

She choked: 'Am I the first? Has anyone told you?'

Ben crouched and handed her the water. He put his hand gently up on her shoulder. 'What is it, Marcelline?'

'Your – your – ' she could not say her name.

Ben said: 'Take your time.'

'Your wife is dead.'

Ben looked at Pearl. 'Thank God!' he said, and was sorry for ever after. 'Oh no. Vane can't be – '

'Vane is dead!' sobbed Marcelline. Her teeth chattered on the glass.

Ben put his arm around Pearl. 'What happened?'

Marcelline had never quite lost her love for Vane, and now her features broke up with naked grief. 'She committed suicide last night. She threw herself from a third-floor balcony of the Mena House Hotel.'

'Who phoned you?'

'Miss Barker, the children's nanny.'

'Are the twins all right?'

'They know nothing about it. It's too horrible.'

'Was there a note?'

'The police say it was an accident. Poor, poor Vane!' Ben took Marcelline's empty glass, feeling her shaking hand. She looked at him. 'You had no idea?'

Ben shook his head.

'She never got over you,' Marcelline wept, 'she loved you still. You did truly love her once, didn't you, Ben?'

'Yes, I did.'

'She knew it too. In her heart of hearts she was trying to get back to you.'

'Tell me what happened, Marcelline.'

'She killed herself out of love. Love, that's the most dangerous force in the world, Ben, and in the end she took it seriously. She tried to be like you.'

Ben repeated: 'What exactly happened?'

'She fell in love with a man.' Marcelline's secret loathing broke through that last word like a horrid smell.

'Go on,' Ben said.

'We'll never know what happened. She was in his room. It was late. I'm sorry, Ben. An Australian, Peter Mackelroy.'

Ben said: 'Oh my God.'

'It was his balcony she jumped from.'

'Fell from,' Ben said.

'Fell if you believe the police. They just want to keep things quiet, the situation in Egypt has been rocky since the British forces withdrew to the Suez Canal Zone.' As the wife of a Member of Parliament Marcelline would know about such matters. 'They've let Mackelroy go. The maid confessed she'd let Vane use her master key to get into his room. There was no trace of any violence or any . . . lovemaking. So he's clear. The balance of her mind was disturbed, she simply chose the wrong door. Accidental death. But it wasn't, was it?'

'It doesn't sound as though Mackelroy was guilty of anything,' Pearl said.

'Men are always guilty somehow,' spat Marcelline.

'I blame myself,' Ben confessed. 'I lent Mackelroy a thousand pounds to get him home and set him up in business.'

'Then you are a murderous bastard,' Marcelline said.

'Love isn't a crime. I'm sorry Vane's dead,' Ben told them. 'I'm sorry for her and sorry for us. But life must go on.' He turned to Pearl. 'This is our opportunity.'

'Oh, Ben, you can't . . .' Pearl said.

Suddenly he strode across and pulled open the door. They followed him into the outer office. David, the manager, was looking at Ben with startled eyes, his mouth dropping. Alice Cypress was pushing herself back in her chair. Ben had slammed his fists on her desk.

'Get on the phone to Caxton Hall,' he was saying, 'I want to get married to Pearl, I want a special licence, I want everyone there, and I don't care what it costs. And I want it now.'

'Dear God,' Marcelline said, 'how can you?'

'Watch me,' Ben snarled at her.

Then he put his arms gently around Pearl. He looked tenderly into her eyes and when he spoke Pearl knew that this moment, this touch, this look, these words, were the truth. This real love.

'Darling,' he said, 'will you marry me?'

Hawk stood proudly in Caxton Street with the leaves from St James's Park blowing around him, waiting for the happy couple to come out. His pockets were full of confetti, which it was against the rules to throw. There was a notice forbidding it. But he was going to do it anyway.

Bert Simmonds was there too, in the crowd, looking as miserable as sin. David and Harriet Jones were holding up their little girl, Cathy, pointing at the steps from Caxton Hall: any moment now, they were saying – and Cathy had pockets full of confetti to throw too, Hawk knew, because he had given it to her.

Alice Cypress was chatting to the statuesque black figure of Natasha Cetawa, Pineapple's wife (though the studio said she was single), daughter of 'a real chieftain, Prince Cetawatunga of the Zulu nation', and that part of the publicity was at least based on truth, although he had lived comfortably in Oppidans Road in Hampstead for many years. Ben had a holding in London Film Productions and had got her the part in a Korda film.

Pineapple was standing by the Rolls, a wide smile on his face. The Nigerian chauffeur approved of marriage – he was very strict in such matters, and he enjoyed a wedding, even one that was so plainly late as this one was, with the bride eight months gone. 'Better late than never,' Pineapple grinned, matching Hawk's opinion exactly. Millionaires could do anything.

Hawk knew that the morality of ordinary people did not dominate millionaires in the same way. People said that Ben London was bust, but Hawk had always known that being the millionaire was about more than money. He got the most beautiful women, but not because he was rich. He demanded loyalty, he commanded respect, but not because he had lots of money. Hawk had never believed in love.

Ben kissed Pearl at the top of the steps. Flashbulbs popped, but they both remained relaxed and defiant of the murmurs of outrage, shouted dirty jokes, the nudges and winks of the crowd that had gathered behind their friends and guests – indeed, they seemed not to notice them. The only moment of tension came when a photographer knelt on the steps directly in front of Pearl, almost tripping her before scrambling out of the way. Pearl, dressed in blue-grey, clasped her hands over her stomach.

'Are you all right? Ben asked.

'Yes. Let's get in the car.' Rice showered down on them quite painfully hard, then flurries of brightly coloured confetti thrown by Hawk and little Cathy. Pineapple opened the car door and they climbed in.

'London's,' Ben said. The reception would be held in the ballroom at the hotel and they would meet everyone there.

The Rolls turned along Caxton Street into Buckingham Gate. It was full of people – some sort of demonstration or hunger march coming up from Victoria Street. The gleaming Rolls-Royce was a target for bumps and kicks, with angry faces pressing at the windows, then the crowd parted and the car pulled away. As they passed in front of Buckingham Palace, Pearl's face drew up. 'I think I've started,' she gasped. 'I won't be able to join you at the reception after all, Ben.'

'I won't leave you,' he said, then tapped on the glass. 'Drive straight to the hospital.'

'Please, you don't have to come.'

'Anytime my wife is going to have a baby,' Ben said, 'I am going to be there.'

In the magnificent ballroom Hawk was dancing with Alice Cypress. Beneath the glittering chandeliers the girls from the Post Room were giggling with the clerks from Dispatch. Peter Harrison the chief buyer was deep in conversation with Clifford Ford the accountant, about butterflies. Clifford's invalid wife Mary sat in her wheelchair on the edge of the dance floor, tapping her fingers to the music. Hawk had drunk three glasses of champagne, enough to take the edge off his shyness and ask the formidable Alice for her next dance too, and he had eaten a great deal of caviar. All this show proved the rumours about the millionaire were untrue, he reflected, because it had obviously cost him a fortune.

'You dance well – Alice,' said Hawk, greatly daring.

'Now you know my secret,' she said, 'I am a young flapper at heart.'

'One of those, eh,' said Hawk, towering over her, trying to match her tiny footsteps.

Smiling, she gazed up at him. 'You know, Mr Hawkins, you're really much nicer than they say.'

'We haven't heard from the hospital for hours,' said Hawk worriedly.

Alice did an astonishing imitation of Pearl's voice. 'Listen, Hawky, just concentrate on the champagne, huh!'

The orchestra went silent and everyone stopped dancing. They turned towards the platform. Then nobody moved in the whole room except the toastmaster who stepped up to the microphone.

He coughed and the system whined feedback.

Then he smiled.

'Mrs Pearl London has given birth to a perfect little baby girl. She weighs five pounds eleven ounces. Her name is Victoria.'

The frozen tableau of the dance floor broke up in loud applause.

CHAPTER FIFTEEN

1

Good King Wenceslas looked out, on the Feast of Stephen . . .

Vic looked at the children fondly. It was a scene as lovely as a Dickens Christmas card. Muffled in scarves and overcoats too big for them, the children were gathered around a glowing brazier outside the Workhouse singing carols, apple-cheeked and innocent with their round mouths and upturned eyes.

. . . When the snow lay round about, deep and crisp and even.

This street-snow had already melted to slush in the sun. One toddler too young to sing, reaching up almost on tiptoe to hold his sister's hand, was dressed in a poncho made out of a horseblanket, and his clogs were so big that they fitted his little feet like boats. Vic tousled his hair and called him a scamp.

He stared up at the black walls of the Workhouse running with melt, then dropped a few pennies in the hat, still staring at the Workhouse vast and dark against the sky, all in shadow. The Poor Law was being swept away and Nigel was full of shiny talk about the bright and fair world just around the corner, where the Local Authorities would look after everyone, and no one would suffer . . . Vic knew the world would always be dark, even on the sunny days like this one, dark and unfair and full of suffering. Nothing could bring back the smile to his little brother Jimmy's drowned face. Nothing would ever put Ben London back in the Workhouse where he belonged . . . could ever close the Pandora's Box that Ria had opened with her feminine wiles when she helped him escape from there.

Damn him! . . . and damn Ria.

Vic hurried past the Workhouse.

He found Rixby the bookie in the same old place, the courtyard off Poplar High Street, taking bets from runners under the steps. Though still profitable it was a primitive system, with small bets and enormous volume making for a lot of work, but Bill Rixby was too old to change. Vic sat in a last angle of sunlight – clouds were looming above the rooftops, heavy with the promise of snow – watching the old man work. Rixby kept looking at him nervously; he was guilty.

'No hurry,' smiled Vic, 'I'll wait until you're finished.' The sun went out. Vic sat surrounded by shadows in the darkening courtyard.

He had come here often as a child. You could bet on anything with dear old Mr Rixby – though he would rook you if he could – horses, cockfights, badgerbaits, the price of hay come Michaelmas. Many children had been terrified of him because of the fine white web of scars that twisted across his wrinkled face beneath his thin beard, and made smooth scores across the palms of his hands, a razor-slashing from many years ago.

When Rixby had totalled up he came and sat beside Vic on the bench. Vic told the lookout to buzz off and when they were alone, he turned to the old man.

'Why are you insulting me?' he asked, in a friendly voice, giving him the opportunity to explain.

'Never, Vic,' whispered Rixby. He began to shake.

'What have you got on Nigel, you dry old stick?' Vic demanded.

Rixby shook his head. 'I swear it!' Their voices echoed.

'You watch you don't cut yourself shaving,' Vic warned amiably. 'Great big lies like that, you've got to be very, very careful.' Rixby dreaded razors, and he curled his hands up like claws, then sat huddling them in his lap. 'One hundred pounds every four weeks, I seen it in black and white,' Vic accused. 'You rook me of a penny or two here or there, Bill, I know it, I don't mind. But this is a very big insult and I will have your skin.'

He waited.

'He promised you'd never find out,' Rixby complained in a high voice.

So it was true. Vic dug down in his pockets to restrain himself from lashing out with the blades he held hidden in his fists. 'Tell me,' he said calmly, 'tell me before I carve you like a chicken and you make your wife and children scream, tell me.' His voice rose.

'I don't know it all,' confessed Rixby desperately.

'I don't want to know it all,' Vic said simply. 'Tell me.'

'Nigel pays me a small commission to cover him. He said there was no risk.'

Vic smiled encouragingly.

'Ray Trott has something on him,' Rixby said. He continued speaking.

Vic felt as though he was floating. He heard almost nothing, he was all a rage of emotion. Nigel was a traitor.

Worse, he was a *weak* traitor: he had paid.

He had not trusted Vic to help him.

Vic squeezed his eyes shut: he could hardly bear the shame he felt. 'I would have done anything for you, Nigel,' he groaned.

Rixby prattled on.

Once before Vic had been so enraged. Instead of Rixby's voice, he heard Ria begging for Ben London's life. Vic had struck her with his fist, his sister who he loved more than anyone else in the world, struck her down mad with envy.

But then too there had been this calm in Vic, this floating calm which enabled him to remain a calm and rational person, and when Ria had made her unforgivable threat, *we'll all tell on you and you'll go to prison and you'll rot!* she had intimidated Vic, she had stayed his hand.

By letting Vic keep her, she had saved Ben London's life.

'Don't!' Rixby screamed. 'Don't slash me!' Vic stared at the cut-throat razor in his hand, then slipped it back in his pocket. This was not a disciplinary matter. It was much worse than that.

Vic said: 'My own brother-in-law is blackmailing my brother?'

For his arrogance and ingratitude, Ray Trott must die.

'No one dared tell you, Vic,' Rixby snivelled. 'Ray has been bragging about it to his friends.' Vic knew the sort of friends Ray had. 'Something important only to Nigel. The War, a long time ago. Cowardice, a Blighty wound, I don't know.'

'But everyone knows Nigel!' Vic howled. 'What man could be more of a coward than Nigel?' No one could be braver than Vic; he remembered Nigel's terrified face peering through the car window while Ted Trott battered at the glass.

'He is what he is because of me,' Vic said dully. Nigel's failure was his own.

'Mr Ben London?' asked the man in the fine mohair overcoat. Ben noticed the shoulders speckled with white. So it was already snowing outside.

'Yes, I'm Ben London,' Ben said.

'I have something for you, sir.' Smiling, the man pressed a piece of paper into Ben's hand. 'Thank you, sir.' He turned and disappeared in the store.

Ben unfolded the paper. He had been served with a Summons to appear at Bow Street magistrates in respect of claims for monies due. Ben went into his office and laid it carefully on his desk beside the stack of bills.

So the first crack had appeared. Soon, very soon now as the word flashed around, this trickle would become a flood that would sweep them all away.

He went over and closed the door, returned to his desk, and dropped his head in his hands.

What will you do to win?

Pearl was happy. She was so happy she hardly dared to believe it. She sat on the Art-Deco sofa with the cushions piled behind her back, looking down at her baby sucking on her breast. Victoria was so beautiful, so *hers*, that it seemed almost a sadness to Pearl that she should have such luck to know such love, such a joy of giving: distantly she was aware of all the unhappiness in the world, a Spanish revolution, the class genocide of the Russian Kulaks, the airship fires and the business suicides, but it seemed to have nothing to do with her. All her being, all her feeling, was concentrated on her baby. Only Victoria's lips suckling her nipple were important. Only Victoria's striking blue eyes, so like her father's, gazing up adoringly into her mother's face, making Pearl smile, seemed to matter. Victoria clenched her tiny fists and reflected Pearl's smile gorgeously.

It was already dusk outside; these English winter days were so short. Pearl picked up the phone to speak to Ben, hoping he'd finish work soon and come up so that she could share Victoria with him.

'I'm afraid he's gone out,' Alice Cypress said.

'Where?' He hadn't told Pearl he was going out. He always told her. 'Where's he gone, do you know?'

Alice sounded worried. 'About ten minutes ago he just put on his hat and coat, and said he was going out for a walk.'

Pearl glanced at the window. Cold fingers closed over her heart.

'But it's snowing,' she said, then put down the receiver, staring. She had been obsessed with Victoria – had she been cutting Ben out? Had she missed something in him that as the wife he loved she ought to have seen?

Holding her baby at her breast, Pearl stared out at the falling snow.

'Where are you going?' Ria asked.

'Out,' Ray said. He shrugged on the new leather trench-coat with very wide lapels over his dinner suit and turned up the collar. 'Just out,' he said when she didn't back down.

'Are you meeting anyone?'

He chucked her chin, laughing at the opal fire that sparked in her eyes. 'Jealous, my love?'

'It's horrid weather,' Ria said. She selected a filter-tip

from the gold cigarette box and held it in two fingers for Ray to light. She liked looking at him, he was so impossibly handsome – if anything more so for the small bar-fight scar now running from his mouth. She still liked to be seen on his arm.

But he tossed her his gold lighter. 'We're a good team, Ria.'

She lit the cigarette herself, glancing at him through the flame.

'I respect you,' he said. 'I didn't mean that lousy password.' *I've slept with Ria.* 'The funny thing is,' he said, 'no one has, have they? The perfect protective coloration for you.'

'You're too bright, Ray.'

'You are my star,' he said suddenly, then gave his scarred, crooked smile. 'I'm glad I married you.'

'We could have been worse,' Ria admitted. She led a busy and contented life and Ray was a better and more considerate husband than many girls had. She was never left short of money, and he never forgot their anniversaries or her birthday. And she had Will to think of and send doting parcels to on the *Mercury*, and holidays with him. Yes, her life could be much, much worse.

'Everything's for the best,' winked Ray cheerfully.

No, it wasn't, Ria knew.

From the window she watched him walk out into the snow along the Strand, then looked down at her hand. He'd forgotten his cigarette lighter.

Tom was cooing at the lovebirds when Nigel popped in to say good night to Terry, but he was already asleep. Esther looked up from the *Radio Times*. 'What is it, darling?' Snowflakes the size of sixpences covered his hat and shoulders.

'Business,' Nigel said. 'Got to go out.'

'Not on a night like this,' Esther said. She patted the arm of her chair. 'You sit here beside me, darling, and we'll hear the weather forecast together.'

'I can see what the bloody weather's like,' Nigel said, showing her his hat.

'It's so nice to have you at home for once,' Esther said tearfully, squeezing his hand. Nigel didn't have the heart to tell her that his home was the Old Bull and Bush now, so just this once, he explained.

'Vic wants to see me.'

'It's unlike my Vic to be so inconsiderate,' Esther said. Perhaps it was another bag of money. She trembled.

'Oh, let the boy go, he's making a draught,' Tom said. Lovebirds were very sensitive to draughts. Nigel escaped gratefully.

Tom said to Esther: 'I reckon he's got a girl!'

Esther's face lit up. That was a wonderful idea. She spent all the rest of the evening dreaming up plans, wondering who it could be.

Ben walked down St James's Street, his footsteps muffled in the white. Each street light carried a dense curtain of falling snow within its circle of illumination. Lights were on in Stafford House, then a man in London County Council overalls came out winding up his tape measure. Ben went up the drive.

'What are you doing?'

'It's being re-rated,' the official said, putting his gear into the back of his van. 'Valuation department,' he explained, opening the driver's door and stamping the snow off his feet.

'Must cost a fortune,' Ben said.

'That's why County Hall are getting rid of it,' the man laughed, starting the engine. 'You can buy it for nothing, but the rates are ten thousand a year, and then there's the upkeep. Good night!'

'Good night,' Ben said. Melting snow trickled down his back and his feet were numb. He stamped them, staring up at the house. The windows were now dark and snow draped the crumbling pediments. This great edifice too was falling down.

★

Driving with his right hand, Nigel swished the handle for the windscreen wiper from side to side to clear the snow. His progress along West Ferry Road into Limehouse was strangely silent, the falling flakes seeming to absorb all sound. The engine started to overheat so he got out and cleared the radiator, then started again and turned down Narrow Street, wrestling with the steering wheel among the warren of turnings. Smoke and snow swirled between the grimy slum walls around the warehouses. This area was not meant to be approached from the land: the warehouses were all served by the river.

The car bumped across a drawbridge. Nigel glimpsed Regent's Canal Dock on his right, and the dark waste of the river on his left, then the walls closed around him again. Vic owned everything round here, the warehouses and the people who worked in them, but not a soul showed on a night like this.

Nigel inched the car into an alleyway and turned off the headlights and the engine. In the sudden darkness and silence he heard the chilling slosh of water below. The Ratcliff warehouse was built out on pilings over the river.

He squeezed out between the car and the wall, found the private door, and went inside. Vic maintained a small flat above here for times of trouble, comfortably furnished and warm, but Nigel had never liked it. It was Vic's place. He crossed the dark space, smelling wet hemp rope and navigating between the crates by feel, then went up the stairs. Vic opened the door at the top.

'I know about Ray Trott,' he said.

'I'm sorry, Vic,' Nigel said.

Vic wrapped his arms around Nigel, embracing him. The firelight showed tears in his eyes. 'You're my brother,' he said. 'Come on. Come on in, Ray's coming. I told him to be here at seven.'

Nigel threw himself in an armchair and covered his face, then looked at his hands and said: 'What are you going to do?'

'I'm going to send him away,' Vic said.

Nigel shuddered. 'But he's married to Ria!'

251

'I married them,' Vic said.

The brothers waited. This time, Nigel knew what was going to happen.

They heard footsteps on the stairs. Vic glanced at his wristwatch. 'Right on time!' he said, snapping his fingers as the knock came on the door. 'Good old Ray.'

'Vic, don't,' Nigel begged. He closed his eyes.

Vic opened the door and spoke in a smiling voice. 'Good to see you, Ray.'

Ray came inside. 'What, having a nap, Nigel, darling?'

Nigel looked at him. Ray laughed and shook the snow off his collar.

'You've been blackmailing my brother for years,' Vic grinned, closing the door.

Ray was unabashed. 'Do you know what he did?'

Nigel cringed, but Vic was amused. 'I don't care, Ray. He's my brother.'

Ray slapped the snow off his hat. 'Well, I'm sorry you found out about it, Vic.' He sat down on the arm of Nigel's chair, put a cigarette in his mouth.

Vic lit it for him. 'It's got to stop, Ray,' he said.

Nigel said: 'Vic, please.'

'Fair enough,' Ray said.

Vic said: 'It's always been a bit too easy for you, hasn't it?'

Ray blew smoke. 'What does that mean?'

'You know. Easy.'

'I have never laid a finger on Ria, I promise you.'

'I know.'

'That's all that matters, isn't it?'

'Yes. That's all that matters.' Vic picked up the poker. Ray looked at it, then into Vic's eyes, unafraid.

Vic stoked the fire, the rising flames sending shadows flying around the room.

Nigel said: 'Vic, please. It was all my fault. I – '

'Don't tell me,' Vic said, 'I don't want to know.' He held up the poker.

'I'm not frightened of you, Vic,' Ray Trott said.

Vic laughed and replaced the poker in the pretty rack

along with the smart brass fireplace brush and the elegant tongs. He put his hand on Ray's shoulder. 'I know you aren't, Ray,' he said, 'but you should be.' He seized Ria's husband with terrible strength and Nigel cringed, hearing the bones crunch in Ray's neck. Nigel crouched with his forehead on the fireside rug, his hands over his ears, his eyes clamped shut, feeling the awful thunder of Ray's heels vibrate the floor.

Then there was only the crackling of the fire.

Vic took another minute to make sure, then stood up. He was holding a garotte of electric wire in his hands. He'd cut it off the Hoover, Nigel could see the writing stamped on the cord, round and round and round.

Nigel said: 'You killed Alan Stark, didn't you.'

'Yes,' Vic said, popping the cord back in his pocket.

'Where is he?'

'Same place this one's going,' Vic said, kicking the fancy leather trenchcoat.

Nigel stood up. 'This is the last time, Vic. I'm not doing it any more.'

'You are implicated too deep ever to save yourself,' Vic said economically. 'Remember Blumenthall. Remember Ted.' He lifted the leather arms and Ray's head flopped forward. Vic held him up with effortless strength. 'You know the ropes. Come on Nigel, turn round.' Nigel groaned, but he turned.

Vic slung the dead man's arms around Nigel's neck, and Nigel pulled up his hands under Ray's knees and piggybacked him obediently downstairs. Vic's hand led him through the dark, then they stopped and Nigel heard a trapdoor opening. A faint light showed from below. They went down wooden steps to a weedy platform below the warehouse, and more steps led down into the water. Vic shone a torch on a rowing boat moored to a ring, its bow high and stern weighted down low. The water made the same sloshing noises Nigel had noticed earlier, but much louder down here, and the wet stank.

Vic pulled the boat up. 'Drop him in there.' Nigel released the knees and Vic let the body flop down between the boards. There was a big block of masonry in the stern that must weigh a hundred pounds or more, a length of slimy chain attached to it. Obviously it had been used to weight a mooring buoy. Vic wound the chain around Ray's legs and neck.

'Get rowing,' he told Nigel, holding out an oar. The rowing boat wobbled under Nigel, then he sat down. On the river, the snow fell on them in a steady dark curtain. Only between the lights of the shore did it float like white streamers. The water and the sky were black.

The rowlocks squeaked as Nigel rowed. It was almost slack high water and nothing seemed to move, but soon the lights glimmering ahead of them were the same brightness as the lights behind. 'The river's fifty feet deep here, sailor,' Vic murmured. 'Does that boy Will ever write to you?'

'No,' admitted Nigel, glad of the distraction. 'Not since I – ' But his meeting with Ben London at White's Club was another secret. Nigel's good turn had alienated him from Will in ways he did not understand, and Will never wrote now.

'Stop rowing,' Vic said. 'Did you kiss Terry good night?'

'We don't kiss,' Nigel said. He would have to drop Ray's body in the river.

Vic wrapped Ray's arms around his brother's neck. 'Last time,' he said.

'Promise?'

'I promise,' Vic said. Vic always kept his promises.

'I'm sorry I let Arleen come between us,' Nigel said. 'You've never had a woman love you, Vic. I loved her.'

'I know what it's like,' Vic shivered.

'Do you, Vic? Do you, really?'

'Yes,' Vic swore. 'Yes!'

The two brothers stared at one another in the dark, Ray's head propped on Nigel's shoulder over his wrapped arms like some grotesque child being given a ride. 'Let's get it over with,' Vic said. He dragged the masonry block out of the bottom of the boat. For a moment he balanced it on the gunwale. Then he pushed it over. The chain snapped taut. Ray jerked, then dragged Nigel pell-mell backwards over the side of the boat in his stiff, dead arms.

Tears poured down Vic's flat cheeks and sobs of grief broke from his throat. The rowing boat rotated in the centre of the river, streamers of light from the distant shores slowly circling Vic as he wept his heart out. He was ashamed – deeply ashamed of Nigel. Nigel had not trusted him; that was what hurt. He had not trusted Vic to help him until finally Vic could do nothing for him however much he loved him.

And Nigel had known that.

Vic touched the splintered scores in the gunwale where Nigel's scrabbling nails had ripped the wood. Even as Ray's deadly embrace dragged him down into the depths, Nigel had gasped his last breath from Vic's mouth. Even as his face bubbled down under the black water, dwindling and shrinking, he had not taken his eyes off Vic's.

It was not forgiveness, but it was understanding.

Vic understood.

2

Ben strode along Cable Street into the East End, his collar up, his hands thrust deep in his pockets. It was the walk of a determined man, a man who knew what he had to do to win, and he looked neither to the right nor the left. It was very late, and the snow fell in curtains around him, draping his head and shoulders, covering his shoes.

He had taken the Underground to Mark Lane and come out by the Tower. Everything was silent under the snow, there was no traffic, even the trams were in the depot, it might have been a dead city. Ben knew this area well. He had not been here for many years, but he would never forget it.

On his right – he did not look – were the steps where

Ria had taken him down and ended everything that he had known before, and begun everything that was to come, by giving herself with her act of love, and taking him. He had fallen.

Below those steps, hidden by the tide, was the weedy platform where Vic had come to take his revenge.

Die; or live. Ben had chosen life.

That was not one choice but many. It had brought him here tonight.

About halfway along Cable Street a pair of tyre tracks turned in from the right, coming up from Ratcliff and the river. He walked in them down the middle of the road. The Old Bull and Bush, Vic's pub, seemed to stand alone ahead of him, almost on its own island, its lighted windows gleaming through the snow. The tyre tracks ended at Nigel's white tourer. The engine still ticked, cooling.

Ben pushed open the pub door and went inside.

It was hot. Vic was sitting at the bar, his feet propped on the brass rail. Physically he had hardly changed – Vic had been born old – but his presence was more powerful. Ben remembered that he rarely drank much alcohol, but now there was a tumbler of rum at Vic's elbow on the counter. He sat with his back to Ben, staring at him in the mirror above the bar.

There was no one else there.

The fire crackled.

Ben stood beside Vic. Then Vic turned towards him, smiling, plenty of colour in his cheeks.

'Going to hit me again, Ben?'

Ben didn't answer.

'I am never going to let you go,' Vic said. He waited.

Then he went behind the bar, poured Ben a glass of rum, came back. Ben drank it down.

'I have an offer you can't resist,' Ben said. He smiled.

'What,' Vic said flatly.

'I want you to give' – *give* was the word Ben used – 'give me a quarter of a million pounds.'

Vic nodded. 'My parliamentary friend Henry Stoughton told me back in the summer that you'd have difficulties.'

'Never mind what Henry Stoughton says. Or Marcelline. Give.'

'You know what you're getting yourself into,' Vic said. Suddenly he shivered, then looked at Ben, wanting to be sure.

'I know,' Ben said. They were closer than brothers.

'Round here they call me Mister Forty-eight per cent,' Vic admitted. 'More than that's usury, see. Got to keep a reputation for being law-abiding.'

'Don't justify yourself to me.'

'Of course I charge more than that to housewives, a few quid here and there for food and coal until Friday. Draws their men into the net.'

Ben almost laughed, and Vic flushed. 'Shut up,' Vic said, then, in an enraged voice, 'God damn you, how do you do it?'

'I'll pay you commercial money market rates.'

'Double that,' Vic said. 'And I want the Emporium. You owe me that.'

'It's in trust to Ralph and George for when they come of age.'

'There's five or ten per cent of shares in other hands.'

Ben frowned. 'But – '

'I want five per cent, or no deal,' Vic grinned. 'I mean it. I'm going to keep my eye on you.'

'You never give up,' Ben said.

'Did you really kill her somehow, poor Vane?' Vic asked eagerly.

'Why do you always think I'm like you? Stand up for yourself, Vic.'

'I'll never forgive you.' Vic was like a dinosaur in a tar bog, and the more he struggled, the more it dragged him down. But there was something new in Vic's black eyes that Ben glimpsed tonight . . . as if Vic was gradually casting himself adrift . . . a truthfulness that had not been there before.

Ben said: 'Do we have a deal?'

Vic nodded. They didn't shake hands. The deal was done. Ben knew that a banker's draft would be on his desk come Monday morning whatever Vic had to do to get it, beg, borrow, steal, it would be there.

Ben went to leave. You could always trust Vic.

'You'll pay for it, believe me,' Vic called after him. Nothing was given for nothing.

Ben looked back from the door. He turned up his collar. 'That I know.'

Pulling on his gloves, he went outside into the snow. Suddenly the door was dragged open behind him. The red firelight swam over Vic's angry face.

'You could have had anything,' he shouted furiously after Ben. 'Why only a quarter of a million?'

The car engine ticked. Snowflakes hissed on the street light that cast its gassy blue glare across the alleyway.

Ben turned. He had won.

He said: 'Because you aren't a millionaire, Vic, and you never will be. All you'll ever have is a million pounds, or ten million pounds, but you won't be the millionaire. Ever.'

Vic stared into the snow after him long after Ben was gone.

'Damn you, Workhouse bastard,' he whispered, 'why won't you leave me alone?'

PART III

CANDLES IN THE WIND

CHAPTER SIXTEEN

The *Daily Herald*, as usual, did Ben proud.

MILLIONAIRE BUYS STAFFORD HOUSE
RENAMES LONDON'S GRANDEST MANSION
LONDON HOUSE
Vows to Spend Vast Sums on Refurbishment

'I have come from my house,' Queen Victoria once told the Sutherlands, who then lived there, 'to your palace.' This was true – and Ben remembered that Buckingham Palace had looked considerably more ornate in those days before the War. As the London Museum, his house had become sadly run down. The entrance hall echoed, deserted. Rooms off the corridor to the left had until recently displayed relics of prehistoric London, the milk tooth of a mammoth found in Pall Mall, the jaw of a rhino dug up under the Old Bailey. Boars had been hunted in this neighbourhood until five hundred years ago. The post-chaise used by Wellington at Waterloo was kept in the basement, and in the Children's Room were dolls' houses and other toys used by members of the royal family. On the right of the entrance hall was the old Roman boat found twenty years ago during the excavations for County Hall. All gone now; and the gutted interior needed the stamp of a personality on it.

It needed to be lived in.

First thing after Christmas Ben had gone to the London County Council offices at County Hall and negotiated the sale. There were several other bidders, including a St James's Club, but Ben clinched the sale by promising to refurbish the property 'concomitant to its situation'; between Buckingham and St James's Palace was a poor place for the eyesore London House had become.

'It's going to cost us a fortune,' Pearl had gasped, entranced, when he told her that he had bought her a proper house and they would no longer have to live in the apartment. She looked through the railings, holding up Victoria. 'What do you think of it, baby? Lots of room to play. And a lovely garden! Oh, Ben, can this really come true?'

'We'll exchange contracts in a month or two. We'll be moving in by spring.'

'It's like a wonderful dream,' Pearl said. 'How did you pay for it, Ben?'

He looked away. 'Don't spoil it,' he said.

'I'm so happy.' She held his hand. 'I'm over the moon, you're such a success now, darling. You've got everything you wanted. Everything's come right for us.'

'Your happiness is all that matters to me,' Ben London said.

The plane trees lining the Mall were showing green buds, and St James's Park was speckled with the cheerful yellow heads of early daffodils, when Ben and Pearl walked hand in hand along the Mall towards their new house. The contracts would be completed at noon, and it was now ten minutes to twelve.

As they reached the railings, the church bells began to chime midday, and Ben recognized the fast tolling of St James's Church from the direction of the Emporium, St Martin-in-the-Fields slower and more distant. The title to London House was now legally theirs: from this moment they were the new owners. The caretaker swung open the gates, saluting – he was an ex-RSM – and they walked up the drive.

Ben pushed open the door then turned to Pearl with a smile. 'Must do this properly,' he said. Pearl giggled as he picked her up. Then with everyone watching he kissed her and she looked seriously into his eyes.

He carried Pearl London across the threshold.

A whistle blew and a flood of workmen with ladders followed them in, bricklayers, plasterers, joiners, and soon the rooms echoed to the busy noise of hammering that

Ben and Pearl would come to know so well during the next six months. It was not until evening that she was able to walk around alone.

Pearl already loved her house. Most of the family rooms were downstairs. They were smaller and would take modern decoration well – this crumbling Louis XV style seemed overpoweringly ornate. Pearl dusted her hands and planned.

She was determined to have her own kitchen put in with an up-to-the-minute, clean electric cooker and fridge. This room was fine: she would have a counter put out to make a breakfast area. She walked through into what would be her private lounge. This expansive room would simply have to be Art Deco, with low comfortable sofas for the lovely corner view across St James's Park, and to the right the broader expanse of Green Park where the sun was setting.

She went upstairs and found Ben. These big rooms would be used for entertaining, and they would be redecorated keeping the Louis style, whose sumptuousness matched their scale perfectly. Ben wanted to sleep upstairs – ever since the Workhouse he disliked sleeping on ground floors – and there was a spacious room that would catch the dawn light. 'I want a huge four-poster!' Pearl chanted, then peered into yet another dressing room. 'Aren't there any ladies' rooms up here?'

'In those days they used the windows,' Ben said.

'I insist on en-suite bathrooms,' said Pearl firmly.

'Look what I found.' Ben took her hand and led her past the long gallery into a room with a breathtaking view. 'This is my office.' Skirting ladders and buckets, they looked from the window, and Pearl gasped. The view was a green panorama of the centre of the city, Buckingham House and a corner of the palace gardens on the right, the many varieties of trees casting long shadows towards them past the tennis courts. Beyond St James's Park the gothic rooflines of Westminster glowed in the amber light; to the left the steel helmets of the Household Cavalry drilling on Horseguards Parade glittered in reflection of the setting sun. A flight of duck wheeled over the lake. It was an idyllic scene.

'I love you,' Pearl said.

Ben joked: 'You just like a man who treats you right.'

'I love you,' Pearl said simply. 'I want a family with you here.'

Ria had cried for her husband, of course she did. Although she had not loved him, she had grown used to Ray and even to like him: his defiance, his wit, his nerve. Ray had used her as camouflage, but she did not mind. He had protected her from Vic, and now he was gone, and she cried for him.

Officially he was a missing person, but Ria knew that he was dead. She lit a cigarette from the gold lighter he had forgotten on the night of his death. Wherever he had gone that night, it had been with an easy mind. Vic, who had been drinking at the Old Bull and Bush with Spike, suspected a gangland killing. Nigel had disappeared at the same time, and that made it an affair of honour for Vic, and Ria knew that he would not rest until he found his brother dead or alive.

Ria prayed that Ray was not implicated in Nigel's disappearance.

Nigel's death.

Ria felt such guilt and remorse about her brother that she did not know how to bear it. She had been so hateful to Nigel – even as children, she had used her tongue like a weapon, humiliating him because . . . because he was not Vic. Nigel was a soft target for her frustrations, and now she hated herself for hurting him: she had never told him that she loved him or anything good about himself, she had never thanked him for the way he had looked after Will, or for going to see Ben, the ultimate nerveracking experience for Nigel. Now Ria felt awful about all the cruel words she had said, and all the kind ones she had not.

She stared at the smoke spiralling into her eyes. She would have to shut up Trott's for a few days and return home to the Isle of Dogs. Mum would be mad with grief, and in times of trouble, a family's place was together.

Esther was devastated by Nigel's disappearance. The worst thing was not having a body to weep over, a display of mourning to comfort her, the ghastly relief of *knowing*. She sat in her armchair wondering if Nigel was dead. He was. (That bag stuffed with money.) He was not – he had disappeared for days after Arleen died, that was why he never seemed able to get on with Terry, the reason Terry was closer to Vic . . . had disappeared that time, and come back.

Yes, perhaps Nigel would come back again, and that was what she had said to Vic yesterday. 'You never know, Mum,' Vic had replied, embracing her with tears in his eyes, 'you just have to live in hope.'

Her face buried in his comforting shoulder, Esther nodded. That was all any of them could do.

'But the last thing he said was that he was coming to see you,' she said. 'Those were his last words. *Vic wants to see me.*'

'Don't say that, Mum.' Vic was in a terrible state. 'You make me feel awful.'

'I'm sorry, darling.'

'He never arrived,' Vic said.

'His last thoughts were of you,' Esther whimpered. 'Oh, Vic, try and find him.'

'I've driven up and down the streets,' Vic said distractedly. 'Mum – I don't know how to tell you this – I think it was Rixby. The police are questioning that dry old stick now and he doesn't have an alibi for the night Nigel disappeared.' In the morning Nigel's white tourer had been found parked in a sidestreet near Rixby's place. 'I think he'll confess,' Vic promised.

That was yesterday. Esther had not slept all night. Now she sat in her armchair, devastated by grief and exhaustion. Ria had phoned – they had a phone now because of Tom's heart condition – and said that she would be over this afternoon, and Esther did not know if she could face the fierce vivacity of her daughter. Then she heard the smooth sound of Vic's Daimler. She looked through the net curtains and saw Vic getting out. He looked uneasily at her window. Esther closed her eyes.

She heard Vic come in behind her.

'They found him in the river,' he said.

'Fetch my hat and coat,' Esther said.

Vic parked the Daimler near the Branch Road mortuary in Stepney where Nigel's body lay. Esther plodded implacably along the pavement. This was her other side: only Ria understood Mum in this mood. Vic walked with her silently.

'Sorry about this, Vic,' Inspector Jarvis said. 'Mrs Price, Vic can identify – '

'Where is he?' Esther demanded flatly.

'I don't think – '

'I will see my son,' Esther said.

Jarvis glanced at Vic, led them into the identification room. Something lay on a white porcelain slab. The pathologist lifted the blanket concealing the face.

Esther looked down. 'Yes, he's Nigel.' She brushed a lock of hair out of his eye with her fist, hard and caring.

'How can you?' Vic gagged.

She stared at him. Then she bent down and kissed the icy lips.

'Take me home now,' she said.

Esther sat in her armchair staring motionlessly at the photographs of the royal family. She was alone. Twenty years ago half the street would have been round with condolences, but all that was changed. Death was a secret, a burden to be borne alone. Even funerals were slipped through with the minimum of fuss. Tom was sitting quietly upstairs; he only had Vic left now. Esther sat without twisting at the handkerchief in her lap or drinking her tea. She thought of that street party when they had welcomed Nigel home from the war, but she couldn't really remember it, just the happy crowd like a huge family together, and her crying for joy. Now Esther sat with her face set like stone.

The door opened without knocking and Ria stood there holding a suitcase, her face tragic. 'I've come back, Mum.'

'Tea's in the pot,' Esther said flatly. 'I went and saw him. Nigel's dead.'

Ria dropped her case and flew over, her golden hair wild, her opal eyes brilliant with tears, and flung her arms around Mum. Esther sat without moving, then a tear wound down her own face. She patted Ria's hair.

'You were always the most difficult of my children, Ria, my girl,' she said.

'Oh, Mum!' sobbed Ria. She gave herself up and radiated her grief in a way no boy ever did, not even Vic. Esther patted her daughter's head in her lap. That genuineness tore at Esther because she did not deserve it. *Oh, Mum.* Esther tried to press her eyes shut to hold back her tears.

'Nigel used to say that – *oh, Mum.* He was a Mum's boy, always was. He would never have moved away but for Arleen. He never loved another girl.'

Ria stroked Esther's face softly. Suddenly the memories tumbled out of Esther so fast that she hardly knew what she said, crying her eyes out. . . . Then she realized that her tea was cold, and that Ria was squeezed beside her in the armchair, warm and comforting, her gentle eyes glowing. Esther had never seen her daughter like that before. 'I've worn this handkerchief out,' Esther said, feeling closer to Ria than she ever had. 'Listen, girl, we're going to give Nigel the best funeral the Isle of Dogs ever saw!'

Ria smiled.

Vic insisted on cremation. Such a show made it a strange, unfashionable affair. The long black cortège wound through the narrow streets under pelting rain. The horses' plumes hung down, and the raindrops rattled on the mahogany coffin and dripped from the silver fittings. The band played sombrely, and people looked from behind their windows to see the family pass, walking behind the carriage, Esther weeping loudly. Vic wore a top hat and held Terry's hand. They were all dressed in plain black, except Ria, who couldn't resist an opal brooch to stop it getting too gloomy. Behind them followed mourners carrying umbrellas, everyone Esther could think of to ask. As they approached the crematorium a boy of about sixteen dressed in a sailor's blues came dashing up behind them. Ria glanced back out of the corner of her eye, then stared. It was Will. He looked awful.

'I just got your letter this morning,' he panted, sweeping the cap embroidered TS *Mercury* off his head, wiping his hands over his drenched hair, then putting it back on. 'I had to come. Nigel was my friend.'

As though a light had been turned on, Ria realized that Nigel had made more of a success of his life than they knew. She asked out of the corner of her mouth: 'Did they grant you compassionate leave?'

'Compassion?' whispered Will, but there was a jeering look in his eye. 'That lot don't know what compassion is. I ran away.'

'Bloody hell,' Ria said.

'They won't take me back,' Will said defiantly. 'They expel you if you run off, it's the worst thing you can do.' He tried to explain. 'I want to be like Nigel if only he'd had the chance. He gave me a chance. I want to use my brain. I want to go to university.'

They filed into the crematorium chapel. Between hymns Ria hissed: 'You can't, you have to read books and everything.'

'I can do it and it's worth doing,' Will said, and Ria saw a flash of his father's determination in Will's deep eyes. Then he looked at her uncertainly. 'Am I doing right?' In the silence the curtains closed behind Nigel's coffin.

'I'm frightened for you, darling.' Ben would never have asked such a question in such a way. She squeezed his hand impulsively as they filed out and Nigel's body began to burn. Ria lifted her veil. 'You do whatever you decide, Will, but do it a hundred per cent.'

'Do you think he would have approved?' Will asked, glancing back.

'Approved?' Ria said. 'I can't think of anything that could have made Nigel prouder.'

His ashes were to be buried beneath a tablet of remembrance next to Arleen at St Luke's. Vic held Ria's hand. 'Rixby confessed everything,' he confided. 'He's been blackmailing Nigel for years and Nigel couldn't live with the shame any longer. He told Rixby he was going to the police. Rixby panicked. He says he didn't mean to kill him, mitigating circumstances and all that. He'll plead guilty to manslaughter.'

'But it doesn't sound like Rixby,' Ria said.

'Who knows,' Vic said, 'the secrets in a man's heart?'

And for some reason, as he said that, Ria was looking at Esther, and Esther looked away. She was hiding something from her daughter.

And Ria suddenly understood that Mum always had been hiding something: mother and daughter were both mixtures of openness and concealment, alike in more ways than they wanted. Always that closeness, always that distance between them. Ria knew all about secrets, knew all about hiding and withholding herself – and so did Mum. That was a bitter hurt to Ria.

Back home, Ria sat at the kitchen table with Esther. Tom was in the front room listening to the wireless. He had developed a surprising fondness for classical music since his heart stopped him gardening. Ria closed the door with her foot. 'I won't stay. I'm going back to the nightclub,' she said, expecting Esther to fight it.

'It's all for the best,' Esther said. Nigel's death had changed something.

'Will's coming with me,' Ria said, watching Mum, 'he'll do his studying there.'

Esther nodded wearily, not fighting it. She was alone now, except for Tom. 'I'm getting what I deserve, I suppose.'

Ria said: 'Mum, is there something you want to tell me?'

'Not until the day I die,' Esther said. She stirred sugar into her tea.

'Is it about Vic?'

Esther stirred in another spoonful. Her eyes wandered longingly to the cupboard under the sink.

'Vic loves you,' she said. 'God help me, he's loved you all his life, before he could walk, before he could talk. And now Nigel's dead.' Her chair squealed sharply as she pushed it back. Esther plodded over to the sink, pulled out the bottle in the brown paper bag, and filled a tumbler with gin.

'Go away, Ria,' she said. 'Get away from us. Leave this house.'

Ben knew, against common sense, that there is no better time than a Depression to make money.

He took advantage of that strange peculiarity of human nature: that few people had the nerve to purchase when prices were low. Investors preferred to buy on a rising trend. They were herd animals, reassured by the spiralling prices their trampling approach caused. By then it was too late. Only the leaders would make real money.

Ben London didn't follow. He led.

He had cash in hand, and he had the confidence to buy cheap. Land, houses, companies, services, were never of lower cost and there were no delays waiting for busy workmen, they were always anxious to start tomorrow. The Depression, horrible in so many ways, proved a marvellous foundation for a fortune, and with nerve and hard work he was able to buy for a song assets he would never have dreamed of affording a few years ago. The more he bought, the more he was seen to be able to afford to buy, and the easier it became for him to attract money.

The richer he was perceived to be, the richer he actually became.

If he invested in houses, house prices rose.

If he put his money in manufacturing industry, share values in Morris, Ford and Harland & Woolf recovered.

Many men, rubber barons, steel magnates, were richer than he, but small investors did not perceive them as millionaires; they eagerly followed Ben, creating the wealth they earned, and then spending it.

They occupied the most expensive suites in London's. Their wives shopped at the Emporium.

Within a few months Ben paid Vic back with interest – a matter as simple as signing a cheque, and then forgetting about it.

But Vic insisted – through their intermediary, Captain Smythe of the London & South-Western Bank, in which Ben was a major investor – on retaining his token but psychologically effective holding of the Emporium's non-voting stock.

Ben shrugged. It entitled Vic to look at the books, that was all.

Remember me, Vic was saying, but he could not hurt Ben now. They lived in different worlds.

CHAPTER SEVENTEEN

1

Dreams come true. Ben stood in the great window of his first-floor office at home, a brandy in his hand, looking contentedly down the gravelled sweep of his driveway. It was the height of summer and the evening was a dusky purple glow after a baking day, the trees viridian green in the still air. Soon their first guests would appear. He glanced at his watch and walked to their bedroom.

'Would you do my zip?' Pearl said, turning her back obligingly. She was wearing the most magnificent over-the-top Chanel ball gown that Ben had ever seen – a sheath of oystershell white embroidered with flowers that looked absolutely fresh. The effect was stunning. Ben touched his nose to one of the silken blooms. 'I thought it was real,' he said.

'None of that hanky-panky. Have you kissed Victoria good night?'

Fastening his cuffs, he walked along the softly carpeted corridor to his daughter's room. She was lying with her eyes wide open, not pretending to be asleep. Victoria never pretended about anything. Her toys were all neatly put away except for Spotty dog, her favourite, laid by her pillow. She was so pretty.

'I want to go to the party, Daddy.'

He sat on the edge of the bed. 'It's much too late for little girls. Give me a kiss good night or I'll tickle you.' He tickled her, then snatched a kiss. 'I'll tell you all about the party in the morning.'

'Who will be there?'

'Everyone,' Ben said.

He waited until she closed her eyes then went through to Ralph's and George's room. Miss Barker was fussing around them – they were old enough now to wear formal clothes without looking cute, and Ralph looked stylish. 'Can we smoke Sobranie cigarettes?'

'You're so fashion conscious, Ralph.'

'That means no,' George said. Vane's death had affected him.

'Suppose someone offers one to us?' Ralph asked cunningly. Ben looked at his incorrigible, good-natured son and shook his head.

'He smoked a mentholated cigarette the other day,' George sneaked.

'Don't get into trouble, Ralph,' Ben said languidly. Ralph never did; it was always George who got caught.

'I'll keep an eye on them,' smiled Miss Barker. She was a pleasant woman with an open face, good at keeping the peace between the twins. As soon as they started boarding at Westminster School – they were old enough to be quite a handful at home – she would take over full time with Victoria. Ben wished he had more time with his children.

A footman knocked at the door. 'First guests are just arriving, sir.'

'Is it true that Charlie Chaplin's coming?' George asked.

'Straight from San Simeon, he's been staying with the Hearsts. Call him Mr Chaplin and don't ask him to do party tricks,' Ben said.

'Wouldn't dream of it,' Ralph said, and Ben laughed.

He and Pearl descended the grand staircase together. Upwards of three hundred guests would be arriving for the housewarming.

The Prince of Wales held his drink between two fingers and talked about unemployment with Lansbury, Stoughton and Tom – Sir Oswald Mosley. 'Parliament's a talk-shop,' Tom Mosley was saying, tall and pantherish, stabbing the air with his finger, 'it ought to be a workshop. Winston agrees, sir.'

'Politicians talking,' Lansbury whispered to Ben.

'I thought Tom had left Labour?' The rich socialist was often photographed surfing at Juan-les-Pins, but the *Daily Herald* was favourable to him.

'Tell the rank and file.' Lansbury would soon head the Labour Party. 'They love him for resigning from the Government. Tom has gifts that must be used.'

'He's a dangerous man,' Ben said, but Lansbury shook his head benignly.

'Parliament was excellent at handling the political issues of the last century,' Winston was saying, looking small and rotund beside Tom, 'however, this century is dominated by economic forces.' Pearl drifted away, uninterested.

'Decisions should be taken by five wise men,' Tom said.

'Come, come, Tom,' called Lansbury, 'why bother with the other four?'

Mosley said: 'You know I'm right, don't you, Ben?'

'Right or wrong, you're ten years too late,' Ben said. He shook hands with Adolf Münchener, his old enemy now his friend, a senior Reichstag Deputy. Dolfo looked ill at ease, but his wife Karin was enjoying herself, a big florid woman with blonde tresses who attached herself to Pearl.

'You should serve Sekt. It is far superior to champagne.' She followed Pearl upstairs to the long gallery where the starstruck – which included Pearl and Karin – were enjoying the glamorous swirl of famous faces.

Chaplin was doing his breadrolls-on-sticks act for Ralph. Pearl thought how similar the comedian's face was to Tom's: both men had the same trick of smiling with all their teeth which in Chaplin looked appealing, but made Tom look hungry and ferocious. Ben was right: Stoughton was an opportunist, but Tom Mosley was a man of force and vision, and he was dangerous. Walford Selby was chatting with Irwin, just back from India. Winston had come up and was complaining about something in a Stanley Spencer picture. She noticed George hanging back in a corner, glancing at the breadrolls and sulking.

'Join in,' Pearl encouraged him, 'enjoy yourself.'

'I am,' George said, but he seemed unable to accept happiness. Pearl squeezed his shoulder. It was George she worried about.

Downstairs, Dolfo Münchener said quietly to Mosley: 'To cure unemployment, Tom, you must first crush the worker's machine. The petty factions of socialism and the trades unions must be replaced by one man, one vision, one leader.'

Tom gave him a euphoric look. 'One nation,' he said.

Dolfo gave a small bow. 'A united Europe,' he smiled. 'There is no conflict between British and German interests, don't you agree?'

Upstairs Karin told Pearl: 'We are sending our son Fritzi to a British public school.' Pearl went on to talk to Jean-Marie Jolie, who was explaining earnestly about costume design to Alexander Korda, the film producer. Then she joined the intellectuals who had formed a clique of their own, Harold Laski and Aldous Huxley on opposite ends of a chaise-longue looking up at the Titian painting. She passed by a few squabbling Bloomsberries, and then by the staircase found a tired-looking Julian Huxley chatting with Herbert Wells, who looked older and more gloomy than she remembered.

By the window Cleremont was talking to a peroxide starlet who must have been sewn into her gown. Cleremont saw Pearl and came over. 'I see Ben's still putting those advertisements in the paper.'

'That's right.'

'He'll never find her, you know. His mother.' He sipped his mineral water, then waved back at the starlet, whose name was Margot – with a silent *t*, no doubt. Turning back to Pearl he said: 'Lisa is gone. Just part of the past.'

'Yes, he knows. He keeps trying. He's chasing a dream.'

'He has all this,' said Cleremont, sweeping his arm round the glittering ensemble but not taking his eyes off Pearl's, 'you, his children, this house, everything a man could desire. Yet still he persists in his painful quest.'

'Ben never gives up.'

'Do you understand him?'

'Sometimes I think . . . sometimes I think that all this is not enough for him.'

'There's nothing more.' Cleremont finished his soda.

'I'm very happy for you, Pearl.' He looked up. 'I am happier now than I have ever been in my life, I think.' He grinned at the starlet. 'Aren't these wonderful people?'

Tonight was the night it all came true. Ria stood in the dark watching the stream of guests arrive. Ben London, the foundling she had rescued from the Workhouse, had won everything everyone dreams of: power, wealth, standing, a beautiful wife, a fine home.

He had it all.

Ria watched. Her vivacious face was infinitely sad. She was no Cinderella. All this could have been hers. Out of arrogance, full of dreams of love, demanding all or nothing, she had lost everything.

Gleaming limousines still swept up the drive. She saw the magnificent entrance hall through the welcoming open doors, and in the lighted windows glimpsed elegant women in wonderful clothes who talked and laughed soundlessly, or danced in the great rooms upstairs, and she heard the strains of an orchestra carrying on the still night air. Not everyone was wealthy: she had seen half a dozen poets enter at least, and imagined their talk in the salons. There were politicians and professors of philosophy, diplomats, an Air Marshal from the Royal Air Force (she guessed from the colour of his uniform) vaudeville artistes, actors and . . . and everybody.

In the spring of 1914, two dirty-faced pauper urchins had stuck their heads through the railings and dreamed of having this house. Now Ria clasped the iron alone. Even then, something in her had known. Life was inevitable.

You wouldn't let me in.

He had said: *Of course I would!*

The last guest had arrived, and now the great doors swung closed.

Ria walked into the dark.

Of course I would!

Her childhood words had come true, and his had lied.

It was still dark. Ben's phone was ringing. For a moment he wondered where he was, then he felt a rush of guilt jolt him awake.

He had forgotten to ask Ria to the party – simply forgotten.

She had been the last thing on his mind.

The phone rang insistently. Pearl's soft arms encircled him. Ben kissed her and struggled across the four-poster. The luminous face of the alarm clock showed 4 a.m. – they had been in bed less than two hours since the party ended, and half that had been taken up making love.

He kicked Ria out of his mind and lifted the earpiece. 'Who is it?'

An officious voice he did not recognize said: 'Is that Ben London?'

'Yes.' Pearl saw the time and groaned, then Ben heard her turn over.

'My name is Gus Ferrers, sir. You don't know me. I am a Head Porter.' Head Porter – that phrase and the prideful tone in which it was said sent an evocative chill down Ben's spine, and he remembered Peter Pungle, the lodger who had lived with him and Edith Rumney, the nurse who looked after him when he was very small. Head Porter, the job Peter Pungle had been so proud of, that had made him such a prize for Mrs Kent . . . Pungle, so infatuated with lust for the prostitute that he condemned a child to the Workhouse.

'Are you there, sir?'

'Yes, I'm here,' Ben said wearily.

'I am the Head Porter, sir, at the Mile End Workhouse Infirmary.'

Just four hundred yards from Lichfield Road where Edith and Peter had lived. 'Yes,' he said, 'I know it.'

Ferrers said: 'I've got a Mr Pungle here, sir. A Mr Peter Pungle.'

'He can go to hell!' Ben almost hung up. 'I don't want

to know anything about that man. He's done enough harm.'

'He asks to see you, sir. He says he wants to confess – '

'It's all in the past,' Ben interrupted. 'I have no interest in those memories.' *Remember.* 'Goodbye,' he said.

'He's dying, sir. Sinking fast.' Ben rubbed his hand over his eyes. Ferrers said: 'He says he has something of value to give you. It's his dying wish, sir.'

'Damn him,' Ben said. Then: 'All right, I'll be over in half an hour.'

Pearl was fast asleep. Ben dressed in a white open-neck shirt and casual trousers, threw a Jean Jolie sporting jacket over his shoulder and went downstairs. He drank a cup of instant coffee in Pearl's modern kitchen, then in the basement garage fired up his new 6½-litre Speed Six Bentley, the unblown motor that had won last year's Le Mans, and let the night breeze ruffling his hair cool his temper as he drove down the Mall at seventy miles per hour.

He had forgotten. Simply forgotten. It was all in the past, long dead, long buried. Why did he feel he had done such a dreadful thing to Ria?

He growled angrily. Trafalgar Square was deserted except for a few startled pigeons in the headlights, and even the Strand was dark. He ignored Trott's nightclub passing on his right, its arch of coloured lights spangling the name over the low entrance. As he came through the City into the East End and the high buildings fell behind, he saw the rambling low rooflines of the Jewish ghettoes framed against the first star-speckled glow of dawn. The saplings he remembered planted along the Mile End Road were full-grown trees.

At the People's Palace he turned left up Bancroft Road, then right into the Workhouse grounds. The infirmary was behind the main building, overlooking the Great East-ern Railways coal depot and Regent's Canal. Ferrers came down the steps cringing and washing his hands with oily servitude, his eyes flicking between the car and Ben's fine clothes. He realized what he was doing with his hands but didn't seem to know what else to do with them.

'Lead on,' Ben said, and followed him down a long corridor.

'He said I'd know you. Yes, you're him all right,' Ferrers said over his shoulder. 'Many's the time I've enjoyed a pint with old Mr Pungle at the London Hospital Tavern or the Lord Tredegar.'

'Get on with it.' Ben shuddered as they walked: the same old Workhouse smell, Lysol, coal dust, cold stone, and no hope.

'He told me you'd be ungrateful,' Ferrers said smugly, now at ease in his familiar surroundings. 'One out of three old people still die in Workhouses, though of course they're changing the name to something nicer now. We're administered by the London Hospital.'

The pauper nurses sewing shrouds by the bedsides of dying patients had gone, but nothing really changed. This ugly ward of dying men was wholly familiar to Ben, though he had never been here before. The nurse gave him a professional stare, disliking Ben's expensive clothes on sight. Once Ben had been condemned because he was poor; now they condemned him because he was rich.

'We had to put him in his own room,' the nurse said, 'not that he is receiving special treatment in any way, but his screaming disturbed the other patients.'

'Is he in great pain?' asked Ben.

'Great remorse,' she said coldly, as if it was his fault, opening the door.

In a high-ceilinged room Peter Pungle lay in an iron bed. Only his skull on the grey pillow seemed to remain. His nose was a sharp white ridge of stretched skin between bruised, hollow eyes and collapsed temples. His forehead was rough and taut, and his whole face was the colour of lead. The lobes of his ears were turned out; he was *in extremis*. He might die before speaking.

Ben pulled up a chair and sat.

At last Peter's right eye turned slowly towards him.

'Knew you'd come,' he murmured, 'couldn't resist one last kick at Peter Pungle, you ungrateful bastard.'

'Save your strength, Peter.'

'I'm sorry,' Peter gasped. 'I'm sorry if I did you wrong.'

Ben shrugged.

'Ooh, you're hard,' groaned Peter. 'You always were. Can't touch you now, can I? Nothing can.' He raised one quivering hand, tested the cuff of Ben's jacket. 'You'll become what you swore you'd never be.' His hand dropped away and he closed his eye.

Ben thought he was dead. He waited. At last Peter Pungle drew breath.

'I lied,' he said.

Ben leaned close.

A single tear hovered in Peter's eye. 'I lied to you, Ben. That day in the pub when you only gave me a few coppers and sprowsie sixpences. Revenge.'

'It was all the money I had. What lie?'

'I said I didn't know where Edith's effects were. All those memories. But I did know. She left a trunk and I wouldn't tell you. Forgive me.'

'Where is it, Peter?'

'Forgive me!' Ben heard the fused bones in Peter's neck ratcheting as the dying man turned his head to point into the corner. A large, battered trunk stood there. Ben remembered it from Edith's bedroom, where it had stood against the wall covered with a pretty chainstitched Victorian sampler.

Now he went across, opened it, and inhaled the sudden camphor smell.

Memories.

Here was his past.

He picked out Mr Benjamin, the yellow teddy bear with a single brown, shiny eye and his name stitched on his collar, his ears neatly re-sewn by Edith. Ben stared down: long his favourite toy, long forgotten. Childish letters and drawings of his own lovingly preserved in ribbon, a tiny pair of shoes that must have been his. An aquatint from

Lancaster's Portrait Studio of a smiling Edith holding a swaddled baby, him. He would be able to order prints.

Here, in this camphor-smelling box, was Ben London's early childhood preserved, much forgotten, much only now prompted back to his memory. And so much that he had never known – he found a torn fragment of blue silk headscarf; a letter from Marcus Rumney, Edith's brother, confessing he had lost all her money; and in consequence, an uninsured loan agreement from the London and South-Western Bank in the name of Edith Rumney quoting number 35 Lichfield Road as security, so they had lost the house after her accident; a faded daguerreotype of a man in a black Victorian coat with a stethoscope around his neck.

'The only man Edith ever loved,' Peter grunted, 'he was a doctor, he died helping others, his name was Benjamin too. She hated it when I called you Ben.'

Ben found something in the bottom of the trunk.

'I fought a man called Ben,' Peter slurred, 'fought him for his job, and won. That's why I called you it. I always wanted to win, damn you.'

Ben pulled out a woman's long cape, of a very dark navy-blue colour, woven of the finest wool and lined with satin, trimmed with fur at the collar. The label was Fenwick's, in Old Bond Street, just up the road from the Emporium.

'Your mother wrapped you up in it,' Peter said. 'That's what we found you in, abandoned on the eleventh step of the London Hospital. God, that was a cold morning.'

'Did you see my mother?'

Peter said: 'No, I never saw her, then.' He added: 'Never met her until a few months after I saw you last . . . New Year's Eve, it was.'

Ben dropped the cape and took two strides back to the bed. 'You – '

'Don't hurt me!' Peter said. 'I'm a dead man.'

Ben's left hand clenched into a fist. It was not a threat. It was anguish.

'She did that too,' Peter remembered. 'In the Lord

281

Tredegar it was, and she bought me a bottle of Mackeson, just like you.' Peter's voice was almost inaudible, and Ben had to lean close, feeling the dying man's breath cold on his lips. 'Ben? Understand your old Peter Pungle. I hated myself. I'd always hated you for coming between Edith and me. Without you I could have made her love me, but it was always you, you, you. And later I hated myself for what I'd done to you. When Lisa came I went mad with my own guilt. Out of spite I called her every name under the sun, I didn't mean it. It was all against me.'

'You poor old man,' Ben said in pity and disgust. 'It made no difference, she went to Regent's Park and saw by chance who she most wanted, and most feared.'

'Who's that?'

Ben said: 'Me.'

Peter gasped as if remembering to breathe. The automatic functions of his brain were failing, and his waning awareness was maintained by his conscious, despairing will.

His right arm began to shiver.

'Ben – ' Peter gasped. He panted, then stopped. 'You see – Lisa knew I lied. Gave me her address. In case. I changed. My mind.' The breath whistled from his open mouth.

'What address?'

Peter raised himself up with maniacal strength, his fingers digging into Ben's hand. 'Forgive me!' His eyes glittered with remorse and desperate pleading.

Ben said: 'Of course I forgive you, everything, ever.'

Peter gave a great cry and fell back, dead.

Ben gently pulled the dead man's hand off his own. A piece of crumpled paper fluttered to the floor.

He picked it up.

On it was written: LISA YORK, 81 CHEYNE COURT, CHELSEA.

Lisa York. His mother had reverted to her maiden name. Ben held his head. He must have been blind. It was what he would have done; she had done it. But his father had said she was still wearing her wedding ring . . . Ben drove along the Embankment with the sun rising over his shoulder, past the Houses of Parliament and into fashionable Chelsea. He turned right by the botanic gardens and looked for number 81.

The fanlit door was answered by a young maid. She shook her head. 'No one by that name, sir. Admiral Storks has lived here since he retired.'

Ben's hopes slumped. 'Perhaps she left an address?'

'I'll inquire of the Admiral, sir.' Ben followed her through. At the gleaming dining room table a man in pyjamas was eating a plate of kedgeree. There was a big brass telescope in the window overlooking the walled garden and a masculine jumble of naval memorabilia, including an astrolabe, with paintings of gunboats off Hong Kong and such things crowding the walls.

'Lisa York? I never met her. She had a rather bad name around here. Didn't care too much for her neighbours. Sit down, my boy. Tea? Lapsang soochong.'

Ben drank gratefully.

'Children all over the place,' grunted Storks, eating. 'Noise. Mess. Little brats apparently. Dirty, too. Kedgeree?' He was lonely.

'Were they local children?'

Storks stared at him. 'Certainly not. We don't have children like that round here.'

Ben helped himself to another cup. 'So the neighbours forced her to move?'

The Admiral pressed a piece of rice into the corner of his mouth. 'Unsuccessfully. Will of iron, wouldn't shift.'

'So what happened?'

'They say she ran out of money – spent it all on the brats. They aren't grateful, you know. Those types. Or their parents. Half of them don't know who their parents are, of course.'

Ben looked round, hearing a sound behind him, and saw two boys standing in the doorway. The older boy was about fifteen, lanky and obedient. The younger, hanging from his brother's hand and looking down at the polished mahogany floor, his thumb in his mouth, was no more than seven. Then he stared up at Ben and smiled suddenly – a happy smile, and Ben felt that those thoughtful eyes missed no detail of his clothes, or the way Ben sat, or even how he held his cup – little finger underneath so that the fragile bone china would not rattle or chip when it was set down, just as Edith Rumney had taught him.

Admiral Storks glared at the little boy. 'Thumb out!' he shouted. The boys disappeared, and Ben heard their footsteps running upstairs.

'So you can't help me at all.' The Admiral shook his head. Ben got up to go.

At the door the maid whispered: 'I know who you mean, all us kids loved her. She was good to us. I don't know what happened to her, but you could try the estate office – number 36. Ask for Mr Peers.'

Ben looked up the hallway and saw the boys' heads peering between the first-floor railings, then they were gone.

Vincent Peers was old, but his eyes were bright. 'I remember her well. My grandchildren sometimes went to parties in her garden.'

'Do you know where she moved to?'

'I can look it up.' He consulted the estate ledger. 'Glebe Place, just off the King's Road. Rented accommodation, I'm afraid.'

Ben left his car and walked away from the river. In London poverty and elegance lived cheek by jowl. Some houses in Glebe Place were genteel residences freshly painted, with cooks and maids in the basement – others were run down, with peeling doors and long rentier lists indicating their conversion to flats. His mother's dwelling was one of these. He ascended the creaking stairs. A woman came out on the landing holding a wooden spoon in one hand.

'I'm looking for Lisa York?'

'No one called that here.' She went back in and slammed the door.

Ben started knocking on doors as he went up. Sometimes people didn't answer and he shouted through the keyholes, but none of them had heard of her. Finally, on the point of giving up at the attic flat, an old lady opened up.

'Lisa York?' She laid her finger against her cheek. 'Now that does ring a bell.' Ben showed her one of Petherton's photographs. 'Yes! I remember her, striking-looking lady. Never thought of herself, poor woman. She was strange. But very kind to me when I was ill – my hip, you know. Cooked broth, went to the shops. Terrible job carrying coal up these steps. We've got electricity now, mind you.'

'But she doesn't live here any more?'

The old lady shook her head. 'She had to let her maid go – couldn't afford her, see. Then she was ill. I didn't know – well, she wouldn't ask for help! Not that I could have, being poorly myself. Pride cometh before a fall, I say. She got over on her rent and they chucked her out.'

'You've no idea where she went?'

The old lady pointed vaguely. 'Try up Manor Street way.'

Ben went downstairs. He felt something on his wrist. It was a flea.

He walked along the King's Road and opposite the town hall turned into Manor Street. Graceful houses adorned its southern end, near the river. This end was a slum. Washing was slung across the road and it was dark. Such poverty was familiar territory from his youth, but sadder, because West End poverty had no pride. This was where people lost themselves. He saw several policemen, too, which was rare down East. The tenements were crumbling and rat-infested, leaving stinking rubbish piled in the alleys. Kids, dirty, hopeless and cunning, followed him everywhere. One dark girl tucked her skirt in her bloomers and shimmied up a backyard wall, gave a practised roll over the top and was gone. Older women in long shabby dresses swore at Ben, their grey hair hanging in greasy Victorian plaits, then pushed their way with muscular arms towards him through the crowd of kids.

Ben faced them. 'I'm looking for Lisa York.'

'Get out of here.' They thought he was a nark. One of them shouted for the men to come.

Ben dropped out of sight through a narrow alleyway, but heard footsteps running after him. He turned left then right, then stopped in a dead end, a tall gloomy courtyard surrounded by grimy walls and black, broken windows. The dark girl who had disappeared over the wall came to one of the doorways. She was leading a woman with a strawberry birthmark blazoned stiffly over half her face.

'That's him,' the girl said. 'He was asking about her.'

The woman with the birthmark said: 'You are looking for Lisa?' When Ben nodded she said: 'I was her maid for as long as she could afford me. Now I am her friend for as long as she will have me. My name is Helen.'

'I am her son.'

Helen shook her head sadly, as though she had long feared this day must come. 'She knows all about you. She does not want to meet you, Mr London.'

'Let her be the judge of that.'

'She is so proud. And so ashamed.'

'I forgive her, I forgive her everything.'

Helen grunted with amusement. 'Of you. Proud of you. But also ashamed.'

'Why?' Was she mad?

'Look at you. Because you are what you are.'

Ben shook his head.

She accused him: 'The millionaire, when so many live in poverty.'

'I can help her.'

'Money?' said Helen tiredly. She wore no shoes; her feet were black, her toes bruised, her dress was patched and torn. 'Lisa is so very ill.'

'I can help her,' Ben repeated.

'No one can help her,' Helen said. 'It is more than a sadness of the spirit. She has tuberculosis.'

Ben closed his eyes. Long ago, his best friend had died of that dreadful disease in his arms, beneath a sycamore tree. Helen saw his face.

'I will take you there,' she said at once.

*

Ben walked slowly after Helen. Children were queuing outside the butchers' shops for leftover scraps to take home to their mums. A small boy passed them toiling behind a pram filled with brown coal – no gas or electricity down here. A group of girls scampered past carrying wooden Denver blocks in their skirts, stolen off roadworks down the elegant end of the street – now that traffic ran on rubber tyres the councils were ripping up the old hardwood surfaces and burning them in bonfires. For many families one of those worthless tarry blocks would make the difference between a cold supper and a hot one – or no supper at all.

Frustrated housewives swore at one another between windows over the narrow alleys, always angry. This was the underbelly.

Ben thought: *No wonder I need to forget*.

Canary Warren had been worse, much worse, but that had been *then*, and this was *now*. Places like this were not supposed to exist in these enlightened days. 'Mother,' he whispered, 'did you give it all up for me? Did I drive you to this?'

He did not see that it was he who drove her still.

Ben London followed Helen down a narrow passage-way, stepping over piles of garbage, until they came to a doorway in a crumbling wall. He could hardly see the sky. This was another courtyard, part of the same development.

She pointed soundlessly.

Ben ducked through. Steps rose into the dark. He climbed to a landing then turned onto a final flight of creaking stairs. It ended in a door.

He opened the door without knocking and looked into the shadows. It was a small room, almost square, with a single window in the angle of the roof. He pushed in and gasped at the smell – damp cardboard, damp plaster, bare rotten boards – there was no carpet. One table, one chair, one bed. On the bed a figure moved, turning away from him.

'You know who I am,' Ben said.

It was too late. Once, in her heart, she would have welcomed such hurt, just to see him, really see him for a few moments, however terrible the price, but now she knew she did not have the strength to face him. She was burned out and ashamed. In her weakened condition, drained by tuberculosis, her guilt consumed her spirit. She no longer cared. She turned away from him and laid her head against the wall.

He strode angrily across to her.

Gently, but brutally, he turned her to face him.

'I know you are my mother. Don't deny it.'

How piercing blue his eyes were.

He showed her a red felt collar on which was sewn a name: Mr Benjamin.

'You left it with me,' Ben said. 'That is where my name comes from. Even as you abandoned me, you named me. You can't escape our blood, Mother.'

Her father's name.

'Mother,' Ben said, 'come home.'

She twisted her face away from him.

'Forgive me,' the millionaire said cruelly, '*I* could not help being born. Don't pretend to blame yourself: you're blaming me.' She stared at him, amazed. 'You can't help these people, not like this,' he said roughly. 'I will help you. I am your son. I am *you*.'

She shook her head.

He held out his hand. 'Help me,' he said.

He did not think she could resist, but she did. Her thin fingers reached out towards him, but then she drew them back. He turned furiously away from her on his heel, then stared for a moment from the cracked window at the broken-backed roofs, the dark well of the courtyard below, seeing no people now but feeling the unspoken despair of their trapped, proud lives all around him in the vast sordid structure of the tenement.

'Who owns this place?' he asked in a voice dark with rage.

Lisa lifted herself up.

She said: 'You do.'

He looked at her as though she had struck him in the face.

Then he said nothing more. He simply swept her up in his arms, and carried his mother home.

3

Without nightmares, there would be no dreams. Lisa woke to cleanliness and light. She lay in a wonderful room with sunlight pouring through tall, sparkling windows. The bedroom furniture was elegant yet simple, and through a high doorway she glimpsed another room with sofas, a painted ceiling, a lovely carpet. Without being told she knew that this was home.

'You are in London House, m'am,' Helen said.

Lisa turned her head on the white pillow. Helen smiled. 'It's all come out right,' she said. 'You won't know what to say. It's perfect.'

'I feel better,' Lisa whispered, still dreaming. She blinked, and realized that it was real. She lay in an enormous bed with soft white sheets. On the bedside table stood a carafe of water and various medications.

'There was no stopping him,' Helen said. 'A nasty crowd had gathered, don't you remember? He stood on the step with you dangling in his arms. You must remember!'

Lisa closed her eyes. She only remembered his face as he swept her up in his arms to carry her home.

'But when they saw the look in his eyes . . .' Helen said, 'they let him through.'

'I don't deserve all this,' Lisa fretted.

'You do.' Her son's voice. Ben London let the door close gently behind him then walked over and took his mother's hands in his, gently though firmly, no longer needing to match her brutality to herself. He had won.

'Mother, this is your proper home,' the millionaire promised her, 'with me.'

'But I must get back,' Lisa said, though now only pretending to struggle.

'That place no longer exists,' he said coldly, staring at her with that look in his eyes. 'You see, there is one very serious question I must ask you,' he said, still holding both her hands. 'When you held me as a tiny baby in your arms all those years ago, that frosty morning outside the London Hospital, did you abandon me on the steps to die – or to live?'

Lisa raised herself, trembling, with all her strength, to stare up into his face; their faces almost touching.

'I knew I could not look after you!' she cried. 'I loved you – loved you so much that I knew I had to let you go. *Because* I loved you, Ben!'

He said something incredible. 'I understand that,' he said simply. He nodded. '*Because* you loved me.'

Lisa clasped him to her in a hug with all her strength, and dropped her head against his chest. She was crying – crying for joy.

She had come home at last.

Lisa had never dreamed of such happiness.

A disease once invariably fatal could now be alleviated with modern drugs. The best doctors were Lisa's family around her, the best hospital her loving home.

By Christmas, Lisa could take a few steps out of her wheelchair.

By Easter, she could walk with a stick.

It was no surprise to Ben that she got on so well with Pearl – he was the spark that joined them. Pearl's light, quicksilver personality, her swift deftness of touch, coupled well with Lisa's solid strength of will and stopped the older woman taking herself too seriously. Looking at them, because they were so different, yet so close, Ben was reminded of an older and younger sister. Pearl could always soften Lisa with a laugh, and soon Lisa learned to laugh at herself too. To Pearl's infectious spirit there was always a lighter side, and Lisa came gradually to realize that Pearl was as determined about this in her way as Lisa was determined in hers. Lisa always fought the dark, but Pearl always sought to brighten it with laughter, to defeat it by not taking it seriously. But still, for all her love, Pearl could not fall pregnant again.

Both women enjoyed the weekly ritual of driving out one afternoon to a *thé dansant* at the Spider's Web up the Great North Road, or enjoying a cream tea in some thatched country village. Lisa relaxed in Pearl's genial company.

They never talked about Charles Cleremont.

Pearl told Ben: 'I like your mom.'

'Mum,' he said, glancing up from his work with a smile. 'Victoria likes her too.'

'Victoria *adores* her.' He put down his pen. 'Lisa's got a way with children. I wish – What a shame she refuses to meet my father.' He stopped, then shrugged.

Pearl sat on the edge of the desk, looking very slim and desirable in a café-au-lait trousersuit. 'They'd be so unsuitable,' she laughed. 'God knows what brought them together. She'll never forgive your father his lies and the pain and grief his weakness has caused her. He ruined her life, Ben.'

'I don't know,' he said. 'He couldn't help himself. And he didn't mean to deceive us about her wedding ring. It was her mother's ring. In a sense Lisa has always been wedded to Charles Cleremont, however much she denies it.'

'What about Edwin Petherton? Didn't he count at all?'

'No,' Ben said. 'He was much too nice for this world. Lisa *loved* Charles.'

Pearl said thoughtfully: 'Sometimes you do frighten me, Ben.'

He hugged her with a smile. 'That's because I love you,' he said.

He showed her some architect's plans on his desk. 'The Collingwood Road Estate.' Grinding poverty could be cured with money and bulldozers. 'Don't tell Lisa,' he said, 'it's my secret.'

CHAPTER EIGHTEEN

1

Vic was standing in bright sunlight outside Coutts' bank in the Strand, looking up the angle of broad road towards Trott's. The friendly arch of coloured lights was turned off, and the steps down to the cellar door, where people queued at night, were in shadow. It looked enticing, those narrow steps down to the golden door, but somehow dead and menacing by daylight.

He crossed the street.

Vic hated places to be shut. He hated to be excluded, because he wanted to be happy, and people were his only source of happiness. Vic loved crowds, loved people. Shut doors were like an insult. Keep Out. Closed.

Vic had been sad and lonely since Nigel drowned. For a long time he struggled not to admit it, but he had needed Nigel. Not just because of the business, though no one was as good as Nigel with the books, or came up with such clever ideas. While Nigel lived, Vic hadn't realized how much he depended on him.

Loved him.

It was very quiet at the Old Bull and Bush without Nigel.

Little Terry got on Vic's nerves sometimes. He had cried a lot, missing his daddy more than Vic would have believed – it had started after the funeral, as though Terry had only then realized his daddy wouldn't come back. For weeks the little boy had been inconsolable, nearly driving Vic out of his mind. At last Vic took him back to the little house at Havannah Street. When it really came down to it, home was where Mum was.

'I knew you'd come back,' Esther said, not very welcoming. Then she held out her arms to young Terry. He stared at her with his black eyes. 'He's forgotten me!' she said, turning to Vic. Terry ran out to play in the back yard.

'He's not been the same,' Vic shrugged. 'I always got on with him much better than Nigel did, but – '

'I'll make him some nice tea,' Esther said.

'No milk, he doesn't like milk.'

Esther was horrified. 'But milk's good for you.'

'I'm going to move back in here for a few weeks,' Vic said, sitting.

Esther sighed. 'I knew you would.' He realized she had changed. She was drinking again, she had that high colour, but whereas the spirit used to elate her, now she seemed depressed. Tom told him Esther wouldn't let Ria stay here, even though she had come ready with her suitcase, and her old room kept dusted too.

'I've come home,' Vic explained, but Esther just turned away helplessly. 'It won't be any trouble, I'll use Ria's room,' he said.

'Vic, I don't want you to stay.'

'But it'll be our family together again, just like the old days.' Her refusal was incomprehensible to Vic. She must be mad. 'Have you been drinking again?'

'I'm sober as a judge,' Esther said. 'I love you, Vic, but that's the way it is.'

Vic almost despaired; he couldn't control her. If only he'd brought her some little gift. His frustration nibbled at the edges of his temper. 'Ria's been poisoning your mind against me.'

'Don't be silly.' Esther was trembling; dying for a drink, a sip of peace.

'Ria is the cause of all my troubles,' Vic said.

Esther gripped his arms, and Vic actually flinched. This was a family matter where his real emotions were involved, not the smiling face he showed to the world, and he was defensive.

'Don't you blame Ria for anything,' Esther hissed. 'Blame me.'

Vic threw his arms around her. 'Mum, you know I'd do anything for you!'

'Yes, I know.' Then Esther took a breath and asked the question that she had avoided all her life. 'Vic, are you mixed up in crime? I mean bad crime?'

He stepped back, then smiled, and at that moment his real relationship with his mother ended.

'No,' he said. He slid his arms around her gently, but she embraced him as though she was saying goodbye.

'I love you,' she said, taking the hardest decision of her life, 'and Terry can stay here as long as you like, but this isn't your home any more, Vic. Your home is the Old Bull and Bush. It's for your own good.' Vic pulled away from her.

'I'll take Terry back with me,' he said distantly. When he left, he glanced back and saw her face full of doubt, and he knew she was wondering if she had done right to make the break with her two surviving children. Very well; so she would lose Terry, her grandchild, too.

But for the first time in his life, Vic felt like an outcast.

He prowled around the many rooms of the Old Bull and Bush. Chi-hiking with the punters gave him no pleasure, all his relationships were shallow, no one knew him – not the real him, the kind and loving Vic who would do anything for anyone for love, the soft and vulnerable Vic who had to be defended and concealed: because people were to be feared. Feared more than anything.

And so they must be made to fear him more.

This was the source of his courage.

Without Nigel to manage the boring details, business was levelling off.

Some afternoons, when trade was slack and it was sunny, Vic went for a walk. At first it was only as far as the Tower of London. Then he dropped down into Billingsgate, but the market was quiet in the afternoons. If he went as far as Blackfriars, he could catch the tram to Cleopatra's needle and sit quietly in Victoria Embankment gardens with the Adelphi and York buildings behind him.

And Trott's Nightclub.

Vic bought a bunch of daffs off a flower-girl and went through the side door into Ria's hallway. He stood looking up the stairwell towards her flat.

His footsteps echoed as he went up.

He hid the flowers behind his back.

'Hallo, Ria,' he said when she opened the door.

'You'd better come in,' she said at last.

He looked around him. It was nice, very nice. Low gilt tables, very ornate, and plenty of handwoven Turkish rugs. Ria had gone arty since Ray died. Her long hair was shingled and marcelled to make it look short, and it was lovely. She wore an oriental housegown, midnight blue with the moon and clouds on it, like Salome. Her movements were as graceful as a singer knew how to make them. She was as mysterious and enticing as a slave-girl from the *Rubaiyat* of Omar Khayyám, and as remote. There had always been this veil between them. Ria was playing, and he hated it. He wished she wasn't so lovely. She hadn't changed at all.

She pointed at a half-open door. 'Will's home from Balliol. He's doing brilliantly, all these are his books. He's studying if you want to see him.'

'I don't.'

'What do you want then, Vic?' She was blind.

He realized the gramophone was playing jazz very softly. 'The Chant', by Jelly Roll Morton. Ray's favourite. Let her play it. Vic didn't care how much she remembered him.

'Look Vic,' Ria snapped, 'what do you want?'

'Simply to be friends,' he said, holding out the flowers.

For the first time he saw something real in her eyes: confusion.

Will, very much the smart young man in his Oxford bags, smoking a pipe, stuck his head around the doorway. Vic smiled at him.

'All right.' Ria put the flowers in a pot of water. 'Friends.'

Later everyone remembered the thirties as the golden
years. The lull between two wars was a glowing interval
of peace compared with what had gone before, and what
would come. If lives are candles blown by the wind, then
for a little while they burned brightly in still air, in the
eye of the hurricane.

Hawk stropped his razor and brushed the hot lather on
his face. His moustache was white, and his hand shook a
faint warning. He carried on. He could no longer walk to
work but sat contentedly downstairs on the bus reading a
paper. Like most people Hawk both admired and dis-
trusted the little Austrian corporal who was doing so well
for Germany. Bert Simmonds, the ex-chauffeur, summed
it up nicely in the pub. 'Napoleon did jolly well for France
too, Hawk, look at the trouble he caused us, and he
was just a little corporal.' Bert was knowledgeable about
history. 'Where he tried to invade England, you can still
see the canals and earthworks and martello towers and
that. We shouldn't forget, Hawk.'

'What are you frightened of?' said Hawk.

'Who, me?' said Bert Simmonds bitterly. 'Nothing. Did
I tell you Algy Courtenay killed himself? The old floorwalker jumped off Blackfriars bridge. Drowned. And he
was doing so well – opened up a men's outfitters, ran it
with his family. Never been happier, blessed the day Ben
London kicked him out. But committing suicide like that.'
He blew the froth off his beer. 'Can't understand it.'

'I hate getting old,' Hawk said. 'I'll never retire.'

'He'll kick you out too,' Bert said spitefully, always
jealous of Hawk.

'You're ignorant, Bert,' Hawk said, 'because you think
everyone's like you.'

Now Hawk stood in the sunlight on his patch of polished flag in front of the Emporium, old and content. He
smiled at the tourists and the window-shoppers, and he
even tolerated pekinese dogs. He pulled out his fob-watch
and studied it. Now that she could walk, Mr London was

bringing his mother to the Emporium, and Hawk was looking forward to meeting her.

Instead, the Rolls-Royce was wafting Ben London smoothly along the King's Road. 'But I thought we were going to the Emporium!' Lisa said. She wore a smart blue dress and cloche hat.

'I have a surprise for you.' Ben looked across the back seat at her, the extraordinary glance that took in everything. 'How do you really feel?'

Her face was tanned and she looked in striking good health since her return from the sanatorium in Switzerland. Her energy was coming back, although she was supposed to take things very slowly. 'The doctors say I am in remission.'

Ben had noted the tiny lines around her eyes. 'But you're still in pain.'

'The knees. Only a little.'

'You're fretting,' Ben said. He always knew what she felt. It was useless trying to hide anything from him.

'I'm not used to doing nothing. It's terribly hard, all this luxury.'

Ben tapped on the glass. 'Turn left here.'

'There's a big crowd,' Pineapple said over his shoulder. He hated driving near crowds since their rough treatment at the hands of the mob at Buckingham Gate that had provoked Victoria's premature arrival. Pineapple had never been so frightened in his life – terrified the baby would be born dead, and it would somehow be his fault. Pineapple had no children of his own – Natasha refused to for the sake of her film career – and he doted on Victoria.

'You can stop here if you like,' Ben offered.

'No, sir!'

Of course not. Lisa knew that Ben had been certain of Pineapple's pride. Ben would not allow her to walk a hundred yards – but he had the confidence to let Pineapple fail him, sure that he would not. So easily he added to Pineapple's self-esteem. That was a rare quality of leadership.

They got out of the car. Many amongst the jostling crowd were cheering, the kids waving balloons, but Lisa heard some boos. She noticed that Ben seemed surprised. He took off his top hat and they shook hands with the Mayor.

Ben had been as good as his word: the old slums had been razed, and Collingwood Road was now a bright estate of new houses. He had spent more money than he would ever receive back, and showed her round proudly: trees had been planted in the small grassy malls, and every home had gas and electricity laid on. They were simply but sturdily furnished, and all had bathrooms.

'I dreamed of houses like this when I lived in Canary Warren,' he said enthusiastically. 'Central heating. Proper windows.'

But still the crowd booed. Ben pushed a path angrily back to the car. Pineapple reversed into the grimy street. This was only a bright oasis in a desert of poverty, and money was not enough. Lisa saw it, but Ben did not. He had done his best to make a fresh start for them and been rejected. She saw through the anger in his eyes to the pain which he hid beneath.

'You can never change Canary Warren now,' she said gently. 'It's all in the past.'

'I wanted to please you.' At last he said: 'Why won't they let me help them?'

Lisa tried to explain. 'Because you are the millionaire,' she said sadly, as Pineapple drove to the Emporium.

Pearl was already arriving with Victoria. They would all be taking lunch together at the Waterfalls. 'Hiya, Hawk, how's it doing?'

Hawk smiled then picked up her little girl. 'Hallo, Victoria!'

'Hallo, Hawk,' Victoria said seriously, then smiled her father's smile. Pearl glowed, then said, genuinely concerned: 'Hawk, you've cut your face shaving.'

Hawk was acutely embarrassed. 'I'm terribly sorry, m'am.'

'It's not much,' she called after him, but Hawk retreated

to his room and dabbed cotton wool on the tiny cut. Everyone nicked themselves shaving occasionally; what appalled him was that he had not noticed. For the first time his eagle eyes had failed him. He had been making a fool of himself; everyone going inside must have noticed. Hawk's hands shook. He was deeply disturbed, and he didn't come out until Pearl had gone.

He returned and stood to attention. Old Bond Street was a traffic jam as usual. Not many people were coming into the shop today, and a wintry wind blew. Suddenly the Rolls-Royce cut through the traffic and pulled up at the kerb. Hawk opened the car door and saluted the woman who followed her son into the Emporium. At the last moment Ben turned back.

'Are you feeling all right, Hawk?'

'Yes, sir,' Hawk said. Ben went into the store. Hawk's face twisted in pain.

He was not all right. His memory was unreeling like a cinema projector running backwards at ever-increasing speed. He was standing here as if for ever, at this exact spot, his square of polished flag, his place. *Her hot blue eyes.* Young Lisa, Mr London's mother, stood in front of him, desperate and alone. She wore a blue cape. She was going to have a baby.

'*Help me,*' she said.

'Oh my God,' Hawk whispered. Pain slid down his left arm. Someone asked him the way to Burlington Arcade, and he pointed with his other arm, desperately doing his duty. People walked around him. He could hardly hear them. Everything Hawk had known was disintegrating, as if his whole life had been made of sand.

His heart hammered, and ceased.

For a few moments longer his body continued to stand to attention. Then he fell like a tree.

Hawk had more friends than he knew; more than two hundred attended his funeral and many more sent flowers – his coffin was almost hidden by the brilliant sprays. Hawk, for all his faults, or because of them, had been a treasured landmark to clients who had shopped at the Emporium for most of their lives. They liked a man who knew where he stood, and Hawk had died where he would most have wished, doing the job he loved. No man could ask for more than that.

'But he died with an expression of remorse on his face,' Ben said, 'the most terrible remorse.'

He offered Hawk's job to Pineapple, who had the strong physical presence needed to step into a Head Doorman's shoes. 'It's a great honour, sir.'

'It's a big decision. Talk it over with Natasha, but don't let me down.'

Natasha was not at home, but as soon as she arrived he broke the good news. 'The pay is the same but the job's worth three hundred a year in tips.'

'Three hundred a year, that's nothing,' Natasha said. How he loved her when she was like this; the superior line of her high cheekbones, her haughty eyes. 'You realize who is in town? David O. Selznick from Hollywood.'

'But you're under contract to Korda.'

'A puny contract that can be broken. I can go to Hollywood, and you will come too. I have my big chance. I have the talent to succeed.'

Three times she had said *I*. He said: 'Your place is with me.'

'Dillibe, when will you snap out of it! Selznick is casting for a really big movie, they know how to do things out there. *Gone with the Wind*. He's bought the rights for fifty thousand dollars.'

Pineapple held her hands. 'But you're black,' he said gently. 'It doesn't matter how talented you are.'

Natasha's temper flared. 'You sound like a bloody Uncle Tom, my own husband. I'm ashamed of you.' She stormed around the mean little flat as if its confines were suffocating her. 'You might be happy toadying to people who call you funny names to humiliate you and spend your life opening and closing doors, but I'm not. Hollywood is where my future lies. You can come with me, or stay.' She said something she didn't mean. 'I don't care which.'

'You're my wife and you'll do as I say! Why can't you be proud of my achievement?'

'Head Doorman!' sneered Natasha, but it was only her flashing temper speaking, he told himself, and the frustration of her thwarted ambitions. She demanded: 'Why can't you have faith in me? Because I'm a woman. I can call you my manager or my agent, don't worry, people won't know you're a kept man.'

This was the source of their trouble: that with her talent Natasha earned more from her unreliable profession than he did from his safe one, which carried a pension, job security and self-respect.

Natasha put her long fingers with their scarlet nails on his shoulders. She spoke into his eyes. 'Have faith in me. Believe in my talent.'

'I have always believed in you,' Pineapple said calmly. 'I will be here.' Her face crumpled. He sat there unable to believe that she would really go, listening to her pack her things. Right up to the moment the door closed behind her, he did not believe she would go. And then it was too late.

To expunge the awful picture of his wife's weeping departure from his mind, Pineapple threw himself into his new job, determined by his success to prove to Ben London that his confidence was not misplaced. Pineapple's happy smile and willing demeanour, his authority and diplomacy in dealing with the thousand problems that came a Head Doorman's way, soon made him a popular and respected figure. He spent his days surrounded by people. All night he was alone.

He lay staring up at the ceiling. He was married heart and soul to Natasha. He was so lonely he might die.

He did not blame her for going. The worst part was knowing she would fail.

Will loved Oxford. Being here was an incredible privilege. The work was hard – as hard on his brain as the TS *Mercury* had been hard on his body. The year after the Nazis were elected in Germany he worked in the holidays for the election of a pacifist as the Member of Parliament for Fulham East. He participated in the Oxford Union debates on the pacifist side: he would not fight for King and Country in the event of another war. Ben came to hear him speak, and Will had never been more proud.

'Have you read Douhet?' Ben asked in the teashop afterwards.

'I will do, sir.'

'The bomber will always get through. Within the first few hours of a major war London will no longer exist. Neither will Berlin or Paris. You realize what this means.'

'That war is impossible.' Will believed in neat solutions.

But Ben shook his head. 'No, in reality it means that a war would be fought by civilians. The survivors.' Wars were always vast and impersonal, but Ben knew that the real battles were always fought on the personal level.

Will looked at his father and shuddered.

'But surely it can be prevented!'

'Surely?' Ben poured them another cup of tea. 'Yes, it's worth doing anything to prevent. Anything.' He added quietly: 'But what?'

Will realized that his father was not so intimidating as he had thought – in some ways they were so close. The more he knew his father, the more he knew how much closer he wanted to be.

Next academic year Will won the coveted blazer of a rowing Blue. He was cycling past the Roman Catholic church behind the High Street, his panniers laden down with books, when someone called out to him from the doorway.

'Will London?' He had adopted his father's surname, another aspect of the growing distance between himself and his mother. Will braked, looking back over his shoulder. A student a few years younger than himself, wearing plus-fours, waved and ran down from the porch. 'You are Will London, I believe?'

Will nodded.

The other boy smiled, stared into his eyes, and stuck

out his hand. There was something vaguely familiar about that straightforward approach.

'You don't know me, so permit me to introduce myself. My name's François Enguerrand.' It was an extremely attractive accent, with flawless English. 'I am the Count of Coucy – whatever that means in these days of the Third Republic.' He had a droll manner that was most engaging and encouraged easy friendship.

'Pleased to meet you,' Will said. The two boys shook hands.

François said: 'My mother is Chouchou.'

Will had heard her name mentioned by Pearl at London House.

'Your father is an old friend of ours,' François explained as they walked together. 'When the trains were not running he flew my mother to be by my father's side at the convalescent home in Deauville. Thanks to Ben London, they had a few happy weeks together. My father was almost well again when he suffered a thrombosis and suddenly died.'

'I'm sorry.'

'Many died for France. This was in World War One you understand.'

That was a chilling phrase in vogue, the title of a book. 'Do you think there will be another war?' Will asked. 'I am a socialist.'

'Then you will be marching off to Spain?'

'It's so difficult to know what to do. I am also a pacifist.'

François was logical. 'So is everyone, until the fighting starts.' The two boys laughed together, liking one another instinctively. François said: 'Let's go and consume a drink, I am growing to like warm beer. I have been invited to London House for the weekend. Will you be there?'

It was dark and raining. Vic jumped the queue waiting outside Trott's. '*I've slept with Ria.*' He pushed past the bouncer and took off his coat and hat, handed them to the cloakroom girl. She shook the water off before hanging them neatly, another change from Ray's time, when the cloakroom attendant was a spiv who probably went through your pockets before throwing your clothes on the floor. 'Thank you, sir,' she said, bobbing nicely and handing him his ticket.

Ria ran a tight ship. The only person she couldn't look after was herself.

Vic went through and was shown politely to his seat. It was a much smarter crowd than in Ray's time. The buzz of conversation was discreet and friendly. One dividing wall had been knocked down, and the place felt much bigger. The dance floor was still intimate and dark, the many tables crowded around the border each with its own candlelit white linen tablecloth and red rose. Vic sniffed appreciatively and crooked his finger at the waitress. 'Champagne, the best.'

'Only the best is served at Trott's, sir.'

The entertainments were very varied. Texas Guingan and her raunchy girls had played here, but so did Mozart quartets, jazz ensembles, ragtime bands, solo violinists. It was a connoisseur audience – they didn't know what they were going to get, but they knew it would be good. *L'oiseau* had sung here on her sole London engagement, but tonight Vic had come to hear Ria.

He studied her beneath the spotlight.

In the latest fashion, Ria had unloosed her hair again. Golden curls fell to her shoulders. Matching her eyes, her flashing blue dress was hip-hugging and slashed to the knee. Vic frowned. She was dressed like a tart.

But it was all part of the act.

It was a shock. She sang very softly – quite unlike what he had expected. Her voice had an amazing quality of innocence. Was this the real Ria? Her voice, her body were captivating instruments. She knew how to hold a note as gently as a caress, or draw it out into a rough, scorching edge that transformed sentiment into a sudden truth.

It was power. She had it.

A politician told Vic that real power is emotion – that was Tom Mosley, after the Cable Street riot of his blackshirts spread towards the Jewish ghettoes. Vic had known this all his life: make them laugh, make them cry, make them pay.

Never mind truth, make them pay.

But Ria's act was true emotion. Vic did not know what to make of it. Every gesture, every stillness, revealed feeling. She made her audience feel her heat, she forced them to respond. How they loved her sadness, her wonderful innocence. Vic sat with tears pricking the backs of his eyes.

Ria, who was more guilty than any of them.

Vic got out before the lights came up.

Ria took her pins out and undressed. She wrapped herself in her dressing gown. It was late, so very late that it was early, and the sounds of traffic had faded away. She was exhausted, but she was not sleepy.

She lifted her hair and stared at her face in the bedroom mirror.

Ria was lonely. Ria was hard. Ria had no feelings.

What has happened to my life? All her feeling was in her singing. She felt little sense of her own individuality. She did not know where she was going.

So she wore her hair down, she sang her sweet songs on stage, allowing herself to be vulnerable, telling herself she was happy without a man, living her own life, dressing as she chose, reading what books she chose.

She had redecorated her flat in blue.

Her visits home had tailed off; it was more than a year since the last.

Will would graduate from Oxford soon. She didn't see him nearly often enough and knew she had failed him, but she didn't know how. Or know how she could have done better. All she could do was stand with her hands in her hair staring at herself in the mirror.

In the silence, she heard footsteps on the stairs.

She ran to the door, twisted the key, fumbled with the chain, pulled it open.

Vic stood there. The stairwell light shone on his wet black hair.

She said: 'Vic!'

'Didn't you know it was me?'

'I thought – I didn't think anything, honest, Vic.'

'Aren't you going to let me in?'

'Will's here, asleep.' He glanced past her, knowing she was lying.

'If that's the way you want it,' he said.

'It's late,' she murmured, 'you can't come in.' She pressed her hands against the thin panels, pushing the door closed against him.

'Who would I need to be?' he asked in an amused voice, then let the door slam, and she heard him laugh. It was the game they played.

She threw herself on her bed in despair.

The family life in London House started with Ben getting up around dawn and looking at Pearl asleep beside him; she was so beautiful that his heart always beat faster for her, and he always kissed her, and she always smiled in her sleep.

They slept naked – summer and winter, London House was the same temperature inside – and if they did not make love, or discuss their forthcoming business trip around the world, Ben slipped from the four-poster and put on a silk dressing gown, then padded along the corridor to Victoria's room.

His daughter usually slept with her hands above her head, her face on one side. She was developing Pearl's lovely bone structure and would be a beauty one day. She looked very peaceful, and he loved to see her.

Ralph's and George's bedrooms were further along, past the night nursery and Elise Barker's rooms. In the school holidays they sometimes had friends to stay, often Fritzi Münchener, who was Ralph's great friend. Both were natural athletes, and Fritzi was the best swimmer and diver Ben had ever seen. For this reason Fritzi would have no trouble entering Heidelberg university, and Ralph would be eagerly accepted by Cambridge.

'They go out drinking together and have lots of fun,' related Dolfo Münchener tolerantly – his job on the Foreign Affairs Committee often brought him over with all expenses paid, and he lived like a gentleman. He grinned into his brandy. 'They probably have the same girls, too.'

Pearl had been astonished. 'Has Ralph discovered girls?'

Both men laughed. 'Years ago,' Ben said. He added: 'It rather excludes George, though. He's not so fast, and he feels left out.' The twins had drifted apart, and they now had separate rooms, so that George could get on with his studies while Ralph, presumably, had fun. Ben imagined how it must gall George to slog faithfully through studies all night while Ralph partied – work that Ralph would dash through in an hour next day for the same grades.

Now as Ben padded past Ralph's door it opened and Ralph stuck his head out, yawning. 'You look awful,' Ben said.

'Late night,' groaned Ralph. 'What time is it? I said I'd drive Fritzi to Croydon aerodrome.' It was an advantage of his father's position that Fritzi could always get a seat on Lufthansa. On such small details rested great decisions, Ben knew. He didn't like the idea of Fritzi returning permanently to Nazi Germany.

Fritzi came out carrying his valise, wearing smart tweed plus-fours, a cold briar-pipe stuck jauntily in his mouth. He looked more English than Ralph. 'Goodbye, sir,' he said, sticking his hand out. 'Thanks for everything.'

'Your father and I are great friends. Tell him I think he is complacent.'

'My father has the greatest respect for you, I know.'

Ben said: 'You don't have to go back.' Fritzi laughed, shaking his blond head, not taking his eyes off Ben. 'Don't go back,' Ben repeated. 'Remember I said that, Fritzi. And tell your too-tolerant father I said it.'

'I'll remember it, sir. But I can look after myself.'

'We are your friends,' Ben said. 'Never forget.' He

watched the two young men walk away. It disturbed him deeply that Fritzi, who had so easily adapted to English ways, would undoubtedly as easily adapt to being German again – and nowadays, that meant Nazi.

'Good riddance!' said a voice behind him, and Ben jumped, unaware that George had been eavesdropping. George witnessed Fritzi's departure with satisfaction. Ben understood. George thought that now he would have Ralph to himself again.

Then the oldest twin turned away and slammed his bedroom door.

Ben went down the staircase into the imposing entrance hall with its Meissen china collection that so amazed Dolfo Münchener when he stayed, saying it was the finest he had ever seen outside Germany. Ben could take no credit: it had been left him by Sir Ozwald Benton-Benson along with the Italian paintings in the long gallery, Easton Manor, and a considerable fortune. Ben had been sole beneficiary, Sir Ozwald had no one else. Ben was the son he wanted: a chilling compliment from a magnate Ben had despised as a victim of his wealth and sworn never to resemble. The only picture that meant anything to Ben, he could not purchase: Will had seen the Mantegna that had saved the Emporium in the Ashmolean Museum, where it would never be for sale.

He walked through to Pearl's garden room with its comfortable modern sofas, her many framed photographs scattered to record their lives together, and picture windows holding a wonderful green view, then fetched a bowl of milk from her kitchen and left it out on the grass for the hedgehogs. At night there were badgers, and once a fox had come and lapped warily at the milk while he watched. He sat on the terrace, his elbows on his knees, relaxing. The dawn was still and calm, and the air as warm as a caress.

He was richer than anyone imagined.

He felt Pearl's hand touch his shoulder and she sat beside him wrapped in a loose-fitting kimono. She was holding some of the photos. 'Love you?' she said.

'Love you.'

Each year a photographer came up and took a formal picture of the family lined up with London House behind them. They giggled at the first: Ralph and George looking very young in their school blazers, and Victoria racing her pedal car across the grass with a child's furious concentration, scratched elbows and muddy face – Lisa, in a wheelchair, was holding out her hand. 'Look,' Pearl said, 'she's saying "Just keep still for a moment!" ' Ben smiled. Lisa's joy was Victoria – as a grandmother she was helping to bring up a child she never had of her own, and between her and Pearl, poor Elise Barker hardly got a look in.

In the next photo Fritzi, wearing the same school blazer, was standing behind Ralph making rabbits' ears with his fingers, and Ralph, already in love with fast cars, girls and parties, not taking life seriously, was laughing. George stood apart with a scowl, his expression strikingly like Vane's. Will, preparing to leave for Spain, was smiling at Helen, and François sat on the steps next to Ralph, his expression at once open and reserved, ironic and self-contained. Lisa was standing with a stick, strong and smiling, and now with a firm grip on Victoria, who was gazing earnestly at something out of picture – probably the little pedal car she still adored.

In the last picture, in colour, Ben was astonished at how different the identical twins looked by now – Ralph stylishly dressed in a dark blue suit, slim and exuberant, George wearing a faded green tank-top pullover and bags, rather unconfidently affecting a pipe. Ralph and François together held Fritzi, waving, on their shoulders – this must have been just a day or two before François returned to Chouchou at Coucy. A girl with long dark hair Ben did not recognize stood shyly beside Helen – probably Ralph's girlfriend of the day, there were so many of them. Will had returned deeply disturbed by the devastation he had witnessed on his assignment to Madrid for the *Daily Herald*, and Ben had arranged with Lord Cleremont that he should recuperate in the northern peace and quiet of

Clawfell. Victoria, her hair cut in pudding-basin tomboy style, was sitting proudly on her new bicycle.

Behind them all in every photograph stood Ben and Pearl. Pearl was always tall, elegant, seeming untouched, yet holding Ben's hand, and Ben's easy smile commanded the tableau.

Yes, he had never been richer.

It was impossible to believe that there was truly any wickedness in the world or that war would come.

3

Breakfasts were family affairs. Juanita, the Spanish maid, laid out cornflakes, bacon and eggs and croissants on the counter and everyone helped themselves. The breakfast room had been enlarged into a light and airy setting with a long pine table and plenty of chairs. George was reading for his tripos – by sheer hard work he had driven himself within bare reach of a First, and he was never seen without his nose buried in an economics textbook. Ben hoped that he would join the Emporium – in a couple of years the twins inherited their Trust, and he desperately wanted them to feel the life of the great enterprise as much as he did, before he relinquished control to them. But his sons did not understand Ben's driving ambition. Ralph popped through to gobble a croissant before going off racing for the day, and a horn blew as his friends arrived to pick him up.

'I don't think Ralph has time to think,' Lisa said, glancing up from her lists. Her garden parties for the children had become enormous affairs requiring as much organization as the fund-raising. The parties themselves, for all the treats and jellies and crisps and sandwiches, with the Punch and Judy man from Southend booked every Friday afternoon for months ahead, were only the tip of the iceberg. There were the schools and orphanages to be contacted and Lisa was a District Commissioner for the

Girl Guides. Many parents and institutions opposed these jamborees at the first, but it was Lisa's genius not to appear stuck-up or patronizing: she felt passionately that these children deserved a chance, and many of the girls and boys thought that they were all her family.

At the other end of the table Pearl was talking with Ben about their world tour. There was a mountain of arranging to be done: Ben had received a letter from François inviting him to visit Chouchou at Coucy, so he decided to join Pearl aboard ship at Cherbourg for their journey to Australia.

'I want to come!' said Victoria, finding the feed for her guinea-pigs.

'It's business, honey,' Pearl said sadly. They would be away from London for nearly eight months, but Victoria would join them for the last three weeks in America and her ninth birthday.

'I'll be here,' Lisa said, finishing her tea and hugging her granddaughter.

Victoria said: 'Can I have a pony?'

'Of course you can.' Pearl always found Victoria's whims irresistible.

'Only if you learn to ride properly,' Ben said severely. His daughter always seemed to have grazed knees and a dirty face. She looked startled by his tone of voice. He winked and she walked down to him.

'I love you, Daddy,' she whispered.

The phone rang.

'Why's there never any peace around here?' stormed George. 'It's like bedlam.'

It was Joan ringing, Lord Cleremont's young nurse who had looked after him since his collapse. He was an alcoholic of course, and the doctor diagnosed cirrhosis of the liver, but Ben suspected a more general malaise: his father was really dying of despair.

'I'll come right over,' he said.

'It's your mother he needs to see,' Joan confided, 'he won't admit it, but that is what's preying on his mind.'

Ben turned to Lisa. 'I know how much you hate him,'

311

he said, 'but I think you ought to go. It's your last chance.'
Or his, he thought, but didn't say it.

Lisa hesitated. 'All right.'

Ben drove her to Lockhart House. It – and Clawfell – would soon be his. He recalled old Rockefeller chuckling – with his shoulders, not his thin lips – as he related the story of some impossible advice: 'My fortune was rolling up, rolling up like an avalanche! I must distribute it faster than it grew! If I did not, it would crush me, and my children, and my children's children.' Rockefeller paused. 'Can't do it, Ben. Money just can't be unmade, not nohow.'

Can't be unmade. That was a truth Lord Cleremont knew – driven by the blood, by the grim demeanour of his successful ancestors, their children, their children's children, staring down the dark stairway at Clawfell, dominating him even here, crushing him with the weight of name and time.

Ben and his mother waited in the hall, listening to the tocking of the clock.

Joan came down. 'He wants to see her now,' she murmured.

Lisa said: 'Is there any hope?'

Joan shook her head. Lisa glanced at Ben. 'Be gentle,' he said.

'I don't know,' she said wretchedly, 'I don't know what I think.'

He waited. She did not come down. The clock chimed softly. He got up and walked around. The air in Charles's study smelt stale and unused. Ben examined the modern paintings without affection; strange that Charles had given up on his own work.

The bookcase behind Charles's desk, half-opened for the first time, revealed a small, dark room. Ben peered inside. It was so sparsely furnished that he did not see its purpose. On the wall hung a single picture.

Ben found the switch for the masked electric light.

He gasped. It was the same view over the Dales, the exact same view where he and Pearl had made love, lying entwined on the grass by the pool. This was there, though it was dated the year 1899.

The painting showed love. The same love, as if nothing had changed. It was truly good, it was over Charles Cleremont's signature, and it was his last work.

Finally Ben heard footsteps upstairs. He clicked off the light and went out. Lisa was coming down.

'He's gone,' she said. He put his arms around her. Her eyes sparkled with tears. 'We had a secret talk. As he died he told me all the things he never found the courage to say in his lifetime.'

Ben helped her to the chair and held her hands.

'He did love me,' Lisa said.

Ben nodded.

'He loved me, Ben, loved me all his life! Only me.' Loved her enough that he never painted again, loved her enough to destroy himself because he did not have the courage to face his feelings.

'He loved me, Ben.' The pathetic loss of Charles Cleremont's life did not matter to her; only his love. At last he had found the courage of it – too late. But Lisa was happy.

'You loved him too,' Ben said.

'He needed me but he was too proud to admit it. As proud as I. We could never have lived closer than we did. But in a way, we were married, always married because of you, Ben. Because you existed.' She touched his face, then shivered. 'He asked if you hated him, and I shook my head. Then at the moment of his death, he said something very strange. "I didn't want to die," he gasped, "with *both* my sons hating me . . ."'

'He must have been thinking of Roland.'

'That must be right. He was quite delirious at the end. His last words were nonsense – a name, I think. *Bula Matari*. That's all. He gazed at me, and said that name. Bula Matari. As if it redeemed him.'

PART IV

THE FIRESTORM

CHAPTER NINETEEN

1

'I shan't give up, Ben,' Chouchou said in a frightened, determined voice.

His calmness gave her courage. 'Giving up never was your style.'

'How well you know me,' laughed the Dowager Countess of Coucy. Age had treated her magnificently. Chouchou's hair was iron grey, and lines of suffering remained entrenched around her lips and eyes even as she laughed, but the rope of pearls around her neck glowed lustrously with that mysterious life-light drawn from contact with her feminine skin, and her eyes had lost none of their rich golden shine: still tiger's eyes.

They climbed up the gentle slope behind the château towards the great ruin dominating the hilltop. For Chouchou's sake Ben stopped, looking back at the village of Coucy-la-Ville below them with its square-towered church and cluster of medieval rooflines, giving her time to catch her breath.

'You are right,' she shrugged. 'I needed to see you so badly.' She inhaled. 'To remember when I was young and all things were possible.'

'But now?'

'I'm frightened, Ben.'

'Tell me how I shall help you.'

'No man can help me this time. I have a cancer.' She clapped his arm and turned uphill, leaning into her stick but climbing with long, determined strides, skirting the patches of wild spring flowers. 'Don't worry,' she called back, 'it is only a very little one. I shall defeat it.'

Ben caught her up. He put his jacket over his shoulder and cooled his face with small flicks of his straw hat, wanting to reach out and help her – she was not as strong as she pretended. It was not death she feared, but failure, that terror or sadness would overwhelm her spirit. They climbed in silence but for Chouchou's gasps. 'Only a very little one,' she insisted.

'Does François know?'

'That, I could not face.'

They climbed through a vast, crumbling entranceway. The courtyard of the great castle covered half a dozen acres, now infested with weeds and shrubs, and trees grew along the mighty ramparts.

'I know the best surgeons,' Ben said.

'It is inoperable. There. You have the truth. A year at most.' She smiled broadly, an awful smile, pointing with her stick. 'Come, let us climb up.'

The walls were thirty feet thick, and a stone staircase led up inside, round and round. They stood on the crumbling stone at the top, without railings to hold them back from the drop, and all of northern France seemingly spread out around them. Coucy had long been the gateway to Paris, the keys to the kingdom. Chouchou leaned against Ben, trembling. To him, she admitted her fear.

He said: 'Will it be very painful?'

She pointed. Behind the plateau lay the ancient town of Laon. Soissons was in front of them down the steeper slope, lying beyond the valley of the Ailette, in the broad valley of the Aisne. 'This is the way an invader must come. Before Christ, the Gauls built a stockade at Coucy to defy the invading Roman legions. Centuries later the barbarian Germanic tribes swept through here on their way to destroy Rome. Four hundred years passed before the fort was rebuilt. This vast construction dominated the middle ages. One house, one family. Yes, Ben, it will be very, very painful to lose.'

'I wish so much I could give you life.'

'You have already done so,' she said gently.

'Will you tell François that he is my son?'

She swung her stick to the right. The hot wind blew in their faces, sweeping thunderclouds above the horizon. In the lurid light Ben picked out a pale green blur. 'The forest of Compiègne, where the Armistice that ended the Great War was signed. No, Ben. François must make his own life. He must never know.'

'I promise.'

'The gateway to Paris.' Chouchou swept her arms out indomitably as if to embrace the panorama. Every single finely worked silver strand of her rope of pearls was stamped with the crest of Coucy. 'All this is worth fighting for. I have no regrets. No regrets. What the lords of Coucy did for a thousand years, they for their castle and their country, I did for my family. My duty.' She tottered, and shockingly, her stick twisted out of her hand and slid into the abyss. A few moments later they heard it clatter on the stones far below. Ben held her, their faces close.

Chouchou whispered: 'I created joy, I regret nothing. I survived.'

Ben must ask now, or never. 'Why did you send Pearl to me?'

'Do you love her?'

Pearl was everything to him. His light, his hope, his world. Chouchou pressed her finger to his lips, seeing it in his eyes. 'Does she love you?'

'Totally,' he said, and knew he spoke the truth.

'Then that is all, and I am content.' She added sadly: 'But now my time is over. My life is in the past.' She trembled.

'Fight,' Ben said. 'Don't give up.'

They stood looking at the shell of the mighty tower dynamited by General Ludendorff. The thunderclouds swept over them northwards.

Looking satisfied, Dolfo Münchener came down the steps of the OKW headquarters on Bendlerstrasse. A member of the Geheimer Kabinettsrat, the prestigious secret council which advised Hitler personally on matters of foreign policy, he did not need to beg favours. No, he had seen the impulsive Luftwaffe chief – Hermann would do anything for a buddy from the Red Baron days – for Fritzi's sake.

The open Mercedes was driven towards the Ku-damm. Berlin was never prettier than at the end of spring, and the girls looked so carefree in their bright summery clothes. At first he hummed cheerfully, then his mood turned down. The air was humid. They had endured this thundery weather for a month now.

War with England would not come this year. The Luftwaffe had neither the strategic bombers necessary to terrorize civilian populations and demoralize family life – the key to effective total war – nor aircraft able to fly at night.

He was still terrified of flying. He concealed this from everyone, even Karin his wife, even Fritzi his son. It was his secret.

But Germany was being sucked willy-nilly into war. He was not sure how it was happening. He had himself believed in the Munich pact and participated in the back-room negotiations. His sincerity had impressed everyone. Yet now it seemed that he counted for nothing, and that they were all servants of forces beyond their control, puppets of the authority they wielded.

At first Karin had simply enjoyed the parties that the Nazis threw so well. He had enjoyed her pleasure. She loved meeting powerful people, the drink, the dancing. Now, just as he began to doubt, she believed. Glorious victory, glorious defeat . . . her heart was hardened. They had long been married only in name.

He still loved her, but Fritzi was everything in the world to him.

His car drew up outside the café Kranzler and he got out. Fritzi, wearing the fine Luftwaffe uniform, stood up from the table. 'Heil Hitler.'

The pale schoolboy who had returned from England was gone. It had been a mistake to send him; then a mistake to bring him back. Dolfo ordered coffee and schnapps. Fritzi was a believer. Such shallowness was wonderful and dangerous.

'I have excellent news, Father. I am to be posted home!'

Dolfo's heart sank. Once the words *father* and *home* would have thrilled him, but their meaning had changed. Now the Party was Fritzi's father, and home . . . home was the Fighter Pilot School at Schleissheim, not their little house by the church.

'Your mother will be pleased to have you at . . . home,' he said. 'But – '

'She is in Berlin. Did you not know?'

'Of course!' Dolfo covered himself. He was losing his son – Fritzi was slipping through his fingers.

'Fritzi, I have spoken with an old friend on your behalf. Field Marshal Göring has a vacancy on his personal staff.'

'I won't be a penpusher!' said Fritzi violently, using the English word. 'I won't die of shame. A young man's place is in the firing line.'

Dolfo dreaded these words – once he believed them himself. But if he opposed Fritzi, the more determined the young man would become. He spoke carefully.

'I wish I had flown in Spain,' Fritzi interrupted. 'You remember Will, Ben London's oldest son? He saw a whole Spanish village blown off the face of the map! Junkers 87 dive-bombers and 52s, Heinkel 111s, Bf 109s for strafing. In ten minutes, only clouds of dust . . . he said he would never forget it. Neither would I! I myself have flown a Bf 109,' he added proudly.

'I could not bear it if you were killed,' Dolfo confessed.

Fritzi finished his drink.

Dolfo stood and had his offer of a lift refused. They talked no more.

Dolfo had himself driven back to his empty apartment. He was a wealthy and powerful man who had made a success of his life – a success that once would scarcely have seemed possible. Now it seemed that what he thought of as success, was failure. He tossed back a drink, then picked up the phone and asked for the international exchange.

Within a few minutes a smart English voice came on

the line. 'London Emporium, Mr London's private office, how can I help you?'

He gave his name. 'I wish to speak to Ben, please.'

'I'm terribly sorry,' Alice Cypress said, jotting his name on her notepad, 'you've missed him by several weeks. Mr London is en route to Australia.'

She thought the man at the other end had rung off, but then he said in a low voice: 'When will he be back?'

'Not until October, I'm afraid.' She doodled, waiting. 'Can I take a message?' With modern communications Ben could run his empire from wherever in the world he wished. 'You could contact him by shipboard radiogram yourself, if you prefer, or send ahead, care of Mr Mackelroy, Perth, Australia.' She listened. 'Hallo?'

'I don't know what I would say,' came the low voice at last, and this time she heard the *ting* of disconnection.

Alice glanced at her watch and timed the call, then marked it No Action. It was hot and she longed to be in her garden. She took off her diamante spectacles and went to the window, looking down the angle of the Emporium's tiered stone façade. Old Bond Street was locked solid with traffic, the fumes rising on the still air. Pineapple stood tall and imposing in his yellow and navy Head Doorman's uniform. He took no nonsense, but was unfailingly helpful to tourists, and Alice knew that he kept half a dozen lollipops in his pocket for children. He had great nobility of manner, and she liked him a lot.

Yet sometimes she sensed the lonely man hidden beneath his skin. He had been married once, apparently, but she had run off. Alice looked for her glasses: that was life. The cure was devotion and efficiency.

Pineapple stepped forward as a taxi swung in to the kerb, and he opened the door, saluting dutifully.

Alice went back to her desk, scrutinized the piece of paper recording the telephone call, and dropped it in the bin. No action.

'Hallo, Dillibe,' the figure in the back of the taxi said.

Then she said, still without leaning forward: 'You were right.'

'Natasha.' She was as beautiful as ever – so beautiful that she must be a dream. Pineapple closed his eyes, shutting her out again, so great was his agony.

'Yes, I failed.' The admission sounded dragged out of her. She had lost out to Ethel Waters for the part in the all-black *Cabin in the Sky* now being cast by Vincente Minnelli in Hollywood; for the first time she had failed not because of her colour, but in spite of it. Her spirit was broken.

'I watched *Gone with the Wind*.'

'Dear Pineapple,' she said coldly, 'so faithful. I don't deserve you.'

'I wrote and wrote,' he groaned, 'but I only got type-written letters back.'

'You weren't on the phone. There's so little time out there.'

He held her hands. They were hot. He knew she manipulated him, but his love for her showed no mercy to him, he could not let her go again.

'Are you getting in or getting out, mate?' the cabbie said over his shoulder.

Pineapple asked his wife urgently: 'Have you come back for ever?'

'Will you have me?'

He gripped both hands tightly, staring into her eyes. 'Promise me.'

'Yes!' Natasha laughed.

Pineapple slid into the seat next to her. 'I had faith in you, I always believed in you. It was ambition that made you go, but I was jealous and ashamed. I'll never gloat. It was the strength of our marriage that brought you back.'

'Yes, yes,' she said, 'that's right.' Four times he had said *I*.

'All right,' the cabbie said, 'out you get.'

'Darling,' Natasha said, 'I have no money – no English money, pay the man for me, would you? Tell him to take me home. I'll be waiting for you.'

'It's off the Edgware Road,' Pineapple told the cabbie through the window.

'Taxi!' George London came running out of the Emporium, arm upraised. His red face was perspiring and he was carrying a new set of tennis whites clasped against his chest. A sneaker plopped on the pavement and Pineapple picked it up. 'I thought you were supposed to open the bloody doors,' George said.

'I was just dealing with this taxi, sir,' Pineapple said, eyeing him for a pipsqueak.

'London House,' George directed the cabbie, snatching his sneaker.

'Excuse me,' said Natasha, 'this taxi is taking me towards Marble Arch.'

George looked around for another cab but there wasn't one. 'Look here, do you mind if I take you half a mile out of your way? I'm supposed to be playing tennis with my brother Ralph but the bloody Spanish maid lost my whites.' George made up for his lack of clothes-sense, which he thought nobody noticed, with fastidiousness about appearing in correct sporting attire. 'May I double up?'

Natasha shrugged. 'If you must.' She glanced at Pineapple.

'Well, I'll pay, of course,' George said, getting in.

'Of course,' Natasha said. Pineapple saluted and closed the door. The taxi turned tightly and joined the queue of traffic. 'Well, you've got a dark, mysterious voice,' George said, making conversation, 'American, is it?'

'I've been in California a few years. The movies.'

'Really! We've had Charlie Chaplin round at our house. Douglas Fairbanks lifted me on the palm of one hand, of course I was younger then. Ronald Colman gave me one of his cigarettes.'

'Should I know you?' Her eyes were large and ironic.

'George London.' George hesitated then shook her languorous hand. 'I own the Emporium with my brother. Or will do, rather, when I come of age.'

'You look quite old to me.'

324

'Thank you. I'm nineteen, nearly twenty.' He leaned forward, peering anxiously through the windscreen. 'Really, it would have been quicker to walk.'

'I'm in no hurry,' Natasha said.

George sat back. 'No. Nor me.' The taxi broke through Piccadilly and turned down St James's Street. 'What's your name?'

'Natasha Cetawa,' she said offhandedly.

Her name rang a bell and he stared at her. 'You're much more beautiful in real life.'

'Thank you. I'm normally made up as a slave.'

She wore a very dark brown silk dress. He came to a decision as the taxi turned into Stable Yard. 'Look, come in and have a cup of tea.'

'I thought you were playing tennis.'

'Ralph's probably forgotten about it anyway. He's got so many friends, he doesn't care about his boring old brother.'

Natasha looked up at the portico. 'All right,' she said casually. George paid off the taxi and held open a side door into the house, looking at her as she moved past him. She glimpsed magnificent rooms through the interior doorways, then George preceded her along the hallway to a sudden small, sunlit lounge. Comfortable sofas were scattered about and she could see a bright green garden through the picture windows.

'We call this the garden room,' George said.

He stood at the glass looking at Ralph play over on the tennis court. He had a girl with him of course, but George couldn't recognize her at this distance. She had to run for a shot and missed, laughing her little blonde head off. Ralph gave her a very gentle serve, and when she missed it he vaulted the net and pretended to show her how to hold the racquet. Very funny. Ralph put his hands over hers and she giggled, then they went to sit in the summerhouse. 'Makes you sick,' George scowled. His lower lip pouted like Vane's. 'They think he's so bloody marvellous.'

'Do I hear a note of jealousy?'

'We're identical twins.'

'He's very handsome.'

George turned. She favoured him with an amused glance. 'What's wrong with having fun. I married my husband when I was seventeen and he was twenty-eight.' She didn't take her eyes off his.

'I'll boil the water,' George said. Thunder rumbled.

'Yes. Let's drink some tea.' She sat on the sofa. She must be twelve, fifteen years older than he, her features strong and wide, black as night.

'Everyone loves Ralph,' George said. He didn't dare sit beside her. This was all very naughty. He didn't normally tell people he hardly knew about his family.

'I think the water's boiling,' she said.

George made the tea and left it to brew. He was starting to enjoy the feeling of naughtiness and made himself sit down very casually beside her. There was a chance that she planned to seduce him and he wanted to see how it worked out. She was a mature, married woman, and that made it all the more interesting. She had red-lacquered nails. He jerked out of his fantasy as she turned slightly, suddenly colossally aware of her proximity. He could feel her heat radiating through her dress, and he felt her weight shifting towards him on the sofa. A thrill of fear shook him. He had never been with a woman, and the authority of her sexuality that she directed at him was quite overwhelmingly unlike anything he had ever imagined, and it dwarfed him. This was the real business, as far from the giggling and petting undoubtedly by now going on in the summerhouse as night was from day. Raindrops splashed on the windows.

'Are you frightened of the thunder?' George asked.

'Terrified. Hold me.' George embraced her desperately, more afraid than he could say that he would fail. He pecked her cheek. She turned her head and her mouth closed over his. George felt the cushions of the sofa under his back and he could hear raindrops pelting down the glass. Her hands came sliding up under his sleeveless pullover and suddenly skinned him of it like a rabbit, although she kept her own dress on, kneeling over him. George gave a groan of pornographic desire, trying to see her body, to grip her breasts, but everything was hidden. Thunder rattled the glass but through it all he heard her deep, slow breaths continuing as she settled down and took him. He gasped between her fingers splayed over his mouth, then whimpered into the palm of her hand.

'Oh my darling,' he whispered at last, gazing up at her. She took the weight off her knees then stood up. Without looking at him she poured the tea and drank a cup, staring out over the beautiful garden in the rain. He still had not seen her body. He rolled off the sofa and found his clothes.

'That was wonderful,' he said.

'Was it?' she said.

'When will I see you again?'

She didn't look round. 'Why should you want to see me again?'

'We could spend longer over it.'

'Why should I want to, little George? Call me a taxi.'

'I love you!' he said. His lower lip trembled.

She glanced at him. Then she laughed, mocking him.

Ria, who had never learned to drive, paid off the taxi at the end of Havannah Street and inhaled the good and familiar odour of the river, evoking memories of her childhood. That river-smell, and the crying of the seagulls wheeling above the narrow streets, and the shouts of the stevedores working in the docks, meant she was coming home.

She looked around her. Even though there were no tall masts now amongst the plumes of smoke and steam rising above the warehouse roofs, and telephone lines and power wires drew cats' cradles between the houses, and there were wireless aerials sprouting from the chimneys and the street was dotted with parked motor cars, this still felt like home.

Probably the car owners wouldn't allow kids to play in the street, not the joyous ball games anyway. That silence, that stillness, was the biggest change. The kids were all indoors listening to Arthur Askey on the wireless.

Ria remembered . . . she remembered too much, and tears burned in her eyes. She remembered taking Ben through her secret alleyways home to Canary Warren – just a concrete lorry park and enormous Canadian grain silos now. Lives were so long, and change was so quick. It seemed like yesterday.

She hadn't changed at all. She was the same person with the same feelings. People changed outside, but never inside.

I'm Ria. I'm special! She remembered Peter Pungle dragging Ben London through the fog . . . nothing was different. It was all still in her head. She remembered walking along here so many times with Will and was seized by an unendurable longing and sense of loss. She had failed her son: failed to love him as a baby, failed to comprehend him as a child. Then those few years of heaven when he visited her on holidays from the *Mercury* and at first from Oxford . . . but they hadn't really understood one another, had they? He had moved more and more to London House, until she had really lost him. Now he had taken up painting and was living on the Home Farm at Clawfell, Ben's derelict Yorkshire castle, also forbidden territory to her.

Territory from which she forbade herself.

Say it again. Nothing.

The cycle of thundery weather had broken and it was blazing hot in the brilliant sunshine. Ria took her jacket off and shook out her hair as she walked up the street. Despite the heat Mum's door was closed. Ria knocked, and heard the bolts being pulled back. The door opened and Esther looked out.

'Hallo, Mum,' Ria said with a slightly forced grin, 'give us a cup of tea.'

'*Go away, Ria. Get away from us.*' Those terrible words were still graven on Ria's heart, all the worse because they had been so without reason. Esther's spiteful effort to split up her family, half out of her mind after Nigel's death, had failed – Ria deliberately came visiting from time to time and so, she knew, did Vic. If Esther had thought she was forcing Ria to escape from her brother and his life of crime, trying to keep them apart, it came to nothing, because Ria had nowhere to escape to except Trott's Nightclub, and he could always find her there – if anything Esther's rejection had driven them closer together. Esther seemed to realize this now.

'You're like a bad penny, Ria,' she grumbled, 'you always turn up!'

Ria grinned openly, knowing she was being welcomed. She and Mum always understood one another hand and glove, they never needed a translation book like for talking with men. As soon as they sat down around the kitchen table they nagged and worried at one another like the two old friends they were. There was only the one mystery remaining between them: that one was the mother, and the other the daughter.

Ria looked in the front room. Tom was sitting in a wheelchair. 'Hallo, Dad,' she called. He was holding a canary in his enormous hands, and the sight of that brought tears to Ria's eyes for no reason. He smiled at her amiably.

'His heart's bad,' Esther said in the kitchen. She was putting on her hat and coat. 'We'll come back and have tea.' She was fifty-seven years old but to Ria's eyes looked ageless: mostly it showed in her old-fashioned manners, even to wearing an overcoat to go out on a day this hot, when Ria looked modern and smart in summer separates, a cool skirt and white silk blouse clean on this morning, her jacket hooked on her finger over her shoulder.

They walked down to Okill's the grocer and bought some flowers, good varieties, Esther selecting them one by one. Ria was going to pay but Esther stopped her. 'I can afford to do this, my girl. Vic sends us money, regular as clockwork, paid into the bank every month. More than we need.' She handed over a pound note and counted her change, then gave a small tip. They turned back up the road towards St Luke's Church. 'Have you seen Terry?'

Ria shook her head. 'Fine young man. Quiet, too. Worships Vic like Nigel did. Well of course Vic's had to bring him up, hasn't he.'

'It's such a shame Vic never married.'

'Where would he find the woman who matched up to you?' Esther blurted, stopping by the church gate.

'Mum, really.' Ria looked shocked.

'I blame myself,' Esther murmured. 'God's punishments come on this good earth. I wouldn't mind spending eternity in hell if only my children were spared.'

'Come on, Mum, that's the gin talking.' Ria bit her tongue.

Esther turned on her fiercely, shorter than Ria but much stronger. 'Vic touched you. I know he has.'

'Don't be stupid.' Ria's colour rose. 'You're thinking of Ben.'

'You admitted it – that day Vic was mad with jealousy because you were pregnant and he went after Ben to kill him. Remember? Remember how frightened you were?' Ria stood in the churchyard with her hands against her head.

'Of course I was frightened!'

'You admitted it: *he has*.'

Ria wept. 'There was nothing in it. It was just rough games. Remember how we lived, Mum – on the bloody floor? Remember having no money, no beds, no bedroom, sleeping all together with only a curtain between us and paper in the windows, sweating together in the summer and shivering together in the winter. That was our family. Vic looked after us! Have you forgotten all that?'

'No,' Esther said dully. 'No, I haven't forgotten hard times.'

'I loved Ben!' Ria said.

'I know *that*, my girl.'

'But I hated Vic more, Mum.'

Esther passed her hand wearily across her face. 'We were all so innocent.'

'Bloody weren't,' said Ria defiantly.

'Sometimes Vic goes along to Trott's now, doesn't he?'

'So what? It's harmless.'

'You're friends, aren't you?'

'Is that such a bloody sin?'

'Don't keep on using that blasphemous language on hallowed ground, Ria!' They both looked away from one another. Ria blew her nose and put on her jacket. She went and looked at Nigel's stone of remembrance set in the bottom of the wall, next to Arleen's. Both were well cared for, but Arleen had had no one in the world except Nigel, so her stone was bare.

But on Nigel's rested a posy of wild flowers, lovingly entwined.

'I always find them there, fresh every month,' said Esther fretfully. 'Wild flowers of the season. Holly with berries on in the winter. God knows who puts them there. I don't know, Ria.' She dropped her shop-bought flowers almost in despair. 'Sometimes I think I don't know nearly everything, and that's the truth.'

Pearl thought Mackelroy was the toughest man she had ever seen. He was a rough diamond, and it was attractive. She saw a little of Ben in him, but with Mackelroy it was all on the surface. He stood with a burly driver and a limousine behind him.

It was the antipodean midwinter, but Fremantle was warm, and Mackelroy stood on the North Quay dockside wearing a dark suit and tie in the European style, looking completely uncomfortable as Ben approached him. Ben held out his hand. He wore an open-neck shirt and looked more Australian than Mackelroy. 'Hi, Pete.'

'Ben, before God, I'm sorry. I wish to God you'd never given me that thousand pounds and none of it had ever happened.' He was talking about Vane's death as though he was obsessed by guilt, Pearl thought.

Mackelroy had forgotten all about Ben's hand so Ben turned and introduced her.

'Pleased to meet you,' Mackelroy said perfunctorily. 'Let's get out of here.'

Mackelroy took the fold-down seat facing them in the

limousine, legs apart and elbows braced on his knees, fingers working, obviously in a state of great agitation. Pearl wondered why he didn't take off his tie as he was obviously dying to do. Ben seemed not to notice the nervous tension, looking out equally at the passing railway yards. As the limousine turned left along Queen Victoria Street Mackelroy said: 'What a way to repay a favour.'

'Forget it,' Ben said.

'I have nightmares. I feel responsible for her death, Ben. I don't know what made her come to my room. A married woman. I promise before God I never touched her.'

Ben knew all this.

'The post mortem proved it,' Mackelroy said. 'Sorry, m'am,' he apologized to Pearl. His attitudes were very masculine. Nothing was more important to him.

'It was natural justice and everyone got what they deserved,' Ben said flatly.

Mackelroy looked uneasy. 'I don't know about that,' he said.

'The subject is closed,' Ben said.

Mackelroy stripped off his tie and Pearl had never seen a man look so relieved.

As they passed the Perth city limits Ben asked: 'We're on a quest. Does the name Bula Matari mean anything to you?'

'No, doesn't sound Australian. African, maybe.'

'That's what we thought,' Ben said, glancing at Pearl.

In Cottesloe the limousine turned up a meandering drive between open lawns to a colonial-style house with verandahs. Mackelroy had been married and divorced. While Pearl went inside to freshen up he led Ben to a table set up on the grass and tossed over a bottle from a crate of Swan lager, the first cold lager-beer Ben had tasted. They stood looking across Peppermint Grove and along the broad sweep of the river to the distant hills.

'I never forgot that thousand pounds, Ben.'

'It was a gift.'

'I struck gold with the last fiver. I didn't let you down.

You said you didn't want control, so you've got forty-nine per cent of Mackelroy–London Mining in your name.'

Ben shrugged.

Mackelroy said: 'Doesn't it matter to you, half a million dollars a year in dividends? And that's not counting the import-export side. I've made a success of it, a real success. I'm the best investment you ever made.'

Ben had other investments which had made more money. He listened to the cicadas chittering in the shrubs.

'Yes,' Ben said, 'you're the best investment I ever made, Mackelroy.'

Pearl came down the steps from the verandah, and he turned to welcome her.

2

On the first day of August Esther found her husband Tom lying beside his wheelchair in the front room. 'Tom,' she said, 'get up, Tom.' The radio was playing and she turned it up, but he was stone dead, and she knew it. Her hands crawled up her face and she screamed, but nobody heard her. In the old days her neighbours would have come running, but all that was changed now, doors were kept shut. Grief was like death, you didn't make a show of it nowadays. Esther knelt down alone and tried to pray, but the radio kept playing some stupid 'Tritsch Tratsch Polka' – forever afterwards, that gay music reminded her of death, and she couldn't bear it.

She held his stiff, cold hand in hers. When she was young she had married Tom not out of love but necessity – her first husband Dick had been the love of her life, though he'd been difficult and sharp, much older than her, but they had less than a year of bliss together and when he died she found herself broke and on the street. It was a man's world in those days, a good girl had to marry or starve, and be hasty about it. Tom had been frighteningly strong, but she knew he only got drunk when he was paid, and he wasn't a brute. And, though he wasn't good with words, she was sure he loved her more than she loved him. She wouldn't move in with him, none of that common law business: Tom was always very proper, and he wanted her as his own true wife. It took three weeks for the banns to be read from St Lukes. On the first, Esther missed her period.

She could still remember praying – just like this – on her knees, on the floor. *Dear God, no.*

Tom was in heaven now; he knew the truth.

Esther's face crumpled in anguish. She hadn't been certain herself – she sometimes did skip a month – not until a couple of years had passed and Vic was born had she been certain. And even then, not at first: Vic had been born with his eyes open, and they had been blue, like the eyes of all newborn babies. Over the next few weeks though, they turned dark, like her's, like Tom's. Tom didn't realize what that meant, and she couldn't bring herself to tell him. And gradually it became too late ever to tell him as the other children followed on, Nigel, and Arthur, and Jane, and Dicky, and Jim.

All dead now; except for Ria and Vic.

Esther got slowly to her feet. She had been a foolish woman, but she didn't see, for her family's sake, knowing Vic, what else she could have done. Life had to be lived from day to day; for so many years, they had depended on him for everything, the meat on their table, the clothes they wore. But her secret had grown more and more appalling. *Go away, Ria. Get away from us.* Futile advice; all she had done was hurt Ria terribly, who'd endured enough pain in her life.

'All my fault,' Esther said, looking down at Tom. She would have to tell Ria the truth now. Esther squeezed her eyes shut; she couldn't face it.

She had to. She picked up the phone. When Ria answered Esther told her: 'This is Mum. Tom's dead.'

Ria gabbled something. Esther took a deep breath. 'Darling, my love, for God's sake come over. No, don't phone Vic. There's something I have to tell you. You

334

alone.' She dropped the earpiece back on the hook. Her hands were shaking as though she had palsy. She needed a drink or she'd never get a grip on herself.

'I'm sorry, Tom,' she said. 'I'll be back in a minute.' She backed out of the room and stooped by the kitchen table, rummaging through the cupboard under the sink for her gin. Her fingers found the smooth neck of the bottle and she took a long, trembling swig, staring back at the front room.

Atrocious pain exploded in her throat and burned her mouth, then the awful burning spread to her stomach. Esther dropped the bottle and doubled up in agony. Burning liquid splashed back into her mouth. She tried to scream but that made it worse. She collapsed, trying to get to the sink, and lay writhing. Finally the agony was so great that she was aware of nothing more.

Mum's call had come just as Ria was going out shopping, so it didn't take her a minute to get downstairs, and by luck the first taxi she saw in the Strand stopped for her. Cabbies didn't usually like going into the East End because of the trouble getting a fare back, but this driver was pleased because he was going home to Cubitt Town and Havannah Street was on his way.

He dropped her at the end of the road and she walked up. It was very hot, but Mum's door was closed, everyone had something worth stealing these days. Ria knocked, then looked through the window. Through the net she saw something lying there that looked like a man's leg. She knocked on the glass, but everything was so still, and then she saw Mum's handkerchief lying all crumpled up on the floor.

Ria ran back and hammered on the door. There was no reply. She turned the handle and thank God this time it wasn't bolted. As it swung open Ria took three quick steps into the front room.

'Dad!' she cried. Tom lay beside his wheelchair with his waxen face turned towards the fireplace. His birds still fluttered in their cages.

Ria went back into the hall. 'Mum? Where are you?' she called. Suddenly her gaze fixed on the kitchen. A blue bottle half out of a brown paper bag lay on the floor in a puddle of clear fluid, and she smelled bleach.

Mum was alive – she was lying in a contorted position, but she was warm and limp. She stank of the bleach and pale deltas of running colour had wormed this way and that down the front of her dress. Her lips were discoloured. She'd drunk the stuff. Ria found a bottle of milk, lifted Esther's head and poured it down her throat. Esther choked but kept it down. Ria got half another bottle down her, then ran to the phone. At first the operator couldn't understand her.

Ria pushed her hand through her hair and forced herself to give the address calmly. 'I need an ambulance, as quickly as you can.'

She hung up and went back to the kitchen. Esther was deeply unconscious but groaning, a terrible sound, then gradually she fell silent. Ria saw blisters had formed in her mouth, and now she realized how very bad this was. If the bleach had got down to Mum's stomach, it would all look like that.

'*Oh, Mum,*' she whispered – just as she had on the day after Nigel's death. 'Don't die, Mum. Don't die.' She lit a cigarette from the gold lighter.

She must phone Vic.

But when she spoke to the operator, she heard herself asking to be put through to London Emporium. She had, in this her hour of need, simply got to turn to Ben. He would know what to do, he would know how to cope. But a smart, rather prim woman's voice came on the line.

'London Emporium, Mr London's private office, Alice Cypress speaking, how can I help you?'

'I've got to speak to Ben,' choked Ria.

'Mr London is not available – '

'That's impossible,' Ria said. 'Put Ben on the line, tell him it's Ria, Mum's dying – tell him Mum's dying.'

'You must be a personal friend of Mr London's?'

Ria closed her eyes. 'We knew one another once.'

'I'm sorry to tell you that Ben has completed his business commitments in Australia. He sailed five days ago from Sydney, bound for South Africa. He's in mid-ocean on the *Doric Star*. However I can have a radiogram sent to him, and I'm sure he'll want to send his condolences.'

'Thank you,' Ria said dully, 'that's very kind of you.'

She hung up.

Then she picked up the phone again and called Vic.

Secretly, their global tour was their honeymoon – the honeymoon they'd never had. Ben and Pearl settled easily into shipboard life, the world of quoits and gin and its, late rising, eating and sleeping – or just walking the deck, hand in hand, with the Indian Ocean vast and deep around them, without worries or cares. Pearl attended classes to learn embroidery. In the evenings it took her an hour to dress for dinner, and she wore her finest jewels – especially the fabulous Mogok Ruby, its pure 'pigeon-blood' red making it more valuable than diamond. He had handed it to her gift-wrapped in brown paper, casually sitting up in bed one morning, but Pearl noted the look in his eyes and sensed inside herself that it was something very special. She opened the package being very careful not to tear the paper, as though it was Christmas. Even so, when she saw what lay wrapped in samite inside, she was stunned.

'Ben!' she gasped. The ruby's glow shimmered across her features. 'It must have cost a fortune!'

'Of course it did. Several fortunes, actually.' He held the stone to her throat, where it glittered with blood-red light. 'Worth every penny?'

'Yes!' Pearl clung to him tearfully. 'It shows how much you love me.' She laughed, holding it against her, then cried again as she kissed him. 'I love you so much. I'm nothing without you.'

'Or I without you.'

'Oh, oh,' Pearl dropped her forehead in her hand, gazing at the jewel. 'I do wish for another baby. I miss Victoria so much, I'm looking forward so much to seeing her.' They would be flying from Durban in a week, meeting Elise Barker in New York with Victoria. 'Can we have another baby, honey, before it's too late?'

He disappeared under the sheets and tickled her toes.

Pearl lay looking up, holding the ruby against her throat for luck. 'I just want another baby,' she murmured, 'I don't mind if it's a boy or a girl.' She closed her eyes and made the wish. 'Before it's too late.'

A few mornings later, they were sunning themselves in deckchairs on the boat deck balcony outside their suite of cabins, Ben with his feet up on the railing and his face turned towards the sun. There was a knock and the steward brought in the day's batch of telegrams from the radio office. This sun was too strong for Pearl's fair complexion and she sat mostly in the shade to one side, wearing a large white hat, working on her embroidery. 'Bring us a cool fruit cocktail, will you?' she told the steward, and he bowed. The only sound was the throbbing of the ship's engines and the surfing wash far below, and occasionally the distant shouts of people playing deck-games, as Ben worked silently through the telegrams. Pearl looked up, watching him affectionately.

'Oh no,' he said suddenly. 'Tom's dead. Esther's in hospital. She was like a mother to me – before I had a mother. Apparently there isn't much hope.'

'Who sent the telegram?'

'Ria.'

'Ben, I'm sorry. You'd better tell Alice to send flowers.'

'Yes, it's the least I can do.' He took his feet off the rail. 'I admired Esther. Mum always believed her absolute duty was to hold her family together, she would give almost anything to keep the peace between us. It can't have been an easy struggle.'

Pearl was wise. 'Are we talking about Esther – or Ria?'

He looked at her with admiration. 'You still surprise me. Everyone thinks you're so bright and carefree, but underneath – '

'You alone know me fully.' Her secret from the cellar.

'Yes, your dark insight.'

Pearl closed her eyes. She wanted a baby so badly it hurt her.

'Only because I love you,' she said, smiling at the sun. 'You're special.'

'That's why you married me. Isn't it gorgeous weather?'

Deep down, she knew, very deep down, there was still a place in Ben's heart for Ria. She was not jealous: no man could eradicate his past, any more than she could. Ben was aware of this as well as she, Pearl knew: that was why he had not even invited Ria to the housewarming at London House, showing Pearl for certain that he was hers securely.

The steward brought cool fruit punch in tall glasses. She drank gratefully.

Ria kept a vigil at Esther's bedside for two days and nights. Vic had arranged a private room on a southern corner of the London Hospital that caught the sun, and it was full of flowers. Esther looked as though she was sleeping, but her hand in Ria's clasp looked almost transparent, and seemed to weigh nothing.

'You did the right thing to dilute the chemical with milk,' the young doctor had told Ria, coming out after using the pump, 'but her stomach has ulcerated.'

Esther was hovering between life and death.

'I'm dying,' Esther whispered once during the night.

'No you aren't, Mum,' said Ria with a brightness opposite to what she felt.

At dawn the nurse came in. 'You'd better get some sleep,' she told Ria.

Ria went to the mirror over the washbasin. She looked awful, with dark bruises around her opal eyes, and her hair was a mass of golden tangles. She splashed cold water over her face and tried to use her comb. Vic gazed at her from the chair on the other side of the bed. He had hardly spoken to her; he looked worse than she did. It was as though, Ria thought, glancing at him in the mirror as she tugged at her locks, Esther's death was part of his own. Sometimes he had been bitterly cruel to their mum, often he had mocked her. But he loved her, and in his way respected her authority and maintained her in it, and now the thought of missing her caused an almost intolerable loneliness in him.

Vic was heartbroken, Ria realized. His red cheeks were pale, and his smart three-piece suit hung off him. He had taken his shoes off and one of his socks needed darning. He looked a pathetic figure, and Ria went over to him. She put her hand on his shoulder in silent understanding.

Vic's position as a gangland leader, with Terry still too young to take Nigel's place, was under threat. Something had gone out of Vic in the last few years, he lost his energy, and in a way it made Ria sad. Vic had always been exciting to be around, just as Ben had been, you never knew quite what would happen next. But that had changed. In the old days Vic would never have come knocking weakly at her door, handing her a tatty bunch of daffs and meekly asking to be friends. He would have demanded, and he would have got.

Vic patted her hand. 'Thanks for being here, Ria.'

'You look exhausted.'

'You look lovely.' A flash of the old fire showed in his eyes. 'Or aren't I supposed to say that about my own sister?'

'I look like a traffic accident.'

'Not to me you don't.'

'Give over, Vic,' she laughed, pulling away. The door opened and a porter lifted in an enormous basket of flowers. 'They're lovely!' Ria gasped.

'I didn't order them.' Vic took the card from Ria's fingers. She had gone quite pale. 'Who is it?'

'No one.' The best wishes on the card were from Ben London.

Vic read the card, then screwed it up and flung it away. 'Can't forget him, can you?' he accused her.

'I didn't mean it. I thought someone ought to tell him. I didn't know he'd send flowers!'

'Can't get him out of your mind,' said Vic bitterly. That was true; but neither could he. The fury left him as suddenly as it had come. 'Look, Ria, there's only the two of us left now. We've got to stick together.'

'I know, Vic, but I'm so tired.'

'When all this is over I'll take you out to the Tooke Arms. It'll be the good old days all over again. Wotcher, Ria?'

'Mum won't die!' said Ria defiantly. She sat in the sun holding Mum's hand.

During the afternoon, when the slanting sunlight had moved across to the other side of the bed, Esther began to talk. Vic's eyes jumped open; because of the heat he had undone his tie and sweat gleamed on his face. He winced against the glare, then pulled his chair forward. 'She's only talking in her sleep,' Ria murmured. They listened for a while, then Esther fell silent.

Vic moved his chair back in the corner where it was cooler and closed his eyes again. Ria's head dropped forward over Mum's hand. Suddenly, it seemed, the room was in shadow, and Ria heard a voice whispering.

'Ria,' whispered Esther. 'Ria.'

'I'm here, Mum.'

It was nearly sunset. Esther's eyes were open, and her head had turned slightly on the pillow. Ria understood that she was hanging on to consciousness by a thread, but she was not delirious. 'Don't exert yourself, Mum,' Ria said. 'You are in hospital. You are going to be all right.'

'No hope,' whispered Esther. 'Got to tell you. No Vic. Vic must never know.'

Ria leaned forward anxiously. 'Don't push yourself, Mum.'

Esther lost her grip on Ria's fingers. 'Tom is in heaven now. He knows the truth, God forgive me. Ria, my darling. My darling, difficult daughter. Listen to what I must tell you.'

'Mum, please rest.'

'Are you listening?' She gripped Ria's hand again with shivering fingers.

'Yes.'

Esther drew a deep breath. 'Ria, why are your eyes blue?'

Ria smiled. 'Why, I don't know.' She had never thought about it.

Esther's hand fluttered. 'Mine are brown. Tom's were brown. Vic has brown eyes, very dark brown. Nigel had brown eyes, just like him. And all my other poor little babies.'

'So what?' Ria said. 'Lots of people have brown eyes.'

'Ria, firstborn Ria. You don't fit in, you never did. Why are your eyes blue?'

'What the hell are you talking about?' Ria demanded in a frightened voice.

'Hell,' groaned Esther. 'My darling, I wanted and wanted to tell you but it was always too late.'

She let the pause go on and on.

Ria suddenly realized that Dick's eyes must have been blue. The truth hit her sideways, it was so bloody blindingly obvious that she had missed it all her life. Never thought about it – but there they were in the mirror every time, saying *look at me*: her impossible blue eyes.

Her real father's eyes.

Dick's eyes.

'Vic isn't your brother,' Esther said. 'He's only your half-brother.'

Then Esther slept. Her blistered mouth dropped open.

Ria glanced across at Vic in the corner. He was looking at her, and she knew that he had heard every word.

Ria covered her eyes, then shook her head, as if by covering her beautiful blue eyes and shaking her head from side to side until it hurt she could deny the truth.

'Stop it,' Vic commanded.

Ria stopped.

He came round the bed and took her chin in his hand, staring into her eyes. Indoors, his looked black, and she could not look away. He stared first into her left eye, then her right eye.

Then he said: 'It's true.'

He touched her hair tenderly.

'Yes,' Ria said, 'it's true.'

It makes no difference, it makes no difference.

But it did.

He leaned down to give her a brotherly peck on her cheek, she thought.

Instead, Vic lifted her chin and kissed her full on the mouth.

CHAPTER TWENTY

But Esther did not die.

Within the week it was plain that she was going to recover, and in a fortnight she was allowed home for bed rest. It was not a happy homecoming. Nothing was going to be the same again.

'I'll help you upstairs,' Ria said.

'I can help myself,' Esther said. Each step seemed to take an hour, and Ria kept just behind her in case Esther fell, but didn't dare touch her.

Esther made it to the top at last. 'Come on, Mum, let's get you undressed,' Ria said. 'I changed the sheets and aired the room.'

'You had no business.'

Esther was bitter. She felt she'd let herself down. She was furious with Ria for allowing Vic to hear. 'After all those years I tried to protect you, Ria,' she had wept. 'You let me betray myself, you took advantage of me.'

'Mum, that's an awful thing to say.'

'I tried to warn you so many times, but you wouldn't see it. You couldn't see what was as plain as the nose on your face. My whole life's been like a nightmare because of that one tiny little white lie I told Tom.'

'Come on, Mum,' Ria said, 'keep a sense of proportion.'

But she realized that Mum had been trying to warn her, even as a kid. It had always been Dick this, Dick that . . . even the peculiar horror of Esther's story, so often trotted out, of Dick's fatal peritonitis had been a kind of warning flag saying *look here, there's something terrible here*, but none of them had realized it, they had just giggled like children. Which of course they had been.

Now Esther turned in her bedroom. 'Leave me alone. Just leave me alone.'

'Mum, don't be like this, don't push me away, it's not my fault.'

'Isn't it?' Esther said nastily.

After he kissed Ria, Vic had stared at Esther with hatred in his eyes. 'Half!' he said. 'Only half!'

He had not returned to the hospital. God knew where he was.

'Don't worry about him, Mum,' Ria said.

'You started this – now you stop it! You know what Vic's like when he gets in a state.'

But Ria couldn't find him. Even Terry, calmly smiling, said he had no idea.

Esther punished Ria to show that she was punishing herself. She suffered; Ria must suffer. And Ria just stood there at the top of the stairs with tears streaming down her cheeks, because she believed it too.

'Our family no longer exists,' Esther said.

Lisa was woken by Victoria bouncing joyously on her. Another day was starting for them at London House – it seemed so empty without Ben and Pearl, and today there would be another departure, yet they were only really strong when their family was together. 'Whoa!' Lisa said. 'I'm not a horse.' She lifted the coverlet for Victoria to slip inside.

'No time!' chattered Victoria excitedly. 'Don't pretend you've forgotten.'

'Of course not. Today you're departing for Greenland.'

Victoria frowned, then smiled. 'New York,' she chided, 'on the *Queen Mary*. Eighty thousand tons. Twenty-eight and a half knots.' Victoria had a factual mind: doubtless she had already jumped on Ralph, who knew such things. Juanita brought in Lisa's early morning tea. Victoria sat with her knees drawn up inside her nightdress, looking at her toes.

'I'm going to miss Marmalade,' she said seriously. Marmalade was her pony, given to her by Ben as a going-away present on condition that Victoria did all the work,

345

the grooming and the mucking-out. While she was away that would be done by one of the gardeners.

'I'll make sure he's looked after properly,' Lisa reassured her.

'What's that book?' Victoria pointed at a fat volume on the bedside table.

'It's about Sir Henry Stanley, the explorer. He was once a Workhouse boy, too, like your father.'

'Gosh,' Victoria said absently, 'where did he explore?'

'Africa,' Lisa said.

They heard Elise Barker calling Victoria to come and have her bath.

'I'll say goodbye later,' Lisa said. Pineapple was driving Elise and Victoria down to Southampton docks at ten o'clock.

Lisa lay back in bed, sipping her tea. In a few minutes Helen brought in the post, her disfigured face smiling brightly. She was pleased because she had got a card from Will at Clawfell, with a silly cartoon on it featuring Helen herself – she had been there on holiday – struggling to carry a waterbucket, a reference to the bucolic pleasures of life at Home Farm. But Will's professional work, his cool, intellectual paintings of his experiences in the Spanish civil war, Lisa found disturbing – perhaps for the very reason that they were so descriptive, so passionless. Or perhaps that was a defect of his skill: to remedy that Will had enrolled at the Slade School of Fine Art under Schwabe, to start in September.

'I'll see you later, m'am,' Helen said respectfully, and left her alone.

Lisa enjoyed her matriarchal status, and she enjoyed the power that money – real money, and Ben's determination to use it – gave her, but without him London House had lost something of its magic. There were rather too many women living here, too much energy with too little to do, and it all seemed rather pointless.

They needed Ben London to pull them together.

Will of course was away, and with François back at Coucy, Ralph and George didn't really count. Ralph was

346

affectionate with girls, and he had something of his father's innocence, but not the force of it, he was too nice. George was mooning around deeply in love, but so deeply introverted that it had no direction. It was himself he loved, and perhaps, in a vague unadmitted way, the memory of his mother.

It was not enough.

Ben had the power.

Ben had never changed, Lisa knew: not in the slightest from the first moment she heard the gate of Tower Hamlets Cemetery squeal, and saw her baby staring up at her with open eyes. The endless moment, the extrovert shock of recognition. Her baby was herself, though to become a man.

By now Ben was in Durban, on business, but at the same time pursuing his strange male quest for Roland, his half-brother. She re-opened the air-mail letter. He had persuaded himself that Roland was not dead: he believed the African air crash of 1 April, 1919, was a fake. Roland, Ben's half-brother, had done what Lord Cleremont never had the courage to do: he had escaped. At least that was what Ben wanted – perhaps needed – to believe.

Lisa was sure that her son's quest was a terrible mistake. Ben London would not find himself in Africa. She knew now who Bula Matari was, and she believed with all her heart that Ben could gain nothing from his search for this man.

Ben's power derived from the women in his life. From Pearl most of all, but also, still, from Lisa – he had not become truly successful until he succeeded in finding her. As they gave to him, so he gave to them. He needed the gentle feminine force of his wife, his family, home life, and London itself, to soften and civilize him, to save him from becoming hard and cold and alone; public success, private failure. Lisa knew this – she felt it in herself. Yet there he was off in Durban, half a world away, with only Pearl – who was dying to get to America to meet up with Victoria and start the process of bringing them all back together again. But suppose something happened to keep

Ben in Africa and Pearl decided to travel ahead? Leaving Ben alone. Pearl, an understanding woman, would never make such a bad mistake.

Alone, like so many men.

Alone, and merely a millionaire.

Bula Matari.

For the duration of their planned three-week stay in Durban Ben had rented a long, low ranch-style house on the Berea. When they woke in the mornings he and Pearl often found monkeys perched on the roof. The head-master of the European school along the road said they often stole fruit from the children's pack lunches. So high near the peak of the ridge, as they breakfasted on the patio Pearl could look over the avocado tree in the steep garden down colourful streets lined with jacaranda and kaffirboom to the shining bay, and the dark Indian Ocean beyond.

During the last week of August before their departure, she looked forward more than she could say to meeting Victoria in New York. It was nearly six months since she had seen her daughter, and it felt to her more like sixty. Victoria had grown an inch; she was the youngest member of the school's under-eleven lacrosse team; she was allowed to wear her hair in plaits. Pearl couldn't wait to hold her. They had so much to talk about.

This morning Pearl walked alone along the Marine Parade. The big white Sunderland flying boat that would take them to Cape Town to join the P&O boat for New York tomorrow had already landed in the calm waters of the bay. A group of whalers lay at anchor by a factory ship off the Bluff. Indian women in brightly coloured saris chattered in groups, and barefooted Zulu men pulled rickshaws at an amazing velocity along the level tarmac. Pearl stopped, watching the women squatting by the rail-ings selling beads, and one woman washing her baby in a basin, playing with her with great laughing slaps of soapy water. Pearl missed Victoria all the more. Children made life worth living.

So she had a difficult decision to make.

Last night Ben had held their farewell party. Hundreds of people had been there, many of them friends of friends they had never met. Among them was Jon Henricks, a white hunter wearing an ostentatious leopardskin band around his hat. He drank too much, but she saw Ben listening to him closely. He looked round for her and waved, then pulled Henricks through the crowd and introduced him.

'Tell my wife what you told me, Jon.'

'Bula Matari isn't only a name, it's a place.' Henricks smiled at Pearl, and she disliked him instantly. He helped himself to a passing whisky. 'A bend in the river. Tributary of the Nile north of Lake Victoria, damn near in Sudan. My father worked that way, he was a pilot. All pretty primitive. Bunyoro territory, very warlike people. Bula Matari was the natives' name for Stanley.'

'As in Livingstone,' Ben said.

'What has this got to do with us, Mr Henricks?' Pearl asked, chilled.

'Stanley converted them to Christianity, m'am. Spears into ploughshares. Last I heard – and this was ten years ago – the trees were being cleared and the land irrigated. Crops.' He shook his head. 'Those warriors gave the British one heck of a rough time during the colonial expansion, butchered a team of military surveyors in ninety-eight on their way to Gondokoro. And now they're growing millet.'

Pearl glanced at Ben. 'What's so surprising about that?'

'Leopards don't change their spots,' Henricks said, 'warriors don't grow crops. They've got a white man with them.'

'Roland,' Ben said. 'Roland Lockhart, DSO and bar, now the twelfth Lord Cleremont.'

'But we're leaving in two days,' Pearl told Ben. She hated Jon Henricks. 'Even our cabin number's confirmed, I spoke to the Cape Town shipping people today. I just want to be with my little girl. Oh Ben, I've been looking forward so much . . .'

Ben said: 'My half-brother is alive and well and living at Bula Matari.'

Pearl touched his hand. 'Our whole family means so much to you.'

'Yet you're longing to see Victoria,' he had said, equally torn.

Now Pearl watched the laughing woman splashing suds over her baby on Marine Parade, and she wanted to cry.

A week ago, Pearl had suffered – and that was the word for it, although there was no pain, none at all – another miscarriage. A thimble of blood, then nothing more, and Pearl knew she would never have another child. She had not told Ben of the secret hope she had carried inside her, so she could not tell him of its loss. Pearl stood motionless on Marine Parade under the burning African sun thinking of the mucky trenches of Europe, the deep, dark cellars beneath, and a single tear trickled on her cheek. If she had been religious, she could have believed in sin. But she believed in love – that was all. Victoria was all she would ever have.

She stared at the Sunderland in the bay. 'It's up to you,' Ben said when she met him for lunch at the Edward Hotel. 'We'll do whatever you say.'

'It wouldn't be fair on Victoria not to meet her,' Pearl said, 'but it wouldn't be fair on you to pass up this chance of finding your half-brother.'

'I won't go if you don't want me to.'

'Let's be democratic, then we both get what we want.' She kissed him on the lips. 'I'll have a good time with Victoria in New York, you go find Roland.'

'It's that easy?'

'Sure,' Pearl said, helping herself from the smorgasbord. 'Come on, let's be happy.'

Early next day Ben hugged Pearl goodbye and watched the flying boat take off into the sunrise, bank to starboard over the sea, disappear behind the Bluff.

Now he was alone.

At first, Ben's wealth made it easy, opening doors, catching seats for him and Henricks with the King's Messenger on the Mombasa mailplane, and from there for the shorter hop to Nairobi. Ben hired a smaller floatplane. For hours he watched the green desolation of jungle passing slowly beneath them. They were entering territory where money had no meaning.

'Thirty years ago the only way through here was by dugout canoe,' came Henricks's voice. 'My father was lost in these parts.'

'I'm sorry.'

'Oh, never knew him.' Henricks checked his rifle.

At the last outpost on the river, the limit of the plane's range, they arranged to fit out the expedition, exchanging mutual pledges with bearers, and local guides led them from Buganda into Bunyoro territory. The jungle gave way to patches of open savanna as the river wound northwards.

'Now you know about distance,' Jon Henricks said. He was by nature a lazy man, preferring animals to people, happy to sit by the campfire half the night drinking whisky, alone but for his rifle and his thoughts. 'No hurry, it goes on and on and on. There's always tomorrow.'

'We strike camp at dawn,' Ben said.

'Don't push too hard, you aren't in your big city now.' Henricks held out his arms in the firelight, and they listened to the sounds of the darkness. 'This is the big shot here. Don't you feel it? This is Africa.'

All day the bearers chanted as they walked, their voices rising and falling in the shimmering glare. Ben studied the grainy sepia photograph in the shadow of his hat-brim: Roland in his late twenties wearing the uniform of a captain in the British Army. That familiar face. *The war turned his mind. He was always intelligent – too bloody intelligent. Threw his DSO off Brighton pier and burned his uniform.* Such actions were incomprehensible to Ben because they led nowhere, changed nothing.

Towards sunset, Henricks called him to the top of a low hill. He pointed. 'There it is. The bend in the river. If your friend's alive, that's where he is.'

The river's broad sweep had been cleared of trees and the dusty earth showed clear signs of irrigation and cultivation. A hungry and nomadic warrior caste was now well supplied with food, and a sizeable village had grown up. He could see toddlers playing between the huts.

'We'll camp here,' Henricks said. 'That lot are Christian, and we don't want any trouble with our Moslem fellows here.'

Ben walked down alone.

Wearing faded shorts and an ancient red-check shirt, his skin burned to brown leather, he was teaching a circle of cross-legged children. It was all in a tongue Ben did not understand, but he recognized an abacus: these Bunyoro children were learning their times tables.

'Roland,' Ben said, coming out of the shade.

The children turned as one to look at the visitor. Slowly the man looked up. His hair was white, his face was lined. He said something to the children. 'I told them we have a visitor.'

Ben shook his head. 'Lord Cleremont, I am your half-brother.'

Cleremont put down his stick very slowly. The two men surveyed one another. Then one of the little girls took Ben's hand and led him across to Roland with casual authority. 'Because you're an adult,' Roland said absentmindedly, 'she believes you cannot see.'

Ben picked the girl up and the other children laughed. Some whispered to their friends who were blind, explaining what had happened, and then they laughed too.

'So he's dead,' Roland said at last. 'Well, I'm sorry you've come all this way for nothing. I shall be Roland Lockhart until I die.'

'Your governess was Miss Bell,' Ben said, trying to find the common ground between them. 'She discovered that one generation of our family hates London, and the next loves it.'

'We certainly seem to have proved her dictum.'

'My mother is Lisa York.'

'I understand what you are saying. Forgive me, it seems so . . . unimportant.' Roland pointed. 'Look, they're coming off the fields.' Short columns of half a dozen workers led by a woman or older children were following dusty tracks up to the village. 'He died years ago. I understood him quite well, and what he was. I would have weakened too. Merely the next Lord Cleremont, repeating the old mistakes like all the others, a prisoner of a privileged, worthless life.'

Ben said: 'He knew where you had gone.'

'Keeping quiet about it was the only admirable thing he did in his life.'

'He understood,' Ben said.

They went to one of the cooking fires and Ben stirred the calabash. 'Millet porridge,' Roland said. 'Not so bad with salt, we barter for that.' He introduced Ben to the people squatting in the circle. 'See how many children we have,' Roland said enthusiastically.

'Why are so many adults blind?'

Roland ignored him in his enthusiasm. 'As we extend our field system into the forest, we can feed more people, so more are born. No tribal wars, no hunting accidents, no starvation.' Following one another by holding onto a long stick, led by a child, another group of blind labourers arrived from the fields.

Roland held out his arms for silence in his tiny domain, and the chattering voices were quiet as he said grace, a scarecrow figure silhouetted against the blazing orange sky of sunset.

The better Ben came to know his half-brother, the more he realized both how close they were, and how far apart. He understood what Roland was trying to achieve for these people.

'This is a war worth winning, Ben.' Roland looked back past the workers toiling in the fields to the village perched on the hill. Everyone seemed oblivious to the flies that swarmed out of the irrigation ditches and clustered around their heads and the corners of their eyes.

'I can help you,' Ben said. Roland couldn't afford medicines for the children or a roof for the school. The hoes and agricultural implements were always breaking. 'Money. Tools, drugs, all the things you need.'

They sat on a felled tree-trunk by the river.

'I won't go back,' Roland said, 'I won't take my seat in the House of Lords. I don't want to live an effective life. This is a good war.'

'Why are they blind?' Ben asked flatly.

Roland turned his filmy eyes on him. 'Onchocerciasis,' he said gently. 'River-blindness is the price we pay.'

Ben stared at him. They were close enough to touch, but the distance between himself and his half-brother was an unbridgeable gulf.

CHAPTER TWENTY-ONE

1

Since the outbreak of war on the third of September everyone had been at sixes and sevens. The first shock was the air-raid sirens setting up an unearthly wail. Suddenly it was all real. London was undefended, the bomber would always get through, and many in the Government believed that the crowded city would be razed to the ground.

Two million men, women and children, they feared, would die within a few days.

London was the front line.

At London House, Lisa took charge. While the sirens whooped and howled she ordered everyone down into the cellars. At first they were all joking and larking about but gradually, down there, the holiday atmosphere faded away. There was no natural light, only a single electric bulb, and Helen was frightened of the dark. 'What's going to happen?' she asked in a trembling voice, 'what ever's going to happen to us now?'

They knew who were the targets in this war: ordinary people like themselves.

'I'm going to join the RAF,' Ralph said bravely, 'just like my father did.' But everyone jumped as something banged upstairs.

'Only a door!' George scoffed.

'But Mr London's always been here before when there was trouble,' Peggy the head maid said in a rising tone. 'Now he's lost somewhere in Africa, and Mrs London's at sea in the middle of the Atlantic with all those German submarines about, and I . . . I just hope Miss Victoria didn't arrive late in New York.' She looked around her fearfully. Her marriage to Oake, the stately butler, had increased her tendency to flap rather than reduce it.

They all looked at Lisa.

'Everything will be all right, you'll see,' said Lisa serenely. She felt obstinately happy, always at her best in a crisis. 'I shall talk to you all later,' she said, taking command. 'We will all have to decide what we must do.'

'The first thing's to get out of London,' George said. 'All this lot's going to go.' He sounded quite pleased at the prospect.

They heard the sirens change to a different note, signalling the all-clear. The bombers had not come.

Not this time.

Much less serene about Victoria's fate than she had let on, Lisa had herself driven to the shipping office to be assured personally that the *Queen Mary* had docked routinely at New York. Of Pearl there was no news, and Ben, somewhere deep in Africa, probably did not even know there was a war on.

Everything was so confused. In a few days a cable arrived from Pearl saying merely in two words that she had arrived safely, but a month passed before her letter arrived from Boston, where she, Miss Barker and Victoria had moved in to Lowell Remington's townhouse. The British consul advised them to stay put: the war at sea had begun within ten hours of the declaration when a U-boat sank the liner *Athenia* with over a hundred dead, including twenty-eight Americans.

One thing was very clear to Lisa: this was her war. Already everyone joked about the phoney war because nothing had happened yet, but she knew it would happen, and it was going to be frightful. George, whose Second in the economics tripos had been announced in July, had explained to her how long it took to get a modern war going, and what a vast economic business it was. But when it got going, George said, no one would be spared. He seemed very calm about it. Not a man of action like Ralph, he was pleased when the Board of Trade offered him a job – there was bound to be rationing and a pricing policy, and with his qualifications he would soon be in a position of real influence.

The evacuation of children to the countryside began on a massive scale, and Lisa knew that this was where she could help – not by making space for them at London House, so dangerously close to the Palace and the great Ministries of Westminster, but by throwing open Ben's properties in the country.

She still had no word from him, but she knew that this was what he would have wanted her to do. Early in December she caught the train to Leeds – standing most of the way, waiting in a siding for an interminable three hours – then couldn't persuade a taxi to take her to Clawfell because of the petrol shortage. Finally she got a lift to Clere on the returning milk lorry and put up at the inn, only two hundred yards from the grimy two-up where she had been born.

In the morning she hired a pony and trap to take her to Clawfell, but as the land rose it started to snow. The driver refused to go further in case the wind got up and drifted the snowfall so that they could not return. She paid him off and went on alone.

'Thee's mad in the head, or sum't!' he called after her, not used to being disobeyed by a woman. Lisa smiled. She was determined. She had made this journey before, and now, for the sake of the children, it amused her to take her place as lady of the manor where once she had been parlourmaid.

The moor rose above her like a white wave beneath the dark, wintry sky. Lisa's joints ached – she was not as young as the last time she had made this journey, jumping playfully in Miss Bell's footsteps, not knowing what lay before her. The brow of the snowfield dropped away with that familiar suddenness, and she saw Clawfell revealed in the distance ahead of her.

No smoke rose from the myriad chimneys; all the three hundred and sixty-five windows were dark. Lisa walked through the trackless snow. Even Home Farm was deserted since Will gave up his dream of studying at the Slade School and joined the Navy as an Ordinary Seaman, Hostilities Only, where his experience as a *Mercury* boy quickly qualified him to train for an officer's commission in the RNVR; Lisa unlocked the door and looked in. As soon as the hurricane lamps were lit and the range set alight it would keep her warm and cosy for tonight.

Going out, she took the farm track then followed the line of the main drive on its long curve. The eighth Lord Cleremont had a fine sense of theatre: his profligate gothic dream, or nightmare, swung suddenly into close view.

For the first time in her life Lisa entered the great house, where she had been brought up and spent the happiest and unhappiest days of her life, through the formal porte-cochère only used by the upper classes.

She knew immediately that this ruin would not do. Clawfell was derelict, with fine drifts of snow around the window frames in room after dark room, thick dust everywhere, and all the furniture damp and horrid. Money was easy, but there was not the slightest chance of obtaining the tons of building materials and small army of workmen that would be needed.

The next day Lisa went south to Stamford. Easton Manor it would be: the house was in good condition, large but not overwhelming. Little work would be required on the immaculate stable block to convert it into dormitories; and at the very least, it would make a safe staging post for evacuated children until they could be found permanent homes.

Lisa returned to London. She sat tiredly over a cup of instant coffee in the breakfast room before dropping into bed. There was another cable from Pearl, frantic for news of Ben. But there was no news.

Dull thudding noises shook the night air, and it took Lisa a moment to realize what it was. On the ordinance factories of Enfield, bombs were beginning to fall.

Our family no longer exists.

The worst thing about the war was that it was so very good for business: close to Charing Cross Station with its enormous throughflows of young men, Ria couldn't help doing well out of it. Deep enough to be safe from bombs, the cellar dance floor was packed solid and everyone was always drunk, the boys just sad or wild, and their girls tearfully pretending to be jolly. All the old atmosphere and unique identity that she had fought so hard to create for Trott's was gone, and Ria hated it.

The top-floor flat would be dangerous – the Savoy only a few hundred yards away had been hit even by the few bombs dropped in the last war – yet that just made her more determined not to leave. But she had Esther to think of.

She had refused to let Esther give up.

Ria was convinced that Esther really felt so guilty about her children that she truly had half wanted to die, as she very nearly had, and Ria didn't like to leave her alone at Havannah Street, so she arrived with her suitcase. Esther, while she was bedridden, had to let her stay.

The older woman wasn't grateful. She ranted at her daughter cruelly.

Vic did not come.

When all this is over I'll take you out to the Tooke Arms, Vic had promised Ria in hospital when he was certain Esther was dying. Since then Ria had avoided Vic, and it seemed he avoided her. He had not been to visit, and Ria supposed he blamed Esther. Half did make a difference, they both knew it did.

Esther had no power over her children any more.

'Fish in milk for lunch,' Ria said cheerfully, coming upstairs with the tray, 'then speciality of the house – rice pudding.'

'I won't eat fish.' Esther turned over in bed. They heard the bell of a fire engine coming down West Ferry Road, then the note dropped and faded.

'Don't be difficult, darling,' Ria said, then bit her lip. The relationship had turned round, and she was the one in authority now – Ria never called Esther *Mum* while she was convalescing, or even thought it. 'I got you a lovely piece of haddock,' she said.

'I was so pleased when you brought young Ben London home,' confessed Esther tearfully. Welcoming the Workhouse boy who Ria so plainly adored into her family home, she had been able to dream without disloyalty that Ben would one day free Ria from Vic. And Ria knew she had almost freed herself – *I'm a woman, stronger than a man.* Now Esther lay like a stone. 'I thought everything was going to be all right. But you played them around just as you play everyone else.'

She was still on Vic's side, and Ria couldn't help rising to it. 'That's not true!'

'You're a hardhearted woman, Ria, and that's the truth.' Esther was talking just like Vic. 'You're plain selfish, with you it's just Ria, Ria, Ria all the time. All or nothing.'

I'm Ria. I'm special.

'Listen,' Ria said defiantly, 'nobody else cares about me. The real me.'

'Ben did.'

'A girl alone's got to learn how to look after herself.'

'You never did look after yourself,' Esther shot back. 'It was always up to someone else. I see that now. In the end you tried to make Ben London crawl to you, but he wouldn't.'

'It wasn't like that!'

'You arranged it like that, because you were afraid of him – afraid of making the commitment. You wanted the money and the fine life, but you were afraid – '

'It was love,' wept Ria.

'Afraid of having the courage to love, afraid of giving your precious self up. It's not love you lack, my daughter. It's courage.'

'That's a terrible thing to say!'

'Isn't it true?'

'Yes,' Ria said slowly, 'it is true.' But she had been courageous once. She had Will to prove that. 'It's true of both of us,' Ria said. 'You too.'

Esther stared at her with luminous eyes. Her mouth quivered. Then she sat up and put her arms around Ria.

'I'll tell you something about love,' murmured Esther, 'I'll tell you something about how lonely it is. We think we've got it so hard. Well, I know who puts those flowers on Nigel's grave.'

'Who?' Ria said.

'It's Betty Stark.' Esther nodded. 'She's a strong, vital girl, you imagine what it must be like, that spirit trapped in her body.' Ria felt it in her own, almost like a physical pain. 'Betty cleans at the hospital to make ends meet. She never tips her hat at another man. Can you imagine her denying herself, how lonely she must be?' Ria could, every day of her life. 'That's love, Ria. And no hope. It makes me shudder.'

'Poor Betty,' Ria whispered.

Ben's telegram from Kampala arrived on Lisa's desk at Easton Manor on a damp and windy day. It was news from very far away – she looked at the cold drizzle sliding down the glass and tried to imagine heat, mosquitoes, jungle, and total isolation after the collapse of air communications. It seemed he had been stranded at the last outpost on the river waiting for a floatplane which never arrived, requisitioned against the Italian menace from the north. Finally Ben trekked out on foot, and it wasn't like a stroll down to the shops. He had been hospitalized for malnutrition and malaria – not that he admitted that, but that was what the accompanying telegram from the Foreign and Colonial Office revealed – and his tone was one of angry impatience to be home rather than relief that he was alive. Lisa read between the lines. Sheer willpower had brought him walking through the jungle with his party intact – every single one of the bearers made it to the mission station.

Lisa looked so relieved that Helen thought she would fall down. 'No, I'm all right,' Lisa waved her away, determined to show no hint of weakness. 'I must cable Pearl in Boston immediately, she's been going out of her mind with worry.'

'Yes, m'am,' Helen said. 'I'll arrange it. It's all so difficult in wartime.'

Lisa looked round as a charabanc hooted in the drive.

Another batch of children was arriving from the East End, each identified by a scribbled parcel-label secured to them with a safety pin. The little mites milled around in the chill grey air looking lost. A woman shepherded them in. The driver unloaded the duffel bags that contained all they had, and then their gasmasks and a gasproof cot – some unmarried mothers were staying with their babies.

'There isn't enough coal,' Helen said.

Nearly all the staff who were too old to join up had been moved here from London now. They and the children were often sent out on twig-hunts for deadwood but there was never enough of anything – of firewood, of meat, of sugar.

Ralph arrived by car. As usual, his life was effortless: he never seemed to have any trouble getting petrol, and his passenger was a pretty, vaporous girl called Kate who plainly adored him. He handed round sweets to the children and through the glass Lisa could hear him telling them rat-tat-tat stories about Hawker Hurricanes.

Ralph had learned to fly with a University Air Squadron and Ben had often loaned him the Tiger Moth, so he had skipped through the year's basic flying training in a couple of months, and this second year, theoretically used gaining flying experience, Ralph was actually spending flying operationally – in other words, in combat. He had made no kills, or if he had he never spoke of them. Lisa was glad. The thought of cheerful, sensitive Ralph actually killing someone, outside of a rat-tat-tat story, was an obscenity.

Lisa met him in the hall. 'I've had a telegram from Ben! Your father's all right, Ralph. He's all right.'

'Thank God!' exclaimed Ralph in an overwrought voice. He looked tired yet full of beans, wearing a silk-lined flying jacket and a crimson scarf, one hand in his pocket to hide his nervous fingers and his arm thrown very casually around Kate. Like most pilots, he was too young to sport the vaunted handlebar moustache, but he was developing a pleasant golden bristle above his upper lip, which he kept taking his hand out of his pocket to scratch.

'He's ever so proud of it,' Kate chuckled to Lisa, giving the moustache a quick scratch of her own with her lovely long fingers. 'He puts Brylcreem on it to make it grow.' Lisa watched them. He didn't take his arm away from Kate once. Maybe it was true love for Ralph at last.

At supper he asked her: 'Do we know when my father will be home?'

'I don't think he has any idea.' Lisa pushed at her omelette, formulated of a kind of inflatable dried egg, with distaste. The blackout curtains lent the dining room a faintly ominous darkness. 'All shipping's in convoys now. Will Chamberlain make peace, will Hitler attack France? The Italians are busy in North Africa and may join the war. Ben's best bet would be to get a neutral ship to Lisbon. But it's all much easier said than done, obviously.'

'Can't your brother help him?' Kate asked as Ralph carved the succulent pheasant which he said he had found lying at the roadside, knocked over by a car. 'George is with the Board of Trade, isn't he?'

Lisa was impressed. The girl was brighter than she looked.

Ralph gave an embarrassed smile as the blade of the knife clinked on shot.

'The only person George helps,' he said, portioning out the black-market pheasant with absolute post-partum fairness, 'is himself.'

The afternoons were the only time George could see Natasha. He had rented a flat in Marble Arch and as soon as the lease was signed he stood in the bedroom turning in circles and persuaded himself he was, or soon would be, keeping a mistress.

Apart from any other consideration, she was much older than him, and the stronger personality. It was often intensely difficult for him to arrange an afternoon off, but she rewarded him almost not at all, demanding to be respected, and often they just sat and talked. George realized how little he knew of the ways of the world, but he was desperately anxious to be mature, and there was much she could teach him. She was an ambitious woman – obviously she wanted money off him, and perhaps the right word in the right theatrical ears . . . at least, that was how it had started off. George wanted to help her, because he longed for a repeat of that wonderful seduction in the garden room. She seemed to assume that their relationship had moved on from there. He hoped that it had not. She seemed oblivious to what was so important to him.

He was aware that seeing her was not mere naughtiness, it was dangerous. No one would ever believe nothing happened. Apart from anything else, her husband Pineapple struck George as a man supremely capable of jealousy. George understood jealousy. He was dabbling with a potentially explosive emotional brew that could ruin his career and cause his humiliation and disgrace in the eyes of everyone he knew, but he was unable to stop.

He loved Natasha, not in any way for herself, but because he was driven to it by the sheer excitement of doing wrong.

He came out of the sandbagged mouth of the Underground. The trees were spring green and birds fluttered, scavenging nest materials – frayed threads from the sandbags were greatly prized and fought over. Meanwhile barrage balloons on wires loomed over the rooflines of the great stores along Oxford Street, and workmen with rolled-up sleeves and swinging shovels were digging shelters. George snorted. Hitler wanted peace, he'd said so.

The lift in the apartment block wasn't working because the porter was afraid of bombs – the bombs that never fell. George climbed five flights of stairs and let himself in.

'I made you a cup of tea,' Natasha said. 'Look, I bought you a present.' It was just a tie, but he put it on faithfully. She fussed over it in the mirror. She wore a long green dress and a turban.

'Do you have any children?' George asked.

'None,' she answered shortly.

He drank his tea. 'I can hardly remember my mother. When she died in Egypt . . . it all seems so long ago. I was the only one who mourned her. I mean really mourned her.'

'It's always very sad.'

'I think my father killed her.'

Natasha shook her head. 'No, no, George.'

'I do mean it. Not directly, but because he is so strong. Or was. Who even knows where he is now? I feel free.' He admitted: 'I've been frightened of him all my life.' There it was; the truth. He revelled in feeling closer to Natasha than he had ever felt to any other woman, except his mother, and told her secrets he would never have dreamed of confessing to one of the girls in the nightclubs.

'Maybe Africa has changed him,' Natasha said in her deep voice.

George put down his cup. 'I love talking to you, Natasha.' He reached out for her, but she stood up, laughing, and swept her coat around her shoulders.

'Try and eat a little more,' she said, 'you're looking thin. I have to go.'

'Can't you stay?'

She shook her head.

All this hope, all this danger, for a maternal peck on the cheek. George closed the door quietly after her, then took the tie off and dropped it in the bin. Yet he felt strangely satisfied. It was enough that she cared for him. That they didn't use the bedroom attested to the depth of their relationship.

He often went down to the Strand when the office closed – it was only a short stroll from Whitehall – and spent the evening in one of the nightclubs. He wore a belted overcoat with as military a cut as he dared, everyone looked down on young men who were not in uniform. And after Dunkirk, men in uniform were everywhere. Now there was a real feeling of the war being fought, the blackout total, car headlights casting only slits of light, the buildings around Trafalgar Square just lumps of darkness. It was the silence that was so unnerving.

The gangsters who ran these clubs still had their shiny black cars though. War created wealth on an enormous scale, supply faltered, rationing had to be introduced, prices fixed, laws passed, and there were always loopholes in them. No one knew that better than George. He worked in a department which had hardly existed when the war started, and now it was bigger than some ministries.

He went down the steps into Trott's, paid a pound to the cloakroom girl who took his coat, and another four pounds cover charge to sit down at a table, but by law the bottle of whisky he ordered cost the same few bob it had before the war.

A face George recognized was there, sitting at a solitary table like his own, but closer to the packed dance floor.

It was Vane's friend, Vic Price. His manner was casual, but his face was ghastly. He looked like a man in torment.

2

Vic prowled the streets of the East End. He stood at the end of Havannah Street looking towards Esther's lighted bedroom window where Ria was, seeing her lithe shadow drawing the blackouts; she'd be returning to Trott's in a few weeks. He gazed down at Nigel's tablet of remembrance by the wall of St Luke's Church, his shiny toecaps almost touching the freshly laid wreath of wild flowers. His face was fixed. His dark eyes showed no emotion.

He had lost his grip.

His fearsome reputation ensured his success. But increasingly that was measured in fear. People had gone away from him, and that was worse than anything else in the world to Vic.

He walked to the river at Ratcliff and stared out, listening to the chop slapping at the pilings, sniffing the wet grey-green smell. Names floated in his memory; just names.

He felt nothing. He was adrift. He walked on.

The change was in him. He knew it, but knowing and feeling were two different things. He had lost his desire, his emotion, and that had always been his power. He was diminished. He didn't feel sad that Nigel was dead, he could hardly remember why. He felt no guilt. Guilt was for Esther.

When old Rixby came out of prison plainly broken by the experience, a pathetic trembling old man who would once have moved Vic to a warm outburst of compassion, he felt nothing. Terry, fifteen years old and still mitching off school just as Vic had at that age to roam the streets, though Terry's fascination was with plans and account-books, knowing more about the nuts and bolts of some operations than Vic himself did; very like Nigel in that. Terry had a mind like an adding machine and a memory as precise as punched tape. Like a one-man dog, he worshipped Vic and no other. No need to pay old Rixby, Terry said, fear alone will suffice to keep his mouth shut. Terry's passionless, still-childish eyes flicking at Vic out of his respectful face: he had learned well. Did Vic still want to keep paying Esther the same amount now Tom was gone?

Vic didn't know. He didn't care. He was uninvolved.

This is Ria. I love her.

Half; only half. Only half a crime.

There was much more to it than love. Vic stopped by St Katherine's Dock and looked around him, seeing nobody. He went down the stone steps to the platform and felt the first touch of fear.

Remember.

Hatred and revenge. Here Ben London had her.

A pure emotion flooded Vic's soul. It was jealousy.

She had let him. It wasn't rape. It was love between them, he was certain of it. All these years he had been deceiving himself, just as Esther deceived him.

Tormenting himself with lies, just as Ria tormented him.

Yes, yes, yes.

3

This was the hottest month in Lisbon. Ben got out of the taxi and batted away the flies that immediately tried to settle on his face. Brown-faced children swarmed around him begging for money. He tossed them his change, surveying the street with keen blue eyes, then held out his pass to the guards on the gate and trotted up the white steps of the British Embassy.

'Shouldn't do that, sir,' the sergeant in the marble foyer said without getting up from his desk. 'Generosity encourages them.'

Ben smiled, and the sergeant knew he'd mistaken his man. The visitor in the cream suit, whose fashionable two-tone spectator shoes had so misled the sergeant as to the nature of their owner, was wound up like a spring. His lean features were tanned brown, but with the slight transparency to the skin that malaria gives. 'What did you say?' Ben asked in a low, soft voice.

The sergeant stood up. He saluted the millionaire. 'You must be Mr London, sir. You look all in, if you'll pardon me saying so.'

'I have an appointment with the under-secretary in five minutes,' Ben said. 'I'd be grateful for a chair. Or are you afraid of encouraging me?'

'Sorry, sir.' The sergeant looked round for another seat, then pulled out his own chair. He stood looking at Ben sit.

'Bloody hot, isn't it, sir?' he asked.

'No, Sergeant. Not compared to Lagos.' Ben closed his eyes.

In the jungle both he and Henricks had contracted malignant tertian malaria. Between bouts of delirium they treated themselves with massive doses of quinine. The quinine had cured the malaria, but then toxic response from the impure drug struck them down with the blackwater fever from which Henricks slowly weakened and died. More than willpower kept Ben going. Sometimes he thought Pearl was walking with him through the jungle.

Without her love, without the sure and certain knowledge of it, he would not have survived. The doctors in Kampala had never seen a red blood count so anaemic; even after three months' convalescence they still advised him not to travel.

In Lagos, the malaria recurred. Rather than risk quinine he endured the rigours of the disease itself until it had run its course. Communication with America was extremely difficult; he had not hidden the seriousness of his illness from Pearl in his letters to her, but he was sure she had not realized it. Norway was occupied, France had fallen, the Battle of Britain was in the balance: in such circumstances, with shipping losses classified but certainly enormous, he could not be sure even if his letters got through. If she wrote to him, hers did not. He was dying to hear her voice.

'It's a bugger, sir, the tropics,' Sergeant Harris said. He had loosened up now. 'When did you arrive in Lisbon?'

'A couple of days ago, on the Portuguese tramp carrying general cargo from Lagos, palm-oil and bananas mostly. I just had time to buy these clothes.' Ben didn't mention that he was staying at the Estoril villa recently vacated by the Duke of Windsor, or that the Ambassador Sir Walford Selby was an old acquaintance from many parties at London House. Ben offered Harris a cigarette and lit one himself, although nowadays he didn't smoke.

'I was in Luanda for six months, that's where I learned Portuguese,' Harris said, inhaling the Sobranie luxuriously. 'I suppose you're trying to get home, sir? Word to the wise, there's sometimes a spare seat on the Sunderland. Maybe not for a few weeks, but . . .' He tapped the side of his nose knowledgeably. 'That's why you're here, right?'

'Yes and no,' Ben said, 'I'm here to speak to my wife.'

Harris frowned. 'I thought you said she was in America.'

'Sure,' Ben said, 'and the British Embassy in Lisbon houses the most powerful radio transmitter on the Iberian peninsula.'

A door opened and the under-secretary came across, his hand extended. 'I'm Wharton. So delighted to meet you. Please step this way.' He held Ben's elbow as they crossed the tiled floor and went upstairs. 'My wife buys her clothes from London Emporium, actually.'

'I'm glad to hear it.'

Wharton was a dapper man in a white suit, white shoes and Old Etonian tie. 'The Ambassador has spoken to me,' he continued in a low voice. 'It's most irregular. Most.' They passed the copying room and Wharton opened a door. 'I trust it's important.'

'Of the greatest importance.'

Wharton held open the door and Ben went down a step into the radio room. The operator stood up and saluted them at a bank of dials. It was warm and close in the little room from the heat of the thermionic valves. 'At ease,' Ben said, offering the young man a Sobranie. 'Now, how do I operate this thing?'

'There's a button on the microphone.' The operator's eyes lit up with enthusiasm as he warmed to his subject. 'I've been talking to them and the ionosphere's good, the signal's bouncing nicely. You're lucky, no solar flares.' Commercial transatlantic telephony had been available for fifteen years, but the bandwidth required for one voice could carry a couple of dozen telegraph channels. The operator was curious. 'What's so important it's got to be spoken out loud?'

Ben asked: 'Who can hear me when I talk?'

'You're on an open channel.'

'What does that mean?'

'You are broadcasting to the whole world.'

Ben gestured him to start. The operator fine-tuned a dial while broadcasting his call signal. When he got a reply he turned to Ben and nodded.

Ben sat on the stool in front of the microphone and loosened his tie. He licked his lips, then pressed the button. 'Pearl?' He cleared his throat. 'Pearl, darling, can you hear me?'

The loudspeaker hissed and crackled. Then he heard her. 'Oh, Ben! It really is you,' she cried.

For all the interference, her voice that he had not heard for eleven months, and it felt like a lifetime, seemed so familiar that in his mind's eye he saw his wife as clearly and imminently as if she were standing in front of him.

'Pearl,' he said, 'Pearl, I love you. That's all. I love you.'

4

Ria had moved back to Trott's six days past.

The phoney war was over. A fortnight ago the first bombs had fallen in the centre of London, only a few dozen, some said by mistake. Berlin was bombed in reprisal. Now London was bombed every night. The East End burned. The Battle of Britain would be fought on the streets.

Vic did not care.

He stood in the dark looking across the Strand. It was warm. The silence was intense. A couple came swaying up the steps from Trott's, a soldier boy and his girl, and across the wide road Vic could clearly hear the tap of her heels, the boy's murmur, her giggle.

His eyes did not follow them.

Vic stared up at Ria's window on the top floor. No light showed yet.

Gina, the hostess employed by Ria while she was away, would be running the show tonight. She was a good girl, Vic liked her. Ria had lost interest in the nightclub apparently; she'd had her dreams for it and they'd come to nothing, just loud music and drunk boys and cheap girls, broken glasses and cigarette butts, and the stink of stale smoke. Ria wasn't softhearted, but she was generous, and too many punters got in free. *I've slept with Ria.* It was safe down there, too deep for bombs.

A searchlight swept across the sky.

Vic waited in the silence.

How he hated her.

Her window showed a dim glow and he sensed her shadow moving, then the blackout was absolute. But she was there. She was undressing. Perhaps a bath, two inches of cool water.

If the sirens went, she'd go downstairs. There was bound to be a Morrison shelter with a mattress in it, or a room set aside in the cellars. Or would Ria defy the bombs? She was the type to do it. Holding out in her lonely, dangerous eyrie with nothing to live for.

Vic knew her better than anybody. He did not know what fear was, but he knew Ria did. She was frightened. She had a conscience.

Vic crossed the road. He used Gina's key on the side door and stood in the hall looking up the stairwell. Very faintly, he could hear music from below. His shoes creaked on the stairs as he went up. He felt little sense of his own individuality, it was as if he were watching himself, but he knew what he was doing, he knew exactly where he was going.

If she opened the door, she condemned herself by her own action: guilty.

He knocked, then waited.

She opened the door.

'Who did you think it was?' Vic said.

She hoped it was Ben, of course.

Ria was guilty, still guilty of love.

'Love me,' Vic said, holding her gently in his quivering hands. 'Look at me, Ria, Ria.'

She looked at him.

'I'm nothing without you,' he said.

'Will's here,' Ria said quickly. It was a lie, and she knew it showed in her face. She was ashamed of herself for trying.

'Let me in,' Vic said.

'No . . .'

She pressed her hands against the panels, but he opened

372

the door and pulled her through into the living room. She was wearing only a dressing gown, staring at him, her opal eyes, her golden hair. Outside, the sirens were wailing. She glanced at the blackout curtains fearfully, then back to Vic. He closed the door.

'Friends,' he said. 'You're the only person who's ever humiliated me, Ria.' He looked in the kitchen and lit the gas. 'I'll make us a nice cup of tea.'

That was how he stopped her from screaming, how prosaic he was. She knew what was going to happen. She loathed herself for knowing what was in his mind, for it had been in her own. He was right; she was guilty. With a dull thud of bombs in the distance, suddenly the lights went out, and she stared into Vic's eyes by flickering blue gaslight.

They glittered with the male imperative. Only in this was a man stronger than a woman. Yet she deserved it; she had felt the similar awesome force of her femininity once, and used it to manipulate Ben London inside her, taking him, exploiting him. She knew from her own experience the thoughts in Vic's head. *I'll bind you to me with ties stronger than chains, stronger than a paper contract, stronger than marriage. I'm a man, stronger than a woman. I always have loved you and I will always love you.* This was what she saw flickering in his eyes.

'I love you, love you, love you,' he hissed.

'No!' she screamed.

Vic clasped her and took her bodily by force to make her love him.

373

CHAPTER TWENTY-TWO

1

And she had felt the flash.

She woke alone, dry-eyed.

Ria was naked. She wore not a stitch of clothes, no nightdress, no rings, no lipstick, no makeup, nothing. There were no bruises on the smooth skin of her body, and nothing might have happened.

But she had felt the flash.

He had taken her utterly.

Ria sat up very slowly. She came out of the bedroom and crossed to the kitchen, where she lit the gas to make a cup of tea. Outside it was late morning. Housewives were queuing at the butcher's and Saxone's and the bus stops. Men were pushing into the Bunch of Grapes. Ria sipped her tea. The linoleum felt cold on her bare feet.

She remembered.

The worst thing was her surrender to his contempt. She could have fought harder or screamed louder, surely. She did not think so. She would always doubt herself. She considered opening the cupboards and pulling down all the plates and cups and glasses and smashing them in her rage. But that would change nothing.

She poured herself another cup of tea, then pulled on a nice dress and went out. She had forgotten to put any lipstick on or to bring her handbag. She was on her own. She was in a state as bad as she could imagine. In a month, when she was sure, she could go to a woman in a backstreet somewhere and have her insides ripped out. But that was not the point. The point was her shame. The act of hate – no forceps could eradicate that. They were not enough.

She could kill herself.

Ria stared over the river. 'Bloody won't!' she said aloud. But she might.

She walked along the Embankment. She sat on a bench. She must have slept.

The light was fading away and the river had dropped right down. The lights on the cars looked bright. Ria walked, she didn't know where. She was going crazy. She had felt the flash, and she was sure.

She carried a baby inside her, and it was her brother's.

It would grow and grow until the memory of the act consumed her, an unbearable curse, witnessing the excruciated distortion of Vic's features above her, feeling the sinuous jolting of his hips against her. Hearing his exultant roar of utter domination, crushing her spirit with his as it gushed into her womb. She remembered it all. And heard her unavailing screams until they deafened her.

Grief, and loss, and hatred, and revenge, these were not enough.

Ria found herself outside the railings of London House, hanging onto the cold iron, staring through. The house was dark. It showed no sign of life.

Suddenly the air-raid sirens began to wail. Ria fled into the night.

2

Charing Cross and Piccadilly were joined by an automatic exchange. All she had to do was dial the number. A smart, rather prim woman's voice came on the line.

'London Emporium, Mr London's private office. Alice Cypress speaking, how may I help you?'

'This is Ria. I'm a personal friend of Ben's. The flowers – remember?'

Can't forget him, can you?

'Yes, of course I remember. I'm pleased to be able to tell you that Mr London is returning home in the next few days.'

Ria licked her lips and lied. 'I wanted to speak to Mrs London.'

'Mrs London is not at home. I'm afraid she won't be coming back from Boston for several weeks at least. There is a war on, you know.'

'Yes, I know. Thank you,' Ria said, and very slowly put down the receiver.

She went through to the kitchen and made a pot of tea. *Mrs London is not at home.*

Ria laid her plans. She would pay for a sin with another sin. She would betray the man she loved, still secretly loved. She would erase hate with love.

Ria stared at herself in the mirror. She made her trembling mouth smile. Yes, she could still play. Even as a child, she had known that the world was full of dark secrets. Now she would create the blackest secret of all, and seal it away into her heart. Only she would know of it. She began to comb her hair. Half of her hoped she would fail.

Ben's four-hour flight from Lisbon, in a Sunderland seaplane swinging far west over the Atlantic to avoid interception by German fighters, at last touched down on Southampton Water. Even after the propellers ceased, all of them – USO entertainers returning from a tour, some smooth gentlemen in business suits – still heard the nerve-drilling roar of the engines echoing numbly in their ears.

Ashore, Ben looked around him. How incredibly green English grass was.

Weather-stained barrage balloons swayed against the peaceful blue sky amongst puffs of white cloud. Girls were wearing shorter skirts again, as always in wartime, with shoulder padding. Stockings were all the rage, and those who could not afford or obtain silk painted their legs with brown stain. For the first time in many months of male company he heard the unforced sound of girls laughing, a group of young mums with prams chatting by a bombed-out house as if the sudden crumbling ruin in the middle of a smart row was perfectly natural. Amongst the neat gardens an old man had dug up his grass to potatoes and carrots.

A horn tooted as a car came up behind him. 'Hop in, chum,' the driver said. Ben squeezed in the back with half a dozen of the girls who had been on the plane with him. Since the flight from the Tagus had been so long delayed, they grumbled, and they had to start their revue-deville at the Windmill tomorrow at two thirty sharp, their rehearsals would leave almost no time for sleep. 'Are we downhearted?' Ben called out the famous catchphrase.

'No!' they chorused. They liked having a man with them, it got them out of themselves and stopped the hardness and tired bitching. With him playing them off the journey would be warm and friendly with lots of talk. Ben inhaled the tang of cheap perfume and cosmetics. It was thirteen months since Pearl flew out of Mombasa and he had slept with a woman. Now he was in the back of a car with a dancing troupe. None of them were beauties, but they were full of life and they enjoyed putting on an act, responding to him.

'We really can call ourselves dancers now,' Doreen confided, slapping his knee. 'It used to be frightfully arty under Mr Van Damm because we weren't allowed to move a muscle, we had to stand like a troupe of blooming statues.'

'It was the law,' Eunice said, 'because we weren't wearing – you know, anything!'

'Except the makeup,' Doreen added.

'And that was heavy enough,' Eunice said.

They went silent as the car drove along an interminable line of rubble, still smoking and ribboned off, where a stick of bombs had fallen along the line of a street; where a street had been. The debris of broken lives stuck out, strips of wallpaper, furniture, an upside-down bath. They hardly noticed bomb damage after that, it was just part of the scenery. Eunice did sewing until the daylight began to fail as they drove into London. It was full dark by the time they crossed Westminster Bridge and reached Parliament.

'I'll get out here,' Ben said. It was only a short walk home across St James's Park. 'Thanks a lot.' The car drove off, the girls waving white hands from the windows, calling him to come and see the show, then he was alone again.

Ben lifted his collar, chilled. He hadn't realized how very dark nights in London now were. Traffic lights had been fitted with long shades so as not to reveal the pattern of streets to bombers, and his pale tropical suit reflected red, then yellow, then green as he walked. He would have to take a war job – the ARP, the LDV, or perhaps he could be more useful to the fire brigade. He crossed the park, following by memory the path through the darkness towards London House.

'Hallo,' Ria said. 'Hallo, Ben.' He heard a match strike, and then her face was lit up in its flame.

They were children. He stared around him at the black shapes of trees, the forms of dark buildings. *I'm going to have this house.*

You wouldn't let me in. He even remembered the feel of her elbow in his side.

The match guttered and died. Ria closed her eyes. *Do you love me?* she remembered. *Will you marry me, one day?* Dreams; just childish dreams.

His voice came out of the dark, still startled. Only a few seconds had passed. 'Ria?' She felt him reaching out. 'Ria, what is it?'

How did he know at once that something was terribly wrong?

'I'm frightened, Ben,' she said, 'I'm desperately frightened.' And she turned half away – she couldn't go through with this. She must tell Ben the truth.

Ria summoned up all her courage.

'Help me!' she said simply.

So he helped her; and damned himself. But Pearl would never know – Ria would never tell her, so what harm could it do to him, the last person in the world she wanted to hurt?

No, no, she was still thinking the wrong way, she must confess the truth of what had happened to her. Ben always knew what to do. But when he touched her hand, that was all, understanding her appeal, and they walked together across the park to London House, Ria could not bring herself to say the words that condemned her – she just couldn't. Because . . . because. Because she loved him.

The house was dark, all the blackouts probably left permanently down since Lisa stayed in the country at Easton Manor. Ben found coffee in the breakfast room, but Ria stopped him. 'I need a brandy,' she said in a shaking voice.

'I think I do,' he agreed. She followed him into another room with a sofa. He found a bottle and poured two glasses, held one out to her. He looked so tired.

'You're exhausted, Ben.' Ria checked herself. *Damnit, don't feel so bloody sympathetic for him, harden your heart!*

Doubtless it was fine brandy, the finest she had ever tasted.

'It's been a long day,' he admitted. Gently he led her round to concentrate on herself. 'You haven't changed at all, Ria.'

Was that so? She touched her face. Surely only her feeling for him was the same. However hard she tried to deny it. She couldn't go through with it.

She could kill herself. She could kill her baby.

He had closed his eyes. 'I miss my wife,' he said. She wondered what he was seeing: Pearl sitting beside him? Feeling Pearl's hand on his? But it was Ria's.

'Tell me about Africa,' she said. She who had never been further than Brighton.

She listened as he began to talk, thinking he was relaxing her. She had begged him to help her, and Ben, of all men, would know she'd never have seen him unless she was desperate. So he talked about Africa, but really the murmur of his voice was relaxing himself, not her, until he had almost forgotten she was there, and when she quietly brought him the final brandy, his hand did not take it. His voice faded away.

'Drink up,' Ria said.

He did not. He was asleep.

Ria brushed his hair off his closed eyelids. She looked at him tenderly.

Now that he was asleep, she leaned down with her lips close to his face. If he was pretending, he would hear; but she knew he never pretended about anything.

'I'm so sorry, Ben,' she whispered. 'I love you, and I know there's some feeling in your heart, deep down, for me. God knows I don't deserve it. Can you hear me? Sleep on.'

Her voice broke, then she continued her whispered confession to his deaf ears.

'Vic raped me, Ben. He took me by force and I feel so guilty. Because I think when it was worst I dreamed of you. I wanted it to be you, Ben, and that's how it happened. God forgive me.'

She kissed his lips.

His breath was perfumed with brandy. 'Come on,' Ria murmured, 'Let's get you upstairs. Good night, Ben.' He looked at her dazedly.

'Goodnight,' he said.

'I'd better help you up,' she said. 'You smell like a distillery. Come on, best foot forward. I'll let myself out.'

He dropped face down on the bed. Ria sat beside him. That was all she did, and the long night passed as slowly as an age.

Ben woke. He could hear the flutter of pigeons' wings on the window sills, and the traffic droning down the Mall. He was home, and he turned over, burning for love. He touched her warm, naked body beside him. Her skin was hotter, her curves more voluptuous, her scent was different – she felt quite different from Pearl. He sat up with a shout, staring.

'Go on,' Ria said in a strange voice. 'That was nice. Yes.'

Ben stood by the bed. She lay with the sheet caught between her thighs, winding in a sinuous satin line across her belly, then demurely covering her breasts. Her replete, smiling face looked up at him from amidst her golden fan of hair over the pillows.

'Oh my God,' Ben said.

'You invited me in. Remember?'

'Remember?' he said stupidly. 'What have we done?'

'Come back to bed.'

'What have I done?' he groaned.

'You were lovely,' Ria said. Her voice broke and she covered it by clearing her throat.

The muscles stood out along his jaw, then swelled across his arms, chest and belly, so furious was he that he looked like a man made of brass.

'Ria! Whore!' he shouted. He hated her, and she deserved it. Ria cringed. All in her was a turmoil of emotion. She loved him. It was the one thing she must never admit. He tore the sheet off her and she lay looking up bravely, not frightened of him at all, certain that he would never hurt her, despising herself. His eyes travelled down her naked body.

He looked in her eyes – her dry, opal eyes. He said: 'Did we?'

'Yes,' she murmured.

'You animal, Ria.' He dropped the sheet over her. 'What have I done? It's my fault. Get out. Out!' He pointed wildly at the door.

Smiling, Ria rolled to her feet and went to the chair where her clothes lay neatly folded. Calmly she selected her underclothes, put on her suspender belt, then rolled her stockings smoothly up her legs, slipped her dress on over her head. She pushed her feet into her shoes and picked up her handbag which was propped tidily against the chairleg.

She turned the open back of her dress towards him. 'Do you mind?'

'I never want to see you again, Ria.'

He thought she shuddered.

He gripped her shoulders in the lightest of touches. One last chance.

'Tell me the truth. Ria, did we make love last night?'

Ria closed her eyes. She must be so strong.

'Yes.'

He did up her dress with fingers that felt as cold as ice.

'Ria, whatever happened, I didn't mean it to happen.'

'Didn't you?'

'I'm sorry about what I called you, I'm just as bad as you. I want you to go now. Ria, I mean it, I never want to see you again.'

Outside in the long, empty corridor, Ria bit her knuckles to stop herself screaming out her pain. The tears she had somehow withheld flooded silently down her cheeks. She choked back the sobbing in her throat.

Ben had stayed loyal to Pearl. Loyalty, next to love the most precious thing in the world. He believed that they had made love. *Whore*. No; Ria dragged him down to save herself.

Yes, yes, yes. Making her baby into the child of the man she loved by loving him.

Love, and loyalty, and happiness. Destroying everything she touched. But saving herself, saving her baby.

But she had hurt Ben London, the only man in the world worth loving.

He was tough; he would survive. But he must keep silent. No harm would come to him if he had the sense to keep their secret; in time he would forget.

But Pearl must never know.

Ben could keep one little secret from Pearl – couldn't he?

Ria walked out of his life.

Vic was exultant.

Since he had slept with Ria, never had he felt so power-ful, never had he been so gloriously in domination of her spirit.

He swaggered into Trott's, ordered a beer and drank it. If only he could talk about what he had done, if only he could brag about his conquest, just as other men did. But of course, that was the one thing he must never do.

It would be their secret.

George London, sitting nearby sipping his whisky, looked across at Vic Price with interest. The only light was from the stage, but there was no mistaking the force and exuberance of Vic's red, jolly face. He was transfor-med. There was no trace of the tormented man George had seen a few weeks ago.

Vic turned his head and glanced over. His black, know-ing eyes took in everything about George at once. Vic knew men. A new act started on stage, and he watched George become absorbed in the dancers.

A little later a bottle of champagne arrived at George's table.

'Who's it from?' he asked Gina.

She shrugged. 'Don't look a gift horse in the mouth. You want a girl to drink it with?' George knew what she was suggesting.

'No, thanks,' he said. Gina put one hand on her hip. Unlike the owner, she did not run a tight ship, and you could buy whatever you wanted at Trott's.

'Suit yourself,' she sneered.

A few days later Spike was driving Vic and Terry in the Daimler along Oxford Street towards Marble Arch. Terry sat upright with his hands in his lap, Vic was lost in thought: Terry sat for all the world like Nigel. They were stuck in the traffic opposite the Palace cinema – Chaplin in *The Great Dictator*. Vic did not find such lam-poons funny; Tom Mosley was in prison – with his own private chef and suite of rooms – and it looked like the

Nazis would win the war. Vic's confidence had come back, and his mind was full of schemes. Someone with a self-engrossed, almost mincing walk that seemed familiar came out of the Underground – he stopped to look at his wrist-watch, and Vic recognized George London.

'Terry, follow him,' Vic ordered. Terry scrambled out and crossed the road, slipping easily into the crowd. His faith in Vic was absolute: Vic who had brought him up like a father. Terry never questioned Vic's hunches: he had a nose for weakness like a shark's for blood in the water, a sense for the soft underbelly.

Terry would faithfully have followed George for miles, but in a few yards his quarry turned right by the Joe Lyons Corner House and walked a few yards up Cumberland Place. He went into an apartment block. The lift wasn't working, and Terry waited in the hall, listening to the sound of footsteps dwindling up the stairs, then silence, then a final flight. Five altogether.

Terry waited outside. A couple came out and three people went in separately, two of them women, but neither going higher than the third flight. Then a black woman came in and Terry hung back – though there were thousands of Jews, Vic said far too many, in the East End there were hardly any blacks – and he was young enough to feel a little afraid of her strangeness, wishing Vic was with him.

The black woman went up five flights, and there was the sound of a door opening for her. Terry left. He had done his duty.

He went back to Marble Arch but Vic had driven off and left him to make his own way home. Terry nodded. He liked having permission to be independent.

He walked along Oxford Street without looking in the shops, then went down Old Bond Street and stood outside London Emporium. The owner had once humiliated Vic. Terry tried to imagine the man who could do that. He didn't believe it.

Then he caught a bus home to the Old Bull and Bush. It didn't take long.

Pearl knew what failure was; but that dark undercurrent in her life was a stain from long ago, before she knew love, this real love.

Her hair, her wonderful hair, vouchsafed that.

Pearl wore her life like a suit of bright clothes. Only Ben knew her secret, only he had unwrapped the layers that laid bare the real she at her core, only with him was she open. There were no secrets between them – or they could not be in love.

He had given her love and redemption, and the miracle of Victoria.

Leaning out of the night-train door, Pearl looked eagerly over the heads of the crowds until she saw Ben through the smoke and steam. He waved and she waved joyously, then flung herself into his arms, her mouth crushed to his, her arms hugging him so tight that he gasped.

'Victoria sends her love,' she said with shining eyes, 'I love you, I'm so happy, take me home, quickly!'

'I love you, I've missed you so much.'

'Are you all right?' He looked thinner.

'Fine!' he said, swinging up her suitcase.

She looked at him in the taxi. There was something harder about him, something in him that had withdrawn. She would change all that as soon as she got him into bed. A man without a woman was a strange creature. For the moment she told him all the news about Victoria and how fast she was growing up, getting rather wild, hooked on everything American – Dizzy doted on her granddaughter with a pony called Windrush and a cowboy to teach her to ride western.

Ben laughed and smiled in all the right places, but his heart wasn't in it. She loved him, he couldn't lie to her. When she thought he was going to say something, she put her finger on his lips.

'I wangled accreditation to Time-Life Incorporated,'

she said, 'that's how I got a cabin on the *Queen Elizabeth*.' She kissed him to stop him speaking. 'How's business?'

'Good. And I've started as an auxiliary fireman – nights, the busiest time. Manchester Square, I've only just come off watch.'

The taxi turned right past Buckingham Palace. The royal standard was still flying, bannering bravely in the wintry early morning light. Pearl touched the goose pimples on her arms.

'Ben, is it true the bombers aim at the fires?'

'Yes.'

She looked at him carefully. 'Then if it's dangerous, it must be worth doing.'

'Pearl, there's something I've got to tell you – '

'Wait until we've made love,' Pearl laughed. Nothing would be so bad then. The cabbie turned up the drive and Ben paid him off. In the hall he dropped the suitcase with an echoing clatter.

'Pearl, I'm a fool to tell you, but because I love you – '

'Kiss me,' she said. He looked torn, then she slid her arms around his neck and kissed him, and there was nothing wrong with his response, his tightening embrace, and she knew he was hers from the way his body tautened as she melted against him. He dropped her coat on the stairs, unbuttoning her blouse on the landing as he carried her up, kissing her body, gentle and longing. 'Ben,' she cried out. She saw her long legs svelte in their nylon stockings as her skirt came off, sent fluttering over his shoulder down the stairwell, then the whisper of the stockings somewhere in the corridor, and felt his fingertips warm and close on her cool, nude flesh. She clung against him as he dropped his head and took her creamy breast in his mouth, her nipple jutting hard against his soft tongue as she locked her legs around his waist, never going to let him go. 'Quickly,' she said as they came into their bedroom.

'No, Pearl – '

'You can't wait. Oh darling.' She trembled; neither could she. He lay her on the bed and she dragged at his

386

belt, his damned trousers. She was open like a beautiful flower beneath him. She caught hold of him and pulled him inside her, then felt him push deeper until she held him like a hot iron in her beating, racing heart. For a frozen instant they were as motionless as death.

'I love you,' he said fiercely – as if love was so fierce it was terrifying.

Pearl stared up. That was the truth. She closed her eyes, and they writhed in the mutual ecstasy of their burning fire.

His furious passion softened, and he lay between her cool thighs. She cuddled him, whispering and murmuring.

Then he sat on the side of the bed, holding her hand. She waited patiently.

'You're going to hate me,' he said at last.

'Never.'

'I've done the most dreadful thing I can imagine.'

He told Pearl about Ria.

'You're right,' Pearl said. 'You were a fool to tell me.'

'It happened.'

She said: 'You need not have told me. I need never have known.'

He shook his head. 'But a secret between us . . .'

'Don't be so hard!' wept Pearl, and he felt how excruciating this was for her.

'We promised each other,' he said.

Pearl was devastated. She had lost to another woman. 'Is Ria pretty as me?'

'Not in the same way.'

'Well, is she better in bed?'

'Pearl,' he said desperately, 'I don't remember.'

Pearl screamed: 'How often has this happened before!'

He laid his hands open on the sheet. 'Never.'

'Just turned up, did she?'

He nodded.

'I can't believe it,' Pearl said.

'That's how it was.'

'In my own bed,' wept Pearl.

'I'll have it burned.' He touched her hands, then when she did not snatch them away, lifted them gently. 'Pearl, I know I've hurt you terribly. I'd rather do anything than that. It happened, that's all. I'm so sorry.'

Pearl got off her bed and looked back at the crumpled covers with an expression of distaste.

'That woman must be a whore. She's so wicked.'

Ben shrugged. 'I don't know. I loved her.'

'She obviously still loves you. Did she ask for money?'

'No. She was . . . calm. In the morning her clothes were neatly stacked.'

'Do you fancy her?'

'Any man would fancy her.'

Pearl looked in his eyes. 'You're so honest, Ben, but I still can't believe it really happened.'

'It's the truth.' Yes; she saw it was.

She knelt naked in front of her husband. 'Do you love me any less?'

'You know I don't. More. I missed you so much. I could never forget loving you . . . Ria *can't* mean much to me, Pearl.'

Pearl stood up and started getting dressed. 'Don't try and stop me! I'm going to sort the little bitch out,' she swore.

5

Obviously it was a myth that all Model Ts were black, because as Pearl strode into the enormous basement garage where the big thirsty Bentleys and the Rolls-Royce were stored up on blocks for the duration, she found standing in the corner a pert white Tin Lizzie Runabout standing on cheerful red-spoked wheels. It was probably used for staff outings, and must have been left behind during the move to Easton Manor. At least fifteen years old, and probably not run for a year, the engine nonetheless started at the first turn of the crank.

Pearl drove down the Mall and parked in the Strand outside Trott's. The bulbs had been removed from the arch of lights over the subterranean entrance, and when Pearl went down the steps she found the golden door in the tunnel heavily padlocked. Down here it was dark and airless, the black brick roof was curved, and she shuddered.

Returning to street level, she knocked on a side door.

Pearl had never met Ria, but she felt certain she'd know her.

The girl who opened the door exhaled cheap glamour like stale cigarette smoke, and surveyed Pearl with dull eyes. Pearl was confused. A man's toy and a whore indeed, she supposed, so this had to be Ria; but Pearl was suddenly convinced that this was not the girl she was searching for.

'I'm looking for Ria.' Ben had loved her; Ria had life, passion, feeling – the alternative, that she was merely a tired vamp like this woman whom Pearl could see through in a moment, was an insult to them all. 'What's your name?' demanded Pearl.

'Gina. What's it to you?'

'Tell me where Ria is.'

'She's not here, ducky.' The door swung closed, but Pearl knocked it back open with a force she had not known she possessed.

'Try the Isle of Dogs,' said Gina indifferently. 'Number thirty-two Havannah Street.'

'Thank you so much,' Pearl said.

She drove east with no very clear idea of where she was going. In the City she had to ask a policeman the way. 'Just keep the river close by on your right and you can't go wrong,' he told her reassuringly.

The East End with all its docks, warehouses and factories was catching by far the worst of the Blitz. But because London was so vast, row after row of mean, low little houses went peacefully on for miles – Pearl had no idea people really lived like this nowadays – then across huge areas the devastation was terrible, as though a giant foot had kicked everything down. Bordering these footprints of destruction, life went on as normal. But Pearl drove carefully, because there were holes in the road where incendiaries had burned through. Beside a heap of stone that must have been a church a huge brass bell stood neatly on the pavement.

The scene was suffused with a grey and wintry light. Pearl turned up her elegant collar and pulled on some gloves. She was frightened. The car engine clattered, then she caught a reassuring glimpse of the river on her right.

She saw children without shoes wrapped in blankets, in this day and age, though they looked carefree and happy. The Jewish ghettos were being blasted out of existence by Hitler's bombers; a man with Hasidic sidelocks, expensive black coat and homburg hat, pushed a wheelbarrow piled with chairs, a carpet, a broken sprung mattress, along the pavement. Later she even saw a dog-cart, as if she were travelling back to Victorian times, dirty and primitive.

Pearl came to a junction. The river was bending away from her, so she turned right down West Ferry Road. Ben must have known this area like the back of his hand, but to Pearl it was strange and alien – a part of his life that she knew almost nothing of, but not because it was secret: she had simply never thought to ask, thinking it was all in the past. No; from the East End came that hardness she sensed in him and loved, part of the brilliant success he had made of his life, covered with a gloss; the East End, always there, but now invisible.

Pearl drove carefully round a final vast pile of debris, then the road was clear. She saw Kosky's fish shop, then came at last to little Havannah Street.

Pearl stopped the car and climbed down. A seagull shrieked and the chill air stank of the river. Looking around her, she stoked up on her rage and jealousy then rapped on the door. A large woman of about sixty with flour on her hands opened it.

'Well, what do you want?'

Pearl could barely understand her accent.

'I – excuse me, I'm looking for Ria here?'

'You're welcome to her,' grunted the big woman, 'she's in one of her moods. I've had it up to here with her. Take her off my hands, for God's sake.' She called over her shoulder, 'Ria, there's a smart woman to see you!' She turned back to Pearl. 'Are you from the club? Never mind, come in.'

The dark, narrow hallway smelt of vegetables. Pearl followed the big bustling woman back into the kitchen. There was a pie on the table ready to be put in the oven. Kneeling in front of the oven trying to get the gas to light was Ria – Pearl was startled, the scene seemed so familiar. Ria had a pleasant normal voice, not at all like Gina's sultry vamp.

'Give us a hand, would you? Turn it up a bit.' Pearl grasped the dial the finger pointed to and twisted it. The gas caught with a satisfying thump. Ria pulled her head out with a snort of satisfaction, shaking out the match as she looked up.

'I'm Pearl,' Pearl said.

The perspiration seemed to freeze on Ria's hot face.

She wore a crimson dress. Pearl had felt she knew what Ria would *not* be like, but now she realized that Ria was exactly as she would imagine her, if only she'd been able to think straight. This pretty; these brilliant eyes so vivid and full of life, and the golden curls cascading over her shoulders. Just the sort of girl men dreamed of – passion in those eyes, too, like flecked blue fire.

All this left Pearl cold.

What made her stare was the Ria she sensed beneath – tragic as a silent actress, mute and unrevealed. Instead of a shallow stream, Pearl found an abyss as deep as the ocean. A dark flash in those shining eyes – eyes overflowing with tears, hope lost. This was far beyond Pearl's imagination, and her tongue jammed in her mouth.

'Bloody hell,' Ria said. 'So he's told you.'

'What's all this about, Ria?' asked Esther.

Ria glanced at her mother, and came to a decision.

'Come on,' she said, taking Pearl's arm, 'if you're going to kick my arse, you might as well do it outside.'

'Ria, what have you done?' wailed Esther.

Ria swung the engine and pointed left. Pearl drove down past the mudchutes to Island Gardens. The two women sat in the car looking at one another.

'Well,' Ria said, 'start kicking and scratching. The outraged wife.'

Pearl said slowly: 'Haven't I got a right to be?'

'If I were you I'd have shot me by now,' Ria said bitterly, 'and put me out of my bloody misery, like a horse.'

This was all different from what Pearl had expected. 'Let's walk,' she said.

They crossed the grass beneath the bare trees and stood looking across the river towards Greenwich.

Ria stuffed her hands in her coat pockets. 'You might as well know the worst. I'm pregnant.'

Pearl screamed and slapped Ria's cheek with her open hand. Ria didn't flinch. Pearl collapsed on a bench and began to cry. After a minute Ria sat beside her and pulled her hands into her own lap.

'Listen, listen, I know what you're feeling.'

Pearl looked into those eyes. 'I hate you.'

'What else?' Pearl stared at her. Ria said gently: 'What else, darling?'

No one knew better than Ria how despicable she had been.

'Why?' Pearl said. 'Why did you do it? Do you love him?'

'Don't ask me that.'

'He said you were a whore, but he didn't really believe it.'

'Do you?'

Pearl searched Ria's eyes. 'No,' she admitted.

'You're very beautiful,' Ria said. 'Even more than you were ten minutes ago. Try and understand me. I'd love to be like you.'

'You're having my husband's baby.' Pearl's dream.

Ria looked out over the river, wringing her hands.

'But it isn't his baby,' she said very soft. This was what she had never meant to say.

Pearl turned away. 'Oh, you're lying, what are you doing to me now?' She searched for a handkerchief but she didn't have one.

Ria grabbed Pearl's shoulder. 'It isn't his baby!' she shouted.

Pearl shook her head.

Ria groaned. She hugged Pearl and told her the truth. Never had she been so naked – certainly not with a man. This was between two women, closer, more secret, alone. No translation book. The bitter tears of rage and shame ran unconcealed on Ria's face as she recounted Vic taking her by force. 'And it was my fault. For what I did to Ben when we were children and we didn't know any better. So it was Ben I ran back to.'

Pearl knew Ria loved him.

'As God's my witness,' Ria said seriously, 'nothing happened.'

'You wanted it to.'

'So that I could live with my baby. Love child, not hate.'

Pearl held Ria's hand. She understood that fierce desire.

'Ben must never know the truth,' Pearl said finally. 'It'll be our secret, shared and halved.' That was how she justified it. 'Ben has done nothing wrong. But I can't tell him, that's all.'

Ria walked to the railings, put out her hands, then turned back. 'But then he'll think my baby's his.'

Pearl faltered. 'Will you have this child?'

'I'm two months gone,' Ria said fiercely. 'Plenty of women have babies at my age and I'm going to.' Pearl understood that determination too. She felt so close to Ria, the girl from the slums, joined to her by a bond of such suffering and hope, and understanding. Darkness had touched Pearl's life – she knew what it was, and remembered that thimble of blood.

393

'Our secret,' Pearl said.

Ria stared across the river at Greenwich Hospital, where Arleen had died in childbirth, and shivered. 'God help us,' she murmured.

'I'm making one very serious condition,' Pearl said, standing.

Ria knew what it would be. 'I promise I'll never see him again,' she said without turning. 'He won't know about the baby.'

'Strictly and absolutely,' Pearl said. 'I won't tolerate you as a competitor, don't even think it. Ben's mine. I know you feel for him as I do, and if I see you near him, Ria, I'll kill you.' Pearl's voice shook.

'I'd kill myself first,' Ria said earnestly. She clasped Pearl's hands.

Pearl insisted: 'Swear it.'

'I swear it before God.'

'I'm doing this for you,' Pearl said. 'I won't endanger my relationship with my husband one bit, because you're not worth that to me, is that clear? I'm doing this for you because of what he once felt for you, long ago.'

Pearl stared at Ria, saw the brave pride fluttering in the opal eyes and the depths beneath, and knew Ria would never be a second woman – she had turned that opportunity down before. To her Pearl was legitimate, the wife, and everything Ria would want to be. But knew she was not.

'Goodbye,' Pearl said. 'We won't meet again.'

She dropped Ria off at Havannah Street and drove away towards the West End.

Esther said to Ria: 'Have you been wicked again?'

'I'm going to have a baby,' Ria said, 'his father's Ben London.'

Esther put her head in her hands.

'Let's have some of that meat pie,' Ria said, 'I hope it hasn't got too much salt in it.'

CHAPTER TWENTY-THREE

1

Pearl was so relieved to get back home from the strange and terrifying poverty of the East End – those horrid slums, and that dark little house smelling of boiled vegetables. Yet Pearl had felt such an empathy of spirit with Ria, she could not get her out of her mind.

Only in one way had Ben done anything wrong: although nothing had happened between him and Ria, *he had been capable of believing that it had*. Only in that way did he deserve punishment. Ria, poor girl, was not Pearl's competitor. Such had been the horror of the slum girl's degradation and suffering that Pearl forgave her – and then realized the power forgiveness gave her over Ben. Pearl had lightly loved and left many men before she married him: but *marriage* was the key word, and now, no longer quite so young, she valued constancy and fidelity more than anything. If she wished to use it, which she did not, Ria had given her a stick to beat him with. Not only that, by agreeing that the baby should be their secret Pearl had done good by Ria, and in return extracted from her the faithful promise that she would never try to see Ben again; and Ria was the type who stuck by her word.

It was a good deal, and Pearl was pleased with it.

In the garden room, she looked behind her uneasily. Such terrible pain as she had seen in Ria's eyes made her guilty to feel so happy.

It could have been her.

Remember.

Ben had left a note to say he was at the Emporium. Pearl changed to get the smell of the East End off her clothes and walked to the store. Ben was standing alone by a counter. Apparently a sub-standard batch of ARP uniforms had been delivered, the stitching already pulling out of the shoulders, and he looked angry.

She took him into the shoe department, which was quiet, and they sat down.

'It's all settled,' she murmured. 'I forgive you, Ben.'

He jumped up. 'I don't forgive myself!' he said.

She held his arm. 'Ben,' she said, 'it's all over.'

'You're a saint to take this so marvellously and I love you so much.'

'Relax,' smiled Pearl, 'let's take the evening out, huh?'

Had she forgotten his duties as a fireman? 'I've got so much work to catch up on. Our suppliers are palming us off with rubbish and quoting war disruption . . . I haven't even had time to tell you about the hotel. London's was hit by a bomb eight days ago, a hundred kilograms of high explosive straight through the roof.'

'Ria has promised me she'll never see you again.'

'No one was killed, it struck the steel water tanks, thank God, or it might have exploded a few storeys lower, and the carnage . . . as it is forty-two thousand gallons of water poured down, mostly at the back, fortunately . . .'

'Ben, I want to bring Victoria back home from Boston. I – I miss her.'

He looked impatient. 'Yes, do it. We'll live at London House.'

'Perhaps while the bombing's so heavy, we ought to move to the country.'

'No, the royal family haven't moved out of their house, so why should we move from our home? The people in the East End aren't moving out of their houses.'

'Yes, Ben, all right.'

He leant down and touched the back of her hand. 'We stick,' he said gently.

She hugged him urgently. 'Ben, nothing's changed, has it?'

'Not unless you think it has. I love you. Believe me.'

'More than ever!' cried Pearl, kissing him, knowing everything was fine between them now.

He caressed her face with his fingertips, looking down

at her fondly. If anything, he knew, she underestimated his feeling for her: he loved Pearl more than words could say. He wondered if she really understood that. It was in the nature of things that a man could never fully show the depth of his feelings.

She had forgiven him, but she had no idea how deeply he felt, because he loved her, that he had betrayed her. *Betrayal*. That was a very powerful word to Ben. She forgave him; he still did not forgive himself.

He disengaged himself from her arms. 'I'm driving on Red Shift tonight,' he explained. 'And I've got a mountain of work to get through.'

George was not quite sure when he fell in with Vic Price. Obviously Vic thought George was the cat's whiskers. It was flattering that Vic admired him and sought out his friendship, but also frightening. That too was part of Vic's appeal. George drank the champagne, but he resisted the too-obvious lure of the girls. Sometimes Vic came over to his table and they chatted about nothing in particular. Vic seemed to understand George's need to get out from his father's shadow, and that his work at the Board of Trade was a way of doing that.

'Terrible,' Vic said casually, 'all these fixed prices.'

George explained Fisher's famous equation to describe the value of money – how prices were set by the amount of money in circulation and the speed with which it was spent. 'Divided of course by the number of transactions,' he added.

'That's clever. My boy Terry would understand all that,' Vic said. 'Well, he's not my boy exactly, but you know what I mean.'

George nodded seriously. They were talking man to man.

Vic said idly: 'You chaps are bringing in more rationing, I suppose.'

'Bound to come.' George finished his drink and found another in front of him.

'Printing ration books and everything,' Vic said.

George shook his head. 'Nothing to do with my job.'

'But you know the men whose job it is.' Vic smiled helpfully.

'Clerks,' George said. He knew a lot more than he was saying.

'The new books are green, I hear.'

George wasn't falling for that one. He held his drink in both hands. 'Vic,' he said. 'Vic, you knew my mother, didn't you?'

'Sure,' Vic laughed. 'Got on well with her as a matter of fact.'

'Vane wasn't as bad as they say, was she?'

'Your father only married her for her money, and he treated her very badly, George. No, she wasn't bad. Vane was . . . lost, that's all. She never did a single thing wrong, and that's the truth.' He smiled sincerely.

'I miss her,' George said. His lips trembled but with Vic he didn't feel embarrassed. Vic knew men. 'I've done a wrong thing,' George confessed.

Vic knew all about the flat in Marble Arch. George was as impetuous and silly as Vane, but such people were useful. Vane's mother Clarissa had died when Vane was hardly older than George had been, and bereavement had affected mother and son in similar ways, he guessed.

'Why can't we get whisky?' Vic yawned as though it wasn't important. 'Even on the black market. The sources of supply have dried up. Surely they're still making the stuff?'

'All shipped off to America,' George said. 'The almighty dollar.'

'Different crates, we could ship a load back,' Vic said idly.

'Why would I want to?' scoffed George. 'Next year the Emporium's mine. When my dad dies I'll inherit a fortune.'

Vic knew many things drove men and women, not just money. He patted George's shoulder paternally.

Ralph loved engines, aeroplanes and girls. He flew

Hawker Hurricanes with the big carburettor-fed Rolls-Royce Merlin V12 in the nose, the same engine as a Spitfire but in a better plane. There was no thrill to compare with the dawn patrol, the engines muttering and grunting with the radiators wide open to gulp the still air of a February morning, each aeroplane trailing a plume of snow in its airwash as they taxied out, correcting the machine's tendency to swing as the power came on, taking off over sleepy Debden in a howl of exhausts, and climbing into the soaring blue bowl of the sky.

Ralph had fought a lucky war. He had shot down a couple of twin-engine Messerschmitts – both pilots and observers parachuted to safety – and he had half of three more claims. Several times he'd come down himself, each time from engine failure caused by coolant loss, only once in the sea. The Battle of Britain, concentrated on the south coast, had largely passed him by – as part of 11 Group, 17 Squadron guarded a corridor stretching from the Thames at Windsor, around the top of London and across Suffolk, only allowed to wander from that territory and have a bit of fun when in hot pursuit.

Ralph looked around. From twenty thousand feet England was wonderfully beautiful – a harlequin patchwork of hedgerows with the comblike Saxon field-outlines and ancient lost villages clearly visible. It was a privilege to be alive.

Ralph was in love. Clipped next to the vibrating altimeter was a photograph of Kate. Ralph licked the leather flying glove over his finger and touched it to her lips on the paper. Kate was different. He had asked her to marry him.

And she had refused.

That made him love her more deeply.

Kate was the only girl Ralph had ever cared about who was not totally bowled over by him. Ralph was vulnerable, pleasantly handsome, sunny of temperament, and rich. He adored girls, and he was a girl's dream. Certainly none had ever found the words to deny him.

Yet not only had Kate turned Ralph down, she said she loved him.

This was far beyond Ralph's comprehension.

He shaded his eyes and winced at the winter sun. No enemy lurking there; he quartered the skyscape automatically, shivering. It was bitterly cold. The cockpit heater never worked and he wore a flying suit, the stiff regulation issue so as not to come it over the other chaps with the fancy Burberry stuff. It was too cold in winter beneath the thin Perspex, and hot as a greenhouse in summer, when they often flew in shirtsleeves.

Last weekend he'd gone down to Sonning, where Kate's father had his medical practice, and had a long talk with her after the lunchtime drink at the pub, walking along the riverbank upstream from the lock. Kate's light prettiness concealed a will of considerable determination. She let him kiss her in the soft afternoon light, but when he tried to caress her she resisted him gently.

'Why not?' murmured Ralph.

She looked down. 'Because there is more than just this to me.'

'Darling, darling I love you.'

'Please take me seriously.' She glanced up.

'I do, I do!' begged Ralph. She had lovely knees, the scent of her close against him and the warm feel of her almost drove him wild.

'You don't love me,' Kaae whispered. 'Just another of your girls.'

'Only you.'

'Another conquest.'

'Just let me kiss you.' She turned her head away and he was frightened that she'd cry.

'Hey, come on, it's all right,' he said. 'It doesn't matter. I love you, Kate.'

He held her close for a while.

'There haven't been so many,' he admitted. 'None that meant anything.'

'That's what I'm saying. I don't mean enough to you, Ralph.'

'Don't you love me at all?'

'I love you very much.'

'Then . . .' He shrugged his shoulders in bafflement, smiling into her eyes.

'You're always joking,' she tried to explain as they walked on, 'I'm just not sure if I'm one of your jokes.'

'You aren't.'

She stopped. 'Of course you would say that.'

'Then Kate, Kate, marry me. I might be dead next week.'

She stared up at him wonderingly. 'Oh, that's brutal.'

'I am not joking, Kate.'

'How could you say such a thing?' She found her handkerchief and held it against her cheek.

Because I'm afraid, he thought. *Can't you see it? I can't help my smiling face, that's the way I am. Because I'm seriously afraid, Kate, believe me.* But she wouldn't; any more than she believed he seriously loved her . . .

The sun made a brilliant glare across the Hurricane's canopy. They'd seen no raiders today, and the flight turned for home.

Ralph glanced at his smiling face in the rearview mirror. He fingered his tally-ho moustache.

He really did put Brylcreem on it, and it was doing okey-dokey.

Lisa decided to remain at Easton Manor. The mass evacuation of children from the great cities had been reversed; most mothers preferred their families to face the worst together, and the majority were returned home in time for the Blitz. But there were many orphans left, and many people with no relatives to go to after they had been bombed out, and Lisa made sure they had somewhere warm to stay until something turned up.

Pearl had come to help out for a while and the two women went walking in the bluebell woods between seasonal showers. The hedgerows were bursting with wild flowers, purple and yellow, and butterflies fluttered amongst the dripping stalks.

'We're getting Victoria repatriated as soon as we can,' Pearl said, 'my mother's had a stroke – '

'I'm so sorry.'

'And Lowell, my father, has never had an easy way with children.'

'Then Victoria must stay here.'

'I must say I agree with you. But Ben insists she stay in London.'

'How are things there?' Parliament had been burned a few nights previously.

'Just dinky,' Pearl said. 'The place lights up like a bonfire most nights. We took a bomb in the garden but the windows were sandbagged. A couple of incendiaries burned out on the roof. The royals were quite glad to be hit, said now they could look the East End in the face.'

They turned towards home. Lisa leaned on her stick.

'Pearl, do you think Ben will be all right?'

'Well, he's still driving the pump escape. He doesn't talk much about it. He comes back with his velours stinking of smoke. Sometimes his face is completely black. I don't like to ask him about what horrors he's seen. They dig children out of the rubble . . .'

'I couldn't bear it!' Lisa shuddered.

'He seems able to,' Pearl said. 'Somehow.'

They walked up the drive as the postman cycled back past them. Helen had torn open a letter from Will in Rosyth, where he was aboard *Dauntless* with the Training Squadron for a couple of months before going back to the *King Alfred* for his exams.

'If he passes he'll be a Sub-lieutenant RNVR,' Helen said proudly. She took a touching interest in Will's career, and he sent her letters covered with funny cartoons of the petty officers japing the cadets with impossible tasks. After some minor infringement of the rules his friend Storks had been given a heavy five-inch shell and told to take it to the galley, where Storks dutifully trotted with his burden, having no choice but to obey. 'Take it to the bosun,' ordered the cook, and Storks tottered around the ship until he found the bosun, who told him to give it to the coxswain . . .

'He always puts nautical words in his letters so I have to look them up,' Helen said. 'When he talks about swarming up ratlines and splicing the mainbrace, it takes me hours.' Smiling, she went off to find the dictionary.

'How I hate this bloody, bloody war,' Lisa said quietly.

2

Ria would not scream.

She was in her old bedroom at Havannah Street in the Isle of Dogs. She lay in her bed on a rubber sheet, wearing a nightie with a blue bow on the front, every detail of which had become familiar to her eyes. This blue bow rose and fell with her breathing, slowly up and down on the mound of her stomach, up as she breathed in through her mouth, then down as she let the breath trickle out slowly from her nostrils. As long as the blue bow was rising and falling she was all right. But then her muscles would tense and the contraction would start, and it went on getting worse, and still the blue bow rose and fell. When it was at its worst the blue bow stopped, because Ria had clenched her teeth together, stopping breathing to stop her scream, and she writhed slowly from side to side in her soundless agony.

Having a baby at the age of almost forty-two was not at all the same as having a baby at the age of fifteen. Not at all.

'For God's sake scream,' Esther said nervously.

'Where's Betty?' Ria cried.

'I'm here, love,' Betty Stark said, wiping Ria's face with a flannel.

'I won't scream,' Ria said. 'I love him. You understand that, don't you, Betty?'

'Yes, love.'

'That's why I wanted you here. I'll never ever see him again. Am I thirsty?'

Betty held the glass to Ria's lips and looked over her shoulder. 'She ought to be in hospital, Mrs Price.'

'She won't go.'

'I think this could take days.'

'She's been wicked,' Esther said. 'All her life, she's been in love with one man.'

'Ben London,' gasped Ria. The blue bow stopped moving. Betty stroked Ria's forehead tenderly.

'So that's why you wanted me here,' she said. Betty understood the love that never dies.

'Ben London's child.' Ria's eyes rolled, then the breath whistled in her nostrils and she lay limply. 'I can't bear it,' she said. They thought she meant the pain; she meant the lie.

'You have a good scream,' said Esther encouragingly.

'Shan't,' Ria said like a litany, her voice rising and falling. 'Shan't. Shan't. Oh no.' She writhed agonizedly, making the two standing women tighten their muscles in sympathy.

'She's been stuck at two minutes for hours,' Betty said to Esther, 'she doesn't seem able to get it any further.'

'It's growing dark,' Esther said. 'Thank goodness the nights are so short. I hate the dark. There go the bloody sirens. There's no chance of a doctor at all.' The horizon flickered and both women, but not Ria, jumped as the thud of explosions carried to them on the evening air.

'That's early,' Betty said. 'We ought to get her down to the shelter.' But she sounded reluctant. Betty's son had died of tuberculosis; the damp in the shelters killed more people than bombs.

'I'm staying here,' groaned Ria. 'I hope a bloody bomb falls on me right here.' She clasped her hands on her belly. 'I hate the little bugger.'

'Don't be like that,' Esther said. She whispered: 'Suppose she dies?'

'Shut up,' Ria groaned, 'I want to die.'

'But suppose she dies?' hissed Esther.

'It's a monster,' cried Ria suddenly, 'I never want to see it.' The rooflines over the street rippled with light and the moon faded into the glare. They could hear the deep, unsynchronous beat of the bombers. Betty pulled the blackout and turned on the bedside lamp – its light seemed brilliantly yellow, and the blue bow on Ria's nightdress rose and fell, then stopped. Her face reddened and her lips twitched, then slowly pulled back from her white teeth.

'Let it out, dear,' begged Esther.

But Ria would not scream.

A pale flash showed for an instant even through the blackout. 'It's very heavy tonight,' Esther said, 'just our luck.'

'It's all your fault,' shouted Ria, then the sound of the explosion went banging past them and the house creaked, settling. They could hear whistles blowing. Betty had the box of matches ready and when the light went off she lit the candle without fumbling. Ria's eyes stared upwards.

'I don't want to see it. My baby . . .'

'Don't be silly, dear,' Esther said.

'I want you to take it out of me without letting me see it and get rid of it,' Ria babbled. 'I want you to throw it in the river. That's the only thing that would hurt him.' She gave a horrible laugh, then grunted in her agony.

'She doesn't mean it, it's the transition,' Betty said.

Then for the first time, Ria screamed: *'I bloody well do mean it!'* She flopped back and whispered: 'Don't let Vic have it.'

'She's off about this again,' Esther whispered, then said reassuringly: 'Don't worry, darling, Vic isn't here.' She shrugged at Betty. The fears and phantoms of childbirth. Ria lay inert as more bombs rocked the house, then there was a colossal thud from the direction of the river, followed by the sound of water falling. Then Ria jumped as the front door banged downstairs.

'Keep him out,' she said frantically.

'It's probably just the air-raid warden,' Esther said.

Ria said: 'It's Vic.'

'Mum,' called Vic's voice up the stairs. 'Are you up there, Mum?'

'Don't let him up,' hissed Ria. 'You know how he feels. Don't let him take our baby.'

'We're up here, Vic,' Esther called. 'Look – go into the kitchen and make yourself a cup of tea, why don't you? I'll be down in a minute.'

'I think we're getting somewhere,' Betty said with a sigh of relief, 'I can see the top of its head.'

'What colour's his hair?' gasped Ria.

'Dark.'

'Oh, oh,' wept Ria.

'Push, love. Do you want a lovely baby boy? *Push*.'

'I don't care if it's a parrot,' Ria gasped, 'I just want it.'

'Push now.'

'Shut up,' Ria said. 'Don't let him up.'

'How's things going up there?' called Vic.

'I'd better go and talk to him,' Esther said, 'you know how he gets in a state.'

Ria sweated and swore. She could feel her boy's head inching into her palms. Now she touched the smooth curve of his forehead. 'Bit more,' Betty said.

Ria screamed.

The door opened, and Vic stood there. Ria stared at him. Her back arched, her nails dug into the rubber sheet running with her blood. She felt the baby's head come slowly squeezing out, then in a sudden rush and a sensation of extraordinary relief the rest of his body came sliding out of her.

Betty held up the wet, shining baby in the candlelight. 'She's a girl!'

Smiling, Betty clipped the cord.

Ria could hardly believe her eyes.

'A girl!' she cried.

Seeing Ria's tears of joy as she came in, Esther said: 'Thought you wanted to get rid of it. But you don't, do you? I hope you're going to make a better job of it this time.'

Ria cuddled her baby. 'Oh, she's *lovely!*'

'Give her to me,' Vic said.

Ria huddled protectively down with her baby, kissing her face.

'What are you going to call her?' Betty asked.

The baby's eyes popped open – opal-blue eyes, and they were beautiful, looking clear through Ria with a baby's wise, unfocused stare. 'Lola,' whispered Ria, 'that's your name. Lola, I love you.'

Lola's fingers slid beguilingly into the corner of her mother's mouth, then were snatched away as Vic lifted up the baby in his great hands.

He grinned victoriously down at Ria, and turned to the door. Betty was standing there, and stared into his face, then at Ria.

'Oh my God,' she said.

'Give her back,' whimpered Ria, then summoned all her strength, reaching out to tug at the back of Vic's jacket. 'Give my baby back! She's mine – even if she's the only thing in the world I have now that *is* mine. Mine! This time I swear it.'

Betty was strong, but more than that it was her implacable features that stopped Vic. He turned, then handed the baby back to Ria with quivering hands.

'You're lucky,' he said. 'Ratcliff's all on fire, I've got to go.'

Esther said to Ria: 'Does Ben know about this baby?'

Vic looked at her and his face deformed into a snarl of rage. For a second all the women cowered as though he would strike them down, then he turned slowly to Ria.

'Ben London!' he said.

'Yes,' Ria said bravely, 'what's wrong with it?'

Vic's face struggled and his eyes glared, but there was nothing he could say – he dare not contradict the lie. The unspeakable could not be spoken. He strode to the door.

'My warehouse is in the path of the fire,' he flung over his shoulder. 'If I'm wiped out, I'll drag you all down with me.'

They heard him go clattering downstairs.

Ria shivered, hugging little Lola to her. The blackout was torn and the window frame splintered, the glass sagging against the strips of sticky tape. They could hear shouts and cries out in the street, and the crackle of flames. Something had landed very close, and they had not even noticed it.

Betty looked at Ria. She knew who the baby's real father was.

Ria, Betty, Pearl and Vic. They were the only ones who would ever know the dreadful secret.

'I think we all deserve a nice cup of tea,' Esther said.

Ria wrapped Lola in a towel and smoothed down her baby's black hair.

'I do swear it,' she whispered, 'this time I'll be the best mother anyone ever had. You'll have everything, I promise you, Lola. There's nothing you won't have, ever, love.'

'She won't have a father,' said Betty Stark.

3

Ben slept on a hard iron bed above the enormous purpose-built fire station at Manchester Square, as he did every night during the Blitz.

At 22:05 hours that evening the bells went down and they had a shout, and turned out. Sleeping only in socks, velour trousers and white shirt, Red Team under Ben were first to run to the brass pole and slide down into the harsh lighting of the garage beneath. It was their duty to be first at the fire, and get any trapped people out down the escape. He could hear the doors already rumbling open, operated by the bells. Ben grabbed his leathers from the cab of the big red Dennis pump escape and dragged them on. 'Where away?'

'Narrow Street, Limehouse, got it?'

That was a long way; it must be very bad tonight. They'd be lucky to get the massive, modern pump escape far into that Victorian warren of warehouses, stores and slums. Ben shrugged on his heavy velour jacket and swung up into the cab, thumbed the starter. The petrol engine started at once off mains electricity and he lifted the clutch, assuming the crew were aboard – tough on them if they weren't – hearing the clatter as the boosters pulled out, and the machine turned into the square with the bell ringing and headlights full on.

Any traffic in Oxford Street got out of the way. The note of the engine rose to a grinding roar as they jumped the red lights. Ben used a clear stretch to do up the fiddly brass buttons of his velours. The fire crew were pulling on their helmets. As they rushed along Holborn into Newgate they could see the skyline ahead of them alive with light.

'Bloody hell,' said one of the auxiliary firemen, even from this distance the flames glowing on his appalled face, 'the whole East End's going up.'

As they passed through Shadwell, the London Docks were burning, the smooth water as red as a reflecting mirror. A bus lay on its side like an enormous slab of corned beef. Ben tramped on the brakes and swung the pump escape down a narrow cobbled street towards the darkness of the river somewhere ahead. Little houses leaned their roofs together over the machine. Men were running with buckets, staring at something ahead. A dog jumped in circles, barking. Smoke came churning down, then lifted, and ahead of them a long dark wall broke into flame. They felt the heat push back at them through the windscreen.

Ben jumped down. Against the wind, steam was trailing from manhole covers towards the blazing warehouse, sucked in by the firestorm. He plugged his phone into the Fire Alarm on the corner of the street, but no more machines were available. He ran round to the front of the building and booted the door down, peering into the lurid space beyond, piled high with crates. This end of the warehouse was not ablaze, but the stifling air seemed to shake, and he knew it soon would be. He peered at the stencilling on one of the crates. Molasses. 'Hoses!' he yelled.

But at the hydrant the mains pressure had fallen so low it was useless. The men dragged suction hoses to the river and started the pump. Water sprayed in long jets, two men struggling with each outlet. Ben pulled one group to the warehouse door and soon water was streaming over the smouldering packing crates inside.

Outside, the air rippled with heat.

A quiet voice behind Ben said calmly: 'Any hope?'

'This one's a goner, chum.' Ben turned to face a slim young man with dark eyes and a very neat, self-contained manner. 'Are you the owner?'

'I know him.' Terry held out his hand. 'Terry Price.'

Ben stared. Terry's face neither smiled nor frowned. So this was Nigel's child from the loss of his adored wife. Their faces shifted like mirages in the shimmering heat.

Ben ignored the offered hand. 'Ben London,' he said.

'Yes,' Terry said.

Ben gestured at the blaze. 'This Vic's?'

'I can't comment on that,' Terry said, sounding both exactly like Nigel and not like him at all; not the Nigel changed by Arleen's death who had advised Ben to save his son. But Terry even held his left hand in his coat pocket in the same way that Nigel had, as if protecting a secret hurt.

'And it's full of molasses, right?'

'That is correct,' Terry said.

A ball of flame burst above the warehouse roof, then a moment later the blast and heat washed over them.

'That's never molasses,' Ben said. He ran towards the groups of firemen struggling with the loops of hose now tangling everywhichway like snakes across the gushing roadway. 'Get back! Back!' he waved, and the men pulled back with the brass nozzles fountaining cool water over their steaming velours. A second explosion shook the warehouse and the heat was intense. The bricks were cracking, and glass from the windows dribbled like spun sugar down the walls.

The men stood around watching the total loss burn higher, then began dousing nearby roofs to stop the flames jumping.

Ben went back to Terry, but the boy was standing quietly in a doorway, and Vic now stood on the street corner. He smiled an awful smile when he saw Ben.

'You!' he said. 'Go home, Terry. This is man's business.'

Terry didn't move.

Ben said: 'Don't tell me it's molasses in there, Vic.'

The fire glittered in Vic's eyes.

'It's whisky,' he admitted finally. 'A whole bloody ship-load of whisky.'

Ben called to a fireman. 'Tell the boys to get back another fifty paces.'

'Yes sir!'

Ben turned back to Vic. 'You bloody fool,' he said, and saw Terry stir. People did not talk to Vic in that tone of voice. But Vic held up his hand.

'One more day,' Vic said, 'and it would have been . . . gone. Dispersed.'

'I hope for your sake you're carrying plenty of war risk insurance.'

'Not a penny,' Vic grinned.

Terry interrupted quietly, coming forward, his voice almost lost under the roar of the consuming flames. 'We're covered for the value of the molasses.'

Vic cuffed him around the head with the back of his hand, the sinews stamping a spreading flush across Terry's cheek. Terry caught his balance with his knuckles on the black, running pavement. He stared at Ben with blank hostility.

Part of the warehouse wall crumbled, revealing the fiery furnace of the interior, the shadows of the firemen stretching back around Vic and Ben on the corner.

'I'm wiped out,' Vic said.

He smiled.

'You came to me once, Ben London,' he said. 'You begged.'

Terry stood with the fingers of both hands pressed to his hurt cheek, staring at Ben with contempt.

'You begged me for money,' Vic said. His face twisted. 'Well, I'm begging you now.'

Terry stared at Vic.

'Shut up,' said Vic, turning, 'I don't like this any more than you do.'

'You can't,' Terry said. 'You've got all sorts of tricks up your sleeve, Uncle Vic – haven't you?'

Vic pointed at the warehouse. The walls fell into a vast column of rising sparks and suddenly they could see the river beyond, and the fire tug *Massey* throwing up long white arches of water. With no intervening building to stop them, before the hoses could be turned down splashes of hot water doused their faces.

Vic wiped away the greasy droplets. Ben's eyes were cold and hard.

Vic stared at him with barely contained fury.

'I'm begging you!' he demanded.

The men were taking the pressure off the hoses, treading them flat and winding them in. Any time now a second or third wave of bombers could come across, and there would be other fires to go to.

'I want my five per cent of London Emporium back,' Ben said.

Vic struggled.

'It's a deal,' he said.

Terry lunged at Ben, his white hands outstretched, but Vic caught his shoulder in a grip that lifted Terry off the ground and made him squeak.

'No,' Vic said. 'No. No.'

4

Ben picked up the inter-office phone. It was raining and the daylight from the window behind him was cool and grey. 'Yes, Alice?'

Alice Cypress said: 'I've got a Mrs Esther Price on the line for you, sir.'

Ben hesitated for a fraction of a second. 'Put her through,' he said. He cleared his throat. 'What can I do for you, Esther?'

Esther spoke very slowly, like a person who did not use the phone often and did not like it.

'Ria has had your second child,' she said.

Ben was dumb.

'I thought that you would like to know,' Esther said. 'How could you do it to the poor girl?' Esther was crying; she was holding her hand over the mouthpiece, but he could hear her muffled sobs. 'I wish I'd never seen you, I wish I'd never heard of you, I wish we'd never taken you in. Vic's right. You bastard. You terrible bastard.'

Ben stood up. 'Don't hang up. Esther, please! Is Ria all right?' No answer. 'At least tell me – is he a boy, or has Ria had a girl?'

She didn't answer. Silence.

Ben shouted: 'If only you can tell me his or her name, Esther. Please!'

The line clicked.

Esther had hung up.

PART V

THE ICE KING

CHAPTER TWENTY-FOUR

1

Over the next few weeks and months, Terry observed Vic. He wanted to learn from him. It was a privilege that a man such as Vic should have snatched his brother's orphan from the women in Havannah Street who would have made him grow up soft like some other boys – still hardly out of short trousers. With Vic, Terry was a man.

Vic had always lived on the streets. He had dragged himself up by the sheer force and attraction of his personality to dominate his environment, and Terry admired that. Terry knew that the East End was made up of tribes – women, the local authorities, Jews, crime, the police, they all had their territories. Vic looked after his people. He was the most violent and powerful man Terry knew, and it was a privilege to be a part of such a man's inner circle by birthright.

In fact, sometimes Terry suspected he was even closer than that. He thought that he was the only person Vic really trusted.

The violence with which Vic treated him reinforced Terry in that view. Vic wanted to teach him because he loved him. Terry admired Vic and desperately wanted to do better. The books were not what he was best at.

Terry could stand back. He wasn't ruled by his feelings like Vic. He could weigh the scales of emotion; he could observe what Vic only felt.

Vic did not know what fear was. Terry, who was shy, was in awe of that.

But there was Ben London.

After that business at the fire, Terry wondered if he trusted Vic quite so much. 'Whisky, nylons, ration books,' Vic had laughed, pouring himself a rum at the Old Bull and Bush when they got back, 'what a bloody mess. Still, could have been worse.'

Terry sat down on the banquette. The mark on his cheek had faded and he was pale and observant. 'Why did London agree to lend to you?'

'Because he was honour-bound.' Vic tossed back the rum and surveyed Terry. 'You wouldn't understand that. It cancelled his debt to me. And he wanted that little share of the Emporium back so much it hurt him. That's useful to know.'

'But you had to give it back.'

Vic looked impatient at Terry's ignorance. 'If you know where a man hurts,' Vic explained in words of one syllable, 'you know where to hurt him.'

Terry noted that, but knowing less, was less convinced. In his opinion Vic had suffered a defeat and was putting a gloss on it.

But Vic laughed, looking very jolly, and then Terry was quite certain that Vic hated Ben London, really hated him. *Ben London can hurt him without even meaning to – and so can Ria*. Terry could not comprehend that. 'I'm not as poor as I pretend,' Vic said, 'I have a few more irons in the fire.'

'What is the reason for this enmity?' asked Terry coldly, and almost bit his tongue. He had nearly said *rivalry*, and Vic would not have forgiven him for it.

'Ria,' said Vic. A terrible rage crossed his face, then was gone. Vic was a success with Ria – but now he had been cheated even of that. 'And more than Ria,' Vic said. He turned on his heel and laughed at Terry. 'Don't worry!' he said.

'I'm not worried.'

'It'll get worse before it gets better,' Vic said.

Spring and fall were Pearl's favourite times in London.

She closed her eyes and relaxed with a sigh of satisfaction, feeling the autumnal sunlight play warmly through the whispering treetops on her face and legs. This mellow English sun would not burn her fair skin but only make it glow comfortably. The deckchair creaked and she opened one eye, watching the sun flicker through the swaying leaves, then turned her head, hearing the drone of voices. Across the grass Ben, dressed in a suit, was sitting at a collapsible table giving dictation to Alice Cypress. Alice must be over seventy now – Ben had to repeat himself occasionally – but she was too devoted to retire. Apart from Ben, probably she alone had any detailed idea of the extent of his business empire. They had been working long before Pearl came out to sunbathe, and they might well be working when she went back in.

Ben looked at a piece of paper in his hand, then glanced over at Pearl. 'George has written me a letter!' he called. This was the first full sentence he had spoken to her today.

Pearl yawned. 'What does he want?'

'He wants to buy Lockhart House.'

'But it's three floors, plus attic, plus basement,' Pearl said.

'It's much too big. Write him a letter, Alice. Tell him no.'

'Politely,' Pearl called. George was self-centred and thought that his father cared nothing for him. Pearl admitted that Ben did sometimes give that impression, wishing that George had more go, more toughness. George still laboured under the burden of Vane's memory and blamed his father for their marriage's tragic failure, but also secretly blamed himself for it, Pearl was sure. That was George's nature, but Ben's child had no reason to feel guilt, she knew, and she was convinced that such deep, dark worries as tormented George about whether he had loved his mother enough had never even occurred to Ralph; it was impossible to imagine carefree Ralph being tormented about anything in this life.

But George chewed over every morsel. And now he wanted to buy his grandfather's dwelling. It was a good thing that Ben had got rid of Primrose House, where Vane had lived, years ago. A sudden thought struck Pearl.

'Who lives at Lockhart House now?'

'It's empty,' Ben said. 'Apart from the pictures.' And

that's the way it's staying, his tone said. Under the terms of the twins' Trust Ben would soon lose the Emporium to his two sons. He would not even have the right of a seat on the board. Over twenty years ago he had dreamed of creating the most glamorous store on earth. Now he must shortly hand over that dream under the sterile terms of old Georgy Leibig's will.

'George isn't having Lockhart House as well as the Emporium!' Ben called.

'Can't you come and talk to me?' called Pearl. 'Does it always have to be work?'

He had changed. Pearl never said it -- *you've changed!* -- but he had. Was it her fault? Pearl couldn't imagine how. She thought it was because he was spending more time on business that he could sometimes seem so cold and hard. With the National Fire Service being set up, he now worked only part time at his fire duties, and he would probably give them up altogether.

'One last letter, then I'll come and talk to you,' Ben said.

Pearl closed her eyes and turned her face to the sun. Some time during the night Victoria's ship would dock at Southampton -- please God, she would have a safe crossing, the U-boats were very bad, really they ought not to have risked having her repatriated -- but Pearl could not live without Victoria. She was going down on the train tonight to greet her daughter first thing in the morning.

'Finished,' Ben said to Alice. While she packed up the papers he sat gazing at the lovers strolling in Green Park. 'See you later, Alice.'

'Goodbye, sir.' Alice waved to Pearl and called: 'Goodbye, Mrs London.'

'Bye,' Pearl waved, and closed her eyes.

She sensed Ben come and sit beside her, and put out her hand. He held it.

Then he said: 'Why didn't you tell me Ria was pregnant?'

Pearl was caught out. 'I was jealous.' She shadowed her eyes with her hand, examining his reaction.

'You're the last person in the world I would have thought that,' he said. But he nodded, convinced, and she realized he knew more of her longing for another child than she ever imagined – and of her lost hope.

'Promise me you'll never see Ria,' Pearl said.

'I promise,' Ben said. 'It was Esther who phoned me.'

That was all right. 'Was it a boy or a girl?'

'She wouldn't say.'

Good. At last the horrid East End was washed out of his blood. She had hated seeing those squalid streets he must have known so well, excluding her; she held him close. 'It's all over now, Ben.'

'You're an angel.'

'Kiss me.' He kissed her, and his face was tender for a moment.

Giving up the Emporium, the quintessential West End store almost forced into existence by the raw will of a mere East End boy, was going to be the hardest thing that Ben had ever done. He had hoped to have a working breakfast in the Waterfalls with Ralph and George to introduce them informally, but Ralph couldn't get leave until the mid-morning, and George declined to leave early from the ministry, although it was a Saturday and he didn't work after midday. Pearl watched Ben dress in a black suit. His face was set into a smiling, invulnerable mask.

'Try and be sweet with George,' she said.

'If George is to make the Emporium continue as a success,' Ben said, 'sweetness is not what he needs.' He still hoped to be invited to sit on the board, and Ralph wanted him to, but George wouldn't countenance it.

'He'd just run the place,' George had complained, 'exactly as he does now.'

'You think you can do better?' Ralph asked humorously.

But George had been enraged. 'I'll show you. He was no older than me when he started out. Our mother had

421

better ideas than him. He isn't so clever. In fact he isn't clever at all.'

Ralph held up his hands against this tirade, laughing. 'I just wanted to protect my investment.' He did not mean that he lacked faith in George, but everything he said nowadays seemed to provoke George to fury. Ralph laughed to ease George's pain, but George took everything to heart, and Ralph knew he was not forgiven. He had scratched his flourishing moustache, amused by his brother's lack of confidence. If only George would relax and open up to people more, he would realize that he was surrounded by friends, not by enemies.

Pearl lay in bed, watching Ben dress.

He tightened his tie. He knew he was going to be hurt today. This smiling, glossy face, the eyes like blue armour, was something a man as successful as he wore to protect himself; he had to learn to conceal his true feelings. It slipped on easier each time, and came off a little harder. Sometimes Pearl hardly noticed it was there.

Perhaps that was because all her thoughts were concentrated on Victoria, whose great grief on returning home had been leaving her beautiful, tireless morgan horse, Windrush, and Marmalade's rough brown coat and four stumpy legs were no consolation. Victoria thought English riding was silly, because the saddles had no knee-rolls, and posting up and down at the trot made her feel ridiculous.

'Don't you miss your American friends?' Pearl had asked.

'What friends?' Victoria cut with her knife and put her fork in her right hand, too. 'This tastes like crud. What is it?' Pearl hid her laughter behind her hand.

'Whalemeat soaked in vinegar,' Ben said. 'Haven't you heard of rationing?'

'The hell with it,' Victoria said.

'Surely you had lots of friends,' said Pearl.

Victoria pushed her plate away. 'Easterners, you know what they're like. They ride like ladies. They were jealous because they couldn't keep up with Windrush.'

'This must seem very tame,' Ben said.

'Sure.' Victoria got down from the table and yawned.

'Sit down,' Ben said. Victoria looked startled, then sat. 'You, young lady,' Ben said, 'are going to go to a school.'

'You know,' said Victoria spitefully, 'you sound just like Grandfather Lowell.' She got up and stalked off.

'She's got a little wild,' Pearl had said indulgently.

Now Pearl straightened Ben's tie. 'Good enough!' she said.

He re-checked it in the mirror. 'Sure you won't come to the Emporium?'

She shook her head. It was going to be difficult enough for him alone, she knew, and it was kinder to keep out of the way. Besides, she was taking Victoria to see over a likely school in north London.

Ben stood alone under the portico of London House staring out. It was raining, just as it had been on the night the twins were born and Peggy had made her epic journey through the dark to the Emporium to tell him. Now with the twins coming of age a full circle was rotating inevitably to its close. He opened his umbrella and walked up St James's Street. As he crossed Piccadilly he saw George vanishing into the Emporium. Ben stopped by the Head Doorman, resplendent in yellow and blue.

'Hallo, Dillibe.'

'Good afternoon, sir.' The millionaire was the only one to call him by his proper name; Dillibe wondered why he did it, and decided that it was friendship. Grinning broadly, he stood to attention on his patch of polished flag, not quite as stiffly as Hawk, but as calm and authoritative. 'Mr George arrived a minute ago, sir, and Mr Ralph has been here about half an hour.'

The shoppers looked up as the sound of twin engines rose to a roar overhead then fell away rapidly. 'Don't worry, folks,' Dillibe called in his deep, reassuring voice, 'just one of them Dornier 17s sneaking in. We heard him, so he's missed us.' The Dornier could bomb at very low level, and the unpredictability of a lone nuisance raider prepared to risk the barrage balloons unnerved the routine of civilian life. People didn't mind so much being bombed all night if they could rely on a break during the day. 'I'll help you, m'am.' Dillibe assisted a woman to pick up her dropped shopping.

Ben walked into the store. The buyers performed marvels obtaining the merchandise they did, and the cheese in which the Emporium had long specialized, though rationed, was still the widest variety to be had anywhere. Long queues attended each counter.

Ben paused at the top of the steps, then felt something touch his right shoulder: the brass switches of the lighting bank. Soon all this would be without him. A momentary impulse seized him to pull up the switches and bury it all in darkness.

No sign of his despair showed in his face.

He walked down and shook hands with David, the general manager, now with premature flecks of grey shot through his immaculately brushed hair. His wife Harriet, who twenty years ago had been a slim girl working in the Post Room, and was today a smooth woman in a fashionably padded dress, though not very much pulled in at the waist, came forward and shook Ben's hand nervously. She had a young girl in tow; her elder daughter was starting in Women's Apparel soon.

'I can't believe this is goodbye, sir,' David said with glistening eyes.

'We always knew it was going to happen,' Ben said.

'Will everyone be looked after?' asked Harriet forthrightly.

Didn't they realize Ben couldn't help them any more? 'That's up to Ralph and George.' He smiled confidently and went upstairs to his office. Ralph in his smart RAF uniform, now wearing the double stripe of a flight lieutenant – he had been an instructor with a training unit for most of the summer – was leaning on the desk casually smoking a cigarette, and George was sitting in Ben's swivel chair. 'Wotcher, Pops,' Ralph said, shaking hands.

''Cher, Ralph. Hallo George,' Ben said. 'Well, my congratulations to you both. I've done my best for the

Emporium, and now it's yours. Like a flower, you'll find it needs water to flourish.'

'I can't believe,' Ralph said, with a glance at George, 'that Grandpa really meant for it to happen this way . . .'

I can. This is exactly what he wanted to happen, Ben thought. *He wanted me to know his pain and suffer in my turn. Congratulations, Georgy, here is your moment of victory over your ambitious son-in-law that you wanted so much.*

Best to get it over quickly. 'I'll introduce you to David and the heads of departments,' he said.

'I wish Mama was here,' George said. He looked at his watch as though he had a more important appointment. 'Do we have to go through with this charade?'

'Let's do it the way Dad wants it,' Ralph said.

They went into the other room where Charlie Bookkeeper was waiting with the legal papers for signature. And suddenly the Emporium was not Ben's any more.

'Good luck, boys,' he said. A cold buffet had been laid on in the Waterfalls where everyone would gather later to welcome the new owners, but for the moment he was determined to show Ralph and George around the departments where the real business was done. An entourage built up behind them. 'This is Frank Dayton, he's been in Accounts with us for many years. . . .'

'Pleased to meet you,' Ralph said with his pleasant charm. Ben knew he had no interest in the Emporium at all, but he was grateful to Ralph for being kind.

'You didn't have to do this, Dad,' Ralph said quietly as they walked on. With his father alone, he dropped his light manner. 'Why make yourself suffer?'

'Because,' said Ben.

'Because?'

'That's all,' Ben said.

'George will run the place,' Ralph pointed out. 'He will come to love it, you know. He feels he has to.' Very like his grandfather in that. 'You could be kinder to him.'

Ben would not admit that George was weak. 'You could give up the Air Force.'

'No,' Ralph said, realizing how desperate his father was and feeling very close. 'I know you could wangle it, but flying a desk, that's not me.'

'Be careful,' Ben said, 'you have been very, very lucky so far.'

'I was born lucky,' Ralph laughed. 'With a silver spoon in my mouth.'

They came down the stairs, pulling ahead of the crowd behind him. On the main sales floor, looking towards the doors, Ben sensed at once that something was wrong. No one else seemed to notice the change, and for a moment Ben couldn't put his finger on what it was. The resplendent figure of the Head Doorman was missing. Then Alice Cypress came out of the lift holding a message. She spoke into Ben's ear in a very low voice. 'There's been a bomb.'

'Not Dillibe,' Ben said, staring at the doors. The glass was intact.

'His wife.' Alice couldn't remember her name. 'Somewhere in Marble Arch apparently.'

'Keep it quiet, keep things going, Ralph.' Ben touched his son's elbow then ran between the counters, up the steps, and forced the door of the Head Doorman's changing room.

Dillibe's great face was running with tears and he was wild with grief, half in and half out of his yellow jacket. First he sat down, then stood up.

'They say Natasha's dead,' he said. 'I don't know what to do.'

George did not hear the news until Ralph whispered it to him halfway through the party in the Waterfalls. George looked at the canapé between his fingers and felt sick. Marble Arch. If Natasha had arrived early at the flat . . . no one would understand how innocent it was. Thirty years ago meeting her – being friends with her – would have been socially incomprehensible; now it was merely unspeakable. He would be condemned (people always thought the worst) for something that had never, or hardly, happened – only in that first meeting when she had taken him with such contempt. But what had started for George as the thrill of a naughty escapade had matured into a genuinely affectionate friendship – Natasha had been kind to him and no one else had ever been; Natasha understood failure, and loneliness, and rebellion. Now she had ruined him: the flat was in his name. George looked around for his father – he would have to confess everything and let his father hook him out of the trouble he found himself in.

To be honest, the trouble he craved. *Look at me! Poor George! Pity me! Here I am!*

When he had his father with him, everything would be all right.

But Ben London was nowhere to be seen.

'He went with Dillibe to Marble Arch,' Ralph said. 'Apparently two bombs landed in Hyde Park and did no damage, but the third hit a building. Some people were killed on the pavement.'

He helped himself to another sherry.

George slipped away. Once free, he ran along Piccadilly until he was gasping, then walked. Sweat trickled inside his shirt. He took off his jacket and ran again, Green Park slipping slowly by on his left, soldiers milling around the big ack-ack battery with its barrel pointing futilely at the sky. He turned up Park Lane past London's, walking wearily now. A cruel stitch jabbed under his ribs with each stride. He began to wander, and hardly noticed the big black Daimler pull in at the kerb beside him. Vic Price got out.

'Terry told me,' he said. 'Get in the car, you bloody idiot. I'll handle everything.'

'I haven't done anything wrong,' George said, then obeyed.

'Doesn't he sing nicely?' Esther prattled as she did the ironing. 'I'm dreaming of a . . . white Christmas . . .' She had a crush on Bing Crosby, and Ria agreed that Bing sounded even more handsome crooning over the Philips radio in their own front room than he looked in the film. And usually Ria agreed with hardly anything Esther said, she always had her besotted head down over that baby.

Well, Esther admitted, Lola *was* lovely.

'Do you remember,' Esther said, leaning on the iron and staring wistfully into the middle distance, 'do you remember in the old days, when we always used to get a white Christmas? We never seem to get them nowadays.' She lifted the curtain and they heard rain beating on the glass.

'Watch it,' Ria warned, 'you'll get the warden knocking on the door about the blackout.'

'We used to have such lovely Christmases.' Esther wanted to nostalge.

'Bloody didn't,' Ria said. 'There was that business about the hats.'

'And Vic always brought us the biggest goose on the Island.'

'I thought we agreed not to talk about him,' Ria said.

'I've been thinking about it,' Esther said, 'and I think you're a bit hard on Vic.' She couldn't help changing her mind for the best about people.

'You watch you don't burn my dress,' Ria said. 'If you even think of inviting him here again, I'm going. Promise.'

'You haven't got anywhere to go to!' Esther said. Ria had always blamed her stage career for getting between her and Will – they had never felt close however hard she tried, because she hadn't loved him enough as a baby. Now that she had a second chance, she was determined to be the most marvellous mother to Lola. Even if it meant the end of her career. Esther had to admire her efforts to be good.

For Lola's sake Ria had sold Trott's out to Vic, for a

pittance, and the word was Gina ran it as a clip-joint. This hurt Ria worse than anything – the club, almost a *salon*, she'd had such dreams for, where Fats Waller himself, carrying her small hand in his huge black one, had taught her to play the left-hand roll of boogie-woogie . . . and all the other memories. The famous sports journalist who kept his own personal deep-freeze behind the bar holding gin and dry vermouth at minus thirty-five degrees Centigrade, and the glasses deep-frozen too, so that Ria's fingers stuck to the stem.

Ray Trott dancing as smoothly as if he had oil in his joints.

Yes; now Ria had nowhere left to go to.

Through having her child, she would come back to her own childhood. She came home.

Ria loved Lola. Nothing was too much trouble if it was for Lola's sake. Never what Esther would have called housewifely by nature, Ria even washboarded nappies and dutifully hung up all the strings of damp baby clothes that festooned the kitchen this winter, though sometimes with a hostile look in her eye, and Esther learned to keep clear and offer to do the ironing.

Sometimes Ria just sat with Lola in her arms and a wonderful grin on her face.

This was what happiness was. She had searched all her life for it, and this was simply what it was.

'No goose this year,' Esther grumbled while Bing crooned, 'and I only got a miserable piece of beef off young Charlie Best, under the counter too.' She glanced at Ria: this was Ria's fault. Once the name Price automatically meant the best service, the finest cuts, and a little extra too. Always kind inquiries about Vic, how was he, do remember me to him and give him my regards, Mrs Price. *And a bit extra slipped under the counter*. Vic was the local boy who had made good, and people liked that, and Esther liked basking in his limelight. But Ria banned Vic from Havannah Street. She was quite unreasonable about it – almost frantic. She really hated Vic this time. Motherhood had certainly given her courage, Esther had to admit that. When Esther took the step of inviting Vic in for a reconciliation, Ria snatched up Lola and threatened to call the police.

That threat was unforgivable.

'I'm so sorry about this, Vic,' Esther apologized. Vic was jealous of Ben; of course he was.

'I only wanted to hold her,' Vic told Esther in a choking voice.

'Of course you did, dear.' Esther looked peevishly at Ria. Ria's face was white but determined, and she was pointing at the door. Her love child peeped sleepily out of the crook of her arm, those entrancing eyes with the big, darkly golden flecks . . . Vic spun on his heel and slammed the door behind him, leaving Esther and Ria alone.

Ria looked relieved. She had broken Vic's hold over her. She had won.

The money stopped, but Ria didn't seem to care. They would make out somehow. Their favoured treatment with the local shopkeepers ceased too, but Ria was fighting her own war. Esther let her have her way, but she didn't quite forgive her.

'One miserable little piece of Christmas beef,' Esther repeated. That was Ria's fault, and she wasn't going to let her forget it. She felt so sorry for all of them. Still, that was life.

CHAPTER TWENTY-FIVE

1

By May Ralph had been transferred back to operational flying in Hurricanes. He flew in shirtsleeves with the sun hot on his soft leather helmet.

He glanced at his squadron leader – an old man of twenty-six, due for retirement. Above and far beyond, the gaggle of Spitfires was still climbing. The calm voice of the sector controller coming in over Ralph's high-frequency headphones was vectoring the Hurricanes towards a bunch of German bombers – given an 'X' designation, meaning number uncertain – somewhere in the blue ahead. The Spitfires would take care of the usual top-cover of German fighters. These traps worked very well if the controllers sprang them properly.

Ralph checked his instruments, then paused. The photograph of Kate was still wedged by the altimeter, but she refused to be another conquest, because she loved him. She couldn't bear not to be everything to him, with him every minute, and of course she could not be. With her, Ralph's magic failed. When he tried to kiss her she thought it was because he took her lightly, so she resisted him, and when he did not try she was convinced he did not really love her. Friends, it seemed, was all they were capable of being.

Ralph wanted more.

He tried to give her confidence in him.

He even gave her house a low-level buzz, risking a court martial, a compliment he could not imagine any girl resisting. Yet the next time they met she seemed to think such a jejeune trick proved his insincerity rather than the reverse.

Kate didn't have the courage to admit that they were in love. She was too frightened that he would be killed.

Ralph had laughed. 'Better to have loved and lost, Kate.' They were walking along the riverbank in the evening haze.

'There you go again,' she said, looking down, 'just making fun of me.'

Ralph stared at her. 'Never.'

'It isn't a joke,' she said miserably. If she had cried, he could have held her; but she turned abruptly and walked away from him along the towpath, and all he could do was follow after her.

Alone in the hammering, blaring cockpit, Ralph squinted up against the sun's glare, then looked down. A mile below, a dozen old Dornier bombers with black crosses on their broad wings moved slowly across the brilliant map of English fields. The headphones squawked, then Ralph armed his guns and the Hurricanes half-rolled and dived. The Dornier crews weaved alertly, and the element of surprise was lost as they scattered.

Suddenly Ralph was close to someone, glimpsing sunlight gleaming on metal and Perspex. The cannons in the Hurricane's wings racketed and it felt as though brakes had come on as the recoil knocked back the machine's speed. As he swooped and climbed Ralph did not know if he had scored a hit – in the nature of air battles, having been for an instant close enough to see the crew's faces, he now couldn't see any aircraft at all. Flying so low, the Dorniers left no vapour trails. A Fenland canal glinted like a silver scratch. The headphones jabbered in his ears then were silent.

'Apany Leader, where the hell are you?' Ralph said, then looked around for his wingman. He didn't like the way those bombers had scattered so quickly.

To his right a tangle of vapour trails hung against the sky, slowly dispersing. Whatever had happened up there was over. Ralph realized to his horror that it had been a trap within a trap – an élite German flight concealing itself perfectly in the eye of the sun.

Above him, a loose white thread unravelled slowly. Looking so close to the sun, Ralph rubbed his eyes, dazzled.

The German machine fell on him out of the sun's glare – the white thread was its vapour trail diving towards him almost vertically. Ralph sensed the thin black line of the wings, a Messerschmitt Bf 109 matching the performance of the Hurricane. Even as he shouted with shock, he banged the throttle full open and the carburettor-fed engine stuttered, starved of fuel, as he dived away.

The 109 had a mechanically fuel-injected engine, which never missed a beat.

Ralph had lost a precious second. As his engine picked up tracers streamed past him. His right wing slammed, and bright circles stuttered across the painted aluminium, the light metal easily damaged, then the airframe behind him shuddered and thumped, but it was covered with fabric that absorbed damage.

The 109's speed carried it past. Ralph fell in behind the other machine and began to close. Now the prey was the hunter.

The 109 turned steeply but Ralph kept the inside position, inching closer. The German machine twisted and turned, white mist streaking back from the wingtips like silk. The sun and fields rotated dizzily around them, then they were in the shadow of a tall pinnacle of cloud, golden above, with rain trailing grey drifts from its thundery base. Ralph's thumb closed over the firing button.

The 109 made a climbing turn and disappeared into the safety of the cloud.

Rain pattered on Ralph's canopy. The Wash gleamed like a dull coin in the distance and he knew the air battle had taken them far to the north. The Messerschmitt must be very short of fuel. The Nazi was a good pilot and a brave one: he had flown his machine ten-tenths, those thin wings flexing visibly . . . Ralph was tempted to leave well enough alone. Honour was satisfied, and he turned along the cloud wall into bright sunlight.

The shining wall of cloud began to shimmer, as if with

the shadow of Ralph's own machine racing with him. But it was not. Their speed snatched the cloud away behind them, and the two machines floated together in an abyss of clear air, seeming to hang almost motionless. They were so close that their wingtips might have touched.

Ralph could see the other pilot, and knew his enemy was his old friend. No doubt about it; the way Fritzi held his head, and the sun slanting brilliantly across his lean face, revealing his features.

It was Fritzi Münchener.

Smiling, Ralph raised his hand and waved.

Staffelkapitän Fritzi Münchener, of II/JG2, the *Richtoven Geschwader* flying from Holland, was every inch his father's son. He wore his blond hair shaved close instead of swept back, as his father had, and his build was heavier than his father's – but in every other way, Ben London would have recognized the man he fought in 1917, and in him the boy who often larked about with Ralph and George at London House in the thirties, who had secretly smoked his first pipe of tobacco together with Ralph in the summerhouse, the schoolboy who ended up more English than the English.

Fritzi stared at Ralph with his mouth turned down. They were alone in the sky; his *Staffel* had turned for home for lack of fuel, their long-range tanks exhausted. Fritzi's Schwarm was an élite unit: at his throat he wore the Knight's Cross of the Iron Cross, signifying twenty kills.

Why had Ralph not opened fire?

Fritzi remembered those old times with affection. However, times changed. They were no longer weak boys – no longer even men. They were warriors, carrying the destiny of nations on their shoulders. War was moral, because without war there were no victors. Only in defeat did right and wrong exist; for the victor it was simple. He was always right.

Still Ralph did not open fire. He waved again, smiling.

Was Ralph such a fool? Fritzi gave him every last chance.

Fritzi remembered his mother Karin weeping tears of joy when he was awarded the Knight's Cross by the Führer himself, in Berlin. Fritzi had turned to his father expecting to see pride reflected there, but found only sadness staining the old politician's face. Fritzi embraced his mother. Later she toasted him in Sekt. 'Here's to the next twenty!' she said with shining eyes.

Fritzi had made no kills today.

He glanced at the fuel gauge. He had less than five minutes left over England. This cocktail party could not continue.

He had given Ralph every chance he could.

At last Fritzi waved. Ralph waggled his wings in farewell, and turned away.

Yes; they had been friends.

Fritzi swung in behind Ralph's machine and opened fire.

The Messerschmitt's cannons sparkled brightly. Surely he did not mean to hit the Hurricane; Ralph did not believe that of his old friend. Then the Hurricane shuddered and thumped and metal sprayed off the wings.

Ralph struggled for control.

The plane fell upside down with the engine stuttering, the clouds and the earth below spinning above Ralph's head. Then the weight of the heavy Rolls-Royce Merlin pulled the nose down into a dive. The Hurricane dropped like a stone into a well of dark clouds.

Ralph looked in the mirror.

The 109 was still behind him, the silhouetted wingtips slowly widening against the brilliant circle of narrowing blue sky as they fell into shadow.

Ralph stared back over his shoulder.

His bullets will come battering through the fabric here, splinters will fly from the airframe around me, the engine in front of me will burn, and still he will keep firing, he will not stop!

It made no sense. They were friends. Fritzi was joking. Ralph screamed.

The cannons flashed. Sparks flew off the engine and there was a terrible noise of disintegration. Smoke streamed back, and Fritzi pulled away.

Ralph choked as smoke filled the cockpit. The fabric burned – he could feel the heat. The smoke was so dense that he could no longer see the lighted world beyond the canopy. In darkness he battered at the emergency canopy release with his fists. The smoke turned orange then a furious blast of heat came back around the firewall as the engine burned. Ralph pulled back his legs from the furnace, but they jammed against the seat. He screamed, tearing frantically at the catches. Flames licked against his thin shirt, then roared around him like a blowtorch as the firewall gave way. In the last despairing moment, the canopy disappeared, and a blast of clear, bright air lifted Ralph bodily out of his harness and flicked him away over the tail. He pulled the ripcord and heard his parachute flap open.

He swung slowly to earth.

2

'Ralph's your favourite son, isn't he?' Pearl said, looking across at Ben driving. The red sun was coming up over the flat, shining fields of Cambridgeshire, so silvery with spiders' webs. It was a little after five in the morning, and the phone call from the Addenbrookes Burns Unit in Cambridge town centre had roused them an hour ago.

'I don't have a favourite child,' Ben said.

'Okay. Different love.' Pearl touched Ben's elbow. 'But he means a lot to you.'

She couldn't penetrate his reserve. 'Of course he does.'

'Ralph's the one most like you,' Pearl said.

Ben turned his head towards her slightly. How little she knew. 'Ralph is not like me at all.'

'For heaven's sake, Ben,' Pearl said, 'ease up, can't you?'

He stared through the windscreen, his knuckles white on the wheel. Ralph had been burned – perhaps terribly burned – perhaps he was dying. Ben couldn't bear the thought of it. He'd only stopped long enough to phone George at the Emporium, where he had taken over the apartment.

'Shot down?' The news had obviously hit George very hard. He sounded overburdened and overwrought. 'I can't take any more. He can't be. Not Ralph.'

'I am afraid he has been burned, George.' Ben's voice was flat.

By his shoulder Pearl had whispered: 'Try to sound more sympathetic. It's hard enough for him as it is.'

'George! Are you there?'

George said: 'I suppose you're going to handle it.'

'I'm going up right away. Do you want to come?'

'I'll get there before you,' George had said.

With squealing tyres Ben turned his car across the pavement into the hospital courtyard. George hadn't arrived yet. A nurse showed them up to the burns unit.

Dr Morrissey was evasive; a doctor does not speak of death until he has exhausted the other possibilities. 'It's wonderful, what we can do nowadays with plastic surgery. Great strides have been made.'

'Let me see him.'

'That's not possible.'

'Why not?'

'He's very weak – and under sedation, you know.'

Pearl asked: 'Has he been very badly disfigured?'

'Perhaps we can talk later,' Morrissey said. He held out his arm towards the waiting room. Ben sat calmly. Pearl tried to read an old *Reader's Digest*. 'How can you just sit there,' she said, looking across, 'sitting there with your face set like stone?'

'Ralph's going,' he said. 'I feel it.'

They heard voices and George arrived. Pearl jumped

up and put her arms around his shoulders, crying. 'They won't let us see him!'

'If he's been burned,' George said, 'he probably looks too awful. It's better not to know.' He wore a suit without a tie, and most incongruous of all, still a pair of bedroom slippers. He pointed at Ben. 'It's his fault.'

'We're all upset,' Pearl said, trying to keep the peace.

'Is he?' demanded George in a quivering voice, then held his fist to his lips. He stood in front of Ben, who was seated. 'Ralph admired you,' he said bitterly. 'He wanted to be the great hero like you.'

Ben looked up without emotion, listening to George rant.

'I don't believe that,' he said.

'Of course he did!' cried George. 'We all did.' His lips trembled. 'How I hate you,' he said dully.

'George, I'm sorry,' Ben said.

George shook his head and stuffed his fists in his pockets. He sat alone by the door. Pearl looked between them both. She realized that Ben had lost George.

'I know what you want,' George called to his father. 'I know.'

Ben stood by the window for hours, looking out.

'He wants the Emporium back,' George said at last.

Pearl defended her husband. 'That's a terrible thing to say!'

'It's true,' George said. 'You don't know him.'

She turned, but Ben stood without moving, his back to them, watching the streams of people walk or bicycle to work. 'Ordinary people,' he said, and there was a note almost of wistfulness in his voice. Did he wish he was like them? Pearl reached out to him, but he did not turn. She did not know what he felt.

'I'd give it all up,' Ben said.

'We'll believe it when we see it,' George said.

Ben remembered the Workhouse. *Did you have a life outside? Are you going to cry?* He could smell the cold stone walls. He had forgotten nothing.

He remembered Knuts's prim voice while young Ben

sat shivering in the initiation bath of icy water, and his hard-won advice. *When they hit you, scream. Let them know they're hurting you.*

Now Ben looked at George. It was impossible to explain his pain to George. 'If only you knew,' he said. He couldn't scream. He was the millionaire.

Who are they? Ordinary people.

'Go to hell,' George said.

Ben demanded: 'Is it true you're great friends with Vic Price these days?'

'Well, what if it is?'

Ben nodded. 'So it is true.' He tried to reach out to George, to admit his pain.

George knew how to hurt: 'Vic comes to the Emporium often,' he said. It was a successful barb: he saw a flicker of hurt cross his father's bright blue gaze. Then Ben turned back to the window, and he didn't look at George again.

When Doctor Morrissey came in, it was nearly noon. 'Mr London? He wants to see you.'

'Me?' George jumped up. 'I am his twin brother, doctor.'

'Ralph asked to see his father alone.'

I can't do it, Ben thought, *I can't bear to see Ralph.*

He nodded calmly to the doctor and followed him out.

George looked at Pearl. 'My father doesn't care about him,' he said. She thought he would cry, but instead George looked very tough. 'He just doesn't give a damn. Well, neither do I.'

'I'm so sorry for us.' Pearl leaned back with her eyes closed. 'I am so sorry for us all.'

Ben was surprised how noisy it was in Ralph's room. The window was half open and all the sounds of the outside world came in: the rumble of a passing dray, the rattle of bottles and galvanized lids echoing up from the dustbin area, cheery voices and fragments of conversation. Ralph lay on a white bed wrapped in petrolatum gauze, only his face and hands uncovered.

He had no face; he had no hands, only claws.

Ben recognized Ralph's eyes – the eyes had not changed. They moved, seeing him, and Ben smiled. 'Everyone's here,' he grinned. 'You're quite a hero, the nurses say.' This was appalling. Ben sat carefully beside the bed. He was terrified of touching anything in case Ralph shrieked.

His son whispered something. Ben had to lean very close, his ear almost touching Ralph's teeth.

'You were right,' Ralph whispered, 'I was lucky.'

The light moved in his eyes. It was a smile.

'Are you in any pain?'

'None,' Ralph whispered. 'Happy. All clear. I want you to have my shares in the Emporium.'

'Don't let's talk about that.'

'You gave me – everything. Life.' Ralph's eyes closed. 'My gift to you.'

'Don't talk. It doesn't matter. It doesn't matter a damn, Ralph.' The tears slid down Ben's cheeks.

'You're crying,' Ralph said wonderingly in his torment. 'It's yours.'

'You are going to get better, Ralph. I promise you.' Ralph was not going to get better. Ben would have made any sacrifice to save Ralph, even to the cost of his own life, but no man's strength could force back death's hand from his son's heart, or explain or deny the ticking and tocking of passing time, or prevent its conclusion. 'I promise you, Ralph,' Ben choked. 'I promise.'

Silence.

A tea-trolley rattling along the corridor. Distantly a nurse calling out something about sterile dressings.

Suddenly Ralph reared up. He gripped Ben's arm with the claw of his hand, with no regard for his agony, his face close to Ben's.

'Tell Kate she was wrong.'

His voice faded away and he slipped back, murmuring, his eyes closing.

Ben leaned down, trying to understand.

Ralph said desperately: 'Tell her, Dad. Promise. I did love her. I do . . . I really do . . . love her . . .'

He reached out to grasp at some invisible image in the air, then died.

Ben sat holding his dead son in his arms.

3

Alone, Ben stood in the village high street. Sonning was a pretty place, well kept, very far from the war. The doctor's surgery was a nice house with a drive, his Morris Eight parked in front of the garage, his wife's Austin just visible in the shadows inside. A USAF Willys Jeep was parked by the steps to the front door, but the waiting room was around the side.

Ben stood by the gate. No expression showed on his face. He did not know where Pearl was. Cambridge, or perhaps she had gone back to London. He had got Kate's address from Lisa. He alone knew what he had promised.

To tell Kate the truth of Ralph's love. To leave her with that knowledge.

He watched the door open and a nice-looking girl come down the steps on the arm of a dark-haired American Air Force officer. He was a leaf captain, without wings, legal branch maybe, wearing rimless spectacles, a GI necktie and a clean class-A uniform. And he wore a class ring on his finger, but no other. His manner was serious, and he treated her with respectful Connecticut or New England manners. If the Jeep had had a door, he would have opened it for her with a small courteous bow – and really meant it. She could depend on him. He was safe.

The girl was obviously Kate; and from the way he looked at her and held her politely as she got in the Jeep, it was equally obvious who he was, and that she would probably marry him.

Ralph would have swung her in over the side with a laugh; Ben could almost see him doing it.

But Ralph was dead.

The captain did a neat three-point turn and drove out of the gates.

For a moment Kate glanced at Ben as if wondering whether she recognized him, something familiar about him – wondered what she saw in his eyes that disturbed her happiness.

The Jeep accelerated away down the road with Kate looking over her shoulder.

Ben went back to his car and drove in the opposite direction. Some secrets were too awful to be told.

He broke his promise. For the first and last time in his life, Ben broke his word.

He left Kate with her happy, guiltless memories of Ralph, and that was what Ralph would have wanted most of all. For someone, for Kate, Ralph would be still alive.

Ben stopped the car and covered his face with his hands.

4

Fritzi breezing back to Berlin on leave had never looked in better health, more vibrant, more alive: young men had such gifts to give away. The bad news from Russia and the growing air raids, American terror fliers coming over by day and British by night, had shaken the morale of the civilian population. But Fritzi would say that there was no such thing as a civilian in this war – and of course, he was right.

Fritzi respectfully drank the vile coffee his father poured for him.

'Fighting units get the best,' Dolfo said apologetically.

Fritzi shrugged. Battles were won by blood, not by coffee. He had come here hoping to see his mother, who at least he could talk to. His father's conversation was that of a defeated man, and this realization alarmed Fritzi. Tonight he was going out for a good time with Reini and Dietrich, but meanwhile he had to suffer this stilted conversation.

'Would you rather it had been me who had not survived?' Fritzi had always suspected his father's motives in
sending him away to England as a child . . . *sending him
away*.

'A man showed me mercy once,' Dolfo commented
mildly, 'or you would never have been born.' He did not
turn. An anti-aircraft battery had set up in the park, and
explosive concussion had plucked the yellow leaves from
the trees. Children played around the perimeter of sandbags. The war was very close.

'Mercy? Who was that?'

'You wouldn't understand.'

'No, it is you who do not understand,' Fritzi said
angrily.

Dolfo knew that war was more terrible than any of them
could imagine. *I could not bear it if you were killed*. The
monster was his own flesh and blood, created by him. It
was himself. This was war. What they thought was victory
was defeat.

'You are frightened,' said Fritzi.

'I am ashamed.'

Shame, when he had expected pride. Fritzi stood up.
'I am sorry, Father, I cannot stay.' Fritzi longed for
reassurance. It did not come.

'Then I must be going!'

Adolf wondered if Fritzi would betray him; he had
failed Fritzi.

'I shall retire home to Schleissheim,' Adolf said, when
he heard the door open.

'I did my duty,' Fritzi said. 'Goodbye, Father.' He
closed the door quietly behind him.

Adolf poured himself a glass of schnapps. The
Geheimer Kabinettsrat had not met since the war began.
For the last three years he had presided over another
sinecure, the Committee for Commercial and Economic
Warfare. That was still the way things were done in the
Third Reich, for men of rank. He would take the train
back to Munich. He believed in mercy. He was still fright-
ened of flying.

CHAPTER TWENTY-SIX

1

For six months Ben allowed George free reign to prove himself at the Emporium. Or perhaps, for those months, he simply could not bring himself to care; Lisa was not sure. Like her, he hid the things that truly hurt him inside himself. Pearl said he and George had an absolutely explosive confrontation in the hospital courtyard, when George accused Ben of unfairly pressuring Ralph as he lay dying to change his will in Ben's favour. 'What nonsense!' Lisa had scoffed to George.

'He's capable of it,' George said.

Later Lisa asked Pearl: 'Is there any truth in this extraordinary rumour?'

'None at all,' Pearl said, 'but George believes it. And through Ralph Ben *has* come out of it with what he's always wanted, a real share of the Emporium – only half ownership, but real power, this time.'

'Ben's a successful person, that's all,' Lisa said. 'He gets what he wants.' Then she coughed. She had moved back to London House because of her failing health, no longer up to running Easton Manor. The tuberculosis had come out of remission and the secondary infection had spread to her lungs. The medical treatment was rest and relaxation, so that the healing process just about kept pace with the damage. She looked well, her complexion pale and beautifully clear as so often in these cases, but she had lost weight.

'He won,' Pearl said, 'and that's what George can't stand. In a fit of pique George said he'd sell his fifty per cent to the highest bidder, but a few days later he changed his mind. I don't know why. You know the sort of cronies George has. Ben was furious, I think.'

'Don't you know?'

'He has his businesses,' Pearl said, 'I have my home.'

'And Victoria.'

Pearl smiled. 'I don't think any school's ever going to tame that girl. You know St Joseph's chucked her out? Thirteen years old,' Pearl said proudly. 'Nothing serious,' she added, 'just wildness.'

'I bet Ben wasn't pleased.'

'I should reckon not. I think he was secretly on her side though.'

'How did this row in the hospital courtyard pan out?'

'They were standing between the cars. George was berserk, but Ben was . . . calm. He just looked at George and George shut up. He crouched as though he thought Ben was going to hit him.'

'Ben wouldn't have done that,' Lisa said positively.

'You didn't see how calm he was,' Pearl said. 'He was icy. George was crying. Ben just said: "You have six months to prove yourself. If you can make a go of it in that time, the Emporium's yours. I won't interfere. I promise." '

And now that time was up. Lisa glanced at the ormolu clock over the fireplace of her sitting room. God help George if he had failed. Now in a more senior grade and transferred to the Ministry of Supply, he had put very little work into the Emporium. It wasn't his fault. What was easily got was little appreciated, Lisa knew. Having valued it because of its importance to his mother and father, George was intimidated by the reality of the Emporium. Lisa had not known Vane, but she saw a little of Charles Cleremont in George. She checked the clock again and made sure her hat was at the right angle – a proper hat with a brim and a pin, not one of those vulgar turbans that were everywhere – then went out and let Ben help her downstairs. He was having a lift put in specially for her. Heaven alone knew where he had obtained it, but Lisa was much pleased by the compliment.

As he drove up St James's Street she made small talk. Ben wore a smooth, heavy overcoat and his shoes were brightly polished. He looked successful and invulnerable – she suspected he was making a very great deal of money out of the war, he could hardly do otherwise. His cheeks were pale, his manner cold.

Lisa cleared her throat. 'Pearl said I was to make sure you weren't too rough on George.' Pearl was away doing an assignment on American auxiliary nurses in Britain for *Time-Life*.

'George is a man now,' Ben said.

'And your son. At least be fair on him.'

'I'll give him credit where credit is due. He can't have special treatment.'

Lisa touched her handkerchief to her lips and it came away with a bright red speck that was not lipstick. She hid it in her hand. 'It's a family relationship,' she said, 'not a business relationship.'

'How else can I communicate with him?' Ben said. He could not face being hurt any more.

'Oh, Ben,' said Lisa sadly. 'Have a little mercy.'

On George? Or on himself?

Ben had kept his word and not interfered in the running of the Emporium in any way. With his shares he now sat on the board, and having Clifford Ford's and David's support – they owed their careers to him – he could have swung decisions any way he wanted. But he had stayed away from the meetings, playing fair, perhaps too fair with George and giving him every chance.

Ben wanted George to succeed.

That subject was obviously closed. Lisa tried to change to something that would gain a more congenial response. 'I hear Will is now a sub-lieutenant on HMS *Anson* at Scapa Flow.'

'A battleship. At least *he'll* be safe!' Ben said, revealing more of his feelings than he had intended.

He pulled up outside the Emporium. No Head Doorman came forward to open Lisa's door – Dillibe had been given the sack, without reason, without notice, as part of what George later called the economy drive. Ben helped his mother out onto the dirty pavement. He had found a job for Dillibe on the night desk at London's, to George's chagrin; he obviously hated the negro.

Lisa crossed the pavement on her stick and Ben pushed open the door into the store. Because of the war heating regulations it was very little warmer inside than out. Ben stood by the lighting bank staring across the main floor. Some lights were out – that wasn't George's fault, bulbs were difficult to get. But the stock was indifferently arranged and a few words with shop-girls revealed how low morale was. George had neither the time nor the personality to motivate the staff, or the drive and leadership to motivate David to do it for him. Even the clients looked dull. George, knowing Ben was coming, had taken pains to be here and he was talking to David in a loud businesslike voice.

Lisa found a chair. 'I think I'll sit here a while, dear.'

George dismissed David and looked at his father with nervous defiance.

'Profits are down, but what do you expect with a war on?'

'I'm listening,' Ben said.

'You're going to take it back, aren't you,' George said. 'You've already decided.'

'If I told you the truth, would you believe it?'

'No, because I know you,' George said. 'You can't keep your hands on it for ever. You'll get old too.'

'I'm on your side, George.'

But George couldn't believe it. 'Vic Price was right about you. He knows how unhappy I am.' His voice broke. 'He understands me, and you never have!'

Ben's face fixed. 'Let's go upstairs,' he said. 'I'm calling an extraordinary meeting right now.'

George jerked away. 'I'll oppose you,' he said. 'I have half. I can block every move you make.'

George was ignorant of power, and Ben made one last attempt to explain to him that he had lost. 'I have Ralph's fifty per cent and I owe it to him to make that count. And I will. Also I have an additional value of five per cent, non-voting, but you'll find it gives me just that little bit of extra clout. And David is with me. And so is Clifford.' Ben followed his son between the counters. 'George! Listen to me. You don't have to lose. Come with me. Come with me, George.' He held out his hands.

George looked back over his shoulder. 'I've got better things to do!' he said.

Later that afternoon Ben was voted chairman and managing director of London Emporium Ltd. In the moment of victory, looking at George down the long walnut table he felt no satisfaction.

He understands me, and you never have.

Vic Price had lost the Emporium, but he had got George, just as he had got Vane. Ben sat watching George's face, feeling the agony he saw there, but what could he do?

Driven by the blood.

Lisa sat watching Ben's face. It was quite blank. It showed neither pleasure nor pain. It was the face of a lonely, successful man.

These were Dolfo Münchener's boyhood woods. The great trees of the forest and the white Bavarian snow – a particular texture of white, quite unique, seen nowhere else – had not changed, but he had. He was dressed in green loden britches and an embroidered jacket. In his right hand he carried a tall knobbly stick. His stiff brown boots crunching the snow made the only sound. Even that ceased as he stopped, leaning on his stick with his clasped fist against his cheek, staring over the lake that he remembered so well.

Here Erich the village blacksmith's child and he had come fishing. When they were older they brought his father's old shotgun for duck, and Erich's labrador dog to swim out and retrieve them, but the dog always swam towards the opposite shore to keep his prize for himself. So many happy memories.

After the first war he came here with his childhood sweetheart Karin for a picnic. It had been her idea. He carried a basket of *Weisswurst*, mustard, rye bread, apples, a stone jar of cider. She had grown up while he was away. He who had killed so many men in combat had been innocent; shocked by the passion in her kiss and suddenly the hot, forbidden, irresistible feel of her. She ate the *Weisswurst* with the mustard trickling down between her bare breasts. Had he really loved such a woman?

Yes, there was Fritzi.

Often he came here quietly with little Fritzi. Fritzi had loved to watch the duck with his father, simply because his father loved watching them.

The duck were gone now. In the winter they had always swum about in the middle to keep clear a dark circle of water, so that the lake looked like a great eye staring up. Now the ice was smooth and white, quite blind.

He listened, hearing an engine echoing between the trees.

Then he nodded. So they knew where to find him.

He turned as a small military *Kübelwagen* bounced along the forest track, followed by a larger car with two officers in dark Reich Central Security Office uniforms sitting in the back.

The engines stopped, and the exhaust fumes drifted away on the silent air.

Dolfo Münchener asked them gently: 'Who told you I would be here?'

2

'Have a good time,' Vic laughed. 'That's all that matters, isn't it? Good old George.' He winked. He obviously thought George was quite a lad, and George was having a hard time living up to it at Trott's. There was a genuine *frisson* of danger here, however safe they were from bombs. American servicemen danced all night and drank black-market whisky, still available at Trott's in limitless quantities at four pounds a bottle. There were often fist-fights and brawls, and once a shooting with an automatic pistol, but George never read about it in the newspapers. Nowadays he would never have come here alone . . . but there was Vic. In George's harum-scarum world, Vic was his guiding light through the storm.

So many things were more dangerous than bombs. Feelings, for example; people. Relationships, love and hate, and trust. But Vic looked after him.

'Come on, drink up,' Vic chuckled, 'no holding back when you're drinking with Vic Price, old lad.'

George smiled the casual smile which he had learned. He liked drinking, but he didn't dare to be drunk. He liked being seen with girls, but not these glittering creatures Vic was so sure he wanted to go with. George liked to be reassured, he didn't want to be overwhelmed. The truth was that George was now frightened.

He didn't dare admit it.

He had no one to turn to. Certainly not his father. George would rather have died than admit to Ben London that he needed help.

George was terrified of Vic – too terrified to break away. Vic knew all about him. There were no secrets from Vic. Vic knew all about Natasha – he thought it had all been perverse and guilty and actually admired George for his courage as if there had been something so terribly wrong and clever about George going with her; whereas he had merely needed her. George couldn't explain the truth that he had simply enjoyed her company because he didn't dare look weak in front of Vic. But Vic always admired cleverness, and strength, and George was clever. And he was trying to be strong. Vic was always asking George's advice. It was a responsibility to live up to Vic's high opinion and George always tried his best to sound authoritative.

George would not have coped with Vic alone, but he liked Terry. The young man was equally in awe of Vic, it seemed. Terry admired Vic like a father – though apparently he was not Vic's true son – and had discovered the perfect foil to Vic's overwhelming presence by seeming icy cool and withdrawn. He was unfailingly polite, and drank only shandy. George wasn't fooled. Inside that shell Terry had feelings all right. He was coming up to eighteen, and had been terrified of getting his conscription papers. George played hard to get, but when Vic dropped the word, George had found a way to help.

They had both been very grateful.

Now George was in with both of them.

It was three in the morning – an hour or two after the unofficial curfew – before Vic was ready to go home. They waited on the pavement for Spike to bring the car, holding up their collars against the driving rain coming down on the wind from the north. There were specks of sleet in it already, and Terry said: 'Maybe we'll have a white Christmas.'

Vic laughed uproariously, then held open the car door for George. 'Drop you?'

'I can walk,' George said. Since his father's palace coup against him, George had been unable to endure the humiliation of the apartment above the Emporium. Finally Ben had relented and allowed him to rent Lockhart House, where George now lived.

'Get in,' Vic said. 'Ria's brat's out in this,' he said looking out of the window as the Daimler swung through the dark, sheeting streets. 'Didn't you know about Will? Transferred to the *Duke of York* on the Russian convoys, based in Iceland and bloody cold in December I should reckon.' George wasn't surprised at Vic's detailed knowledge, Vic always seemed to know everything concerning his sister. The car stopped outside Lockhart House and Spike turned off the engine.

'Going to ask us in for a coffee?' Vic said. 'That's not going to be rationed, is it?'

George put the key in the door. 'No,' he said.

'A lot of people say it will be,' Vic said.

George shook his head. 'There are no plans to do so. Come in.'

He went to the little kitchen he'd had put in one of the rooms behind the stairs, but Vic stayed in the hall. George could hear his feet on the tiles as he looked round.

'Or tea rationing?' called Vic.

George was amused at Vic's naïvety. 'There'd be riots!' he pointed out. 'The day we rationed tea would be the day we lost the war.'

He carried the steaming coffeepot through the hall on his way to the study. Vic was looking at one of the pictures; a Dales scene painted as if from the height of an aircraft, though the date below the *CL* of the artist's signature – Charles Lockhart was not yet Lord Cleremont – was April 1899, before powered flight, so it must be from a hill. Vic looked more closely. There was a clear, deep blue pool in the foreground.

'Lost the war? Too true,' he said, glancing indifferently at George. 'Well, Terry and I will be pushing off now, old mate.'

George was startled. 'But what about your coffee?'

'If it isn't going to be rationed,' Vic said from the door, 'you can afford to waste it.'

CHAPTER TWENTY-SEVEN

1

Lola, her dream-child.

Ria loved her little daughter and loved her and loved her. Lola was her best friend. At last Ria had found out what it really was to be a mother, and she gave Lola all the love, and time, and a good home, and the doting attention which poor Will never knew. She queued all morning for a fresh egg for Lola, and was happy to do it. Once she walked three miles to a banana raffle – and got one, too – with little Lola hanging from her hand to walk for a few hundred yards, then hitched on Ria's hip for another half mile. Ria always gave Lola the best bits off her own plate, pretending she wasn't hungry, and by now her slimness had almost become too thin. But in the main the rationing made sure everyone got enough, and Ria's hair had retained its gloss, and her eyes their fire.

She met the telegram boy on the pavement when she was coming back from the shops in West Ferry Road with her shopping bag almost empty – she remembered that, the empty feel of it swinging in her hand when she saw the little post-office boy standing with the envelope in his hand, then popping it out of sight through the letter box.

'Salt, mustard, vinegar, pepper,' chanted Lola, then looked up with her engaging smile. She had a wonderful memory; she had remembered whole nursery rhymes and been able to sing them tunefully at the age of twenty months, to Ria's great and obvious pride, and now a year later she was trying to understand games. Lola spent hours watching the older children play hopscotch, her bright, flecked eyes missing nothing, seeming to know more than she could say. She looked up at Ria now; her mother's face had not moved, but her hand had gone absolutely cold, and Lola began to cry.

Ria snatched Lola up and held her against her, shivering. It was the day after Boxing Day and great events were being celebrated by the wireless and newspapers: during a great storm – they had felt the edge of it even down here in London – the battleship *Duke of York* had sunk the Nazi battle-cruiser *Scharnhorst* in the Arctic. In those freezing waters only thirty-six Germans from a crew of two thousand were saved.

The bulletins made no mention of British casualties.

'No,' Ria said. 'Please, no.'

The post-office boy scurried past her without looking up. Lola hid her face against Ria's shoulder. Ria dropped her bag – a neighbour brought it in later – and walked slowly to the door. She opened it and went inside.

Esther was standing in the hallway, her bulk cutting out most of the light from the kitchen. In the gloom her eyes looked very white in her pale face. Between both her hands she was holding the envelope.

'It's for you,' she said. 'I'll take Lola.'

'No!' Ria hugged Lola to her with one hand and held out her other hand for the envelope. She opened it with her teeth and pulled out the slip. *Regret to inform you . . .* Ria's face broke up in grief. 'Will has been injured.'

She swayed and only then let Esther take her child, feeling her legs giving way. Esther took the weight and then Ria collapsed. She sat against the wall with her knees drawn up and her hair cascading over her face, her hands.

'Badly injured?' asked Esther in a stricken voice.

'To the head.' Ria tried to read the words through her tears. 'He's in Russia. Oh my God, Russia! He's probably being looked after by some peasant doctor – if they have a doctor at all . . .'

'Now, calm down,' Esther said.

'I won't calm down!' Ria shrieked. 'He's my son – I can't bear it! All the things I could have done for him I never did!'

She began to cry deep, wrenching, genuine sobs.

She cried for hours, inconsolably, and when she stopped Esther knew that she would never be the same again. She heard Ria crying in the night too.

Pearl woke. The phone was ringing. Ben rolled over and turned on the light. He picked up the earpiece.

'Yes?'

So late at night the line was clear and loud, and even Pearl could hear the voice at the other end. It was a friend from the Admiralty.

Ben said: 'No, I haven't heard about Will.'

Pearl heard the voice over the line hesitate. Will had been hurt.

'Oh, Ben!' Pearl said, kneeling beside him with her hands on his shoulders. 'I'm so sorry.'

He did not move.

He said: 'What are Will's injuries exactly?'

Another pause. The tinny voice over the phone came back. 'To the head.'

Ben said: 'Do you mean to his brain?'

'Yes. I'm sorry. It was an accident.'

'What are you trying to tell me?' In a calm, unemotional voice Ben put the question that Pearl could not have brought herself to ask without breaking down. 'Has he lost any functions?' Silence. He re-phrased himself with brutal flatness. 'What functions has he lost?'

The line clicked and buzzed.

At last the other man replied. 'We're not quite sure yet. I assure you he'll be brought back to this country as soon as possible.'

'Thank you. Please keep me informed. Good night,' Ben said.

He hung up. Pearl gazed at him, not knowing what to say, or how she could share his grief. If he felt grief; nothing of what he felt showed on his face. *Did* he feel it? He took a sip of water, turned out the light, and Pearl heard him lie back on the pillow. His breathing steadied and deepened as he fell asleep.

She shook him.

His voice came out of the dark. 'What is it?'

'Your son!'

He said: 'There's nothing I can do. In the morning I'll buy the finest neurosurgeon in the country. But for the moment, Pearl, I need my sleep.'

'You've changed,' Pearl murmured into the darkness, 'you've changed.'

A few weeks later Ria got a letter postmarked Chelsea from Sub-Lieutenant John Storks, who was home on leave. He wrote that he had been friends with Will in their *Mercury* days, when they were cadets together. In the thirties they had gone their separate ways, John to the oriental spice import business run by his father since his retirement as a rear-admiral in the Far East squadron. When war started he bowed to his father's wishes and joined the Navy. 'My brother and I,' he wrote, 'were early trained to follow orders.' He had renewed his friendship with Will at the HMS *King Alfred* officer-training shore establishment at Hove.

Ria held the precious letter to her bosom. So much that she had not known about her son, so much that she hungered to know; his life was hers. John Storks ended his letter by asking when he might visit 'as there is so much that I cannot put in writing'.

John Storks was a pleasant young man and Ria did her best not to intimidate him. They sat around the kitchen table while Esther tactfully looked after Lola upstairs.

'Was Will brave?' Then Ria nodded to herself. 'Of course, you would say that. You all stick together, don't you?' she said, glancing at his officer's pips.

He offered her a Waverley cigarette, then asked her permission to smoke when she refused.

'Will and I were posted to the battleship *Anson* at Akureyri in Iceland together,' he said, inhaling, 'providing distant heavy cover on convoys to the Kola Inlet, in Russia. When Admiral Fraser transferred his flag to the *Duke of York*, he particularly asked for Will to accompany him. So you will know that Will was a brave officer, Mrs Price, and a good one.' He hesitated. 'Almost too good.'

Ria looked at him. 'This isn't easy for you.'

'The most painful visit of my life!' John Storks said. 'You see, my young brother Roger – eight years younger than me – I'm afraid he is the cause of Will's injury.'

He didn't say *accident*. 'You mean it was assault,' Ria said.

John drank his tea and put his cup down carefully, with his finger underneath to stop it rattling. 'Roger struck Will, from behind, with a length of chain. He will be tried for attempted murder.'

'I hope he rots,' Ria said. 'You've got a bloody nerve coming here, mate.'

John's voice shook. 'Wait until you hear what I have to tell you. I – may I have another cup of tea?'

'I ought to throw it in your face,' Ria said.

'You're right to feel as you do.' He looked round apologetically for an ashtray.

'Don't be so bloody polite, use the saucer, can't you?' She poured the tea. John laid his hands flat on the table, the cigarette sticking up between his fingers like a fuse.

'Roger is only eighteen. He's always had . . . difficulties. My father and he never got on, I'm afraid. Roger was the artistic one of the family, obviously – he wanted to be a poet – and since Father returned permanently home from the East, Roger got short shrift. He was never strong.'

'Save your excuses,' Ria said.

'Last year he joined the Navy as an ordinary seaman, hostilities only, as the lowest form of animal life – a messdeck sweeper. He did it deliberately to spite Father, I think. Will was his divisional officer on the *Duke of York*. An officer is totally responsible for the sailors in his division – he makes sure everyone gets his allowances, that his good conduct medals come through on time, that there's no trouble at home. Will seems to have understood Roger well. Apparently Will also had creative ambitions?'

Ria shrugged.

John said: 'I think Will understood him better than anybody.'

'Go on,' Ria said.

'In December it is so dark in those latitudes – every day is as dark as night. The wind sweeps down off the icepack and raises seas like rolling mountains that freeze as they break over a ship. The ships look like icebergs – hundreds of tons of ice hanging from the upperworks – and they're hard put just to survive. But that's not all, you see. These convoys are what keeps Joe Stalin going, and the Germans throw everything they've got at them – aeroplanes out of Norway, capital ships, submarines, the lot. No one has enough sleep. The guns go off at any time. Cold and nervous exhaustion become a torture for everyone. Those godforsaken seas around Bear Island are the closest we come to hell on earth. I believe that hell is cold. Icy cold.'

'Tell me about my son,' Ria wept.

'My brother couldn't take any more,' John Storks said. 'Roger disappeared. Everyone thought he'd slipped overboard – the *Duke of York* was attempting to rendezvous with a convoy at high speed – on Christmas Day a blizzard covered them, and the seas were appalling. Nevertheless, a search was made of the ship, but Roger was not found. Will was not satisfied. He knew that Roger was a careful, methodical sort of chap, with no reason to go on deck, and his wet-weather clothes were still in his kitbag. Will decided that Roger's nerve had gone. He was hiding somewhere aboard ship.'

Ria wiped her eyes. 'Will tried to understand people. He never gave up.'

'I think Will must have asked himself: "Where is the worst place on this ship?" Men who break don't hide themselves away in the place of least pain, but the most. A coward wants to suffer. Will used his imagination. We know he considered the tunnels that carry the propeller shafts, because he spoke to the Chief Engineer, but he was assured that only an engineer could get access to them. So Will tried the paint store.'

'He wanted to be a painter,' Ria said.

'Not this sort. The paint store is right up in the bow, a wedge-shaped room in the narrowest part of the ship, stacked with hundreds of gallons of red lead and turpentine and grey camouflage paint in barrels. Imagine the smell. And the storm, that little room rising and falling sixty feet like the wildest ride at the funfair. Empty paintpots rattling across the deck. The swinging, clanging chains of the painting platforms stored in the racks above, and everything breaking loose. All in the dark. This was the worst place in the ship all right.'

'So Will found him there,' Ria said.

'Crouched behind a stack of barrels. I've been allowed to speak to Roger. Will turned the light on and he seemed to know just where to look – he looked directly at Roger. Their eyes met. Will didn't say a word – didn't try and reason with the terrified lad, as most of us would have done. He simply held out his hand. You see, he understood.'

Ria sank her hands in her hair. Esther said: 'Just what he always dreamed of.' She had been standing unnoticed in the doorway, holding Lola. 'Will always wanted to understand,' Esther said. 'Well, now he does.' Her voice became thick with tears to match Ria's, and Ria held out her arms to her mother. But Lola slipped down Esther's dress and toddled across to Ria to be picked up instead.

Ria cuddled her daughter. 'Nothing's going to happen to you, ever,' she whispered, her mouth brushing Lola's soft black hair, 'I won't let it.'

John Storks said: 'Roger claims that it was one of the swinging chains breaking loose from a painting platform that struck Will on the back of the head. He says it was an accident. He says he shouted a warning.'

'Do you believe him?' Esther asked.

'I don't think anybody does,' John said. 'The Chief Petty Officer who found them swears that Roger was still holding the chain. What it basically comes down to is that nobody liked my brother much and he got what he deserved. He'll go down.'

'Two wrongs don't make a right,' Esther said.

'It's wartime,' John said. 'They do.'

'They won't let me see Will,' sobbed Ria. John knew that such details were important to a woman, although it would make no difference to Will who held his hand. Worse, emotional histrionics might upset him. 'Can't you arrange it?' Ria begged.

'His father's Ben London, isn't he – the millionaire?' John looked around the small, shabby kitchen with one wall distorted by a bomb-blast and the cracked windows held together with tape.

'Yes,' Ria said.

'Will is being cared for by the very best surgeons.'

'That's all that matters,' Ria said bitterly.

'He has a father who cares for him,' said John Storks with a catch in his voice. It was almost envy.

2

'With the end of the war in sight and the completion of repairs making more rooms available shortly, it is anticipated that London's will no longer trade at a loss.'

Ben sat in his office at the London Emporium. Pat, a stenographer from the typing pool, was sitting by the desk taking his dictation now that Alice Cypress only came in part time.

'Is it true?' asked Pat excitedly, 'the war really is won?'

He didn't seem to think it was important. 'The Allies will finish off what's left of Berlin by midsummer,' Ben said coldly. He didn't like to be interrupted while he was working. Pat bent her head over her shorthand – he was as frightening as they said. That coldness; as though he didn't care about anyone at all. He treated his staff fairly, but those harsh eyes missed no human frailty.

Yet sometimes a warm smile crossed his face, and his eyes lit up with life, and she saw the young Ben London revealed behind the stiff mask, brimming with drive and energy and joy, burning as bright as a flame with emotion. It always thrilled her.

Ruthless, yes, and that was what sent a delicious hot shiver up her spine: a man who would stop at nothing.

But instantly it was gone in a flicker of pain, and that mask was back again; what she always thought of as his old Victorian curmudgeon's face. Something in him had given up, and taken this easy way out. He wore it to protect himself.

What did he need to protect himself from? He had everything every man and every woman wanted. And Pat Wallace had spent the whole morning taking dictation from him – the other girls would be green.

She looked at her reflection longingly in the desk clock. It was almost one, and she was hungry. She was dying to show off in the canteen wearing her glasses up on her forehead.

He intercepted her glance. 'You may go now,' he said kindly, 'we'll finish this afternoon.'

That bright, flashing smile made her stop loyally. He was quite human. He'd had so much pain in his life and there were all the troubles, and now the tragedy of his son. She said: 'I really don't mind staying, sir.'

He frowned. 'I'll see you back here at two o'clock sharp,' he snapped.

Pat left the office without another word.

It still hurts. Ben stood up and looked from the window. He was alone. Public success, private failure. He put his knuckles to his mouth. *I have everything, and nothing*. Money was money, but everything of value to him had been lost, except his love for Pearl, and hers for him; and they had Victoria. He loved them both.

But Ralph was dead. That still hurt the worst.

Lisa . . . Ben could not bear to face up to the fact that his mother was slowly fading away. A few nights ago, at dinner, she began coughing weakly, and bright specks of blood appeared in her napkin. A lesion had haemorrhaged in her lung. There was always supposed to be a new miracle drug under development, and he had funded

461

research into several out of his own pocket, but they never worked, and Ben no longer believed in miracles.

Will was slowly regaining his health, but how fully he would recover no one could predict. Most doctors said it was just a matter of time and tender loving care, meaning that they could do no more. Will had regained all his senses, although his balance was still poor. When he was discharged from the naval hospital Helen looked after him in the nursing wing at Easton Manor, wheeling him around the grounds and pointing out the names of familiar objects with infinite patience. It was plain to Ben that she loved him in a way that could now be open and unembarrassed, and Will adored her, staring innocently up at her pretty face with its disfiguring birthmark, nodding his head and grinning happily.

Ben did not like to come between them. He was almost unable to communicate with his son. He had bought Will an exquisitely illustrated and extremely expensive antique book of Redouté roses.

'Say thank you, Will,' prompted Helen gently.

'Thank you,' smiled Will obediently – at Helen.

'I'm sorry, Ben,' she said.

'It doesn't matter!' Ben said.

He had given some Easton boys a shilling to wash his car round the back of the stable block. It was a Saturday, and he was returning to London as soon as they had finished. He was going across to hurry them up when a bus pulled up at the gate and Ria got down. For a moment Ben froze, but she turned back towards the bus without looking over.

Ria, who had used him so unmercifully.

But Ben kept his word to Pearl, moving behind an outhouse wall where Ria would never see him; they would not meet. He heard the bus move off, the engine grinding. Then birdsong came through as though there was not a war on, and he heard Ria's footsteps approaching on the gravel. Two sets of footsteps. She had someone with her.

Ben had peered through a narrow gap in the boards. There was Ria's face. Thinner, but she hadn't changed, in fact she looked better. Full of life. Happy. How could she be happy? Her son Will being pushed about in a wheelchair grinning like an idiot at all and sundry . . .

A child bobbed along beside Ria kicking cheerfully at the stones. Ben stood on tiptoe, his forehead pressed against the unyielding wood, to see down to her. She was about three, with long black hair flowing from beneath a navy-blue beret, and lovely blue eyes with very deep tawny flecks – almost as dark as old gold. Her cheeks were red from her exertions.

'If you scuff those new shoes, my girl, after all the points I had to save up to get them,' came Ria's voice, 'I'll discombobulate you.' They had gone past and Ben heard the little girl chirp something, he couldn't hear what. 'You just watch you behave proper,' came Ria's voice drifting back.

Ben dropped down on his feet with aching knees, and he was shaking. He was shaking all over.

He had seen his daughter.

He opened the outhouse door and watched them walk up the drive with yearning eyes. She was enchanting; but he did not even know her name. Now he knew his own mother's agony, and the force that had driven her to try and find Ben London even after twenty-five years, and then to hide in hope and fear for a further five or more: it was himself. He felt it now. The call of the blood.

He watched Helen push Will across the grass in his wheelchair towards the visitors. When Will saw Ria the most gorgeous expression of elation filled his face and he reached up as Ria ran to him, then tottered forward on unsteady legs towards her until they embraced. Ben could feel the radiant heat of Ria's joyousness from here, and hear them laughing and crying together while he stood alone, watching them from the distance like a stranger – a stranger whose throat was choked with grief and who for a moment did not care if they saw him. But they did not. They saw only their own happiness.

Ria took the handles of the wheelchair and the group

moved away in front of the house, leaving Helen standing on the grass looking after them.

'Helen,' Ben said softly, coming close, re-living Lisa's pain.

She turned, startled – or perhaps it was his expression that startled her.

Ben choked: 'What was her name?'

Helen was flustered. 'Who do you mean?'

'The little girl,' said Ben. 'Please tell me her name!' he begged frantically.

'Oh!' Helen said. 'You must mean Lola.'

'Lola,' Ben murmured. 'Lola, yes.'

'Isn't she sweet?' Helen said, looking at the distant figures going out of sight around the side of the building.

'Yes,' Ben said. 'She is.' He watched them disappear.

'Perhaps you could see them later.'

'I must get back to London,' Ben said.

He did not know that he had seen his first love and her daughter for the last time in many years.

On the night of Monday, 7 May, Ben finished work late, though no later than usual. The offices were silent as he went through them turning out the lights which the girls had forgotten in their excitement. Victory-Europe Day was officially tomorrow, when Winston told the House of Commons, but everyone knew that the war was really over tonight.

He went downstairs and crossed the darkened Emporium. 'Good night, Mike,' he said to the watchman. The old man nodded through the glass doors at the crowds outside. 'Haven't seen anything like this since Mafeking night!' He turned the key and the Auto-Eze automatic doors imported from America hissed open, and Ben went out.

Bonfires were blazing in Piccadilly. People jostled everywhere, in uniform, out of it, waving flags, clashing cymbals made out of dustbin-lids. He heard the rattle of thunder-flashes, and rockets weaved in the night sky. A Dutch sailor swung an ATS girl up and kissed her, Poles and Czechs danced arm in arm. Novelty vendors were selling out of paper hats and streamers. Children sat on the kerbs watching the processions, eating apples from Canada, or running out amongst the crowds to pick pockets.

Ben walked down to London House with his shoes rapping on the pavement, swinging his tightly folded umbrella; it had not rained after all today, and he did not even need his overcoat, for it had been sunny and warm.

He saw Pearl in the garden by the reflected glow of the anti-aircraft searchlight battery in St James's Park, which was starting its display. The iron railings had been taken to help the war effort, and now she was almost standing in the Mall. The night breeze fanned her hair and she was very beautiful. He went down and stood beside her. She put her arm around him. The searchlight beams made flashing white fingers across the sky.

'You've got your overcoat on,' she said, concerned. 'Are you cold?'

The victory celebrations seemed unreal to Ben. 'I'll lay odds that most Germans are still sound supporters of Hitler.'

'Hitler's dead,' said Pearl determinedly.

'What will de-Nazification prove? Another victory for propaganda, just another demonstration that people's minds can be directed what to think by newspaper and wireless . . . making good democrats . . . like herds of animals.'

'Don't give up on us,' Pearl said, linking her arm through his and putting her head on his shoulder.

'Rationing won't stop. The future looks so bleak and dreary. No brave new world.'

' "The battle for peace has begun," ' Pearl chanted. She loved slogans. Then she turned serious. 'Are you going to fight the battle for George?'

His face tightened. 'George has made his own bed. Let him lie on it.'

'Relax,' Pearl said. They watched the searchlights. 'Do you care enough?' she asked.

'George is lost.' His voice brooked no argument.

But Pearl did argue. 'Help him, Ben. You can save him.'

Ben shook his head.

'What purpose does it serve,' Pearl goaded, 'this endless fight with Vic?'

Ben laughed at her, knowing she didn't understand. Pearl still had no conception of evil, no real idea how attractive and how deadly it was, how casually it destroyed. Poor Frankie was her limit. There were piles of rubble in the roadway and patches in the roof of her own house, and still she did not understand.

'Which you have lost,' she said. 'Is that why you don't believe in victory?'

He shook his head at her, and turned away.

Pearl ran after him. 'There's nothing you can do for Ralph or Will but there is something you can do for George,' she whispered fiercely, tugging at his elbow, but he kept walking. 'You can't abandon your son just because you don't like him, or he doesn't suit you. You created him. George is the one, the only one you can save.'

'You don't understand, Pearl.'

'Why have you given up on him? Why are you so determined you're beaten?'

'He's got a good job.'

'Without his father that's worth almost nothing. Isn't he worth fighting for?'

'I can't fight George's battles for him, Pearl!' Ben shouted.

They stopped, glaring at one another in the glowing dark, listening to the crackle of bonfires.

'You could do it,' Pearl said. 'Don't leave George alone – like you did Vane.'

That was the cruellest she had ever been, and for a moment his calm face revealed the terrible pain he felt inside, that he normally concealed.

'Don't hide from me, Ben,' Pearl said softly.

'You don't know Vic.'

Pearl scoffed: 'You're frightened.'

He didn't answer. Was she attracted to Vic?

Pearl said earnestly: 'Don't give up, Ben.'

'George's life is his own. He knows what he wants.'

'He wants his father.' Pearl explained the obvious. 'He needs to know his father loves him.' Why did Ben feel that she did not understand? She had seen George walking in Whitehall a few months ago, smoothly dressed in a conservative pinstripe and bowler like a thousand others. She had seen in his eyes that he was a lost man; he did not dare to be anything else.

From then on, Pearl had decided to work for a reconciliation with Vic.

'Ben,' she said in a bright, sure voice, 'make a success of George.'

CHAPTER TWENTY-EIGHT

Pearl was not sure when Ben began to regain his faith in himself and the good order of the world he lived in. Perhaps it was just a month later, when a letter at last came through from liberated France to inform them that although Chouchou was dead, Ben's son the irrepressible François was alive, well, and married. And that the new Countess was expecting a baby. Yes, perhaps it started then, with the news of his first grandchild. Ben's smile was incomparable.

Or perhaps, Pearl thought, it was that strange, hopeful meeting with Will – the first real ray of hope for Will's total recovery. During the autumn Ben took the decision to close Easton Manor, which had outlived its usefulness and was virtually deserted. The staff had all returned to London House, where Will would continue to be looked after by Helen. But she said he wanted to move to the Home Farm at Clawfell.

'It's the place he's always loved more than any other,' she told the family when Will came down to visit the Harley Street specialists. 'If anywhere can make him better,' she said defiantly, 'it's there.'

'I agree,' Lisa said.

'It's a long way from help,' Ben pointed out.

'He doesn't need help,' Lisa said quietly, 'he needs love.'

Helen fetched the Redouté book Ben had given them and forgotten. 'Look, he's learning the names of roses.' She said urgently: 'I can make him better, Mr London. Will doesn't need doctors. Just me. And a place we can live – a place where Will can learn . . . learn himself. Where he can find out who he is again. Tell them, Will.'

Will fumbled eagerly with the book in his hands and

his face lit up in a smile. He turned the pages slowly and very carefully.

'Josephine,' he said. 'Wild rose. Albertine.' He looked at Helen for approval.

'That's very good, Will,' Helen said encouragingly.

She took a couple of loose sheets of paper from the back of the book and handed them to Ben. It was a child's drawing of a rose: a red scrawl stuck on a simple green stalk. 'Look at the one underneath,' Helen urged. 'He did it a couple of months later.'

Ben glanced at the second sheet. The lines were much more careful, and it was obviously a rose – the petals were better formed, and the stem carried thorns. Ben looked at Helen's pleading expression and took a risk.

'All right,' he decided, 'you can use Home Farm.'

Yes, Pearl thought, perhaps it was then – that moment when Ben, standing holding the drawings in his hands, dared to begin to hope again.

Perhaps it was in October, when she and Ben finally decided to get a firm grip on Victoria's education. She had been expelled from the exclusive Roedean school based at Keswick for rebelliousness and intractability. However she was all sweetness and light, looking lithe and boyish wearing imported slacks, when Ben questioned her. She was lying to him, thinking that he could not control her. Ben bided his time and arranged a private tutor because she was so far behind in schoolwork. Victoria sulked. But for her fifteenth birthday he sweetened her with a horse, a magnificent black Arab called Pasha, a descendant of his own Sultân from many years ago.

Victoria was a fearless rider, her touch nearly flawless. At dawn Ben drove Pearl to Hyde Park and they stood in the knee-high mist watching their rich, beautiful daughter ride past them between the trees, the wind shimmering in her hair as she crouched forward to whisper encouragement in the horse's ears. They heard the slap of the whip.

'She's a natural,' Pearl said admiringly, shielding her eyes from the sun along Rotten Row. Then again the slap of the whip.

'Not good enough,' Ben said, deciding. 'She's got a lot to learn. I won't have her getting spoilt and out of hand – '

'But, Ben – '

'A finishing school is what she needs – and a thorough one,' Ben said. 'Charlie Bookkeeper says the École Madame LaFarge in the hills above Lausanne is the best. His sister was sent there in the twenties, and came out an angel.'

'But Switzerland's so far away,' Pearl said doubtfully. 'I'd only be able to see her in the holidays.'

'No bad thing.'

'I know you think I dote on her,' Pearl said unhappily, 'but I love her and I like her too. I want everything to be for the best.'

'What she needs is a touch of the whip, just like that horse,' Ben said mischievously, then hugged Pearl's shoulder. 'It's too late for this academic year anyway. Don't worry about the currency regulations – I've had money stashed away there since before the war . . .'

'All this trouble for Victoria,' Pearl said, 'but what about George?'

He glared at her then and walked back to the car.

'What about George?' Pearl called after him. He hesitated, then shook his head. It was working; Pearl hid a smile and turned to watch Victoria cantering Pasha back.

But really it was the miracle of Lisa's recovery that changed Ben.

Apparently, Pearl learnt, he had been funding research for years into all sorts of nostrums and remedies, out of despair rather than hope. Among them was a soil fungus, *Streptomyces griseus*. In its di-hydrous form it had antibiotic properties but attacked the auditory nerve; perhaps a more refined version might be effective against the tuberculosis that penicillin could not cure. By the end of the year Lisa was ready to start a course of treatment with laboratory streptomycin.

'I have to tell you,' the professor said, 'this is an experimental drug, and we have found that there is sometimes a risk of deafness.'

Lisa turned her head weakly on the pillow. 'What do you think, Ben?'

'Go ahead,' Ben said without hesitation.

Lisa looked at him. There was an extraordinary confidence on his face, and she knew that everything would be all right, because he said so.

'She may be too far gone,' the professor had confided to Ben earlier, in a very low voice. 'She's too weak, I fear. That left lung . . .'

'She's stronger than you think,' Ben said, and repeated his words, smiling confidently at Lisa, as the professor commenced the injection.

Ben sat in the silence by Lisa's bed that night, the lights still burning brightly, holding her hand as though he could make her live by sheer force of will. He was terribly afraid that she would die.

But Lisa did not die.

It was a miracle; a miracle of science. Within weeks, the change in his mother was extraordinary. As the lesions in her lungs healed, the colour flooded back into Lisa's face. With the coming of the warmer weather she could take turns around St James's Park, and by the time Ben and Pearl flew to Switzerland to see over Madame LaFarge's establishment and have their first holiday for seven years, she was walking as far as the river.

On the night before their departure from the new Heathrow airport Ben slipped into Lisa's living room and stood silently behind the sofa where she was sitting. He let the door swing softly closed – almost inaudibly.

Lisa's head turned at once.

'Your hearing's perfect,' Ben whispered, coming round and kneeling in front of her.

She said: 'Of course it is!' and her face was shining with happiness.

'It's the best of all possible worlds,' sighed Pearl, drinking from a bowl of milky Swiss coffee. They were sitting on their hotel balcony breaking croissants and looking down on the ultramarine-blue lake nestling between soaring slopes of alpine green. A sailboat tacked patiently to and fro. 'Isn't it so peaceful?'

'Victoria starts in September,' Ben said.

Madame LaFarge's establishment was several kilometres back up the road behind them, set in fastidiously neat grounds. Despite herself, Pearl had been impressed. There was no spot of dust anywhere, the girls were helpful and polite, and they seemed to enjoy the discipline and the rules that governed their lives every moment of the day.

'But I can't send her to that place,' Pearl explained, 'she'll hate it.'

'Only at first. I'm not having her get out of hand, Pearl. I won't lose her. Not like George.' Ben had seen George walking with Vic and Terry in the Strand a few weeks ago, and it had been like looking at a stranger. Vic had not changed at all, he was absolutely familiar. He had grinned and made as if to cross the road towards Ben, secure in his victory, but George held back, pretending his father was not there, refusing to meet him.

Pearl put down her croissant and laughed at Ben's expression. 'You can't get George out of your mind, can you!'

'That's what Vic wants.'

'Oh, Vic, Vic, Vic!' she scoffed. 'You beat him before, you can do it again.'

'I wish it was that simple.' He could not explain what she could not understand.

She shook her head. 'It's exactly that simple.' Perhaps she was right.

Pearl really did love Ben London; her faith in him was absolute, total. The millionaire could do anything. Her view of him had never changed.

'You really do want me to do it,' he said.

'I really do love you,' she agreed, 'and I hate to see you fail at anything. I want you to be a success, Ben. I want my husband to be a success at everything. I want your money, your heart, your happiness, your family, and you. Let's go back to bed.'

Ben stared at the sailboat tacking to and fro, to and fro.

'All right,' he said finally. 'It it makes you happy, I'll give Vic a call as soon as we get back, and arrange a meeting.'

'Yeah!' Pearl said. She had won.

CHAPTER TWENTY-NINE

'*If you know where a man hurts, you know where to hurt him,*' Vic had said once, and Terry had never forgotten that. The Daimler pulled up at the kerb and before the hotel commissionaire could react Terry had opened the car door for Vic, then George got out. The car pulled away. They stood looking at the imposing entrance to the hotel.

'Do I have to do this?' George muttered.

Vic barely glanced at him. 'Can't lose,' he said, and George's back straightened loyally. He was heavily on the booze now, all of his own will, and his eyes were still watery from last night. He'd taken a few hefty wallops from the brandy flask on the way here, too. George was afraid – afraid of what Vic would do to his father. Yet he was powerless to stop it.

Vic yawned, standing on the pavement like he owned it, surveying the façade of London's. It had taken more than two decades to reach this moment: he was carrying the battle back into Ben London's territory. The heartland. And this time, he would win.

George would pay for Ria.

Nearly a quarter of a century had passed since that night Ben London had burst into the Tooke Arms, just where Vic felt safest, and taken Ria from him, and driven off in the back of the Rolls-Royce with her, leaving Vic to imagine what they did together . . . imagine everything that happened between them all night in the back of that big, big car.

Only then had Vic truly understood how much Ben hated him.

Vic would never forgive that night he had spent in hell in his mind's eye, imagining them. Ever. Even though Ben London had lost her and Ria had come back . . . of course she had. But for the right reasons? Who knew the secrets in a woman's heart?

But she had come back. That was what mattered.

As any lawyer knew, possession was nine points of the law. And no one would know that better than the millionaire. Vic was beating the man of property on his own ground.

Vic yawned again. He was savouring this moment, Terry knew. First Ben London had lost the woman he had loved to Vic, and now he would lose his son.

No one could stand against Vic.

Terry thought: this is the price men pay for love.

And it couldn't go wrong. Terry touched the automatic pistol in his pocket for luck, not letting Vic see. Vic was old-fashioned about such implements.

They went into the hotel foyer. There was the famous black man on the desk, whose courtly manners charmed the tourists. 'Let's go up,' George said nervously.

Vic laughed. He was carrying a small black Vuitton case, obviously heavy. Terry didn't know what was in it, perhaps a bomb. Explosives were as dead easy to come by as guns after the war. Terry looked at him admiringly. Vic wasn't nervous at all.

They took the lift to the top floor and a bellboy directed them into one of the large, bright rooms often hired for meetings by commercial companies – so Terry knew that Ben London would feel at home here.

That worried him. They should have met at a neutral place, but Vic wouldn't tolerate neutrality in places any more than he would in people. The bellboy left, closing the door softly behind him.

The view from the tall windows was a panorama across the golden treetops of Green Park, then all the varied autumnal hues of Buckingham Palace gardens to the great buildings of Westminster beyond, silhouetted against the brassy river under the morning sun.

The posh room was dominated by a long walnut table as smooth and polished as the dashboard of a Rolls-Royce.

It held their faces like a mirror. At the head of it sat Ben London.

Beside him stood a woman, Pearl London.

Terry had seen her from photographs, but he'd never met her before.

Ben and Vic stared at one another and Terry could have cut the atmosphere with a knife, but Pearl said in a businesslike way: 'Why don't we all sit down?'

Terry glanced at Vic, surprised, but Vic took it in his stride. He pulled out a chair for George. Pearl came and shook hands with them, smiling. Yes, it was a business meeting where they would air their differences and come to a sensible, businesslike conclusion to the mutual benefit of them all. Terry hid his smile and held out his hand politely. She shook it. Her hand was cool and gentle.

Ben London did not move from the head of the table and he did not shake hands. Terry observed him to be a very dangerous man . . . a man of feeling after all. He observed too that Vic, putting his case down neatly by his chair, didn't take his eyes from his adversary for a moment.

Ben said: 'Pearl will say a few words.'

Terry walked around the perimeter of the room. If she had been twenty years younger he would have fallen for Pearl London. She had star quality, a presence as imposing as her husband's. She was very tall and statuesque, and the lines around her mouth were from happiness. Yet there was something goofy about her too – something light and not quite serious. He didn't rate her. She wasn't afraid of Vic, for a start.

Terry stopped by a door in the wall and checked it: only the circular fire escape dropping down a long way into a dim courtyard.

Pearl was looking at Vic with interest. He didn't look such a terrible ogre – more like a successful businessman, a man accustomed to getting his own way. He looked the sort of man she could do a deal with, and she was quite sure that half the stories about him must be untrue. Pearl had never forgotten her day in the East End. Anything bad that he had been driven to do must largely be the fault of his terrible background – the whole family sleeping in one room, and him being left to roam the streets by his ineffectual parents, and having to care for them and look after them from such an early age. It must have been an awful burden for a small child – and she remembered too what Ben had admitted long ago: *Perhaps I myself made him what he is* . . .

When Vic grinned at her, she looked at him almost with sympathy. All his life, he felt that he had been wronged, and so of course he had done wrong. It was time for this vicious circle to stop, she decided.

Pearl had prepared a speech; she cast it away. She must appeal to their hearts.

'You stupid men,' Pearl London said, staring at Ben as well as Vic, 'don't you ever learn?'

Ben's eyes did not move from his enemy, but Vic looked startled that a woman could talk like that, and Terry waited for him to slap her down.

'You stupid men – all of you,' Pearl said. 'What are you fighting about? It's time someone knocked your silly heads together.'

Ben nodded slowly. 'I think Pearl is talking good sense, Vic.'

'Why can't you all live in peace?' Pearl demanded.

This was the most ignorant thing Vic had ever heard, but he looked tolerantly at Pearl. He didn't want to frighten her; he wanted her out of the way. 'I agree,' he said casually.

'Thank you,' Pearl said. 'George, come home with me.'

George shifted uneasily. The emotional charge he felt in this room made words into dangerous weapons. It was not so simple as Pearl made it. He licked his lips. 'Why?' he said.

'Because we love you.'

George's face struggled. So simple, yet so effective. Pearl said gently: 'We love you and we want you home.'

'Me?' George said.

Vic interrupted: 'George is old enough to choose his own friends.'

Pearl said: 'Is he happy?'

George hesitated.

Terry watched Vic, waiting for orders, putting his hand ready on the shooter in his jacket pocket.

Vic considered how far to go. He went all the way.

'Who killed your mother, George?'

Even Terry gasped.

At last Ben London said quietly: 'If you believe that, George, go with Vic.'

George said: 'I don't know what to believe.' He looked around the circle of their faces. 'I don't know what to believe!'

'Love exists,' Ben said.

He sat back. He didn't need to say anything more. He knew he had succeeded. Terry looked at him in confusion.

Pearl touched George's shoulder. 'Vic hates you,' she said, 'do you see?'

'No one knows me,' George said in a quivering voice.

'Don't be so sad,' Pearl said, 'live your own life.' She held out her hand, and then slowly George reached out and took it.

Pearl thought: a victory for reason. She sat by George, holding him. He looked so like Vane; as if in the end reconciliation and redemption could defy even the grave. And so could forgiveness too, perhaps.

Vic didn't move. He wanted to smash them apart. *This is what happens when you try and help people*, he thought bitterly, with a blaze of the old anguish inside him. George would never be happy. Pearl London was innocent, as Ben had been once. That was not a virtue, but a damnation. He began to move his hands towards them, but knew that Ben would be on him. He forced himself to sit still, but he could not help rubbing his mouth with the back of one hand, remembering.

Pearl stood up with George. She looked back towards the head of the table. There was something unknowable in Ben that accounted for his power over her love, but now she felt she knew everything about him. He had stage-managed this meeting, he was a winner; that was what she liked.

'I'm sorry for you, Vic,' Pearl said.

George looked back too, and Ben gave a soundless clap of his hands and smiled with his whole face – a beautiful happy smile, and George found the same smile on his own face, and found that he had automatically given the same childish handclap without even thinking about it. He stared down at his hands in bewilderment. *What exactly happened there? Now why did I do that!*

'You think I'm a criminal,' Vic called out to Pearl, 'but I'm not the one.' He pointed at Ben. 'He's the criminal, he always breaks the law. He broke the law the day he was born, the bastard.'

'Why can't you be friends?'

'You're a stupid woman,' Vic said, still rubbing his mouth, 'but I admire you. I admire you for the sacrifice you made,' he said obliquely. So he too knew her secret. 'You're one of us.'

'You despicable animal,' Pearl said quietly, but Vic only grinned.

'You and me, Ben,' he said, 'we're not so far apart. All we care about are our children.' He let the pause linger, then said no more.

'Take George home,' Ben told Pearl.

'But aren't you coming?'

'Exchange is no robbery,' said Vic.

The three men watched the door close behind Pearl and George. Terry gave Vic a worried look. But Vic was calm and unconcerned, so Terry did nothing, reassured. Personally, he was frightened. This was getting out of control.

Ben London said: 'You've got five minutes, Vic.'

Vic picked up the Vuitton case and dropped it on the table in front of him.

'You've lost for the second time, Ben.'

It was a bomb. Terry cringed, pushing himself back from the table, his chair teetering. Ben London didn't move. Vic's blunt fingers snapped the locks open. Vic was going to take them all with him. Terry jumped up.

'Too late,' Vic said. He always sensed what Terry was thinking. Terry's pale face flushed brick red with shame.

Vic said: 'This is between me and him. Is that clear?'

Terry nodded. His hands were shaking. But Ben London sat calmly, as if he knew what was coming.

Vic upended the case and money flooded across the table. The pile buried Ben London's hands. Bundles dropped over the edge of the table and Terry hurried to pick them up. Money in one-pound notes. Thousands and tens of thousands.

'Leave them,' Vic commanded in an awful rising voice. Terry snatched his hands back.

Vic walked round and stood over Ben London, his fists clenched. 'You did this to me once. Eat it.'

Ben laughed, and Vic's features darkened with rage. His lips drew back from his broken teeth.

'I mean count it,' he said. 'Count it, damn you!'

But Ben still laughed. Terry gazed at Ben London laughing at Vic. He waited for Vic to smash him down or shiv him – he waited for that shiv to come flickering out between Vic's fingers, but it didn't, and Ben London was still laughing.

'What is all this?' Ben asked, amused.

'It's the money I owe you. You remember.'

Ben shrugged. He had almost forgotten the night of the firestorm, but Vic hadn't. It raged unabated in his heart. *Can't get him out of your mind, can you?*

Ben said in an amused voice: 'We go back a long way, Vic. I recall that at the Tooke Arms, Nigel always counted the money.'

'Nigel,' Vic said. His shoulders slumped in defeat. 'Oh God, Nigel.'

Terry stared at the despair on Vic's face.

'Terry can count the money,' Ben said.

'No,' Terry said. He came round the table shaking his head.

'Do it,' Vic ordered dully. 'Oh God, what have I done?'

Terry shouted: 'No! You can't let him defeat you – not *you*!'

Vic slumped down into a chair, the back of his hand against his mouth.

'You wouldn't understand about Nigel,' he said. His brother's face bubbled down into the black water.

'Nigel was a brave man,' Ben said. 'You didn't know he came and saw me.'

Vic squeezed his eyes shut.

'No!' Terry shouted, pulling out the pistol to give Vic time to get the shiv. But Vic didn't move. He slowly opened his eyes, seeing Terry swing the pistol at Ben London.

'Don't!' he shouted.

Ben moved like a boxer, knocking the pistol aside and striking Terry down with his fist. The even white teeth came splattering out of Terry's mouth and he sprawled amongst them across the carpet, then scrabbled to his feet. Vic cringed away from Ben, trying to protect his own face with his elbow.

'Don't,' he whispered.

'Go,' Ben said. 'Leave me in peace.'

Terry, standing with both hands pressed over his face, stared through his fingers at Vic's dark, terrified eyes.

Fear.

Vic was afraid of Ben London.

The scales fell from Terry's eyes.

Still cringing, Vic scrambled for the nearest door. A gust of wind blew in, and he swayed above the drop, then he was going down the fire escape, round and round, faster and faster, his shoes ringing and skidding on the iron.

They heard the echo of his footsteps running over the cobbles far below, then silence.

Ben picked up the pistol with distaste and sat down at the head of the boardroom table.

'It was never your fight,' he said to Terry, 'I'm sorry you were hurt.'

Terry didn't move a muscle. If he could have spoken he would have said: 'Finish it.' He waited for the bullet.

'Go away,' Ben told Terry, 'it's all over.'

Terry backed out into the corridor. He was a free man. He turned and walked along the elegant passageways, but he did not know where he walked. Ben London had crushed Vic Price, who meant more to Terry than anyone else in the world. Terry did not feel the agony of his shattered teeth, he felt nothing. Only the unendurable pain of his loss.

Ben closed the door.

'It's all over,' he repeated.

For the second time in his life, he had been merciful.

CHAPTER THIRTY

'Merry Christmas!'

She walked slowly through the streets of London, her daughter hanging from her hand. The bells were ringing out above them over a Dickensian scene. The snowy pavements were a festive, hurrying, scurrying swarm of people, young clerks freed from their desks pelting for the tube or the bus, and smartly dressed secretaries pausing to look in the lovely window displays brightly lit against approaching night. Everyone ignored the woman in shabby clothes. Packed red omnibuses inched through the crowds. Last-minute shoppers, swaddled in overcoats and mufflers, were waddling wearily homeward clutching their gaudy parcels. Regent's Street was a blaze of lights, she saw, with long grey icicles hanging from the wires, and chimneys churned filthy yellow smoke into the black sky.

She stopped at Piccadilly Circus, hesitating, not knowing what to do, feeling the small warm hand holding on to her trustingly.

She walked on.

She followed the street lights shining like stars into the distance along Piccadilly, packed solid with vehicles, as usual. At intervals barrow-men blowing into their half-gloves were selling hot chestnuts, watery-eyed from bending over the smoking braziers.

'*Nice 'n' hot, piping hot, who'll buy my nice hot chestnuts?*' She watched.

'Thruppence . . . thank you kindly, sir. Merry Christmas!' The old man selling chestnuts crackled open another bag and looked round for the next customer. The woman was still watching hungrily.

'You still here? Get on with you!'

The woman with the little girl – she couldn't be more than five or six years old – was standing in the roadway where they wouldn't get jostled by the crowds. This had been Old Tommy's patch for almost a lifetime of winters, close by Fortnum and Mason's. He was well known, and now he frowned. Many fancy people coming out bought a bag, their faces lighting up with the nostalgia of childhood memories as they tasted the hot, nutty flavour in their mouths, and these two hanging about in their shabby clothes were bad for business.

'Geroff!' Tommy shouted, pretending to chase them.

The little girl had enormous, innocent eyes. The woman looked at him defiantly, and she had older, knowing eyes as fierce as fire. Doubtless an edge on her tongue too.

'I'm not hungry, Mum,' the little girl whispered, tugging at her mother, 'really I'm not.'

The woman stared at Old Tommy until he backed down.

'Look, I'm packing up soon,' he said. 'If there's anything left over – '

'You can keep your leftovers to yourself mate,' the woman said aggressively. 'We pay full price.' She dug in her purse and pulled out a thruppenny piece from the lining. Old Tommy shrugged and scooped a bag.

'I want it to the top,' Ria said. 'You can take that burnt one back too.'

'I was really starving,' Lola said as they walked, juggling a hot chestnut in her fist.

'Of course you are, love. I could hear your stomach rumbling from here.'

Lola crunched the chestnut with difficulty. 'It's ever so dark.'

'Yes,' Ria said wretchedly. 'You're not cold, are you, love?' She made sure Lola's old overcoat was done up to the top button.

'Are we going home?'

'No, love, this is the West End. Don't you like the lights?'

Lola said: 'I know you're worried, Mum.' She looked up with a child's wisdom, then followed Ria's eyes to the brilliant shopfront that stretched away from them up the road to their right.

Lola read: 'London Emporium.'

'Come away!' her mother said, pulling her on. The crowds were thinning but soon the evening crush would start. Ria and Lola sat on a bench amongst the stiff black trees of Green Park, huddled together for warmth, eating the last of the cooling chestnuts.

'What are we doing here, Mum?' Lola asked finally.

Woman's intuition. Ria didn't quite know how to put it in words, but she had never been able to hide her feelings from Lola. After the bust-up with Vic, Terry had flown back to the little house next door in Havannah Street and lived there very quietly, alone. Ria rarely saw him, he was a proper nightbird and these days she was not, but she could never meet him without feeling guilty – he reminded her of Nigel. But she could hardly make contact with him at all, he was so cold and polite, holding it all bottled up inside himself. Just as Nigel had, until he met Arleen and damned himself. But Terry had no one.

Ria didn't like him.

When she had asked him what had happened between him and Vic, a look almost of contempt had crossed Terry's face. 'Nothing,' he had said calmly.

Once Vic had been everything in the world to Terry; maybe he still was. 'Don't worry, you'll get back in his good books soon enough,' Ria had tried to reassure him. 'Vic can be quite forgiving when he wants.'

'But I am not,' Terry had said in a voice like ice. Ria knew something had changed all right. Later Esther said that apparently there had been another row with Ben, but she had heard no details, and Ria hadn't wanted to hear them anyway.

She had promised.

Esther had flapped the newspaper. Mr Ben London was holding a huge Christmas party in the ballroom at his hotel for all his family and friends. It was the social gala of the year, believed to cost him more than ten thousand pounds.

'We could do with some of that. I'll never forgive him, never,' Esther had said vindictively, glancing at Lola.

'Oh, Mum,' said Ria wearily.

This morning Lola was helping Ria bake the sweet pies and they used more sugar than they thought. Ria went next door to get a cup off Terry. He couldn't have been more helpful, but there was something wrong about his manner. He was furtive, and there was a very faint, strange smell in the house – Ria almost commented on it.

It was familiar, faintly acid, a bit like bath scale cleaner. But it wasn't that.

Ria couldn't place it, but it made her uneasy. It was the smell of danger.

Ria thought about it all the time the pies were baking. She walked up and down the kitchen nagging at herself, prey to nameless fears. *Woman's intuition.* She told herself she was on edge because of their money troubles, there would only be poor presents for Lola this year, nothing shop-bought – except a wooden doll with a curly red painted mouth, and Ria had knitted the doll's clothes herself, reducing adult patterns to size and wrestling with the long needles when Lola was asleep. But now she couldn't get that acid smell out of her mind.

'Let's go for a walk,' Ria had said suddenly, and fetched Lola's overcoat.

She must have been mad; here they were sitting in the park without so much as a bus fare home. Lola must be ever so tired, poor little dear, but she never complained. Suddenly Lola pointed across the park, her face lighting up with joy. A gilt Cinderella coach with classical paintings on the doors, pulled by four white horses with white plumes, passed in a golden blaze under a street lamp, then almost disappeared in the pit of shadow beyond. Then another street lamp, much closer, covered it with light and inside Ria glimpsed a face she knew.

Ben didn't see her, because Ria pulled Lola behind a tree.

The coach turned into a sidestreet off Piccadilly. Ria looked down and saw that the gaze of childhood wonder had transformed Lola's face, as it had her own once. Ria knew that coach. It was an old, old dream from long ago.

'Come on, darling,' Ria said gently, 'it's time for you and me to walk home.'

'Oh, what a wonderful idea.' Pearl was clapping her hands and laughing as they rode in the coach, which was as sumptuous inside as out. 'It's like a dream come true – I've always wanted to do this. It's *magnificent!*' She pretended to be worried. 'But will it turn into a pumpkin at midnight?'

He shook his head. 'You're my princess,' he said seriously. 'Dreams come true.'

'For us.' Pearl was wearing her diamond tiara and a slim pale blue evening dress with a cape, and long gloves. Her diamonds flashed under the glare of floodlights as they turned out into Park Lane and stopped outside London's.

A darting postillion opened the door and pulled down the step. The commissionaire saluted. 'Hey, it's Pineapple,' Pearl greeted him, 'I didn't recognize you in the new rigout.'

'Special clothes for a special night,' the black concierge smiled. 'Don't you go calling me that old Uncle Tom name no more,' he chided, 'we're living in enlightened times.'

'I'm sorry, Dillibe. You make sure to ask me to dance later?' Pearl kissed him impulsively, then turned to Ben. They went up the frosty steps with their breath hanging about them like smoke.

They welcomed their guests in the foyer, where footmen took their cloaks, then moved up to the ballroom gleaming in white, scarlet and gold, a sea of people – the men in white tie and tails, the women showing off their brightest, finest gowns. They were rebelling against the drab egalitarianism of postwar life where rationing was still the order of the day. Tonight, waiters circled smoothly amongst them with trays of champagne.

Ben bowed to Pearl. 'We have the first dance,' he said.

'The Charleston!' Pearl guessed correctly.

He had lost none of his grace, and this time she did not miss a step.

Next he danced with Lisa, her face glowing with health.

Later the orchestra played waltzes, David and Harriet from the Emporium dancing together, and Ben asked their daughter Cathy to dance, a pert girl of about twenty-two who now managed the handbag department. Next was Pat Wallace, her large spectacles glinting anxiously, and he knew he was going to have to dance with the whole typing pool.

'I don't know where Ben gets the energy,' Lisa told Pearl. 'Why isn't Victoria here?'

'Her plane's been delayed by the weather in Geneva, it's such a shame coming at the end of her very first term. But she called from Cointrin to say she expects to arrive at Heathrow early tomorrow morning.'

'Too late for the ball. Poor Victoria.'

'She'll be wild,' agreed Pearl. 'Apparently they don't have boys in Switzerland.' She nodded as Ben crossed the floor. 'Ah, Ben's got the post room lads to liberate him from the typists.'

Clifford Ford, looking more cadaverous than ever since his wife died, was dancing with Alice Cypress. George, immaculately drunk, was being steered around the floor by Cathy. François was showing off his new young wife, a delicate creature with luminous sloe eyes and an alert, delightful smile. She wore the chain of Coucy pearls at her slim throat.

'May I introduce the new Countess,' François said.

'Your dancing enchants me.' Ben welcomed her in French with a deep bow, effortlessly charming her. 'You have studied the ballet.'

Smiling, she shook her head.

François said anxiously: 'You are aware that she is unable to speak – '

Rachel held Ben's hands. They communicated perfectly, her muteness confined only to her tongue and not at all to her eyes, or her hands, or her smile. She knew suffering, just as Chouchou had. Ben nodded. Without a word, they moved lightly together onto the dance floor.

'She dances beautifully, François,' Lisa complimented him. 'Did she really study to be a ballet dancer?'

François shrugged with his hands palm-upwards in a very Gallic gesture of baffled amusement. 'Who knows? Apparently! One day I will tell you.'

Across the floor, Cathy stared longingly at Pearl. 'Isn't she beautiful?' she whispered to George. 'I remember the day when they were married. Hawk gave me confetti to throw. He was such a sweet old man.'

'You must be drunker than I am,' George muttered. 'He was a Grade A swine.'

Cathy shook her head. 'Dance with me again,' she said gracefully.

George stared at his father. 'Does he think all this glitter is worth anything? Who does he think it impresses?'

'It's called being alive, and it's dark outside,' Cathy said. 'It's against the dark.' She was a young woman in love. She touched his lips with amusement. 'You needn't try to sound so nasty, George. You aren't, so don't pretend, not with me.'

An American band took over and the youngsters started holding close. Ben took Pearl out and they smooched.

'Cheer up!' he said.

'I'm having the night of my life, really I am. I just wish Victoria was here.'

'She will be tomorrow.' He glanced at his watch. 'Today, now.'

'I know,' she said, cuddling him.

The late buffet was served. Ben sat at a large round table with a snow-white cloth of Egyptian cotton and glittering silver. Except Victoria, all his family was gathered around him, Pearl on his left, Will in the wheelchair on his right with Helen to help him, then François, Lisa, George who was getting very slurred now that Cathy was not there to hold him back, Rachel . . . Ben watched them all with a smile but Pearl saw there was a great sadness gleaming in his eyes, and he suddenly put down his knife and fork. Pearl squeezed his hand. She knew what he was thinking.

'Ralph,' Ben said. 'Ralph's not here.'

He got up. Spontaneously and unrehearsed, he jumped up on the bandstand and held up his hand for silence.

Everyone watched him. He smiled. No more unhappiness.

'My lords, ladies and gentlemen. I will propose only one toast tonight.' He held up his glass. 'To absent friends!'

They chorused: *'To absent friends.'*

Ria lay awake – it seemed the night back home in Havannah Street would never end. Lola had been asleep on her truckle-bed for hours; sometimes her breathing shallowed, and she muttered as she dreamt. Ria looked for the bedroom fireplace but could not even see it, the last embers no longer glowed. For the hundredth time she looked at the luminous hands of the clock. Still hardly after three. She turned over and pulled the pillow over her head, muffling the tick, tock of passing time.

When she lifted her hand and looked at the clock again, it was five minutes later. Lights swung across the window and she heard a car engine.

Ria sat up.

The sound approached, then stopped. Not the smooth purr of Vic's Daimler; the sportier note of Terry's MG. Footsteps crossing the pavement. A key in the lock, then the thud from next door of the door closing.

And there, sitting up in bed, Ria remembered the smell of nitroglycerine explosive from her work at Woolwich Arsenal in the first world war – she had been a lyddite canary, and handled trinitrotoluene too, but as she sat there now it was another smell she remembered: the acid odour clinging to the clothes and skin of some other poor girls in another department, whose job it was to saturate silica with nitroglycerine to make dynamite.

Ria shook her head.

The cistern in the loft next door made a hissing noise.

Terry was taking a bath. Ria stared into the dark. Her heart was hammering.

She jumped out of bed, then stopped. *Don't be stupid, Ria.*

She got back between the sheets.

Then she got up and went onto the landing, and turned on the light. But she was stark naked. She went back into the bedroom and pulled on a threadbare dressing gown, then went downstairs wrapping it round her. She stopped in the hall looking at the phone. The phone book lay beside it.

Don't be silly, Ria.

Ria sat on the bottom step, her hands in her hair. She had promised.

But perhaps something dreadful had happened.

She opened the phone book, then picked up the phone.

The lights were going down and pairs drifted lazily around the dance floor. 'We're staying here in the hotel overnight,' Helen told Ben, 'and taking the train north to Clawfell in the morning, before the moors are cut off.'

'You should stay down here,' Ben said. Pearl and Lisa stopped chatting and looked at him, hearing his tone of voice. It was the same old disagreement.

Will looked at Helen. 'He's happier up there,' she spoke for him. 'This isn't his life any more, down here. Home Farm's redecorated – all by Will. You wouldn't understand, being so successful no one can touch you. But Will's vulnerable.'

'You have to face facts, Helen.'

She shook her head. 'We know you think he can't live an effective life, that he's running away – but I think you ought to see this.' She lifted a slim, flat parcel onto the table. 'It was to be a Christmas present, but I think Will would like you to have it now.'

'I l-l-love you, Dad,' Will said. Ben held his son's hand.

He tore the wrapping with his free hand and they all stared at the painting inside. A bombed Spanish village from the civil war – Will had been there, this experience locked up inside him all these years – blasted walls, a stormy sky, the sunset like a dusty rose. It was full of feeling and Ben knew it was good, but he did not understand *how* it was so good . . . so untaught, so real.

Lisa said softly: 'He has inherited Charles's talent. The talent Charles did not dare use.'

Someone came up to say goodbye, and Ben glanced at his watch. Lisa's chauffeur arrived to drive her back to London House in her car, and Ben told him to park in the drive because the carriage, borrowed off the London Museum, couldn't be left outside.

Ben and Pearl said goodbye to the last of their guests, then were driven back home through the darkened streets. The first milkfloats were already chattering slowly along the Mall. 'Well, you were right,' Pearl said, tapping her foot on the carriage floor.

He looked at her inquiringly.

'It didn't turn into a pumpkin,' Pearl said. He kissed her.

'Tell you something,' Pearl yawned as they got down. 'Betcha Cinderella didn't have to get up in a couple of hours to fetch her daughter from the airport.'

They crossed the entrance hall, squinting against the bright lights, and Pearl was halfway up the stairs when the phone rang. 'Oh, bugger it,' she called, 'don't answer it, darling.'

But he picked up the receiver. 'Ben London speaking.'

He heard an inhalation as though the person at the other end almost spoke, then nothing. He heard a distant rattle of milk bottles over the open line.

'Hallo?' he said. 'Hallo? Hallo?'

He replaced the receiver.

Pearl said: 'Who was it?'

'No one.'

'Who are you talking to, Mum?'

'No one,' Ria said, putting down the phone. She had kept her long-ago promise to Pearl. She had not spoken

492

to Ben London, but the mere fact that he had answered had laid her stupid fears to rest.

'I'm not sleepy now,' Lola said. 'You woke me up.'

'I'm sorry, love. I just felt that something wasn't right.'

'I don't like Uncle Terry,' Lola said.

Ria looked at her daughter. 'You've got an attack of woman's intuition too,' she said, unlocking the front door to fetch in the freshly delivered milk.

'What's intuition?'

Ria reached out for the bottles, then slowly turned back.

'Woman's intuition says, go and get your hat and coat on,' Ria said, and as soon as she said it she knew she was right.

EPILOGUE

Pearl's alarm clock rang. She looked across at Ben, still asleep, then kissed his shoulder and swung her long legs quietly over the edge of the bed. After dressing in warm casual clothes with a long scarf, she went downstairs and drank some coffee, but the excitement of meeting Victoria had already driven the tiredness out of her mind and she left it half finished. Outside was the first grey light of dawn, and the snow was grey, and grey snowflakes whirled slowly down between the grey trees.

Lifting her collar and blowing into her hands, she got into her car, turned on the ignition, and thumbed the starter. The motor churned over slowly, then stopped, so she went over and tried Ben's Silver Wraith. As she turned on the ignition, out of the corner of her eye she thought she saw a dark figure with waving arms running towards her up the drive, then there was a blinding flash.

Ben woke hearing a woman's voice screaming: 'No! No!' He ran downstairs still half-asleep, his bare feet slipping on the marble, hurting his ankle. The fanlight above the doors glowed with a brilliant illumination, casting shadows, then the windows blew in around him and the lights went out.

Ben lifted himself on his hands. His face felt icy cold. He heard the sound of tinkling glass sliding off his back. He turned his head from side to side then crossed to the door, hands outstretched, but there was no door. It was completely dark outside and he fell down the steps.

'Pearl!' he bellowed.

He heard a woman scream.

Pearl was dead.

Ben crawled across the hot wet gravel towards the heat, immersed in smoke. He couldn't find her.

'Help me!' he shouted. 'She'll be all right.'

He felt a hand on his shoulder. 'Pearl?' he whispered, staring up. 'Pearl?'

Lisa's voice echoed distantly from the top of the shattered steps. 'Tell him, he always wanted to know the truth. Tell him.'

'I was too late,' came Ria's griefstricken voice, close by. It was her hand on his shoulder.

He looked up into the darkness.

Ria knelt beside him. Like a stitched thread, often unseen but always unbroken, holding her life together and giving her hope against the darkest days, her love for Ben had never wavered.

Once she had turned him down because he had everything.

Now he had nothing.

Lola was playing innocently in the snow.

The dawn was bright, and Ben's eyes were as white as flame.

Where do you go, when no one will help you, and you have nowhere to go to?

He roared: 'Help me!'

Ria put her arms around his shoulders.

'I will help you,' Ria said. With her fingertips she turned his face gently to the right, towards Lisa. 'I will help you.'

Lisa gasped when she saw her son. She understood.

A selection of bestsellers from Headline

FICTION

THE MASK	Dean R Koontz	£3.50 ☐
ROWAN'S MILL	Elizabeth Walker	£3.99 ☐
MONEY FOR NOTHING	John Harman	£3.99 ☐
RICOCHET	Ovid Demaris	£3.50 ☐
SHE GOES TO WAR	Edith Pargeter	£3.50 ☐
CLOSE-UP ON DEATH	Maureen O'Brien	£2.99 ☐

NON-FICTION

GOOD HOUSEKEEPING EATING FOR A HEALTHY HEART	Coronary Prevention Group	£3.99 ☐
THE ALIEN'S DICTIONARY	David Hallamshire	£2.99 ☐

SCIENCE FICTION AND FANTASY

THE FIRE SWORD	Adrienne Martine-Barnes	£3.99 ☐
SHADOWS OF THE WHITE SUN	Raymond Harris	£2.99 ☐
AN EXCESS OF ENCHANTMENTS	Craig Shaw Gardner	£2.99 ☐
MOON DREAMS	Brad Strickland	£3.50 ☐

All Headline books are available at your local bookshop or newsagent, or can be ordered direct from the publisher. Just tick the titles you want and fill in the form below. Prices and availability subject to change without notice.

Headline Book Publishing PLC, Cash Sales Department, PO Box 11, Falmouth, Cornwall, TR10 9EN, England.

Please enclose a cheque or postal order to the value of the cover price and allow the following for postage and packing:

UK: 60p for the first book, 25p for the second book and 15p for each additional book ordered up to a maximum charge of £1.90

BFPO: 60p for the first book, 25p for the second book and 15p per copy for the next seven books, thereafter 9p per book

OVERSEAS & EIRE: £1.25 for the first book, 75p for the second book and 28p for each subsequent book.

Name ....

Address ....

....

....